A Waltz for

Matilda

A Waltz for

Matilda

Jackie French

📖 Angus&Robertson
An imprint of HarperCollins*Publishers*

Angus&Robertson
An imprint of HarperCollins*Publishers*, Australia

First published in Australia in 2010
by HarperCollins*Publishers* Australia Pty Limited
ABN 36 009 913 517
harpercollins.com.au

HarperCollins*Publishers*
Level 13, 201 Elizabeth Street, Sydney NSW 2000, Australia
Unit D1, 63 Apollo Drive, Rosedale, Auckland 0632, New Zealand
A 53, Sector 57, Noida, UP, India
1 London Bridge Street, London, SE1 9GF, United Kingdom
2 Bloor Street East, 20th floor, Toronto, Ontario M4W 1A8, Canada
195 Broadway, New York NY 10007, USA

National Library of Australia Cataloguing-in-Publication data:

French, Jackie.
    A waltz for Matilda / Jackie French.
    ISBN: 978 0 7322 9021 4 (pbk.)
    For children.
    Swagmen—Australia—Juvenile fiction.
A823.3

Cover design by Darren Holt, HarperCollins Design Studio
Cover images: girl by Tim Flach/Getty Images; all other images by shutterstock.com
Author photograph by Kelly Sturgiss
Typeset in Sabon 10/15pt by Letter Spaced
Printed and bound in Australia by Griffin Press
The papers used by HarperCollins in the manufacture of this book are a natural,
recyclable product made from wood grown in sustainable plantation forests. The fibre
source and manufacturing processes meet recognised international environmental
standards, and carry certification.

A love song to a land, and to a nation

To the seven generations of women who taught me the
lessons in this book

Publisher's Note

The song 'Waltzing Matilda' arose from a collaboration between A.B. 'Banjo' Paterson, who wrote the poem in 1895, and Christina Macpherson, who was responsible for the earliest version of the music.

Over the years, a number of different versions of the song have been sung and recorded. The National Library of Australia refers to three versions, one being Paterson's and another being the arrangement by Marie Cowan in 1903. We cannot be certain whether Cowan obtained the original version directly from Paterson, or whether she heard it sung and transcribed it.

However she came to write it, it is Cowan's version that most of us recognise, and which is sometimes referred to as the 'popular version'. It is this version that appears on the back cover of this book.

Readers interested in more information on this most famous of all Australia's 'bush poems' can go to the National Library of Australia website: www.nla.gov.au/epubs/waltzingmatilda

Apology

This book is set from 1894 to 1915, a time of widespread racism, some of it quite unconscious. The desire to pass new comprehensive laws to 'keep Australia white' was one of the reasons many supported the federation of states that became the nation of Australia. Writing about those times has needed racist words and racist assumptions that are not — and should not be — in common use today. But without them it would be impossible to show the hatred of those times or the ideas that made today's Australia.

Jackie French

Chapter 1

Dear Dad,

I hope you are well.

Did you get my last letter? Mum and I are not at Aunt Ann's now, we are living with Mrs Dawkins in Grinder's Alley. It is a boarding house, we only have one room but Mrs Dawkins is kind, she found me a job. It is in a jam factory. I pretend I am fourteen not twelve so I get paid three shillings a week. The boys get six shillings, which is not fair.

A bullock dray fell on Aunt Ann. She did not get better. Mum and I could not pay the rent. The bailiffs came and took our furniture. Mum had to go to hospital for an operation, but we do not have the money for doctors now. Mum is very thin and cannot do her sewing, but she says she will be better soon.

I hope you are all right. We have not had a postal order from you for more than a year, that is why I wonder if you got my letters, and know what happened to Mum and Aunt Ann.

It is very different in Grinder's Alley from Aunt Ann's, all the houses are squashed together. The smoke from the chimneys just sits above the houses. Our rent is a shilling a week, I buy day-old bread and spoiled vegetables to make soup and Mrs Dawkins lets me use her kitchen, but there is not enough money to buy medicines, so I hope you will send a postal order soon.

I miss Aunt Ann and my friends at school. It is too far away for me to see them; also I have only Sunday off each week. I am worried about Mum too. She says she is all right but I do not think she is.

Give my love to the sheep and the lambs, I wish I could see them and your farm some day, and you too.

Do you have a dog? I like dogs.

Your loving daughter,
Matilda

PS It is hard for Mum to breathe in Grinder's Alley. If we could come to the farm I think she might be better.

PPS If somebody else is reading this because Dad is away shearing could you send it to him please, I think maybe he does not know where we are now, or that Aunt Ann died.

It was midnight in Grinder's Alley. The gas lamps flickered in the darkness. Somewhere in those shadows lurked the larrikins of the Push, with their hot breath and cold knives.

Matilda put her chin out. The jam factory was only three streets away from Mrs Dawkins's. She'd managed to escape the Push before. She'd make it tonight too.

She clutched her shawl closer as she slipped down the boarding-house steps. Since the bailiffs took their alarm clock, she didn't dare sleep all night with Mum. There were too many women with hungry children who'd take her job if she was late.

The houses crouched like mushrooms behind their iron railings. Matilda ran as fast as her skirts would let her, staying close to the fences, one shadow among many. The night air smelled of smoke from coal fires, and the big furnaces of the jam and tin factories. Someone was cooking sausages too. Her tummy clenched into a knot.

She'd eaten nothing since Tommy's sandwiches yesterday. She'd told Mum the factory gave the workers dinner. It was a lie: Mr Thrattle's cockroaches ate better than his workers. But Mum was so thin these days. Two shillings a week only bought food for one.

Why hadn't Dad sent money? Shearers had to go places without post offices, but he'd always managed to get money to them every few months.

A shadow moved in the dimness further up the alley. She stepped back into a shop doorway, then relaxed, as Ah Ching emerged from the darkness, pulling his vegetable cart.

Aunt Ann had said that Chinese men wanted to kidnap white girls and sell them into slavery. Impossible to think of Ah Ching doing that.

Mrs Dawkins said that when the Push had tried to steal Ah Ching's vegetable cart, Ah Ching had moved like the wind, chopping, leaping, a knife of his own suddenly in his hand. Impossible to think of this small gentle man leaping with a knife too.

But the Push never troubled Ah Ching now.

Matilda watched the small, grey-headed man pulling the handles of the big cart, piled high with tight green cabbages, bunches of carrots, beetroot, leeks and wooden cases of fruit, each piece wrapped in newspaper to stop it bruising. Ah Ching's wrinkles changed into a smile when he saw her.

She bowed her head and right knee slightly, then looked down. 'Qing An.'

Ah Ching had taught her the words and how to bow properly weeks ago, when they first met. She had no idea what the words meant. But Ah Ching's smile deepened when she bowed and spoke.

'Qing An.' He bowed back — a lower bow than hers — then reached into his cart. His hand brought out a crumple of newspaper. He bowed again as he handed it to her.

Matilda unwrapped it carefully. A peach! Even by the lamplight she could see its blushed white skin, like Mum's cheeks. She lifted it and smelled its sweetness.

'Duo xie!' She bowed again, wishing she knew more Chinese words to thank him properly, then slipped the peach into her bag.

Ah Ching waved his hands. He said something she couldn't understand, then made chewing motions. He meant that she should eat it now.

How could she explain how badly Mum needed fruit like this, if she was to get well? She hesitated.

Ah Ching's smile changed: became deeper, gentler, rich in understanding. He picked out a second peach, then held it out to her, bowing.

She looked at him, speechless, then unwrapped it slowly, letting the smell seep into her nose. The first bite was like slipping into the waves at the beach or clean white sheets. The juice exploded down her chin. She wiped it, embarrassed.

4

Ah Ching laughed softly, as though delighted at the compliment to his peach. He watched her steadily as she ate it all, using her nails to gouge out the last peach strings from the seed.

Matilda bowed again. 'Gai ri zai lai, qing zou hao.' They were the only other Chinese words she knew.

Ah Ching nodded. For a moment she thought he would say something more. But instead he simply bowed, and began to trot toward the market.

Or maybe he's going to sell his fruit and vegetables from house to house, thought Matilda, listening to the creak of the wheels fade out down the cobbles as she turned alone into the next shadowed street. She and Ah Ching knew nothing of each other, except this brief friendship of the night, linked by fruit and darkness.

'Got her!' A fist reached out of the darkness and grabbed her by her collar. Another boy's hand seized her arms. Snagger Sam carried a bag of pennies, dangling from one hand. Mrs Dawkins said he'd blinded a cove with those. Todger Bailey held a knife. She didn't know the names of the others, short-coated bullies with lengths of lead pipe or knotted cord and beery grins.

Aunt Ann said drinking spirituous liquor drove men mad. Matilda gazed from one boy to another.

No point struggling. No point screaming either. No one answered screams round here. The Push carried matches and cans of kerosene. If you crossed the Push you'd find your house burned down, and with you in it if you didn't get out in time.

'Out late again, little girl?' Todger Bailey stuck his knife up to her throat. 'You know what happens to little girls who go out in the dark?'

Snagger Sam laughed. 'They learn to do what they're told. Ain't that right, boys?'

'You gunna do what we tells you?' whispered Todger's beery breath in her ear. 'You gunna be nice, little girl?'

She couldn't let fear take her now. She had to get to the factory — and she couldn't if she'd been taken by the Push. But Tommy had told her what to do. Tommy knew everything. Or she hoped he did.

She let her body go limp.

It worked.

The hands let go of her for a precious second as she slumped into a bundle of skirts and shawl on the footpath. She rolled twice, till she was past their legs, then surged to her feet, lifting her skirts so she could run faster all in one movement. She was a yard away from them before they knew what had happened.

Laughter echoed along the lane behind her. A twelve-year-old girl couldn't out-run the Push, or not for long. But she only had one block to go before she reached the factory.

She could hear the clomp of boots behind her, almost feel their hands reaching for her, but there was the factory, dark and silent at the end of the street, the metal fence around it.

'Bruiser!' she shrieked.

She hurled herself over the fence, landing hard, heard boots thud onto the ground next to her. 'Got yer, yer little —'

Todger screamed. It was a good sound. Matilda stood, trying to get her breath, as Bruiser tugged and tore at the young man's arm. Blood dripped onto the gravel.

'Bruiser, down.'

The big dog glanced at her with one yellow eye, as though to say, 'Don't stop me. This is fun!' No one knew what sort of dog Bruiser was, not even Tommy. Part German shepherd, perhaps,

6

or something even larger. Part lion, more likely, Matilda thought, escaped from a circus.

'Let him go, Bruiser,' she said again.

Bruiser opened his mouth.

The young man cradled his arm to his chest, his breath coming in deep sobs. Suddenly Matilda wanted to cry too, to run back to Aunt Ann's and the safe days of love and buttered toast. But those days were gone. She had to stop the Push waiting for her again. Mum depended on her now.

She tried to keep her voice steady. 'Better get the doctor to disinfect that bite. Bruiser's got rabies.'

She stroked Bruiser's ears. 'See all his spit? That's mad-dog spit. Anyone he bites goes mad, unless they get it disinfected fast. It's called hydrophobia. If you see a drop of water you'll start screaming and screaming and you won't be able to stop.' It wasn't true, but she hoped it sounded terrifying. The other boys watched warily over the fence.

Matilda smiled at them grimly. 'If Todger touches you, you might go mad too. Better stay away.'

She turned her back, forcing herself not to run. Bruiser followed at her heels as she walked to the factory doorway. By the time she'd sat down, with her shawl around her, the Push had gone.

It was cold huddled in the doorway, even with Bruiser for comfort. The big dog gnawed the soup bone she had brought him. There was no meat on it — not after two days' boiling on Mrs Dawkins's wood stove — but the dog seemed to like it.

Matilda stroked him again, the torn ears, the scars on his side from kickings. Bruiser cowered whenever Mr Thrattle came near. Anyone else he savaged. Except Matilda. Matilda was his friend.

Now at last she could sleep. She huddled down, her shawl around her, trying to ignore the ache of her bruises and the cold of the concrete below her. She couldn't afford to lose this job. Not with rent to pay and food for Mum.

Matilda smiled in the gaslight shadows. Tonight Mum could eat the peach.

~~◦◦◦~~

'Oi! Wake up, young coot. Breakfast's here.'

Matilda opened her eyes. Tommy lounged in the doorway, grinning at her, showing off the gap in his teeth where one of the Push had hit him when he was a kid.

Tommy was fifteen now, and the best mechanic around. If Snagger or Todger wanted to keep their precious bicycles on the road they needed to stay in good with Tommy these days. She stood up stiffly, and stretched.

'Here.' He handed her a packet wrapped in greaseproof paper. Tommy had brought her sandwiches since her second day at the factory, when he saw she didn't have any lunch.

Matilda bit into the first one eagerly, then grinned up at him. Roast lamb and chutney, with big cold hunks of butter. Six big chunks of bread, so lopsided he must have cut them himself. She'd eat two sandwiches now, keep one for her lunch.

'Thank you.'

'No worries. Them arms of yours look like a match with the wood shaved off. We need to fatten you up.'

Tommy nodded at Bruiser, standing at her side and growling at him softly. 'Tie him up, will you, so I can get inside. Need to see to the big pulley afore I start the burners. That pulley's almost rusted through, but the old bast— er … *biscuit* is too cheap to buy a new one. The whole dashed place runs on spit and rubber bands.' He grinned again. 'I got a new idea too.'

Matilda swallowed the mouthful of bread and meat. 'What is it?' Tommy had built half the machinery here, even the big thing he called a 'conveyer belt' that carried the cans of hot jam. He was so full of ideas she expected to see them leak out of his pockets.

'Grapples,' he said triumphantly, then saw her blank face. 'To hold the cans of jam with, like, so you girls don't burn your hands all the time.'

Matilda gazed down at her hands automatically. Three months had left them scarred and callused. 'Can you make them today?'

He shook his head. 'Will on Sunday though.'

Trust Tommy, she thought, to spend his only day off working. But for Tommy, machinery was never work.

Tommy blew on his hands to warm them. 'Come on then. I want a good scrounge in the junk heap for bits and pieces to make 'em afore I light the burners.'

Matilda nodded, her mouth full again. She led Bruiser over to the fence and tied the rope to his collar. She hated to do it. A dog like Bruiser needed to run. She'd go mad too, tied up all day. But the dog was Mr Thrattle's, not hers.

Behind her Tommy had already slipped inside the echoing factory. Matilda felt her eyes closing again. Just a few moments more of sleep …

'No time to be napping, young lady. This is a place of work. Put your apron on and look lively.'

Matilda pushed herself to her feet. The sky was grey with dawn and smoke. 'Yes, Mr Thrattle.'

Women straggled along the street. Inside she could hear the whoosh as Tommy hosed down the floor.

The day had begun.

～⁂～

Six hours later her feet ached. Her back ached. Even her elbows ached from keeping them close to her side so she didn't jostle the aproned women next to her.

The world had shrunk to the few feet of space by the conveyer belt, can after can after can, the air thick with smoke from the fires under the giant vats of water and the steam from boiling fruit. Her hands stung from checking the seals on each hot can, then pressing on a label.

The sooner Tommy worked out his grapple thing the better. She glanced around quickly, wondering where he was now — the pots of hot jam came too fast to look away for long.

Men trundled boxes of fruit or barrows of coal, the older women slicing, slicing, slicing at the endless mounds of plums and chokos. Chokos were cheaper even than plums, and no one was supposed to know the difference, just like when Mr Thrattle added marrow to the strawberry jam, with red food colouring to make it look good.

Another hour till lunch, then five hours more till she could go home. At least the endless stench of jam stopped her hunger. She'd never eat jam again ...

For a second she heard Tommy's laughter close behind her. She hoped he didn't come up and talk. The women weren't allowed to speak while they were working. Mr Thrattle wouldn't sack Tommy, but she didn't dare attract the boss's attention in case he docked her pay.

She risked another glance up. Tommy winked at her, then moved away, past the vats where the fruit stewed, to the big coppers where the sugar was added. The mix had to be stirred by hand, two men working giant paddles back and forth, till the jam was thick and bubbling like a volcano, ready to be tipped out into the giant funnels that filled the cans.

Matilda was glad she wasn't on the filling station. Hot jam could burn you to the bone. Jam burns got infected. Mrs Dawkins had told her about one of the women who'd lost an arm, and two of the women worked nine fingered.

Can after can … pick up a label, dip it in the glue, slap it on the hot tin, pick up a label, dip it in the glue …

Beside her women coughed, deep coughs that wracked their bodies, made worse by steam and smoke. Everyone who worked at the factory coughed after a few years. It was the factory cough.

Pick up the label, dip it in the glue, slap it on a tin, wait for the next …

Her hands kept working even when her mind was elsewhere — back at Aunt Ann's cottage, or Dad's farm … she had never seen it, couldn't remember her father either. But Aunt Ann had had a book about a farm. The farm kitchen was painted white, with a yellow cloth on the kitchen table and a fat brown cow peering through the window. And in the background white lambs with wriggly tails and fat pink pigs.

She peered up at the factory clock again. Forty minutes to go. Behind her the brackets creaked as another vat of plum jam was swung over into the funnel.

Something cracked, loud as lightning. Men yelled.

She turned in time to see the giant vat swing off its hinges, spilling the jam onto the floor.

Tommy had said the whole thing was rusted ... for an instant she felt nothing but pleasure that he'd been right, that Mr Thrattle would lose the profits of a whole vat of jam. Maybe he'd even let them take some of the spilled jam home ...

And then she saw a shape among the red.

Chapter 2

'It's young Thompson!'

'My oath! Help him, someone!'

Matilda's skin crawled cold, despite the steam. That shape was Tommy, half buried in the still bubbling jam.

Why did no one move? Were they afraid of getting burned? Her mind moved faster than her body … pulling him away from the jam wouldn't be enough. The jam would stick on his flesh, still burning to the bone.

Somehow she was already at the giant hose, turning it on full force. Within seconds the crowd was saturated. They moved apart, some in anger, others seeing what she was trying to do.

It had to work! It had to!

The top layer of jam began to sizzle. Slowly it began to move, washing back bit by bit, showing the details of the shape beneath.

Matilda let out the breath she hadn't known she was holding. She had imagined Tommy burned to a skeleton. But part of the mechanism had sheltered him. Only one arm and the side of his face had been burned: they were revealed, red as the jam, as the water washed him free.

Men moved now, using the jam stirrers to move the still-hot cauldron away from him. Tommy's face stared up, mouth open, eyes shut, one side stark white, the other blistered red. His left leg was folded under him at a strange angle.

'Is he dead?'

Matilda didn't know who spoke. She stood, the hose still in her hands, vaguely aware that someone had turned it off.

'Move away there.' It was Mrs Eastman, the steadiest of the women on the line. She held her skirts up out of the jammy water while she kneeled by Tommy's body, her hand on his neck, then ran her hands along his sides.

He didn't move.

Mrs Eastman looked up. 'Bring one o' the doors. Now!'

Men moved. Mrs Eastman nodded at Matilda. 'Good work,' she said shortly.

'Is he ... is he alive?'

'He's breathing. One leg broke, I think. Might lose the arm too.' She spoke with the dispassionate voice of a woman who had lost ten of her twelve children to disease and a husband to drink. 'He'd have been a goner if you hadn't got that jam away. You saved his life.'

'Here, you!' she called more loudly. 'You men, put him on the door. Gently now: don't jar that leg. Don't touch them burns, neither. You.' She fixed her eye on Mr Thrattle. 'Get a taxi cab to take him to the hospital.'

'But who will pay ...?'

The woman fixed him with her eyes. 'You will,' she said.

The man opened his mouth as though to argue, then hurried to do her will.

Chapter 3

They wouldn't let Matilda see him at the hospital. One of Tommy's brothers sat with her in the wide hospital corridor, with its wooden benches and smell of antiseptic, awkwardly twisting his hat in his hands, as though he had no idea how to handle a crying, jam-splattered girl who refused to leave till she knew how his brother was. 'He ain't woke up yet. But Ma says Doc told her he should be all right, long as it don't get infected. Doc has set his leg.'

'Will he be able to use his hand?' Matilda tried to keep her voice steady. Impossible to think of Tommy not using his hands. Tommy, grinning as he took machines apart, creating new ones from scraps of cogs and wire. Tommy, grinning as he watched her eat his sandwiches.

'Don't know.' The young man's voice cracked. He's trying not to cry in front of a girl, thought Matilda. The image of a one-armed Tommy must be as hard for him as her.

'Tell him … When Tommy wakes up, tell him I was here. Tell him I'll come back tomorrow night.'

'Might not let you see him.'

'I'll come anyway. Tell him.'

'I'll tell him.' The boy had his voice under control again. 'That old lady said you saved his life.'

Matilda shrugged.

'Thank you.' The words were even more awkward. 'Tommy's …' The young man bit his lips. 'Tommy's a good 'un.'

'Yes,' said Matilda softly. 'He is.'

The smell of boiled cabbage and stale wash-rags lingered around the front door of Mrs Dawkins's boarding house. Matilda slipped upstairs as quietly as she could.

For a few seconds Matilda let herself linger on the memory of Aunt Ann's tiny cottage up above the beach, the salty sea air, the scream of seagulls overhead. It was only an hour's cart ride away, but it was gone from her life as surely as the jam had burned the flesh from Tommy's arm.

She shuddered, trying to shut away the image, and fixed a smile on her face.

Mum lay under the grey cotton sheet. Her eyes opened at the click of the door. They seemed too vivid for her white face. She managed a smile.

'Matilda …' Her eyes darkened. 'Rabbit, what's wrong?'

How could she think she'd hide the truth from Mum? The tears that wouldn't come before erupted in a giant choke. 'Tommy. There was an accident at the factory. He's burned.'

'How bad?'

Mum's voice was just a thread; there was no breath behind it.

One thin hand touched hers, its fingers long and soft. The nails had grown since she'd stopped sewing.

'I don't know. He's at the hospital. They said they think he'll live …'

'Oh, my little rabbit.' Matilda could feel Mum's warmth as she lay next to her, the comfort of her arms. 'Come, lie down. He's strong, little rabbit. He'll pull through.'

Matilda nodded, her sobs easing. Tommy was too — too bright to vanish into death. But his arm, his hand … how could he be Tommy without two hands?

'Have you had something to eat?'

'Yes,' lied Matilda. She'd go down soon and make Mum's soup. She glanced over at the bowl and cup she'd put out before she left. Both were empty, and she could smell the chamber pot had been used too. Surely that must mean Mum was getting well. In a few weeks she'd be up again.

'How's the pain?'

'Better. Much better.'

But Mum said that every evening, and every day she was weaker still. Weariness flooded Matilda suddenly, as though her bones were liquid. Just a few more minutes before she went downstairs. Just a few moments to dream.

'Mum, tell me the story.'

For a moment there was silence. Matilda lifted her head. Was Mum too tired to talk? But Mum was smiling again. 'Once upon a time …'

Matilda nestled back into the warmth.

'Once upon a time,' whispered Mum, 'a golden man rode into town. He had brown eyes, deep as a well, and a smile as bright as lamplight.'

'Tell me about the horse.'

'It was a big horse, black as night.'

Night isn't black, thought Matilda, not with the gaslights and the lanterns in the windows. The horse would be as black as Mrs Dawkins's velvet dress, the one she kept for funerals …

'Go on,' breathed Matilda.

'Most men stopped at the hotel. But the golden man came into the Presbyterian Ladies' Tearoom.

'"I could eat a horse and chase the rider," he said.

'The waitress had never seen anyone like the golden man. "We don't sell horses here," she said. "There's cheese on toast, or creamed asparagus on toast, or cinnamon toast. You couldn't fit a horse on toast."'

Matilda smiled. It was the best joke in the world: the most familiar too.

'"You smell like spices," said the golden man.

'"That's the cinnamon," said the waitress.

'"Then I'll have a pile of cinnamon toast right up to the ceiling," said the golden man. And he did, all of it dripping with butter.'

Matilda felt her tummy rumble. She hoped Mum didn't hear it.

'He had cup after cup of tea, and so much toast the kitchen ran out of bread. Then when the tearoom closed he walked the waitress home. That night there was a church dance. The golden man and the waitress danced every dance, and then they waltzed, out through the door and onto the verandah. The moon shone a golden road down the sky. "One day I'll take you along a golden road," whispered the man. "We'll go to my farm."

'"It's a golden farm,"' said Mum softly. 'That's what he said. Hills of golden grass and golden paddocks. He'd build us a house there, and one day we'd waltz in the paddocks, under the moon —'

She stopped to cough. But just a little cough, thought Matilda. She held the water to her mother's lips. 'And six weeks later you were married, and a year after that there was me. One day we'll go to the farm and see the golden hills.'

Mum nodded. 'One day,' she whispered.

'There'll be the sheep,' said Matilda dreamily, 'and lots of lambs, just like in Aunt Ann's book, and a dog for me and a big chair out on the verandah for you to sit in.' She felt Mum nod next to her.

Matilda shut her eyes. Sometimes she thought she remembered her father: a big man, with strong hands. But it was so long ago, and maybe the person she remembered wasn't her father at all.

All that she really knew of him were the postal notes. No letter with them — men didn't like to write, said Mum. Dad was off shearing to earn enough money to build their house.

But one day the golden man would come again. He'd take them to their house. Mum could sleep in the sun on the verandah, away from the city smoke, and get strong enough to waltz in the moonlight. And Matilda could have a dog, and books, and Tommy could come and stay —

Tommy! Her eyes opened. She wished she could go back to the hospital to see if he had woken up or over to the Thompsons' house to see if there was any more news. But she needed to make Mum's broth, and empty the chamber pot.

She sat up. Mum was asleep, smiling. She always smiled when she talked about the golden man. Matilda stroked her cheek. It was so soft, so …

Cold.

'Mum! Mum!'

The shadowed eyes didn't open.

Chapter 4

Dear Dad,

I hope you are well.

Mum is dead. I am sorry I do not know the polite way to write that to someone, they didn't teach us that at Miss Thrush's school. We could not pay a doctor but Old Mother Basket down the street who delivers babies said Mum had a growth inside her that spread. I do not know if that is true but Mother Basket is good at delivering babies.

The grave does not have a headstone. It cost too much. It is a pauper's grave but I bought a proper coffin and Mrs Thompson has a rose bush and she gave me some flowers. There aren't any other rose bushes near here, not like at Aunt Ann's where there were lots of flowers. The book on farms I read said they have lots of flowers like wattle and boronia and native honeysuckle. I wish I could have picked a big bunch for Mum. There were only five roses on the bush.

Please could you come to the city? I know you are very busy,
but I do not know what to do.

Your loving daughter,
Matilda

PS If someone else is reading this could you please send it to my
dad quickly?

－⁂❀

The hospital floor was so polished her boots kept slipping. They were Mum's boots, worn with newspaper stuffed in the toe, to look respectable for Mum's funeral. The black dress was Mum's too, the hem hastily taken up and the sides tacked in. 'No point cutting good cloth,' said Mrs Dawkins, when it could be let out again later as Matilda grew.

Tommy's bed was at the end of the row of neat grey blankets and white sheets, and men's white faces too. Tommy looked younger and smaller, somehow, on the starched pillow. One side of his face was still puckered and red, but at least the jam had missed his eyes. She looked down at his hand. His arm was still bandaged, but now he held a small rubber ball in his fingers. She could see the sweat on his forehead as he tried to clasp it.

'You should wait till your hand has healed.'

He looked up at her and tried to smile, one half of his face twisting while the other stayed still.

'I need to stretch it before the scars set. I was reading about a cove who kept working on his muscles when his leg was crushed. Got his leg working again after six months. Arms and legs are just like machines, except they got muscles and tendons instead of cogs and pulleys.'

It was so like Tommy to have read how arms and legs worked. 'I'm sorry. I should have bought you grapes or something.'

'Ma brought those.' He gestured to the bowl by his bed. 'Go on, eat them. I'm that sick of grapes.'

'I'm not hungry.'

'Eat them.' The voice was gentle, but firm. She nodded. It was funny, everyone wanted to feed her now, even Mrs Dawkins, but her appetite had gone.

'How was ...'

'The funeral.' She forced herself to eat another grape. 'It was just me and Mrs Dawkins. But it was a proper coffin, not a pauper's. I pawned Mum's wedding ring.' She glanced up at him. 'I'll get it back one day. Bury it with her.'

He nodded. 'What now?'

'I don't know. Mrs Dawkins has let our room to someone else. I'm sleeping with her Monica. She says I can stay, as long as I go on working at the factory. My wages will pay for my keep.' She shrugged. 'Or I can go to the Destitute Children's Home.'

'No!'

She gave up on the grapes. 'I heard they send the orphans to school.'

'Only till they're big enough to work. They'd farm you out as a maidservant, working all hours just for your keep.'

'Oh,' she said slowly, 'I didn't know.'

He sat forward, grunting a little with the pain, and reached out to her with his good hand. 'Stay at the factory for now. Maybe ... maybe you can live with us. I'll be out of here soon.'

No, you won't, she thought. And when you do you'll need nursing. She'd met his ma two days ago, thin-faced and anxious. She'd thanked Matilda over and over for saving her son. But she had eight children already in that small house, and now

Tommy not working. Matilda couldn't add another burden to that tired face.

She said steadily, 'There's one other thing that I can do.'

'What?'

'Go to my father.'

Tommy stared. 'You don't know where he is.'

'Of course I know where his farm is. It's called Moura, north of Gibber's Creek.'

'Gibber's Creek! That's beyond the black stump.'

'What stump?'

He gestured with his good hand. 'Just a saying. But Gibber's Creek's hundreds of miles away from here.'

'I know. I found it on the map when I was at school. But even if he's not there, there has to be someone looking after his farm. Don't you see,' she added urgently, 'it makes sense.'

'No, it doesn't. Write to him, send a telegram, and wait for him to come to you.'

'No.'

'Why not?'

Matilda sat silently. She wasn't even sure she knew the answer. Just that so much she loved had vanished. Mum, Aunt Ann, even Tommy, though he'd come back (wouldn't he?). She needed something of her own, and there was only one thing left.

Her father.

'You don't even know how to get there.'

'There's a train.'

'The train'll only take you as far as Drinkwater. That's just a big property, not even a town.'

Drinkwater. She stored the bit of information up. She should have known Tommy would know the nearest train station to anywhere.

'How do people get to Gibber's Creek from the train?'

He lay back, suddenly exhausted. 'I don't know. Someone picks them up in a cart. Maybe there's a mail coach. I don't know everything. Matilda?'

'Yes.' She leaned closer.

'Why didn't your dad help you before? When your ma was ill?'

'Because he's off shearing,' she said patiently. 'I told you.'

Tommy shook his head. 'They don't shear all year round. Why doesn't he ever visit you?'

'He's ... he's busy on his farm. He's building us a house to live in.'

Tommy watched her from his bed. 'He ... you do have a father, don't you?'

'Of course! Everyone has to have a father.'

'Not everyone,' he said gently. 'Sometimes ... sometimes men don't want a family.'

She shook her head. 'My dad's not like that. He sent us money, up till last year. I *told* you, remember? I went to school and everything.'

'Are you sure that wasn't your Aunt Ann's money?'

Matilda shook her head. 'I saw the postal orders. And Aunt Ann didn't have any money, just what she and Mum got from sewing. Besides, Mum wouldn't lie to me.'

She took his hand again, the good one. 'All sorts of things can happen when you're out shearing. Floods, so that letters can't get through, or he could be a long way from a post office.'

He shook his head, too tired to argue further. 'Promise me.' His whisper was urgent. 'Promise you won't do anything till I'm outta here.'

The gong chimed at the nurses' desk to say visiting hours were over. Matilda leaned over and kissed his cheek, the one that wasn't burned, and smiled as he blushed. 'We'll see,' she said.

Chapter 5

Dear Mrs Dawkins,

I am sorry to leave like this. I hope you don't mind. I am going to live with my father. I am sorry I did not pay you my wages yesterday. I need the money for the train.

Thank you for all your kindness.

Your obedient servant,
Matilda O'Halloran

The railway platform was almost deserted, smelling of old soot. A woman in shabby black dozed with a child either side of her on one of the benches, brown-paper packages at their feet. Somewhere a train snuffed and snorted, but the big train on the country platform was silent, and even its lights weren't lit. She hadn't dared wait back at the boarding house, or Mrs Dawkins might have tried to stop her leaving.

All she owned was wrapped in the old shawl: her spare dress, Mum's dresses and Mum's good shoes too. Everything else had been sold in the last six months, even their hats.

She'd hoped there might have been a letter from her father, hidden under the mattress maybe, something Mum kept treasured, too secret to be shown. But as Mum had said, men just didn't like to write.

The scent of roasting rabbits wafted in from the stand on the corner of the station. Her stomach rumbled so loudly she hoped anyone who heard it would think it was a train.

'You waiting to get on, lass?' A man in a uniform peered out of the guard carriage.

'Yes, sir.'

'You all on your ownsome?'

'My father is meeting me.'

'Och aye.' He had an accent like Mr Macintosh, who'd rented the room below theirs. It was funny to think she'd probably never see Mr Macintosh again. Funny leaving the factory last night, knowing she'd never set foot in it again. She hoped someone else would bring Bruiser a bone sometimes. She'd have to ask Tommy. But at least she'd never see Mr Thrattle's piggy whiskers again either.

'Old biscuit,' she said under her breath.

'What was that, lass?'

'Nothing.'

He looked at her kindly. 'Well, seein' you're on your own, you'd better step into the carriage. It's warmer there. No one'll bother you, I'll see to that.'

'Thank you.' He must have seen the relief on her face. The station had been too big, too empty.

'I'll be makin' myself a drop o' tea, afore we set off. I'll bring one along to you, and a biscuit or two as well. Second-class carriage is the fifth one along.'

'Thank you,' she said again. She picked up her skirts, hefted her bundle more firmly under her arm, and headed toward the carriage. No more mornings hiding from the Push. No more Bruiser or Ah Ching. No more Tommy ...

She felt her breath catch. Impossible to think of not seeing Tommy. But he could come and stay with them. They had machinery on farms, didn't they? Ploughs and hay balers and things. He could practise fixing things with one hand.

It was warmer inside the train. She lay on one of the hard bench seats, so unlike the green leather ones she'd seen through the windows of the first-class carriages, pulling her skirts and shawl around her.

Matilda slept.

— ✿ —

Rented a fence ... rented a fence ... rented a ... rented a ... rented a fence ...

She'd slept again after the train had left the station, the guard's tea and biscuits warm in her stomach, and woken up hours later with the words in her mind. They didn't make sense — who'd want to rent a fence? But that was what the train wheels were saying. *Rented ... rented a ... rented a fence ...*

It was strange to have the world rush past you. She'd never been on anything faster than an omnibus before, the tired horses clomping up the road to Aunt Ann's.

Now the nearby bushes outside the train window blurred by, too fast to see. Things far away moved more slowly, as though it

27

was the world outside that was travelling at two speeds, while she and the train stayed still — except for the rattling.

It was fascinating, seeing things she had read about but never seen. Trees with giant white trunks, not just a small park of them but seeming to go on forever; ragged children sitting on a fence and waving, then they were gone again.

More trees; trees with rocks; trees with no rocks; trees and a small ferny creek; then trees and grass; then finally hard baked ground, a few trees holding thin limp leaves.

How could anything live in a land as dry as this?

Suddenly movement flickered. Those must be kangaroos. She had seen kangaroos in books and seen them close up, but never in a mob like a wave sweeping across the ground. She had never dreamed of a land so big, so flat. Its size and drabness were frightening: so different from the gardens she had known when she had lived at Aunt Ann's.

The other passengers in the carriage dozed or stared out the windows like her, except for one man in the corner, thin and intense in his shabby dark suit and tie, who was scribbling something in a notebook, unscrewing the ink bottle every time he needed to dip in his pen in case the rattle of the train tipped it over.

Even the fat woman with the two small children was sleeping, one child in each arm. They must be hot, all crammed up together, thought Matilda.

She was hot too. She wished she hadn't put on all her petticoats, but it was easier wearing them than carrying them. She'd have liked to open the window, but when she'd done it before big smuts had blown in from the train's smoke, and a cross man with no teeth had made her shut it again.

The trees outside grew sparser. The grass became dust — brown dust, white dust, grey dust — with a few tussocks and the occasional bald hump of a hill. Grey rocks were scattered across the landscape. It took Matilda a while to recognise that they were sheep, motionless in the heat.

How long till Drinkwater now? She didn't dare shut her eyes, in case she didn't hear the guard's call. He'd said they'd reach Drinkwater around four o'clock, but no one in the carriage had a watch. She craned her neck, trying to see ahead, but there were still no houses or even fenced paddocks with horses or vegetables or cows, just dust and trees and lumps of sheep.

Suddenly the train began to slow. A sheep on the line, she thought — they'd had to stop five times already so the guard could shift livestock sleeping on the railway tracks.

'Drinkwater! Drinkwater! All out for Drinkwater!'

For a moment she thought she must have imagined the call, but then the guard came bustling through the door, a smut on his cheek from swinging between the carriages. 'You lassie, you're for Drinkwater, aren't you?'

'Yes ...'

He was already swinging her bundle down from the rack. 'Come on then.'

Behind her the thin man stood up too, putting on a battered bowler hat and grabbing his Gladstone bag. The fat woman peered out the window. 'Why, lovey, that must be your dad, come to meet you.'

'But he doesn't know —' began Matilda, then stopped as she saw a white-bearded man in a wagon outside. The train only ran twice a week. Maybe he'd got her letter and decided to come to the station! But surely that man was too old to be her father.

She followed the guard and the thin man out to the corridor then down the stairs.

The heat hit her like a slap, then seemed to drag the moisture from her lungs. It had been hot in the train, but that heat had been damp with sweat. This heat would dry a loaf of bread into breadcrumbs in a second.

The flies followed. Flies in her eyes, flies crawling at her mouth. She shuddered and tried to wave them away.

She looked around. Why would anyone want to stop here?

No railway station. No platform: just dust, worn hard by feet and horses' hooves. A rough wooden sign, with *Drinkwater Siding* burned into it with a hot poker. Trees that seemed larger than they had from the train. A white track that seemed to lead to nowhere.

For a moment she thought the man and the wagon she had glimpsed from the train had vanished. But as the last train carriage moved away, leaving gusts of smoke behind, she saw the cart again, across the tracks. Two men stood next to it, both younger than the man in the cart. They smiled and raised their hats to her politely, but made no move to come over to her.

Matilda took a deep breath, then coughed as she swallowed a fly. She tried not to imagine it crawling around inside her.

Was one of those men her father? None of them looked like the golden man of her mother's stories. They weren't rushing over to greet her either.

'Well.' The voice beside her was deep and well bred. 'I do think your Uncle Cecil might have been here to meet us.'

'The train was early, Mama.'

'That is no excuse.'

Matilda looked around. Besides the thin man who had been in the carriage, two other passengers from the first-class carriage had alighted: a woman in plum-coloured silk, three feathers in her net-veiled hat, and a girl a couple of years older than

30

Matilda, dressed in white, despite the risk of smuts from the train. Matilda was vaguely glad to see a large grey smudge on the back of the muslin skirt, staining the lace and the ruffles. The girl's hat was heavily veiled too. No flies under those, thought Matilda enviously.

'You Patrick O'Reilly?' The yell came from the driver of the wagon. He waved the stone jug in his hand, as though in welcome.

The thin man nodded. He picked up his bag and began to cross the tracks.

Matilda hesitated. Instinct told her to stay with the woman and the girl, not to talk to strange men, especially ones as rough-looking as these. She didn't like the way they passed the stone jug from one to another either. She was pretty sure it contained what Aunt Ann called 'spirituous liquor' and Mrs Dawkins called 'rotgut rum'. But neither the woman nor the girl had even smiled at her, and the men seemed friendly, at least.

She grabbed her bundle and followed the thin man across the shimmering train lines.

All four men were in the cart now, the thin man and the white-bearded driver, the other two in the back. The three locals were dressed alike: big hats, grey trousers tied up at the ankles with string, stained shirts that might have been any colour once, but now were grey as well. Two of the men had strange bits of string and corks bobbing from their hat brims, so it looked like they were behind a bamboo blind. Only the men's beards were different: one white, one red, one grey and one brown.

The old man looked down. 'What you want, girly?' His breath smelled like the garbage bins in Grinder's Alley. She clenched her fists to give her courage.

'I need to get to Moura.'

'You mean Jim O'Halloran's place?'

She looked up at him eagerly. 'You know my dad?'

'Your dad!'

Three of the men stared down at her. The fourth, the thin man from the train, was checking his notebook again.

'I ... I've come to stay with him.'

Grey-beard stared, open-mouthed, showing gaps in his long yellow teeth. 'Jim O'Halloran's got a daughter?'

'Shh.' Brown-beard nudged him in the ribs, not gently. 'Bloke's got a right to have a daughter, ain't he?' He took a swig from the jug and passed it on.

'Then why ain't we ever seen her? You mean Jim O'Halloran had a wife too?'

'I had a wife once,' said Brown-beard reminiscently. 'Way back when I was working on the Murray. Dunno what happened to her, but.'

'Mum and I have been living in the city. But she ... she died.'

'Ah, too bad,' said White-beard. But there was no real sympathy in it. White-beard sounded as though he'd need worse than the death of one woman to show real sympathy.

'Woman's got a right to live in the city,' said Brown-beard. 'Got a right to live anywhere she chooses.'

'Nah, she ain't,' said Grey-beard. 'She oughtta be at home cookin' her bloke's tea. That right, Mr O'Reilly?'

The thin man looked up. 'Our fight is for the rights of working men *and* working women.'

'Women got a right to work, sure enough. But they should be doin' it in the kitchen,' Grey-beard concluded.

'Or the bedroom.' Brown-beard chuckled.

'None o' that,' said White-beard. He grabbed back the stone jug. 'Ladies present.'

'A man's got a right to say —' began Brown-beard.

'Please,' said Matilda. Her head was swimming. 'Can you take me to my father?'

'No worries, girly. Your dad's a union man, ain't he? One o' our own. You don't leave one o' your own in the dust.'

'Got to stand together, arm to arm.' Brown-beard bent down a leathery hand. One finger was missing. 'Plenty o' room in the wagon. I'm Bluey,' he added. He gestured to the grey-bearded man. 'This here's Whitey Gotobed.'

'An' I'm Curry and Rice,' said the other man, moving aside as Bluey swung Matilda up as though she was a chicken feather. Matilda shoved a blob of what she hoped was dirt away with her boot, then put her bundle down and sat on it. Could it be as easy as this? 'You'll really take me to Dad's farm?'

'Nah, no need,' said Mr Gotobed. 'Take you to tonight's meeting. Your dad'll be there, all right. He's a union man.'

'What's a union?'

Mr O'Reilly looked up from his notebook again. His voice was dry as the dust but more precise. 'A union is a brotherhood of men, joined together to fight the oppressor.'

'The oppressor is them as owns the stations,' put in Bluey. 'A man has a right to sell his own labour, ain't that right? An' a right to ... to ...'

'To withdraw it too. To strike,' finished Mr O'Reilly. 'A union is where any group of workers joins together to fight for better conditions, whether they be in a shearing shed or factory. The Shearers' Union formed three years ago, when the men who owned the stations tried to lower the pay rates. Shearers across the country came out on strike.' He could have been reading a railway timetable. 'Our job is now not just to force employers to let their men join unions, but to make just laws for the

33

whole country.' He took out his ink, dipped in his pen, and made another note.

'Oh,' said Matilda.

Mr Gotobed scratched his white beard. Matilda hoped he didn't have fleas. Or worse. The men smelled like they'd never had a bath in their lives or washed their clothes. 'We didn't go on strike round here, 'cause old Drinkwater didn't cut our pay. But when your dad started a local branch of the union a year ago, the old bast—'

'Biscuit,' said Matilda firmly. Aunt Ann had warned her that men were inclined to swear if you didn't watch them.

'The old, er, *biscuit* said he'd sack any man what joined. He weren't having no boss on his place but him. So we went on strike, the lot of us. Mr O'Reilly here has come to address us —'

'That means to talk at us,' put in Curry and Rice.

'A man has a right to free speech.' That was Bluey.

Matilda nodded, to seem polite. None of it made sense, except that she'd see her father soon. And maybe ... 'Will — will there be food at the meeting?'

Mr Gotobed looked at her, as though she'd said something that actually sank in. 'You hungry, girly?'

She nodded. There'd been a dining car, but she had only one and sixpence left, and that was for emergencies. The other second-class passengers had brought food with them. The fat woman had given her a couple of the children's rusks, but apart from the guard's biscuits that had been her only food all day.

Mr Gotobed scratched his hair. 'Give you a drop o' grog if you want.' He offered her the stone jug.

'No, thank you,' said Matilda politely. Aunt Ann said that the devil was in spirituous liquors, and anyone who drank them.

34

These men didn't seem to have the devil in them, but she still didn't want to risk it.

'Girl's got a right to eat,' said Bluey. He cupped his hands over his mouth. 'Hey, ma!' he yelled to the elegant woman waiting on the other side of the tracks. 'You got anythin' to eat? This girl's half starved.'

For a moment Matilda thought the woman wasn't going to answer. Then to her surprise she nodded. 'There are the remains of our luncheon in the basket. You are welcome to them if you want.'

'Good on yer, lady.' Bluey swung himself down from the wagon and stepped across the rails. He opened the wicker basket at the woman's feet, then piled the contents into his shirt. 'You don't want a lift too, do yous?'

'No, thank you, my good man. My half-brother, Mr Drinkwater, should be here any moment.'

Bluey's face flushed with anger as well as drink. 'You related to that old bast—' he glanced over at Matilda, '*biscuit*? I should throw this stuff down in the dust and trample on it.'

'And then the child will stay hungry.' The woman's voice was calm. 'If you men wish to dream up new laws for the country, I suggest you learn to think before you act.'

'A man has a right to —'

'Did I say you hadn't? Now good day to you.'

She turned away.

Good for her, thought Matilda. She was stuck up, and hadn't even smiled at her. But in a way she reminded her of Aunt Ann and Mrs Dawkins: women who met the world face on.

Bluey brought the food over the train line, muttering under his breath. He passed the bundle up before he levered himself into the cart.

Matilda took it eagerly. A whole chicken, wrapped in greaseproof paper, with only a few slices and two wings gone. She hadn't eaten chicken since the Christmas before last! Thin-sliced bread and butter, still soft and fresh, what must be most of a tin of digestive biscuits, three hunks of dark moist fruitcake, an apple, an orange ... how much had someone packed for one woman and a girl to eat?

She spread out her shawl to hold it all, with the cake and the chicken on the paper so as not to get fat stains on the cloth.

'Would any of you like some too?'

Curry and Rice waved the jug. 'We're right, girly. You tuck in. Let's get the horses movin',' he added. 'We'll never get Mr O'Reilly to the meetin' if we stand here all day. We got a new nation to make, remember!'

'I'm a goin'.' Mr Gotobed clicked the reins.

Hoofbeats sounded behind them. Matilda turned in time to see a carriage emerge from the trees, shiny blue with yellow scrollwork. Even the big wheels looked clean.

Three horsemen rode behind. It was hard to make them out at first, for the sun was behind them, throwing their faces into shadow and making a golden halo about them all: a man in a white shirt, black necktie and straw hat, and two boys, dressed much like the man, one a couple of years older than her, the other sixteen, perhaps, controlling his big horse so easily that he didn't even have to tug the reins to make it stop.

Matilda caught her breath; Mum's voice was whispering to her again ... *a golden man.*

They all looked golden, the boys even more than the man: skins browned by the sun, not by dirt or grease. But it was the shine of their horses' coats too, the clean, ironed shirts, the pale trousers even out here in the dust, the fresh-looking hats without even sweat stains at the band or rim.

They glowed, as though each had his own special sun.

It was her father. It had to be. A golden man, just like Mum had said. But then she looked at the boys again, so obviously the man's sons. She was her mother's only child, she was sure of that. Had her father been married before he met Mum?

She stood up, wishing she had a dress all white lace with ruffles, like the other girl. If only her hair wasn't limp with dust and travel. Maybe her face was smutty too.

The man lifted his hat. His hair was grey and tightly clipped, and his moustache was white. He turned slightly, so his face was no longer in shadow. He was old, she realised. His upright seat on the horse, a trick of the shadow, had made him seem young.

'I'm sorry I wasn't here to meet you, my dear.'

He spoke to the girl in white. Matilda put up her hand to attract his attention. He thinks she's me, she thought. That's what he'd like his daughter to be. All neat and white, not in a droopy black dress with a bundle. Then she realised the man was speaking to the woman, not the girl.

The woman smiled up at him. 'You are always late, Cecil.'

Matilda sat down. This must be Mr Drinkwater, the woman's half-brother, the man who had employed the men she was with. He must be the boys' grandfather, she thought. He's too old to be their father.

Mr Drinkwater smiled, showing white teeth. Matilda had never seen an old man with white teeth like that.

'I prostrate myself with apology. Will that do?'

'No excuse, then?'

He laughed. 'No good one. The boys and I were out hunting.'

She raised an eyebrow. 'Successful?'

'Just one buck this morning.' That was the older boy. He grinned, showing perfect teeth too, then lifted his hat to the girl. 'I'll teach you to shoot, if you like, Cousin Florence.'

The girl shook her head, her eyes wide. 'Don't be horrid, Cousin James.'

'Ha.' The older woman waved away the flies that were trying to get through her veil. 'Shame on you, James. And Bertram too. You and your father would rather shoot roos than meet your cousin's train.'

'Not roos.' There was laughter in the older boy's voice. 'Natives. They've been spearing the sheep again. But they won't dare try anything for a while after this.' He was showing off to his city cousin, but his words still rang true.

Matilda stared. People? They had been shooting people. And none of these people seemed to find it strange.

Maybe … maybe the boy had been joking. She looked at him again. He and his brother had slid off their horses now, and were helping the carriage driver put the luggage in the back.

'Hey, Drinkwater!' Bluey raised the jug at him. 'You been ter any good fires lately?'

Fires? thought Matilda. What about shooting people?

Mr Drinkwater swung round and gazed at the men in the cart. 'Was that your work?' His voice was quiet, but it burned through the air like boiling water.

Bluey laughed. 'Us? We knows nothin' about no fires, does we, lads?'

Mr Drinkwater looked at them, slowly, one by one. 'Whoever burned my shearing shed will go to gaol. Three troopers arrived on last week's train. Didn't you hear?'

'We heard,' said Mr Gotobed. 'Maybe them troopers o'

yours'll go to the meetin' tonight. Maybe they'll decide not to work fer the boss, but cast themselves in with their brothers.'

'If you have a brother, Gotobed, he is living under a rock. You watch yourself. The troopers will do their duty.'

'I'm shiverin' in me boots,' said Mr Gotobed.

The older Drinkwater boy — James — glared at the men in the cart. 'You remember who you're talking to. You're on Drinkwater land here.'

'This is a public road,' said Bluey. 'Man's got a right to ride on a public road.'

'You put one foot off it and my father will have you arrested.'

'James, Bertram, come on. There is no point arguing with riff-raff.' Mr Drinkwater swung himself down from his horse, and held his hand out to the woman and then the girl to help them into the carriage. The boys mounted their horses again.

Such wonderful big horses, thought Matilda. She had always wanted to try riding a horse. The boys sat comfortably, as though the giant animals were armchairs.

My dad has a farm too, she thought. Maybe next time she met the boys she would be wearing a new dress, with her face washed and her hair long and shiny. The boys would look at her like they looked at their Cousin Florence now.

But these boys hunted people ... or did they?

'Come on,' said Bluey. 'Let's get goin'. I don't like the smell around here.'

Mr O'Reilly looked up from his notebook. 'I would not want to be late for the meeting,' he said, in his small, passionless voice.

Mr Gotobed clicked the reins again.

Chapter 6

The carriage with its two big horses passed them before they had gone half a mile, the riders cantering past without even looking down.

'Why was Mr Drinkwater so angry?' asked Matilda.

Mr Gotobed grinned. 'When we went out on strike, Drinkwater brought in scabs to shear his sheep.'

'Scabs are men who take the jobs of men who are striking,' put in Mr O'Reilly precisely.

'So somehow old Drinkwater's shearin' shed burned down. Can't shear sheep with no shed,' said Mr Gotobed with satisfaction. 'The old, er, biscuit is goin' to have 20,000 wool-blind sheep knocking about his property if he don't allow the union on his place.'

'What's wool-blind?'

'Wool grows over their eyes so's they can't see. Wool gets all daggy too, burrs and whatnot. He'll get half price a bale if he's lucky.'

'But that's cruel — to the sheep I mean.'

Curry and Rice laughed. 'What do you know about it, girly? You ain't no worker. I reckon only workers got the right to say —'

'I am a worker!'

'Needlework?'

'Proper work.' She glared at him. 'I worked fourteen hours a day at the jam factory. Or I did till Mum died last week. I looked after her too. We couldn't pay for a doctor or a nurse so I did it all. That's work too! I slept in the street so I could be sure to wake up in time to get to work because the bailiffs took our alarm clock —'

'Hold your horses, girly!' Curry and Rice held up his hands in mock terror. 'No need to start nippin' at me ankles like a sheep dog. Fourteen hours a day, eh? What were you doin'?'

'Sticking labels on cans of jam.' She held up her hands when the men began to laugh. 'The cans have to be hot or the jam doesn't seal. Your hands blister at first, then they get tough.'

Curry and Rice blinked at her skin. 'Them's scars right enough. All right, girly, you's a worker too. Now you eat yer tucker an' enjoy the ride.'

Matilda took another bite of chicken, then looked at the man curiously. 'Why are you called Curry?'

'Used ter cook for the shearers, that's back before the strike, o' course.'

'How long have you been on strike around here?'

'About a year.'

'How do you make money then?'

'This 'n' that.' Mr Gotobed shrugged. 'No one's got money with the drought. Sell a few possum skins now an' then.'

Matilda pulled at a piece of chicken. Had that been why her father hadn't sent money for so long? But he owned a farm ... and yet the men had said he was a union man, that he'd even started the union around here.

The horses pulled along at a good pace. They might be dusty, not brushed shiny like the Drinkwater horses, but they kept their heads down and moved well, even on the uneven track. It looked like it would vanish any second into the dry dirt either side.

Then we'd be lost, thought Matilda, for all the trees looked the same, all the clumps of grass and giant mounds of orange clay.

'Who built those?' she pointed, a chicken leg in her hand.

'Them's ants' nests, girly,' said Curry and Rice. He burped, and handed the jug over to Mr O'Reilly. O'Reilly shook his head, and passed it to Mr Gotobed. 'Good things, them ants' nests. You can dig a hole in them an' light a fire and them's the best oven yous ever seen. Or spread 'em over a dirt floor an' wet 'em and tamp 'em down, and it sets hard as rock.'

'Oh,' said Matilda.

I'd better not ask any more questions, she thought. Adults often got impatient if you asked too many questions, and these men were drinking spirituous liquor. They could go mad at any moment.

Besides, she couldn't ask the real questions. What was her father like? Why hadn't he ever been to see them? What was his farm like? Mum and Aunt Ann had drilled it into her that private things were ... private. And you especially didn't talk about your family to men like these.

The wagon rumbled along. She finished the chicken — she didn't want to leave any, in case the flies got at it — and the bread and butter. She wrapped the fruit, biscuits and cake in her shawl, then used it as a pillow to lean against.

The men were silent now. Even the dust from the Drinkwaters' carriage had vanished in front of them. There was just the clop of the horses' hooves, the silence of the trees above, the almost noiseless cluster of the flies. She put an arm over her face to keep the worst of them away. And despite the heat, she slept.

─◦◦◦─

It was growing dark when she woke.

The wagon had stopped.

She sat up. All four men had gone, leaving the empty stone jug on its side next to her. She peered around.

So this was Gibber's Creek. There was a street — a proper one, she was glad to see, with what looked like a town hall next to her, lit up with gaslights, and shops on either side, dark now, the glass in their windows reflecting the last of the sun. There seemed to be no street lights here.

Further down the road were what looked like houses — nice houses, with gardens, and cottages too, lamplight glowing from their windows.

Horses were tied to the rails all along the shops, single horses and others still hitched to carts or buggies or sulkies. There were so many that it took her a moment to realise that she was the only person in the street.

There were people nearby, though. She could hear yelling, the stamp of feet and the hum of chatter, all coming from inside the hall.

Her father would be there. Her heart thudded at the thought of finally meeting him. She brushed her hair back over her ears, wishing she could wash her face, look nice for him.

But why hadn't he come out to look for her? Had the men even remembered to tell him about her? She doubted it, after so much spirituous liquor. She picked up her bundle in case someone stole it, and clambered down from the cart, then stepped up into the hall.

The noise broke over her as soon as she was in the door, and the smell too: old sweat and bad teeth, musty clothes and unwashed bodies, the stale smells of horses, tobacco and spirituous liquor.

Most of the crowd was made up of men, standing in the hall below the stage, but here and there women sat on chairs against the walls, some with children on their knees or by their sides: weather-stained women, with faces creased from work and sunlight. Even the young ones looked dried from the sun.

And every face looked hungry.

Not just hungry for food, though many, especially the women, were hollow cheeked. The crowd gave off a curious sense of expectation.

The stage above was dark.

Matilda clutched her bundle closer. Her father was in here somewhere — or was he? She couldn't see anyone here who looked like a 'golden man', the way Mr Drinkwater and his sons had looked. Golden boys with black hearts, she thought, remembering the careless way the older boy had spoken of shooting natives.

Maybe there was more here than she understood. Aunt Ann had often spoken about sending missionaries to civilise the natives. Some natives were cannibals, weren't they? She remembered a cartoon of natives cooking a missionary in a big pot.

She shivered ... maybe, maybe the natives here were savage. Maybe Mr Drinkwater and his sons were trying to keep everyone safe.

It was impossible to feel a lurking hope that her father was more like Mr Drinkwater than the men in the cart.

The crowd was growing restless. All at once the room quietened, like when the foreman at the factory turned off the machinery. A man walked onto the platform, carrying a taper. He bent down at the edge of the stage. Suddenly lights flared, one by one, washing a glow across the boards.

'Oi, Slippery Lucas, we ain't here to see you!' Laughter rippled across the crowd. Even some of the women smiled.

The man on the stage smiled cheekily, then walked off behind the curtains that hung on either side. The crowd stayed quieter now, muttering instead of yelling, watching the stage instead of chatting to each other.

Mr O'Reilly walked on.

He still looked small. The knees and elbows of his suit shone in the gaslight. He cleared his throat.

'Men and women of Australia!'

It was the voice of the man in the cart, but it was different too. This voice was pitched to carry to the back of the hall. It reached in and spoke to people's hearts.

'Tonight we stand on the brink of a new nation: one nation, no longer separate colonies. A new, big-hearted nation where each man has the vote — yes, and each woman too. A nation where each has the right to work — and to withdraw their labour when the bosses grip too hard; the right to worship freely, Catholic as well as the church of the English Queen; the right to wages a man can keep a family on ...'

The crowd was cheering now, but O'Reilly's voice thundered across them. A small man, thought Matilda, but with big ideas.

'Tonight in slums across our cities children sleep in gutters; they work in factories and never see the sun. Today women die

45

without money for a doctor, while their children weep, hungry and helpless.'

He had been listening, thought Matilda. Watching and taking notes ...

'Today the rich live on plum puddings while the children of the strikers starve. Today squatters bring in scab labour, forcing white men out of a job. Today the bosses bring in kanakas and Chinese who work for little money or none at all, tearing the bread from the mouths of the children of decent working men.'

The cheers had changed now to a steady call of, 'Yes! Yes! Yes!'

'I see a new world opening! Hand in hand you and I will build it. The nation of Australia, a brotherhood, a new nation where no man travels second class, for all men are created equal. A just nation, where no man can profit from his neighbour, but must share with all.'

The audience members were silent now, as though imagining a world like this took every fibre of their being. Suddenly Matilda could see it too. A land where people shared, with someone like Tommy, maybe, in charge of the factory, and the money made by Mr Thrattle shared out with everyone who worked there.

A free nation with laws to keep out the Chinese and the Islanders ...

The spell broke. Chinese. That was Ah Ching. Dear Mr Ah Ching, her friend of the dark mornings. He didn't take anyone's job ... or maybe he did, she thought, but did it matter? Why shouldn't he work too? She would rather have a land of Ah Chings than the boys of the Push.

Mr O'Reilly was still speaking, the crowd still drinking in his words like they were rain on the dusty world outside. Outside, she thought. I need fresh air and quiet. There's no chance of finding Dad in this. Today had been too much …

Was it only this morning she had been creeping down the grimy street, sleeping in the silent train, journeying through dust and trees?

At least she was at the back of the hall, with no one to notice as she left. She slipped out of the door and down the stairs, then sat on the lowest one, breathing in the quiet and the darkness, trying to ignore the voice inside.

Big ideas, she thought. Too big perhaps for her to understand. Too big, maybe, for most in the room too — maybe even too big for Mr O'Reilly.

Aunt Ann had spoken about the agitation to unite the states into one nation, where even women would have the vote. Aunt Ann was for it, especially the votes for women. She was sure if the women of a new united Australia voted, they'd back the Women's Temperance and Suffrage League, and ban spirituous liquors from the land.

Somehow Matilda didn't see the crowd behind her cheering for that.

But Aunt Ann hadn't had the passion, the intentness of that crowd. Maybe because her life was full with her church and her sewing, her temperance work, with her sister and her niece, till the dray tipped over crushing it all out so thoroughly.

Matilda reached for her bundle. She sat on the empty steps and began to nibble the leftover fruitcake.

What now? The crowd had been too thick to find Mr Gotobed and the others, and anyhow, she doubted they cared what happened to her. They'd been heading to the meeting, and so they'd brought her here. Probably her father wasn't even inside.

How far away was Moura? She could just start walking till she found it. But the road ran in two directions. She might head in the wrong direction, and maybe there were other roads out of town too.

She was just so tired. For a moment she allowed herself to dream that when she woke she would be back with Aunt Ann bustling about and giving orders, a dust cloth in one hand and a jar of her home-made lavender polish in the other, telling her to polish the sideboard once a day for a week, once a week for a month, once a month for a year ...

Something creaked along the road. Matilda opened her eyes. Mr Ah Ching walked toward her, pulling an empty cart along the road.

She blinked, and suddenly it wasn't Ah Ching, but another man, a few years younger, though still with Ah Ching's pigtail and black pants and top. But this man's feet were bare.

He was a stranger, but in a funny way he was the most familiar thing in this long day. A Chinese man and a vegetable cart coming toward her in the darkness. Without thinking she stood and bowed, her head down, and said, 'Qing An.'

The man looked up, seeing her for the first time. The rattle of cart wheels stopped. He spoke rapidly, so fast that she couldn't tell if any of his words were ones she knew.

He stopped, then spoke more hesitantly. 'You speak Chinee, missee?'

'No, I'm sorry. A ... a friend taught me a few words. I don't really know what they mean.' Somehow she had the feeling that the man in front of her understood her English, despite his halting speech. 'You don't know Mr Ah Ching, do you?'

She felt embarrassed as soon as she said it. There were lots of Chinese people in Australia. She had a vague feeling they'd been here just about as long as the English and Irish. Why should he know Mr Ah Ching?

'Sorry, missee.' He stood there, as though considering her. 'You need help?'

Was it so obvious? She stood up uncertainly, brushing crumbs off her skirt. 'I need to find my father, Mr Jim O'Halloran.'

He looked around the empty street. Yells and cheers came from inside the hall, even louder now. She had a feeling that more spirituous liquor was being drunk in there than Aunt Ann had ever dreamed of. 'Mr O'Halloran of Moura?'

'You know it! How do I get there? Is it far away?'

He seemed to come to a decision. 'You get in cart.'

'You'll take me there?'

He neither shook his head nor nodded. 'You get in cart.'

She hesitated. What if Aunt Ann was right? What if he was going to kidnap her and sell her as a slave? No one knew she was here. No one would even look for her. She would just vanish in the darkness.

Laughter erupted behind her. Two men lurched out of the hall, each carrying a stone jug. The stench of old sweat and spirituous liquor grew stronger. 'Hey, lassie,' called one of them. 'All alone?'

Suddenly the risk of being kidnapped by a white slaver felt less likely to harm her than sitting here unprotected in the darkness.

She stepped toward the cart.

Chapter 7

She ran through the smoky lanes, lost. Somewhere in those faceless houses were Mum, Aunt Ann, Tommy, her father too. She only had to find them.

No, she wasn't lost. They were lost. She was asleep in bed. Soon Mum would wake her to go down to the factory. Matilda pulled the sheet over her head. She'd just sleep a little longer.

She woke, abruptly. It was a blanket, not a sheet ... no, not even a blanket, just a hessian sack. At least it looked fairly clean. She was still in the vegetable cart, her head on her bundle. The warmth was sunlight, not a bed. The world smelled of fresh soil and — cabbage?

Flies clustered at her eyes as soon as she opened them, hunting for moisture. She rubbed them away and felt the grittiness of dust. She sat up and looked around.

The sun was just rising, washing its light across the land. She was in a garden, or rather a farm, vegetables all around her. Cabbages, carrot tops, pumpkins curled among the flat leaves of other vegetables she couldn't recognise, some with silver-purple flowers, a shock of lushness among the grey of dirt and clumps of grass. Hens scratched in the dirt behind a rough branch fence.

Beyond the vegetables flowed a shallow river, wide as a city block, winding through broad flats of bright white sand. Light glinted on a thin channel of water, curling through the sand and then through dirt, till it reached the garden.

She turned her head and saw a hut the size of a carriage house, with bark walls and a bark roof. Beyond the hut two men, both dressed in black, bent over the vegetable beds, each hacking at the soil with some sort of long-handled tool.

One of them was the man she had met last night. What magic did they have to create such greenery in a dead land like this?

She shifted uneasily. She needed to use a chamber pot. Now. Should she go into the hut and try to find one? But you couldn't just use a stranger's chamber pot, especially a man's.

Maybe she could squat unnoticed among the cabbages. She slid down from the cart, and waited for the men to look at her. But they seemed intent on their work. She crouched down among the tallest cabbages, straightening her skirt when she'd finished, and scuffled over the wet patch with her shoe.

One of the men looked up. She flushed, glad he hadn't looked a few seconds earlier. (Or had he been watching out of the corner of his eye, carefully looking the other way to give her privacy?)

He said something to the other man then stepped over to her, still holding his hoe.

'Qing An.' She hoped it was still the right thing to say, early in the morning when you'd just squatted among someone's cabbages. 'Please. We go to Moura? Find my father?'

He nodded. 'Too far last night. I take now.'

He vanished into the hut, reappearing seconds later without his hoe, holding a china jug in one hand, and a blue and white plate in the other. He held them out, making drinking motions.

She took the jug cautiously and tasted it. Weak tea. She drank it gratefully, then handed the jug back and took the plate. There were flat white things on it, looking a bit like shiny fishcakes, but when she bit into one of them it was more like a dumpling, filled with something dark and sweet.

The first mouthful was almost disgusting; the second not bad. By the time she had finished the first dumpling she had decided she liked them. By the last mouthful, she knew they were even better than Aunt Ann's apple pie. She looked at the man hopefully, but he didn't offer her any more. He gestured to her to sit down on one of the blocks of wood by the hut instead.

Again she had the feeling he understood a lot more English than he was prepared to speak. Somehow he seemed a lot less foreign than the men on the wagon yesterday. 'Excuse me, sir, what is your name?'

He looked at her without expression. 'Doo Lee.'

She bowed, in the way Ah Ching had showed her. 'I'm pleased to meet you, Mr Lee. My name is Matilda O'Halloran.'

He blinked, as though once again she had done something unexpected. 'Mr Doo. Not Mr Lee.'

She bowed again. It felt a bit silly, but it was the only way she knew to be polite.

He gestured to the seat again. She sat. The two men began to fill the cart. They pulled up cabbages by their roots, slicing the stems off with long curved knives, and made bunches of beetroot, radishes, onions and carrots tied with their stems. At last they lugged what looked like a sack of potatoes out of the shed, and a net full of half a dozen strange round fruit, each bigger than a football.

She felt awkward sitting there, not helping. But they moved so expertly she guessed she'd be in the way.

At last Mr Doo gestured for her to get onto the cart too. She shook her head. 'I can walk. I was just tired last night.'

It wouldn't be fair, she thought, for him to have to lug me as well as the vegetables.

Again he neither nodded nor shook his head, just looked at her consideringly before getting between the shafts of the cart and beginning to pull.

She trudged after him, expecting him to head for the dusty track that led to the hut. But instead he pulled the cart between the vegetables, then across the hard ground toward the river, hauling the cart's giant wheels through the sand banks with the ease of long practice. He stopped at the water's edge to roll up his trousers. Once again he gestured for her to get into the cart.

This time she obeyed, trying to find a perch on top of the cabbages. She could swim a bit. Aunt Ann had taught her how to dog paddle in the cove by the cottage very early in the day, when there'd be no men around to stare.

But the water in the river looked deeper now she was close to it and, even if it was shallow, she couldn't lift her skirts up in front of a stranger, much less a man and a Chinaman. She wasn't even wearing any stockings.

The cart wheels splashed through the water. The river was shallow at first, up to Mr Doo's ankles, then abruptly it grew deeper, so he was wading almost waist-deep. The water rose up to the edges of the cart and across the wood beneath Matilda's bottom.

Matilda crouched, trying not to unbalance the cart as well as to keep herself dry. She wished she'd thought to take off her shoes. She had expected the water to be hot, flowing between the sun-warmed sand, but instead the chill almost numbed her toes through her shoes. She reached down and gathered some of the water in her hands, and tried to wash her face and neck and arms while not upsetting the cabbages. The air around her was already hot, the sun a yellow fire beating down on her, quickly sucking away the river's chill.

Mr Doo gave a grunt of effort, pulling the wheels through the sand and water up into the shallows. He stood puffing on the bank, the water dripping off his clothes and down his legs. He glanced at Matilda. 'Road long. This way short.'

Matilda nodded. Somehow his lack of speech made her feel she had to be silent too.

She scrambled out of the cart. Her shoes squelched as she trudged across the sand. She'd have to fill them with newspaper tonight or they'd dry hard and out of shape. Or maybe ... maybe her father would buy her new shoes straight away. Proper young lady's shoes, white, with buckles instead of laces ...

They crossed a paddock now, so flat it was hardly higher than the river, then trudged up a hill, dotted with grey rocks. All at once one of the rocks moved, and she saw it was a sheep. Or was it? Weren't sheep all white and fluffy? It looked much bigger than the sheep in Aunt Ann's book or the animals she had seen out of the train. Maybe this was another animal altogether.

The animal stared at her. 'Baaa,' it said, then bent to pull at the tough grass.

'Sheep?' she asked.

'Sheep,' said Mr Doo.

'Moura sheep?' she asked hopefully.

But Mr Doo shook his head. 'Moura long way. This Drinkwater,' he said.

The train had stopped at Drinkwater. She was pretty sure Mr Doo had headed in the other direction from the station. Drinkwater must be enormous, she thought, looking round. That man and those boys owned all this.

But it was ugly. Not the river behind them, slinking through the sand, but this land of dust and tussock. Even the scattered trees seemed to have been leached of colour, and the bald hills were squashed and featureless. Why would you want to live here if you were rich?

Please don't let Moura be like this, she thought. If Moura was a long way away then maybe the country was different, greener, with grass and proper trees.

They walked on, the heavy-woolled sheep gazing at them curiously, but making no move to either approach or flee.

The hill was steeper than it had looked. Now at the top Matilda looked around. More dusty ground, with a few trees scattered across it like raisins in Aunt Ann's fruit scones, and about a mile away a cluster of buildings around what looked like a large house surrounded by green trees — real green, not the dusty green of gum trees.

The roof of the house gleamed silver in the sunlight. That must be Mr Drinkwater's home, where the two boys from yesterday lived too.

Was this how farmers lived out here? The buildings looked substantial, almost like a village, the greenery soft and welcoming. It wasn't what she had imagined a farm would be like: the cottage with the pigs and cows and roses. But you could be comfortable in a big house like that, sheltered by its trees.

Mr Doo was already pulling his cart down the hill. She hurried after him, the wet edges of her skirt flapping around her ankles. At least she'd dry soon in this heat. She brushed the flies away again.

The buildings grew nearer. Now she could see men working on some sort of structure, heaving up tree trunks to make a framework. A big black smudge spread across the ground nearby, with half-burnt timbers in a heap.

Was that where the shearing shed had burned down? They were near enough now to hear the shouts of the men as they passed a roof beam up, but none of them even bothered to look their way.

Suddenly she realised what she must look like; just another figure in black, next to the black-garbed Chinaman. She didn't know whether to be glad or sorry. Sorry she didn't look like a pretty girl; but glad not to attract the notice of strange men.

The cart bumped its way toward the buildings. The nearest looked like cottages made of slabs of wood, with wooden shingles on the roof, and front terraces paved with stones, each with a stone fireplace. Lines of washing hung out the front. A dog barked somewhere, then hushed as its owner yelled at it to be quiet.

A road ran from cottage to cottage, as though this farm was almost a village. It was easier going on the road. They passed a long, low building made of uneven stones, with a roof of corrugated iron and blocks of wood as rough seats out the front, and a fireplace marked out by rocks. Further along another stone building had a small wooden structure next to it, then a fenced paddock, where two brown-eyed cows munched hay from a trough. A dairy, thought Matilda. Behind the cow's paddock were fruit trees, or she supposed they were, for she could see lemons on one of them. The rest were covered in blossom — white, pink, red — an incredible burst of colour in this land of dust.

Now they were close a hedge of shrubs hid the main house from the road and smaller buildings. Suddenly the hedge stopped. Matilda stopped too and stared.

A wide, gravelled courtyard stretched in front of the most wonderful house she had ever seen. It too was made of stone, grey as the dust in the paddocks, two storeys, with wide high windows and many chimneys. The ground floor was sheltered by a wide verandah, with a purple-flowered vine growing up the poles and big cane chairs with cushions. A white cockatoo in a cage peered out at her.

'Scratch cocky,' it ordered.

She almost moved to obey, but Mr Doo stopped her. 'Not go to house, missee. Over here,' he said.

She turned, and saw where he was heading: another low stone building, with a wide open window. 'Farm shop. Sell vegetables here,' said Mr Doo. He hesitated. 'You wait in garden.' He waved his hand toward the trees.

She understood. Whoever he was going to sell vegetables to might wonder why a white girl was with a Chinese man. It would be easier for both of them if no one noticed.

She nodded, and slipped into the green shade of the trees, then stared again at the big house, wishing she could sneak up to the windows and peer inside.

Green velvet curtains with gold tassels ... a friend of Aunt Ann's had curtains like that. The gravel courtyard was so smooth it must have been raked this morning. Smoke wafted from a big chimney at the back — the kitchen chimney, she supposed, for the air above the other four chimneys was clear.

Someone called on the other side of the garden. She pressed back into the shade, hoping her dark dress would help keep her hidden. Mr Drinkwater had last seen her with the men in the cart and, while he hadn't exactly forbidden *her* to set foot on his farm, she didn't want to be seen, not with wet boots and muddy hem, her dress stained not just with soot, but with the mud from the cart. Her plaits must look like a birch broom in a fit. She ran her fingers over her head, trying to push the straggles behind her ears.

Another voice called, a girl's, and then the first again. It sounded young and male. The younger brother, Bertram? She hadn't heard him speak the day before. The girl must be Cousin Florence. She tiptoed closer, then peered out from behind a tree.

It was almost a secret garden, surrounded on three sides by shrubs and on the fourth by the stone wall of another farm building.

A massive tree spread dark green skirts over startlingly green grass. Cousin Florence sat on a swing hung from one of the branches.

She wore white again today. It looked better here against the green than it had by the dusty railway siding. Her straw hat trailed blue ribbons, and her hair was freshly curled.

'Push me! Come on, Cousin Bertie.'

The boy laughed. He wore much the same clothes as he had the day before, pale trousers, neatly ironed, a white shirt, though with no necktie today, and no hat either, here in the shade. He grasped the swing's seat and gave it a push.

That wasn't much of a push, thought Matilda scornfully. But Florence squealed anyway, lifting her legs in a show of ruffled pantaloons, white shoes, a froth of petticoats.

'Not so high!' she called.

'Scaredy cat!' He pushed the swing again.

'I'm not! Oh, I can see the river.'

'We'll take the rowboat out later, when it's cooler.'

'It's never cool here.'

He pushed again. 'It is on the river. I'll ask Papa if we can have a picnic.'

The girl wrinkled her nose. 'Mama will say "ants".'

'Not on the sand.'

'Mama won't sit on sand. I don't like it either.'

He laughed again. 'Townie! We'll take blankets to sit on, and cushions. Or the men can carry chairs down.'

'I'm not a townie.' She shrieked as he pushed the swing again. 'All right, I am a townie. So are you!'

'I wish I was. Boarding school isn't the same as town.'

'Come and stay with us next holidays then.' She wriggled her feet in the breeze from the swing. 'Mama won't come here next holidays. She says she had forgotten the dust and flies.'

'I'll have to ask Papa. I bet he says ...'

'Missee O'Halloran.' A hiss, loud enough for her ears but not to reach into the secret garden.

It was Mr Doo. She hadn't even heard the wheels of the cart. She blushed, embarrassed she'd been caught eavesdropping. She followed as he trotted down the road, pulling the much lighter, though not empty, cart. Soon the house — the big comfortable house that wasn't hers — was behind them.

Chapter 8

She stayed close to the cart as they trudged down the Drinkwater driveway toward the road. It was a long driveway, almost a mile, she thought, lined with thick-trunked gum trees, their shade welcome now the sun was climbing higher.

It was hard to feel the house and its green garden vanish behind her. That house meant comfort and safety, even if not for her.

The road soon veered down toward the river again, winding along a hill that must be out of flood reach. She wondered if Mr Doo always came this way or if he was making a special trip to take her to her father. Somehow it felt impossible to break his silence.

They had been walking for an hour when she saw the hut. It was made of slabs of wood, like the cottages she'd seen earlier, but instead of shingles this was roofed with sheets of bark, curling at the edges. She wondered how the bark kept any rain off at all.

But people lived there. A skinny cow, its hip bones as sharp as a coat hanger, nosed sadly about the dusty tussocks. Two ragged urchins sat in the shade of the dunny, staring at nothing. A boy of five or six, dressed in a pair of men's pants cut off roughly at the knee, threw stones at three scrawny chickens clucking indignantly in the dust. He was the only one who looked up as they approached.

'Hello,' said Matilda.

The boy's face showed vague interest. 'You goin' ter work in the hotel?'

'No. Why do you think that?'

'Thought that was maybe where you was walkin' to. Me big sister went to work at the hotel.' The boy threw another stone at a tatty rooster. 'Suppose she's married by now.'

'How old was she?' asked Matilda curiously.

'Dunno.'

'Bobby! You watered them geraniums?' The voice was tired; the face and body were even wearier. She was a slump of a woman in a rusty dress half covered with a tattered hessian apron. A naked baby sat on her hip. She hardly glanced at Mr Doo, but nodded vaguely at Matilda.

'Er, good day,' said Matilda. 'I'm Matilda O'Halloran.'

'Mrs Heenan.' The voice was automatic, as though the answer came without the owner even having the energy to speak. 'Bobby, you go and water them geraniums, now, do you hear?'

Mrs Heenan looked tiredly back at Matilda. 'That's men for yer. We're always waitin', ain't we? Waitin' for 'em to come home to yer, waitin' for 'em to do anythin' to help.' Her voice died away.

The boy sighed. He crossed over to the door of the hut and picked up a wooden bucket of greasy washing water, then slung it on a spindly plant crowned with a single bright red flower. He brought the bucket back to Mr Doo, who began to fill it with potatoes and onions. The woman stared at it vaguely.

'Er, is your husband away working somewhere?' asked Matilda. Anything to crack this silence.

'Down grubbin' on the Mallee.'

'He's what?' Images of chasing grubs ran through her mind.

'Grubbin' out tree roots. Older boys too. Ain't had a penny from them in months.' She shrugged. 'I'm past carin' what they do now. Just past carin'.'

Matilda shivered. What had happened to these people? Was it drought? The strike? Or just this land that sucked the life away?

Mrs Heenan absently flicked the flies away from the baby's eyes. More clustered as soon as her fingers dropped. 'How much do I owe ya?' she said to Mr Doo.

Mr Doo held up two fingers. Mrs Heenan reached inside the hut and found two pennies which she dropped in Mr Doo's hand.

Matilda eyed the pennies as Mr Doo slipped them into his pocket. Tuppence seemed very little for a bucket of potatoes and onions. But if it was charity, Mrs Heenan seemed neither aware nor grateful.

They began to walk again, faster now, as though both wanted to leave the hopelessness behind them. Matilda was sweltering in her petticoats. She wished she'd taken them off before they left.

Was Moura like that hut back there? No, it couldn't be! Her father was a golden man, a good man who had sent enough money back for her to go to school, for them to share the house on the cliff with Aunt Ann.

And if the men in the wagon had been right — and Mr Doo — he wasn't away grubbing either.

The next hut was about a mile from the first. There were no children to be seen, though by the washing on the line several lived there. But otherwise it was much like the hut they had left. The empty-eyed woman, her grey hair tied back in a rough bun, the tuppence for the bucket of vegetables, no smile or thanks, or even an offer of a cup of water.

How would these people live without Mr Doo? she wondered.

The third hut was better, as Matilda saw, peering past its mistress: a young woman with only one baby; a driveway marked out by stones; and gingham curtains hanging limply at the hut's only window. The floor might be of dirt — or stamped down anthill, she remembered — but it had been swept till it was hard and dust free, and there was a plaited rag rug by the scrubbed stone hearth. There was even a cradle for the baby, roughly carved out of a tree trunk, with uneven rockers made of curved branches.

But this woman didn't make conversation either, or look straight at Matilda or Mr Doo. Maybe she assumes I'm Chinese too, thought Matilda. She doesn't look, and so she doesn't see.

Once again the cart trundled down the road. She glanced at the sky. The sun was just past noon.

'Moura soon?' she asked.

Mr Doo nodded. She hoped he really understood.

Well, if they ended back at his market garden she would just sleep in the cart again. At least the men would — probably — give her dinner. Then tomorrow she could try to make her way back to town, and ask about her father there.

Or she could go to the Drinkwaters', perhaps — not to the main house (she felt too dirty and ragged to be seen there). But one of the men working there must know her father, know where Moura was.

How much English did Mr Doo understand? 'Those people back there,' she began. 'Why do they live there? I mean, how do they live?'

Mr Doo didn't look at her as he answered. 'Small farm. Hundred acres. Father work, brothers work, send money. Sometimes.'

A hundred acres was a small farm? She supposed it was, out here in the dust and nothingness.

How big was Moura?

The road veered away from the river now. The sheep became fewer away from the water, till there were none at all. There were more trees here, some with dead white trunks, like tree-ghosts who hadn't realised they were supposed to fall and rot, others with bark almost as white, but splashed with grey and red and olive green. They looked different somehow from yesterday's trees by the railway line, taller and longer limbed, though they had the same sickle-shaped gum-tree leaves.

The land began to rise to the blue hills she had seen in the distance before. They were taller than she had realised. The road twisted and suddenly there were cliffs in front of her, high and streaked like massive organ pipes.

Then she saw the sign. It was like the one at the railway siding, though the poker-work letters there had been straight and clear — *Drinkwater*, as if the family and the land they owned were one.

This sign was on a log roughly chopped in half, the letters sloping and unsteady. *Moura*.

She looked over at Mr Doo. He nodded. He swung the cart off the road onto a rutted track, up toward the cliffs. She peered between the tree trunks, trying to see what was ahead.

The cliffs grew closer. For a moment she thought they were going to come to a dead end, blocked by the rock, and then she saw an opening between two hills. They passed between them.

Matilda stared. It was as though they had entered a roofless room enclosed by cliffs — a massive one, as big as a whole suburb in the city. The air was cool and shadowed.

Once, perhaps there had been trees. Now most of the land was cleared. Here, at last, there was green grass, dappled with tussocks up to the tumbles of rock below the cliffs. A trickle of creek ran between grey boulders, then vanished into the ground, though Matilda could see a creek bed where it must flow in wetter times.

There was a square fenced area, made from logs, to hold a horse perhaps or even a garden. A shed, made of slabs of wood, with big wide doors. A pile of firewood, neatly stacked. And then the thing she had tried not to look at.

The house.

It was a house, at least, and not a hut. The walls were slabs of wood, their joins packed with what looked like mud. The roof was made of wooden shingles, neatly overlapped, not flimsy sheets of bark. There was even a verandah, with a proper wooden floor, and a rocking chair — made of rough branches and split wood it was true, but still a rocking chair. A table, a slab of wood, with four smaller slabs of wood for chairs; a bench for sitting — another slab of wood, carefully smoothed — beside it.

'Moura,' said Mr Doo.

She tried to keep the disappointment from her face. It was much better than she had feared after the dust this morning, but so much less than she had hoped after the beauty of Drinkwater. Yet this house was as big as Aunt Ann's cottage; it even had a stone chimney.

Why should I ever have thought my father was rich? she wondered. If he had been rich the postal orders would have been bigger. If he had been rich we'd have been living here, not with Aunt Ann.

A bird sang from somewhere along the cliff, a rich, warbling, almost liquid sound. It made her realise how silent this valley

65

was; there were no human voices, not even the sound of chopping wood.

'Hello?' she called nervously.

The sound echoed from the cliffs. *Hello ... hello ... hello.*

Mr Doo looked at her hesitantly. 'You stay?'

Stay in this emptiness? But if there was no one to greet her, at least there was no one to threaten her either. And there was the house, solid and real, and water from the spring.

'When will my father be back?'

'Not know. Soon. I come back, three days' time?'

She understood. 'Yes. Thank you. Thank you for everything. I'll ... I'll be all right till then.'

He turned busily to the cart. She saw he was gathering up the last of the vegetables, the sack of potatoes, only a tenth full now, carrots and a cabbage, one of the round green fruits. If there were a saucepan and matches inside she could cook food. If there were no matches she supposed she could walk the hour or so back to the last cottage, and ask for some hot coals in a tin can.

'Thank you.' And then she remembered. She bowed. 'Duo xie.'

He bowed back to her, and spoke more words, so fast she couldn't tell one from another. She shook her head to show she didn't understand.

He smiled — the first time she had seen him smile — then took the handles of his cart. She watched him trot back the way they'd come, moving faster now that the cart was empty and going downhill.

He was a stranger, but a kind one. And at least he was another person. Suddenly she was aware that she was the only human left among these shadowed cliffs.

She turned toward the house.

66

Chapter 9

Matilda's footsteps sounded hollow on the floorboards as she trod up onto the verandah. She pushed at the door — a proper door, even if it was swung from loops of leather, instead of hinges.

The room inside was half kitchen, half sitting room. A horsehair sofa — the room's only 'real' furniture — sat to one side of a hearth made of slabs of rocks carefully fitted together. A large metal pot with a hooped handle sat on the other side. A slab table and three rough-hewn chairs ... three, she thought. For Dad, Mum and me. The only light came from the door, but there were two windows, covered with wooden shutters instead of glass. She opened them. Suddenly the room seemed less gloomy, almost welcoming.

Two smaller rooms opened from the main one. The first had a double bed, leather plaited between stumps of legs to make a base, and covered with what looked like the hide of a cow. The other room had a single bed. The only other furniture was two big wooden chests, one in each room, and a chest of drawers made from old kerosene tins. She pulled out the drawers one by one. Folded sheepskins, soft and woolly, almost as white as the sheep in her picture book, stitched together to make a sort of mattress; two blankets, tattered at the edges.

She shut the drawers, staring around at the carefully smoothed walls, the wooden planks so carefully fitted together for the floor. It was like the story, but totally unlike it too. Here was the house he had been building, with a bedroom for her. Here was the farm. But there were no woolly sheep, and no cow or pink pig, like the farm book at Aunt Ann's. Most importantly, no father.

She put her bundle down in the room she supposed had been meant for her, and opened its shutters too, fastening them against the wall with a leather thong to stop them banging in the wind.

The vegetables were still on the verandah. She carried them in, then looked on the work bench. Yes, a box of matches.

There was no newspaper to make a fire, but at one end of the verandah she found a box of dried leaves and kindling. She brought in an armful, then went outside again to fetch wood from the heap. The bird had stopped calling now. The valley breathed silence.

She reached for the top bit of wood, neatly sawn from a tree trunk. Something black slithered from under the heap into the rocks behind.

Snake! She felt her heart leap. If it had bitten her there was no one here to suck out the poison. She'd have to be careful where she trod and put her hands. At least that had looked like a red-belly, not as vicious, or as deadly, as the occasional brown that had hidden in the gardens at Aunt Ann's.

It took two matches before the leaves caught, and then the twigs. For a moment she thought the fireplace wouldn't draw, as smoke puffed into the room. And then the fire flared properly and the air cleared.

She peered into the pot. It had been scoured clean and there was no dust in it either. Which meant that someone (she hoped her father) had been here lately. She carried the pot out to the stream — or pool rather, for the water ran no more than a few feet before it vanished into the stones. She bent and drank, scooping the water with her hands. It was surprisingly cold, with a tang like tin.

A shadow swung above her. She looked up. A cage hung from a branch wedged into the rocks. It looked like the fly-proof cool safe at Aunt Ann's, but bigger, and made of canvas instead of tin. She opened the door.

Food — proper food. A hunk of cheese, a bit dry around the edges. A can of golden syrup, safe from the ants. She took a deep breath of relief. Someone had left these recently. Was there more food inside the house?

There was. The bench was a hollow chest. When she lifted the seat she found a sack of flour, a smaller bag of salt, a tin of tea and four cans filled with old dripping, a candle wick in each. There was a sealed tin of fresh dripping too. She sniffed it. It smelled fresh, rich and fatty, and just faintly of sheep.

She hesitated to use the stores — her father would expect them to be as he'd left them when he returned. But if he did come back, perhaps he'd like to find food waiting for him. She could show him she would be useful.

Her mind shut down on the question of why she needed to prove anything to the man who had brought her into the world.

In the end she decided to make soup, the vegetables that Mr Doo had given her browned in the dripping, with water added. If she cooked it long enough the potatoes would thicken it.

69

She made another trip down to the pool, washing the vegetables in the pot so she didn't dirty the water, then washing the soil out of the pot again. For a moment she wished she had a geranium like the woman in the last hut, to pour the dirty water onto: just one bright flower, in this world of gum-tree green and rock.

There was a knife and a toasting fork by the hearth. It was strangely comforting, chopping, heating the dripping in the pot next to the fire, browning the potatoes, the carrots and the cabbage, just as she had under Aunt Ann's eagle eye or back in Mrs Dawkins's kitchen, holding the now hot handle with her skirt when she took the pot out for a fourth time, to cover the vegetables with water.

The fire needed more wood. She made several trips this time, choosing the thickest pieces — hard-knotted hunks of tree that should keep burning all night if she piled the ashes over them — so she wouldn't have to waste another match.

She felt even hotter and dirtier by the time she'd finished. There was soap in her bundle. She should have washed before she put the vegetables in the pot, she realised. Then she could have washed inside.

She glanced at the tiny pool of water. It would be so good to be clean. Maybe if she wet herself and her hair, she could soap herself, then scoop out water to wash it off, without filling the waterhole with scum.

But to be naked, out in the open! She glanced up at the cliffs, tall and silent. There was no one to see her, except the eagle, hovering above. And she needn't take all her clothes off at once.

In the end she washed her hair first, then under her skirt, undoing the buttons and pushing the top of the dress down to her waist just for a few minutes.

She'd have liked to wash her dress too, and her petticoats. They weren't just dirty — they smelled of old cabbage leaves, and perspiration, and coal smuts from the train. I'll wash them tomorrow, she thought. Tonight she'd put on Mum's second dress — it was her good one, but she wouldn't get it dirty.

The valley was in shadow now. Only a bright rim of gold and red showed at the far end of the gorge. Small scurryings in the shadows could be anything. Maybe snakes …

Why not ghosts too, while you're at it? she told herself. Or bogeymen. It was too cold for snakes at night. The noises were probably just possums, like back at Aunt Ann's. She'd seen their droppings on the verandah.

It was even darker inside. She hesitated, then lit one of the candles. She didn't really need it, not yet, but its light and the red glow from the fire were comforting. She shut the door and the shutters. At least anything that lurked outside couldn't come in now. She took off her still-damp shoes in the bedroom. There was no newspaper to stuff into them, to keep their shape, but they'd dry more slowly here away from the fire, so hopefully the leather wouldn't crack.

She pulled out one of the sheepskins and stretched it over the narrow bed, covered it with a blanket, and arranged her spare clothes and shawl as a pillow, stirred the pot, then wondered what to do next. She had a feeling that once she stopped doing things the loneliness might be too hard to bear.

Nonsense, she thought. I've borne worse than this. I have a roof over my head — a good roof and waterproof, by the look of it. No mouse droppings, no cockroaches scuttling in the corners, no fug of coal smoke, no factory in the morning.

No Mum, no stories whispered as she fell asleep. No Tommy, comforting bearer of sandwiches and friendship. No Mr Ah Ching.

She ran her hands through her hair to get more knots out. It was almost dry now, and reached her waist. The ends looked red in the firelight. She stirred the soup. The potatoes weren't quite dissolved, but she was almost too hungry to wait. Her eye caught the strange green fruit on the table. She cut a slice off the top. It was bright red inside, even in the dim light. She sniffed it. It smelled sweet and good.

It was. She cut another hunk, and another, nibbling the red right down to the peel. The juice left her skin sticky, but she wasn't going out into the growing dark to wash it. She'd have to explore the shed tomorrow, in full daylight, keeping a wary eye out for snakes. There might be a bucket in there, so she could keep water in the house.

The fruit had revived her. Suddenly she thought of the tatty edges of the blankets. At least there were needles and thread in her bundle. She fetched them, then crouched by the light of the fire and lamp, and began to darn, turning the edges over neatly.

The familiar routine was soothing too. She began to hum, and then to sing a lullaby that Mum had sung:

'*Sleep then, my pretty one, sleep,*
Fast flow the waters so deep ...'

The door was flung open.

'Who the flamin' hell are you?'

Chapter 10

She struggled to her feet, her sewing slipping to the floor, then ran behind the table, to keep a barrier behind her and the stranger. It wasn't till he'd hung his hat on the peg inside the door that she realised who he was, who he had to be.

Her father.

He was ... nothing special. No glow of gold. Not tall and handsome as her mother had described, but not ugly either. Just a work-worn man. You could pass him on the street and never look at him again.

Brown eyes like hers; black hair and beard, roughly trimmed; tanned skin, creased about the eyes; pants and shirt washed till they had lost all colour, like most of the clothes she'd seen yesterday; gaping boots tied together with twine; a bundle tied with more twine in his hand.

Strong, though. Had she remembered that?

'Dad?'

'What the —' He stared at her. 'You're not Matilda?'

She nodded.

He let the bundle drop. 'Well.'

Once again, it was nowhere near what she had hoped, but not what she had feared, either. At least he knew who she was. Despite her fantasies she had been half afraid that he might not even remember her, his mind rotted by spirituous liquor, or that he might not return to the house for weeks or even months, perhaps ever. She had even been afraid he might be one of those men who had two families or even more, leaving one and travelling to the north or west, starting afresh, leaving their wives and children never knowing where they had gone or even if they were alive.

But he was here, at least.

He moved his bundle near to the bench, still gazing at her, then shut the door behind him.

'What are you doing here?'

He didn't sound unfriendly or angry, just bewildered.

'I wrote you a letter. Lots of letters.'

He shook his head. 'Haven't had a letter for a year. More 'n that, I reckon. Drinkwater's men pick up the mail bags for round here from the train. Reckon the old bast— I reckon Drinkwater only passes the mail on to those he likes.'

'He doesn't like you?'

It was as though he hadn't heard the question. A smile twisted his face. It looked almost familiar, and then she realised; she had seen that twist of the lips when she'd looked in the mirror back at Aunt Ann's. 'My Matilda,' he said softly. 'I never thought ...'

Tears prickled. It sounded like ... like he really was glad to see her. More than that ...

'You're really here. My daughter. In my house.' He took a step toward her, uncertain. She walked to him in a daze, felt his arms around her, her face pressed into his shirt. It smelled of sheep and sweat.

She had never been hugged by a man before.

He grabbed her shoulders and held her back, staring into her face. 'You've your mother's hair,' he said slowly. 'Your great-gran's eyes. The shape of her face too.'

'You mean your grandmother?'

He nodded. 'Aye.'

Excitement lit a flame inside her. 'You mean I have more relatives? I can meet them?'

The happiness on his face vanished, as though someone had blown out the lamp. 'No. Not any more.' He stepped back. 'Matilda ...' He said that name as though he loved the sound. 'What are you doing here? Your ma —' he added sharply, looking toward the other rooms. 'Is she here too? Why aren't you at Ann's?'

'It's just me.' She didn't know how not to make it hurt. 'Aunt Ann died a year ago.'

He sat on the bench, gesturing to her to take the horsehair sofa. 'I'm sorry. I liked your Auntie Ann.' The smile twisted his lips again. 'I think she liked me too, in a way, though she told your ma not to marry me. But what about your ma? What does she think about you being here?'

'Dad.' Somehow the word and the man didn't quite fit together yet. 'I'm sorry; Mum's dead.'

She expected him to cry, as she had done. Instead he just said, 'I'm sorry, girl. Must have been hard for you. I wish I'd known.'

'You ... you're not sorry for *you* though. Are you?' she said slowly.

He met her eyes — his brown eyes, so like hers. 'No, Matilda. With your ma gone, I'm free.'

She shivered at the matter-of-factness in his voice; there was almost even a touch of joy. He's just happy to see me, she told herself, not happy that Mum is dead.

But it hurt, nonetheless, that the only person who would cry for Mum's death was her.

Suddenly the word 'free' struck her. Free for what? She stared at him, this dark man so different from her imaginings, this father who she knew not at all.

Chapter 11

The pot on the hearth gave a glop.

He glanced over at it, then gave her a tentative smile. 'Smells good.'

'A man named Mr Doo gave me the vegetables. He brought me here.'

'The Chinaman? He didn't hurt you?'

'No,' she said gently. 'He was kind.'

'Yes, well.' He nodded at the pot. 'Let's be tasting it.'

'Are there bowls?'

'False bottom in the chest in the bedroom. I'll get 'em.' He saw her look. 'I'm away a lot. There's bast— *blokes* out there who'd steal the salt from a man's body given half a chance, my oath they would. No need to make it easy for 'em.'

She pulled the pot away from the heat, and stirred it again. The vegetables had caught on the bottom. She hoped her father didn't notice. He handed her the bowls — deep tin plates really — and a couple of spoons. They'd been good once. Now the silver was worn so thin the edges were almost sharp.

'I'm sorry, there was no meat.'

'No matter.' He spooned a bit up. 'It's good.'

She tasted it. 'No, it isn't. It needs salt.' And it had a burned taste to it too.

He laughed. 'It tastes good to a hungry man. It's better than most things I've eaten. Maybe you've got your aunt's touch with cookin', girl.'

'Not my mother's?'

He kept his eyes on his soup. 'Not unless she changed in the past few years.'

'Dad … Why did you stop sending money? Why didn't you tell us the house was built? We could have come out here.' And Mum might still be alive, she thought, if she'd had this fresh, dry air to breathe.

'You and your ma did come here,' he said shortly. 'Any more o' that soup?'

She filled his bowl automatically. 'No, we didn't.'

'You were too young to remember, I reckon. Hardly toddlin'. Fat little thing you were an' all. So pretty. Your hair was almost white then. It's like gold now.'

'I don't understand.'

'Simple enough,' he said flatly. 'Your ma couldn't see me for what I am. Ann knew it. I didn't. Fool that I was back then. Your ma had dreams of what a farm would be …'

'Woolly lambs and white tablecloths,' she said slowly.

He met her eyes. 'That's it. She never lost them then?'

Matilda shook her head.

'I'd paid off this land afore I met her. Proud as a peacock, I was. Built the house by the time you were born. Borrowed a cart off Drinkwater to meet the train … I was still workin' for him back then. I'd even set the table nice for her; the beds were made;

a new rug by the hearth. A possum made a mess of it a few years back.

'Your ma took one look at this place an' burst into tears. Said —' He stopped. 'Some things are best forgotten.'

'But you remember.'

'Yes. But you don't have to hear.' He shrugged. 'She cried the whole damned ... *dashed* ... night. Three days later I took her back to the train, an' you too.'

He looked at her, and Matilda could see that he was telling the truth. 'I wanted to yell at her not to go. She was taking my whole life with her on that train, taking my daughter, all my hopes. I wanted to get down on my knees and plead with her to stay. But I couldn't.'

'Why not?' Her voice was almost a whisper at the memory of pain in his eyes.

'Because I loved her. Because she was right. Your auntie was right. You've got to be strong to live out here. The land would have sucked your ma dry. It was best for her to go back. Best for you too, I thought.'

'You didn't even want to see me?'

He was silent for a moment, and then he met her eyes. 'You want the truth? I tried to forget I had a daughter, growing up somewhere. Tried to forget how you looked, that first morning here, curled up with my dog by the fireplace. Some things hurt too much. You were hers now, not mine. Your ma went back to the nice cottage by the sea, with her parents' polished furniture and her big sister to take care of her, the church down the road and her white aprons with the lace at the tearoom. But every time I worked a shed I sent her all but a few shillings, to keep you an' her at Ann's, to make sure you got the best schooling to be had.'

'But then you didn't.'

'And then I couldn't,' he said flatly. 'We was on strike.'

It was like the flames leaped from the fireplace to her. 'You could have kept on working! We almost starved. Maybe if Mum had the right food she'd be alive. If we'd had the money for a doctor —'

'I wasn't to know that! I thought your aunt would see you right. She was doin' pretty good with her dressmaking. What I sent was for luxuries, to see you schooled and pretty clothes ...'

'Mum sewed too. But when Aunt Ann died she couldn't make enough to pay the rent, even when I helped. We sold all we had, but it didn't bring much.' She looked at him straight in the firelight. 'Would you still have gone on strike if you'd known?'

He was silent a moment. 'You want a lie this time? Nice and sweet like your ma's dreams?'

'No.'

'Didn't think so. You've more of your Aunt Ann in you than your ma. No, girl. Some things matter. It's a new world we're fightin' for here, not just a few more shillings to our pay. We're fighting for the rights of —'

'The rights of working men,' she said tiredly. 'Fighting for a new Australia. I was at the meeting last night.'

'You were? I didn't see you!'

So the men *had* been taking her to her father. 'It doesn't matter.' Suddenly she just wanted to sleep. To sleep and sleep till somehow this all made sense.

'I'm sorry, Matilda,' he said simply. 'I truly am.' He stood up and took her bowl. 'You'll want to go to bed.'

'I need to wash the dishes —'

'You're like your aunt, all right. Can't wash up till daylight —

the breeze'll blow the lamps out if we take them outside. I'll show you where I hid the buckets then. Matilda …'

'Yes?'

'You can't stay here, you know.'

Fright drove away the tiredness. 'Why not? Please … I'm useful. I can cook … and sew …'

'Matilda my darlin', it's not that.' He bit his lip. 'I have to get away for a while. Never mind why. I just came here to pick up a few things. I'll be making tracks in the morning.'

'Where to?'

'Anywhere. Just away till things cool down. Pick up some work, maybe.'

'It was you,' she said slowly. 'You burned down the shearing shed.'

'How did you hear that?' He shook his head. 'Never mind about that. And no, they won't pin that on me — not on anyone. But old Drinkwater's brought troopers down. They'll get me for something, just to get even, to show the union he won't be beat. So I'm going away.' He hesitated. 'You can stay with one o' the women round here if you like. I can give them a few shillings for your keep.'

'No!' She thought of the bare baby, the boy throwing stones at the chickens. 'Please — can't I stay here?'

'Not by yourself. An' I ain't got enough money to send you to boarding school.'

'I know.'

'What about someone in the city — you got a friend you could stay with there?'

It had been a year since she'd seen any of the girls at school, hadn't known any of their families well enough to want to stay with them or even ask for help when Mum was sick. She would be even more foreign to them now, after the year at the factory, even the two days out here. She thought of Tommy's family briefly. She'd just be another burden there. She shook her head.

He looked at her, a slow smile lighting up his face. 'All right then. Come with me.'

'What?'

'It ain't so bad camping out. Stars for your ceiling and the wind in the trees.' He grinned, his teeth very white in the lamplight. 'See if you're your mother's daughter or mine.'

'I'm both.'

'Well, we'll see if you're the bit that can take sleeping in a swag. What do you say? If I do pick up work you can't sleep in the bunkhouse,' he added. 'But there's always room for another maid at places like that. You can cook. Add your wages onto mine. Then in a year, two at the most, we'll come back here. Buy some good ewes, the best ram we can find. A couple of horses. By the time you're a woman we'll have this place as rich as Drinkwater.'

Safety. A life. Someone who loved her. Somewhere she belonged. But once more sleep was almost all she could think about.

'Sweet dreams, Matilda,' he said softly.

She turned to go into the second bedroom. At the last moment she turned. 'Dad? Why did you say now Mum was dead you were free?'

'Because now I don't have to send her almost every penny I make, I can make this into a proper farm. Not with white sheep and baa-baa lambs. Something real.'

He looked at her as though she was a bucket full of gold. 'Your ma took that from me, just like she took you. I'm going to get my life back now.' He crossed the room and took her shoulders again, then kissed the top of her head. 'Sleep well, my daughter.'

Chapter 12

Dear Tommy,

I hope you are well. I really, really hope you are out of hospital soon and that your arm is getting better.

I am leaving this nailed to the front door of my father's house with a penny for the postage. My friend Mr Doo will see it and I hope he will post it to you. Please do not write back, I mean I would love to get a letter from you but I will not get it, as the post is sorted by Mr Drinkwater who is the biggest farmer here, and he is an old biscuit who does not give the letters to people he does not like, which includes my father.

I think I like my father, which is good. He has to go away to work for a while so I am going with him, but I will write to you when we are anywhere I can post a letter. We will come back in a year or two, when we have money to buy rams (they are male sheep with big horns, I have to learn more about sheep now) and ewes. We'll wait till it rains, because there is not enough water for lots of sheep here till then.

Do not worry about me. My father is glad I am with him, and he will look after me. It is dry and hot and there are lots of flies but I like it better than the city. There is space and you can breathe. This morning I saw a thousand green birds, they are called budgerigars. They were on all the trees and the rocks. It was beautiful. Dad says you can eat them too but they are not worth the plucking.

When we are back here maybe you can visit us. Dad says he can build another room on the house easy and that can be for you. He has no machines here yet but he says when we have money he will buy some, perhaps a plough so we can put in crops such as turnips or corn for the sheep to eat (I have learned that already). There is one that can jump over stumps, you would find it most interesting.

Please take care. I miss you.

Your friend,
Matilda O'Halloran

The road shimmered white and dry before them. On either side sheep looked up, hoping the humans had brought hay, then gazed back down into the dust. The only trees ran along the riverside, far to their west.

It wasn't as hot walking today, not with her petticoats packed into the false bottom of the trunk back at the house and her father's hat on her head. It was too big for her and hung down almost to her eyes, but the swinging twigs kept the flies away, and the wide brim shaded her face too.

'Tired yet?'

'No.' She wouldn't have admitted it, even if she had been. Somehow being safe — and loved and wanted — made her feel like she could fly along the road.

Her father had insisted on carrying her things too — not much: another dress, a blanket, needles and thread, her soap — in the big rolled swag that dangled down his back, with a billy dangling from one side. He'd grinned at her. 'We're waltzing our Matilda together.'

She hadn't understood. He patted the swag. 'The men o' the road call a swag their Matilda.'

'Like me?'

'Just like you. Your Matilda is your best friend when you're on the road. Your Matilda and your billy.'

'If I was a boy would you have called me Billy?'

He laughed at that. 'I might.'

'What about the waltzing?'

'That's what you do when you take to the road to look for work. Waltzing your Matilda.'

'Not a dance?'

He must have seen her disappointment. 'You can have both, Matilda my darlin'. We'll waltz the road and the next place we come to with music, I'll show you how to dance the waltz too. What do you say?'

So now they were waltzing their Matilda away from the valley that sheltered the house, its hills faint in the heat and dust behind them.

'No blisters?'

She shook her head. She liked how he worried about her; how he'd made her finish the soup this morning and eat half the cheese; how he'd rubbed her shoes with dripping to make them softer before they set out.

'Won't go too far today. Just get off Drinkwater's land before we make camp for the night, so he can't charge me with trespass or the like.'

'Are we on his land now?'

'Road is right o' way for everyone. But we want to be well away from him and his boys.'

'How much land does he own?'

'About five square miles, up and down the river.' He grinned down at her. 'With a few holes in it, that other folks selected, like our place.'

Matilda felt a smile grow across her face. It sounded good. 'Our place.'

'Old Drinkwater never bought most of his land. He squatted on it, back in the forties. He was just a lad then. Ran his sheep. Made money. Him and other squatters got so rich they was running the government. Made laws to say the land was theirs, if they paid a bit o' rent. Then the law was changed so that some of the squatters' land could be selected. Drinkwater and the like paid their workmen to buy up the good land then sign it back to them.'

'Is that when you bought Moura?'

He nodded. 'I knew I wanted land since I was your age. Saved every penny I could get. Sold possum skins, trapped koala bears for their fur. Everyone wanted land along the river — there's a dozen hundred-acre blocks down there. Moura didn't go for much. Drinkwater didn't know it had water. That stream never goes beyond the cliffs, except in a flood. He was as mad as a hungry bull when he found out.'

'Is that why you … you don't like each other?'

'No,' he said slowly. 'Give him his due, he never held it against me. We was all right, me and the old man, till the strike.'

'What happened then?'

'Drinkwater's one of those who think that because they're boss of one big place they can be king of everything. The bosses have all the power — they say what you can be paid, even if it's not enough for a man to live on.

'They say how many hours you've got to work for.' There was passion in his voice now. 'That's why we need unions. No one man can fight bosses like Drinkwater. But if we stand together we're strong enough to fight for our rights.'

'So he got angry because you joined a union?'

'He was in a red rage because I started the branch of the Shearers' Union around here,' he said flatly. 'Other stations have been run on union labour for years. But Drinkwater wasn't too bad till the price of wool dropped an' he cut our pay.'

'Maybe ... maybe he couldn't afford to pay more.'

'Drinkwater can afford a fancy new carriage and to send his precious lads to city schools. But it were the idea of a union what got him riled. He wants to hire who he likes. We say the sheep'll be shorn union or they won't be shorn at all. He brought in scabs — outsiders. An' then his shearing shed burned down. And Drinkwater blames me.'

'Is he right?'

'I didn't do it.'

'Do you know who did?'

He didn't answer.

She didn't want to spoil it all by asking again. They walked in silence for a short time. 'Tommy got burned because Mr Thrattle wouldn't pay for a new chain for the jam vat,' she said at last. 'Would a union stop things like that?'

He nodded, pleased. 'You've got it, me darlin'. Right on the nail. But it's more 'n that. We need to join the states up to make

87

a new nation. This land needs one parliament to make laws for us all — new laws, fair laws. Laws to protect the workin' man.'

'And woman.'

'Well ... her too.' He grinned. 'You might even get the vote one day. Women voting. What do you think o' that?'

She nodded seriously. 'Aunt Ann was in the Women's Temperance and Suffrage League. The League says women should vote because women are more sober and sensible than men and don't indulge in spirituous liquors. Dad?'

Matilda liked how they both smiled when she said that word.

'Yes?'

'Do you drink spirituous liquors?'

'Yes,' he admitted. 'Don't you worry none, Matilda me darlin'. I ain't goin' to waste me dosh on grog now, not when we've sheep to buy. How about I promise I won't have a drink of, er, spirituous liquor till we've got 2,000 sheep?'

She considered. It wasn't as good as signing the pledge. But she could always argue again with him in 2,000 sheep's time. 'All right.'

'That's me girl.'

She craned her head to look at him from under the big hat. 'Are Mr Drinkwater's sons like him?'

He was quiet for a while. 'They say the chip doesn't fly far from the log,' he said at last. 'James and Bertram only know what he's taught them, him and his kind, how to look down on anyone who's a worker or not their class.'

'Dad ... When I met them at the train James said that they'd ... they'd been hunting natives. Do you really think they did that?'

'Yes.' The word was short and clipped.

'Why?'

'Because men like Drinkwater think they own the whole of God's earth, and no one else has a right to it. If you're a native workin' for Drinkwater you're all right. If you're not, then get off his land.'

'So there are natives about?'

'Yes.'

She wanted to ask more — what were they like, did they really throw boomerangs and not wear any clothes? But once again she sensed the subject was closed.

But it was easy to talk about other things, words slipping into rhythm, like their footsteps, as though the silence of the land allowed the words to flow. She told him about her life at the factory; about Tommy and Aunt Ann; and about Mum's slow death, the pain gradually taking her away.

In return he gave her memories of her mother when they first met: 'Like a spring breeze she was, all fresh with scents and blossom.'

'She was beautiful,' he added. 'I looked into that tearoom and there she was, with her blonde hair and her clean white apron. She was the most lovely thing I had ever seen.'

'So it was true? You met her there? Did you waltz with her too?'

He smiled. His teeth were very white in his tanned face when he smiled. 'Oh yes, we waltzed. Never think, Matilda darlin', that you weren't born with love. The love didn't last maybe, but it was there.'

He was silent for about twenty paces, and then he added, 'Maybe it would have worked if I'd had more to offer her. Or if she'd dreamed less, so she wouldn't have been so shocked with what I had. We could have had a grand place by now, me and her and you. Moura stays green when the rest of the world is brown.'

'But not enough water.'

He glanced at her. 'There's more water there, if you know where to look. If I had money for pipes and troughs. But there's no point in pipes without the sheep, and there's no point in sheep without men to stop 'em strayin'. And there's no point in men without the money to pay 'em.'

'And you'd pay them properly?'

He laughed. 'There's many as don't. Soon as they get enough money to employ a bloke or two they turn into bosses themselves, buying motorcars and pianos while their workers' children go barefoot and in rags. No, I'd share and share alike, put what's needed back into the farm, then share the money with whoever works with me. That's one o' the things the union's working for: a set wage, so no bast— blighter can cheat and say he can't afford no more. Set hours too. No more fourteen-hour days, or men shearing till they're so bent and cramped they can only crawl on their hands and knees.'

Another thirty-two paces — she counted them — then he said, 'There'll be no more Tommys when a new Labor Party rules Australia. A new nation with fair laws, and votes for all to make them happen. A land where waltzing Matilda means dancing in a fancy dress, not pounding the road with yer billy, hoping for a handout or a pile of wood to chop. But don't you worry, Matilda darlin', we'll get something better than choppin' wood.'

'Even with me?'

'Especially with you,' he added honestly. 'Them squatters' wives will take one look at you, with your bright hair and big brown eyes, and give me any job of work that's going. They'll keep me workin' too when they see I keep my nose to the grindstone and don't drink my wages neither.'

'Dad?'

'Yes?'

'Those small farms, down on the river? I saw three of them yesterday. They looked — horrible. Hungry. The children didn't even have proper clothes.'

'Those farms aren't enough to keep a family. Their men are on strike so the families starve.'

'So it's Mr Drinkwater's fault?'

'Yes.' He looked at her thoughtfully. 'Not all his fault though. There's men who promise their wives they'll live like princesses, but drink most of their cheque away. You don't need money to feed your children — there's tucker all around and firewood for the picking up, not like the city. A man with an axe can build a house. A woman with sense will find some bloke who used to be a gentleman before the drink got him; he'll teach her children how to read in return for a plate of dinner and a drink of rum.'

He hesitated, as though trying to find the words. 'That's why we need unions, new laws — because some people don't know how to help themselves.'

Most of the words flowed over her, but one phrase stuck. 'What do you mean, there's tucker all around?' She gestured at the flat white dust around them, the drooping trees.

He laughed. 'Oh Matilda me darlin', you learn this land right and it'll give you everything you need, and riches too.'

She was silent a while. He loved this land. But to her it was simply hot and dry and full of flies. Maybe I'm too much my mother's daughter, she thought uncomfortably. Maybe I'll always see this land as ugly.

He watched her silently, as though he knew what she was thinking. 'Forget about green,' he said suddenly.

She stared at him. 'What?'

91

'Land is always green in books. Green grass and a white farm house, that's what your ma expected. It don't have to be green to be beautiful.'

It was almost like poetry. He looked embarrassed, then shrugged. 'Just look,' he said.

She looked. The trees still drooped, weighed down by heat. The dust hung in a golden haze across the horizon.

Gold, she thought, not green. Gold is supposed to be beautiful too. She let her eyes travel across the landscape, and suddenly she saw it: hills like old skulls, with a beam of sunlight spearing down behind a cloud, turning them to gold as well.

The gold bones of the landscape … it was a hard beauty, but real.

He saw the change in her face and nodded. 'You keep lookin',' he said softly. 'The land'll get to you. Floods and fire may come and those you love may leave you, but the land will still be there.' He gestured into the distance. 'See that big stump over there?'

She squinted. 'Yes.'

'That's the boundary o' Drinkwater's land. Once past that we're free.'

Chapter 13

The sun was hovering above the tree tops when they made camp. They stopped beside a wide lake covered in water lilies, the white flowers starting to close as they lost the sun. A flock of ducks rose squawking, then vanished beyond the trees.

'Gunna be a storm tonight. See the way the ants are scurrying?'

'We'll get wet!'

'Not too wet, I reckon.' He slung the swag down next to a giant white-trunked tree.

A blackened space near the water was surrounded by big rocks. People have camped here before, she thought. Swaggies waltzing their Matildas too? 'It's a pretty lake.'

'This is a billabong,' he said. 'See that bank of sand? This was a bend of the river once. Then a big flood came, or lots of little floods, and made the river go straight instead, leaving this behind.' He lifted his arms and stretched. 'Reckon there's a few fish in there. You see those bubbles? How you feel about fish for tea?'

She'd seen fishermen down on the shore from the cottage and had always longed to try it herself, though Aunt Ann said ladies didn't.

'You've got a fishing line?'

He laughed. He looked so different from the grim man of last night: younger, brighter, freer. With the sun behind him he almost looked like the golden man of Mum's story.

'What good swaggie ain't got a fishin' line? Even brought some worms from the dunny back home. Not the one we're usin' now,' he added when he saw her look of horror. 'Where the old one used to be. Worms like it all soft and damp.'

'Errk.'

'You don't have to eat the worm, girl.' He sounded amused. 'Just the fish. Come on, help me get some firewood.'

He was faster at setting a fire than her, expertly stripping flakes of bark from the trees and snapping off dead twigs from the branches.

'Wood on the ground is always a bit damp,' he explained. 'Even when it's dry like this, there's dew at night. Tree wood catches faster. Once the fire's hot enough it'll burn anything, even green wood, if you don't mind the smoke. Smoke'll keep away the flies and mozzies too.'

She nodded, entranced. His smile grew wider. He was showing off for her, she realised, just like boys playing ball in the street. He wants me to admire him, be glad that he's my dad.

'Take a look at this.' He pointed to the sandy lip by the water, where the grass had worn away. 'See that? That's a wallaby track — that's him coming down, that's him turning and jumping back.'

'How do you know it's a he?'

He laughed. 'I'm not that good, girl. She then, maybe. Now that's a roo — see the tail mark? It stood further away to drink too. They'll all come to drink here later — wombats, possums. Good eatin' on a possum.'

She said cautiously, 'I'd rather have fish.'

'Whatever your ladyship wishes. As long as they're biting.'

'Do other swagmen know all this?' she asked curiously.

He winked at her. 'No. Some are lazy bast— er, *biscuits*. Live on what they scrounge from farm to farm, and don't offer to even chop the wood in return. Others learn a bit while they're on the road.'

'But not as much as you?'

He shrugged. 'I had good teachers. Want to see how to put a worm on a hook?'

'No! Yes …'

'Like this, see, so it can't get off.' He whirled the end of the line and let it go suddenly. It plopped into the middle of the billabong. 'Now you hold onto the line. If you feel a tug, don't do nothin' — the fish'll just be nibbling at the bait. Wait till you feel him really tugging to get away.'

She caught her breath with excitement as she took the string, part of it still wrapped around a stick of wood. His hand was callused, brown from a lifetime in the sun. 'Then what'll I do?'

'Then I'll pull it in.'

'Can't I do it?'

'Not this time. Needs practice. If you pull too hard and *he* pulls too hard the line'll break. You've got to go slow and cautious, let him rest then pull him a bit further. You'll get the knack.'

The line thrummed under her hand. Each time it shuddered she imagined a fish on the end of it. She glanced at her father.

He was lying back against one of the white-trunked trees, watching her.

All at once the line was pulled taut. It jerked wildly, then went still. She shot a look at her father, then back at the water. 'Is it a fish?'

'It's a fish.' He stood behind her now, his big hands on hers. 'Come on, I'll show you how. Just wind it round once, one more ... that'll do it. Now wait.'

She waited. The line jerked again, so hard she thought that it would break, then grew slack once more.

'Is it still there?'

'No need to whisper. We've got him now. Yes, he's still there. Roll him in slow now ... that's it ...'

Another turn ... the fish tried for freedom once again, and then again gave up.

'They never learn, fish. If they pulled against the line and kept on pulling they'd break it. But they give a tug then wait and hope we've gone away.' He winked at her. 'Always keep on fighting, Matilda my darlin'. Don't end like a fish.'

The water rippled, closer to the bank. 'He's a big 'un. Keep the line tight.' He moved quickly and lightly to the bank. A splash and he vanished under the water lilies.

'Dad!'

Suddenly he was standing in the water, a giant fish flapping in his arms, the line still trailing from its mouth. Water streamed from his shirt and head, and a strand of some sort of weed clung to him.

'Got it!' He clambered up onto the bank, reached for a rock, and bashed the fish swiftly and expertly on the head. It flapped a few more times, then grew still.

He pulled a knife from his belt. 'Now this is how you gut 'em.'

'Errk. Dad ... I thought you were going to drown.'

He grinned up at her. 'Not me. I've been swimming since I were a nipper. Can swim underwater right across the billabong, I reckon. My grandma showed me how. I can swim under a duck, grab at its legs and bring it down. Can you swim?'

'I can dog paddle a bit. Aunt Ann showed me how. We'd go out in the early morning, when no one could see us.' The starched tablecloth, the smell of polish, the egg waiting on the breakfast table in its tiny cosy. It all seemed impossibly far away.

'Better make sure you practise. Not here — too much weed. Come a flood, you never know when you might need to swim for it.'

'Here?' She glanced around at the dry land, the sheets of bark, the crisp tussocks.

'Don't let the river fool you. See that grass up in the tree tops? A flood dropped that. Don't even need to rain here, neither. Just a cloudburst upstream. You ever hear a rumble, you run for it. I've seen a wall of water twenty feet high crash down this river. Cows, fences, horses even, all tumbling with it. It always changes, this land.' He glanced up at the sky. 'Don't think tonight's rain'll be much though. A flash and some thunder, and that'll be it.'

She looked up at the sky too. But it was still cloudless, an almost impossible blue.

Her father pulled down a green branch, snapped off its twigs and leaves, and poked it in through the fish's head and out by its tail. The fish looked like it was snarling at them, its eyes wide and staring, its mouth open.

'Dinner,' said her father.

Chapter 14

The sun was hovering on the horizon, sending slanted shadows through the trees, by the time they had eaten half the fish, toasted on two forked branches over the coals, and some 'sinkers' of dough, wrapped around yet another branch and held over the fire too. All at once light cracked open the sky. A noise shattered the air behind them.

Matilda gave a startled squeak.

'Told you there'd be a storm.' He scrambled to his feet and grabbed a hessian bag. 'Best get the food back in the tucker bag before it rains. Stop the flies getting the fish too.'

Matilda looked up at the sky. A black cloud had slunk in behind them while they ate. Even as she spoke the first hard raindrops, cold as melted snow, stung her face. 'How are we going to keep it dry?'

'Like this.' He'd gathered the swag into a bundle again. He placed it under the big gum, then used his knife to slit some giant flaps of the tree's bark and pulled them swiftly off. He placed one on the swag, then sat on it, and gestured for her to come over to him. She sat beside him, snuggling into his shirt as he pulled the other length of soft bark around them. He put his arms around her. 'This'll be over in ten minutes. Half an hour by the fire'll dry us out.'

'Won't the storm put the fire out?'

'Not with that log over it. Ah, that's it, send her down, Hughie!' he yelled at the sky.

'Hughie?'

'The rain, my darlin'. Hughie sends down the rain.'

'You mean God?' she asked, shocked. Aunt Ann was firm about not taking the Lord's name in vain.

'Nah. Hughie's just ... Hughie. What we really need is ten days' rain, but this'll green things up. Good pick for the roos. Travelling man's friend, that's the kangaroo. Never go hungry if there's roos.'

The raindrops grew thicker. Another roar split the sky. The air smelled strange, a bit like hot tin, but fresh too. Her father held her closer as the fire snickered and spat.

Then as suddenly as it had come it was over. The fire still flickered, the coals dark red in the growing dusk.

Her father stood up. 'Come on. Let's warm up by the fire then get some shut-eye. Want to be off at first light, afore it gets too hot.'

'Where are we going?'

'Don't know.' He saw her surprise. 'We been heading south-west, following the river, to get off Drinkwater's land. We can cross the river down at the ford from here, then travel north again, if you like. Or south. Best keep to the river though. We ain't got no way to carry water, except in the billy, and that won't see us more 'n half a day. Besides, most towns are along the river, and the big stations too. What do you say? North or south?'

North would mean going back the way they'd come. 'South.'

'South it is then.' He hugged her again, hard. It still wasn't a practised hug — more like a squeeze and a shake. But it was good. 'Look up there, Matilda.'

'At what?'

'The stars. See, there's the Southern Cross. When we're a new nation I reckon that's what we'll have on our flag. If you wake up in the night and wonder where you are, you just take a look at that cross. Back when I was working for Drinkwater, during the lambing, we men'd take it in turns to check the ewes, each of us on for half the night. Call me when the cross turns over, we'd say before we went to sleep.'

He looked at her seriously. 'You get scared in the night, though, you call me. All right?'

'Even if the cross hasn't turned over?'

He met her smile. 'Even then. I'll be here for you. I'm always here for you now. Good night, me darlin'.'

It felt strange, sleeping among the trees. The breeze out here smelled like it had just had a bath. Young Mr Flanagan, three houses down from Aunt Ann's, slept outdoors every night, but that was because he had the consumption and needed the fresh air. She supposed it was healthy for her and her father too.

It was better than at Mrs Dawkins's, anyhow. The air still smelled of rain and of honey. Maybe from the gum-tree blossom, she thought drowsily. Do gum trees flower? She thought they did. Her father would know. He knew everything …

There was something hard under her back. A rock. She rolled over, wriggling deeper into the sand. Yes, that was better. She could hear a soft snore from her father, a reassuring sound, and then a soft thud. She opened her eyes. It looked like a roo, but smaller. A wallaby, she thought. It twitched its nose at her then, when she didn't move, bounced slowly down to the billabong. It bent its head and drank.

How many other animals would drink here tonight? Wombats, her father had said, and possums. If she could stay awake she could see them all ...

But there were days and days to see them. Weeks and years, travelling with her father, building a nest egg for the farm back home.

Home. It was a good word.

Matilda slept.

Chapter 15

Something was staring at her, two inches from her nose. Something with yellow teeth and a long nose.

She bit back a scream.

'Baaa,' it said.

She rolled over and stood up. The sheep looked at her expectantly. 'Baa?'

It was big — bigger than she'd ever expected from the woolly lambs in the picture book or the distant rock-like animals she'd passed on her way to Moura. It was as high as her waist and as wide as a kitchen table, though she suspected a lot of the bulk was wool.

'Baa?' The sheep edged closer.

Matilda backed away. Did sheep bite? 'Dad!'

'Wrmmph?' Her father opened his eyes, then pushed down his blanket and sat up.

'It's trying to eat me!'

He began to laugh. 'Sheep eat grass.'

'Then why's it trying to bite me?'

'Baa?' said the sheep again, looking vaguely disappointed. It turned away from Matilda and began to nuzzle at the tucker bag.

'Oh no you don't.' Her father sprang up and pulled the bag away.

'I thought you said sheep eat grass!'

Her father held the tucker bag up high, out of range of the sheep's questing mouth. 'Most do. I reckon this one's a poddy.'

'What's a poddy?'

'Pet sheep. If the mum dies you can feed the lamb milk from a bottle, or fill up a leather glove and let it suck one of the fingers. The sheep grows up thinking you're its mum. It'll follow you for miles, given half a chance.'

'Who does this one belong to?'

'Us. See, there's no earmark. We're on what used to be Joe Matheson's place, but he left here five, six years ago, when the drought began to bite.' He looked at the sheep again. 'This one's not that old.'

'How can you tell?' She edged nearer, now she knew it was safe.

'The teeth. Mutton chops for lunch?'

'No!'

He laughed again. 'You thought it was going to attack you a minute ago.'

'Yes, but I know it won't now.' She reached out a tentative hand, and began to scratch the sheep behind its ear, just like she had scratched Bruiser back at the factory. The sheep shut its eyes in ecstasy. Its knees began to wobble, and then it collapsed at her feet, allowing her to pat it.

'It's sweet!'

'You're not going to let me cut its throat, are you?' he asked resignedly.

'No! Why was it going for the tucker bag?'

'After the sinkers, I reckon.' He handed her one. 'Go on then. Feed the blasted thing. But we ain't taking a sheep with us.'

'Why not? We won't even have to feed it,' she said eagerly. 'It could eat grass and —'

'Because we walk faster than a sheep, that's why. After the first mile it'll be panting and puffing, then it'll lie down and wait till it gets cooler. And I ain't carryin' a sheep as well as a swag.'

He watched as she held the sinker out to the delighted sheep, letting it nibble around her fingers. 'You ain't never had a pet, have you?'

She shook her head.

'Make you a deal then. We leave the sheep here and next place where there are puppies you can have a dog.'

She looked up at him. 'Really and truly?'

'Really and truly. Besides, a dog can help hunt roos.' He began to pile wood on the fire again. A thread of smoke twisted into the early morning air. 'I usually have a dog of me own. Last one died, oh, a year ago now. Been too busy to get another.'

She wasn't sure about having a pet that hunted kangaroos. She patted the sheep again. 'Can I give it another sinker?'

'Not if you want breakfast. It can eat grass. You can't.'

She nodded, and then pushed the inquisitive face away. 'Go on,' she told the sheep. 'The rest is ours.'

As though it understood her the sheep bent its head and pulled up a mouthful of tussock. It began to munch.

Matilda slipped back into the trees to go to the toilet. When she came back the sheep was still there, eating. It didn't even look up as she approached.

'They've only got brains enough to think of one thing at a time, sheep. But then if sheep had brains we'd never get them shorn. Here.' He handed her the two remaining sinkers and a hunk of cold fish. 'Get that into you while I boil the billy.'

She'd rarely had black tea before — Aunt Ann always made her tea so it was mostly milk, with two big spoonfuls of sugar. But even though it wasn't cold this morning she felt like drinking something warm.

They took it in turns to drink from the billy, holding it with bits of bark so it didn't burn their hands. She sipped the last of the brew as her father kicked sand over their fire. 'Time to go then. There's a good spot to camp about twenty miles down the river. Big swimming hole too. You can practise that dog paddle of yours —'

Something moved behind them. She turned as a big brown horse cantered through the trees.

Riding it was Mr Drinkwater.

Chapter 16

For a moment Mr Drinkwater looked surprised to see her there. Then he ignored her, as though she were a fly, and stared at her father. 'Well, O'Halloran. Been setting any fires lately?'

Her father met his gaze. 'Only the campfire to boil my billy. And we're off your land.'

'But you've got my sheep.'

'Your what?' Her father began to laugh. 'You must be crazy. This is a poddy — it must have followed us down here.'

'Poddies don't roam as far as this.'

Her father shrugged, turning his back and beginning to fold their blankets. 'Suit yourself. We're off. Take the dashed sheep —'

'And let a sheep thief go?'

Her father looked back, incredulous, as Mr Drinkwater pulled something from his belt. Matilda stared. It was a pistol. For a second she thought he was going to shoot her father. But instead he lifted it and fired into the air.

Her father gazed toward the trees. 'What in flamin' hell are you doing?'

Matilda could hear hoofbeats. Had Mr Drinkwater brought his sons too? But then she saw the horses, smaller, scrubbier beasts than the boys rode: a piebald, a grey with big feet, like it was half draught horse, and a brown mare with a wild look in her eye. On their backs sat troopers, their blue uniforms grey with dust. They reined in their horses then, one by one, pulled out their pistols.

Her father shook his head. He sounded more bewildered than angry. 'Look, I don't know what this is about —'

'It's about the law,' said Mr Drinkwater. 'The penalty for stealing a sheep is about the same as burning a shearing shed.'

'That's three years ... you can't be serious! Three years in prison because a poddy turned up at my campsite!'

Mr Drinkwater said, too quietly, 'Maybe it's time you realised I *am* serious. There'll be no union interfering in how I run Drinkwater.' He gestured to the trooper on the piebald. 'Arrest him.'

The trooper gave a grin. 'My pleasure. Jim O'Halloran, I arrest you in the name of the Queen for sheep stealing. Looks like you're waltzing Matilda with us this time.'

Matilda ran to her father's arms. 'Leave him alone, you ... you old biscuit!' she yelled.

Her father held her close for a moment. 'You leave her out of it, all right?'

'I have no quarrel with the girl. It's you who needs a good cold rest in gaol to sort you out —'

'You'll never take me anywhere.' He bent and kissed the top of Matilda's head, then suddenly swung away. Before anyone could stop him he had flung himself into the billabong.

Water splashed over Matilda, frightening the sheep. It gave a startled baa, and ran to Matilda. She put her arms around its woolly neck automatically. The flat-footed horse tried to shy, till its rider hauled on the reins again.

Matilda stared into the billabong. Her father had vanished.

Chapter 17

Seconds passed, then minutes.

The trooper on the piebald cleared his throat awkwardly. 'You think he's gone and drowned himself?'

No, thought Matilda. She remembered her father's words last night. *Can swim underwater right across the billabong, I reckon.*

How long could you hold your breath underwater? She gazed around the billabong, expecting to see her father's head slip from the water on the other side. The ripples from the splash had died away. The water was still; not even a breath of wind stirred the water lilies. All at once it began to move again, as though the sand under the water shivered. But it was impossible to tell exactly where the movement had begun.

Mr Drinkwater looked uncertain. 'You,' he said to the troopers. 'Get in there and look for him.'

'Can't swim, sir.'

Mr Drinkwater swung off his horse. 'I'll do it myself.'

'I can swim,' said Matilda. She began to slip off her shoes.

'You'll do no such thing. Hold her,' he said to the first trooper.

One of the others put up his hand. 'I can swim.'

'Then get in there, man!'

The trooper swung off his horse. He unbuttoned his shirt, then began to slip off his boots.

'Hurry!' Mr Drinkwater pulled off his own boots and slid into the water. The trooper followed him gingerly. At first the water only reached their waists, then slowly it grew deeper as they trod forward, peering at the surface. At last Mr Drinkwater bent down and began to swim. The trooper waded around toward the other side of the billabong.

How long had it been now? Matilda tried to hold her breath, to see how long she could last. The men were still searching when she let it out. The sheep began to graze again.

Suddenly the trooper ducked under the water by the far side of the billabong, then stood up. 'Sir! I think I've got him. Sir!'

'Help him, you fools!' Drinkwater began to swim across the billabong as the trooper reached down into the water. The other troopers ran around the edge, then leaned out toward the now murky water.

'He's caught in the water weed!'

'No!' Matilda stared. Dad wasn't caught. He was escaping.

The trooper pulled something grey and limp into the air. An arm, in a grey sleeve.

Mr Drinkwater had reached them now. He too pulled at the man in the water. All at once her father popped to the surface, a rope of weed about his neck. Like a noose, thought Matilda vaguely. Her father ...

She felt hot ... or was it cold? The world seemed to swim around her.

'You sit here, girly.' Somehow one of the troopers was back, supporting her, lowering her to the ground. He ran to the others again. The four of them pulled the body onto the far bank of the billabong, laying Dad on his back. Matilda forced herself to her feet.

'Dad!' She ran around the sandy edges of the pool, startling the sheep.

'Baa,' it complained.

She bent down and touched his cold white face. 'Dad! Wake up! Wake up!' She stared up at Mr Drinkwater. 'You have to make him breathe again!'

'I can't,' said Mr Drinkwater quietly. 'Child, I can't do that.'

'You killed him! You killed my father!'

'He killed himself.' Mr Drinkwater's voice was flat. He added quietly, 'I'm sorry.'

She hauled her father's head up onto her lap, desperately seeking some sign of life. 'You know he didn't steal the sheep. You know!'

'Child, you'd better come with us. Up on my horse with you.'

'No!' She kicked out as he reached for her, hitting him on the knee. 'Don't touch me! I'm not leaving him. I'm not!'

'We'll take the body too.'

All at once the breath left her. The body. That was her father. Not a man, not Dad. He was 'the body'.

It had been too quick. This was the man she had dreamed of most of her life; and he was so different — so much more — than she had ever guessed. Now not just the man had gone, but the life she was going to have with him.

She felt cold, but curiously strong. It was like when Aunt Ann died, and Mum couldn't stop crying, and she had had to talk to the undertaker instead. It was like when the jam had tipped over Tommy. Lost. They were all lost. And now her father too.

But she had coped before. And she would now. She just had to get through the … the wobbly bits, the confused time till she could work out what to do.

What did she have, now that they were all gone?

Where could she go? Impossible to face Mrs Dawkins's now, and Grinder's Alley, after she had seen the sunlight on the hills.

A breeze tickled the edges of the billabong, sending ripples on the water and fluttering the leaves. It was almost as though a ghost was whispering.

And then it came to her.

The land. The land her father had loved, had chosen to stay with — in her grief she admitted it — rather than go to the city with his wife and child. His land was hers.

His dreams were hers, as well. She knew what her father wanted for her now, as surely as if he had spoken.

She took a deep breath. She put her father's head onto the ground, then bent to kiss his cheek, like Mum had shown her how to kiss Aunt Ann, like she had kissed Mum, just a couple of weeks before. His flesh felt cold already.

He is really dead, she thought.

She looked up at Mr Drinkwater. His face was twisted, his expression impossible to read. 'I'll come with you,' she said. 'But you have to take the swag. It's mine.'

He nodded.

'And the sheep.'

He stared. 'What do you want with a sheep?'

'It isn't yours. There's no mark on the ear. That's right, isn't it?'

He didn't answer. She took silence for agreement. 'If the sheep is mine it proves my father wasn't a sheep stealer.'

'How am I supposed to transport a sheep?'

Suddenly she knew. 'The same way you brought it here.' One of the troopers sucked in his breath. She knew now that she was right.

Murderer, she thought.

Mr Drinkwater seemed to come to a decision. 'The sheep is yours. Now will you come with me?'

'I'll come.'

Chapter 18

Sitting on a horse was strange. It was higher than she'd expected, and curiously easy, though maybe that was because Mr Drinkwater kept them to a walk, steadying her in front of him while he held the reins. Or maybe it was because nothing felt real now, not even the trees that she and her father had passed only the day before.

Her father. Her father. The man who held her on this horse had killed her father.

One of the troopers rode beside them. The other two troopers walked, one leading the horse laden with her father's body; the other leading his horse and the sheep, a rope around its woolly neck. They were far behind by the time Mr Drinkwater directed his mount into the long, tree-lined avenue to the house.

The sound of the horses' hooves changed as they hit the gravel of the circular drive in front of the house. Mr Drinkwater pulled at the reins. The horse stopped. A man came running and took the bridle. Mr Drinkwater dismounted, then held out his hand. 'Come on, girl.'

She looked at the hand, then at his face. He put his hand down and flushed. He watched as she slid down the horse herself, then began to climb the steps to the verandah.

'Hello, cocky! Hello, cocky!' The big white bird edged back and forth along the perch in its cage.

Matilda followed Mr Drinkwater through a door with stained glass on either side, and wooden latticework above to catch the breeze, then into a wide hallway, with sombre paintings along the walls, and the smell of polish and roasting lamb.

It was cool inside, despite the warm scent of cooking. She stood, while Mr Drinkwater opened a door. 'Wait in here.' His face looked strange, his mouth twisted. He is upset too, thought Matilda. She wondered if it was because her father had finally escaped him. There would be no one to imprison for the burned shearing shed now.

'He's beaten you,' she said.

He blinked, as though his mind was somewhere else. 'What?'

'My father. You can never catch him now.'

'You know nothing about it, child. Go and sit down.'

She stepped into the room as he marched down the hallway. It was a parlour, as big as the whole house at Moura. The floor was dark and polished, like at Aunt Ann's. Bright coloured mats, shining like silk, lay next to three giant sofas. There were soft-cushioned chairs, small tables with carved legs and those deep, rich, green velvet curtains at the windows.

She was afraid to sit down in case she made the chair dirty. This was the sort of house she had always dreamed of. Everything so smooth, from the furniture to the rugs. So many colours ... she felt a pang of guilt at her own disloyalty.

Her father's house — her house — had been made with hope and love. This place had been furnished with money, by the man who had killed her father.

She sat on the nearest chair without even trying to brush the dirt from her skirt.

How long was she supposed to wait here? If it was going to be hours then maybe she could cry.

The door opened. It was the woman from the train. She had evidently been told what had happened — or a version of the story, anyway. She recognised Matilda too. 'My dear, I'm Mrs Ellsmore. We met briefly a few days ago. I am so very sorry about your father.'

Matilda looked up at her face. It was smooth, and white from a life of hats and veils and parlours. But she seemed sincere.

She stood up as the older woman came into the room. 'Thank you.' The politeness was automatic. She wanted to yell at her, 'Your brother murdered him!' But then she might have to explain, and the tears would come.

'Would you like anything to eat?'

'I'm not hungry. Thank you.'

Mrs Ellsmore looked her up and down. 'Clean clothes then. My daughter's should fit you.'

Matilda opened her mouth to refuse again, then shut it. Her dress was filthy. This family owed her more than they could ever give. A dress was nothing. 'Thank you,' she said instead.

The door shut. Suddenly her legs would no longer hold her. She sat — not on the chair, but on one of the carpets, her back against the sofa. There was a painting on the wall: a picture of fruit in a bowl. She stared at it, trying to keep her mind away from what had happened — what was happening now. There was a pineapple, two apples, a pear …

'Who are you? What are you doing in here?'

She scrambled to her feet. It was the older boy. What was his name? James. He wore working clothes, a sweat-stained shirt and dust-stained trousers, unlike his brother when he'd pushed

Florence on the swing. But these clothes were almost new, and had been freshly ironed.

He raised his eyebrow at her, almost amused. 'Maids stay in the kitchen till they're needed, in case you didn't know. They don't sit on carpets either. You won't last here long if you do that.'

'I'm not a maid.'

He stared — at her worn dress, then at her hair. She had plaited it tight yesterday morning, but it must be a mess by now.

'No,' he said frankly. 'You're too dirty to be a maid. So why are you here? A thief?'

'No! Your father brought me here.'

He sat on the edge of a sofa and looked at her, interested. 'Why should he do that?'

'Because he killed my father!' The words tumbled out before she thought.

'What? Don't be ridiculous.' He stood up, as though to leave her.

'It's true! Your father was going to have my father arrested as a thief. My father drowned trying to get away.'

'He shouldn't have stolen then.'

'He didn't steal! You're the ones who are thieves.'

'What?' The boy stepped toward her, his hand up. For a moment she expected him to hit her. 'How dare you?'

'Your father took my father's life. Isn't that stealing? Your father stole this land too.'

'He did not!'

'He did! He just squatted here, pretending he owned it all.'

The boy laughed, and put his hand down. 'Ancient history. It's paid for now. It's ours.'

She stared at him. Her father was dead, and this boy laughed. She wanted to hurt him — hurt him like she had been hurt.

'You're the son of a thief. You can't change that.'

'My father can have you whipped!'

'He can't! I'm leaving here now!'

The door opened. 'Mrs Murphy is bringing the tea tray. I think these should fit you —' Mrs Ellsmore stopped and stared at the two of them, her arms filled with a froth of clothes. 'What is going on?'

'Nothing,' said Matilda. Or everything, she thought. But she wasn't going to explain. Not to them. Never to them. 'Where's my swag?'

'Your what?'

'My father's belongings.'

Mrs Ellsmore looked puzzled. 'There's a bundle on the verandah. Is that what you mean?'

'That will be it.' Matilda tried to find the voice Aunt Ann used to the drunk who tried to dance with her in the street. 'Good day to you.'

She was halfway down the hall before she felt Mrs Ellsmore's hand on her shoulder. But it was a gentle hand, almost an entreaty. 'My dear, you can't go off into the wilderness by yourself.'

'I'm not. I'm going home.' She met the woman's eyes. 'My father's house is just down the road. I can be there in an hour.'

'Not in this heat. Not by yourself.'

'You can't stop me.'

The woman gave a wry smile. 'I probably can. But I won't. I wish though that you'd wait till one of the men can take you in the wagon. Or James could take you —'

'No!'

'My dear, please don't go. Not like this. Do you have any other family? Someone we could contact?'

Matilda stared at her. 'My mother is dead. My Aunt Ann is dead. Granny and Grandpa Hills died before I was born. Now my father is dead too. But I am going home.'

Mrs Ellsmore stared at her. 'You're in shock. I'm not sure what's going on, but I promise —'

Matilda began to walk again.

'Wait!' Mrs Ellsmore peered out at her from the front door. 'What shall I tell my brother?'

Matilda turned. 'Tell him to bring my father's body home. And my sheep.'

It took more than an hour to get home. The swag that had looked so light against her father's back bent her almost double. In the end she held it by one strap and half dragged it, the billy clanking and bouncing through the dust.

But the pain was good. The struggle was good. While she forced her body along the road she couldn't think.

She didn't want to think.

Her mouth felt as dry as the gum trees by the time she reached the shadow of the cliffs. She almost ran the last stretch between them, dropped the swag and plunged her hands into the cold clear water of the pool, gulping great mouthfuls, then drinking more slowly. Finally she washed her face and her hands over and over, as though she could wash away all that had happened today, as if when she lifted her face from the water her father would be back in the house, and she would see smoke rising from the chimney as he put the billy on.

She lifted her face. The house sat still and quiet. No smoke rose from its chimney. She wiped away the tears, and then bent to drink again.

She should have filled the billy with water before leaving Drinkwater. Or asked for food, at least. No, she couldn't have done that. She would never ask them for anything, ever. But all she had was the flour in the tucker bag, the treacle, the salt and the tea. And some money, maybe ... She drank again, slowly now, then picked up the swag.

It was hot inside the house, and stuffy. She put the swag on the floor and opened the windows, and left the door open too. Her letter was still nailed to the outside of it. She picked it off and put it on the table. Her father's table, made with such love and care.

Something moved out the window: a yellow shadow, gone in the blink of an eye. She stared up at the rock face, wondering if she'd seen it at all. A wallaby, maybe, she thought. Could a wallaby get up that high?

A wallaby wouldn't hurt her. She was pretty sure there weren't any savage wild animals in the bush, nothing that could harm her. Except snakes of course. And spiders. And men ...

But the house sat in its well of silence. There were no men here. Just her.

At last she could sit down and cry.

Chapter 19

Dear Tommy,

I do so hope you are well, and that your arm is getting better.

I am back here at Moura. My father died. It was sudden. I do not want to write about it yet. But I have the house he built and the farm so I am quite all right and you are not to worry about me.

I will give this letter to Mr Doo to post with the other one, both will fit in an envelope for a penny. But I am quite all right, really.

Your loving friend,

Matilda

She had thought she'd feel lonely by herself, despite her determination to come here. But she didn't. Not yet, at any rate. Her father's hands had built this house, for her and her mother. He'd carved the chair, found just the right branches to make curved runners for the rocker. Maybe he'd even tanned the sheepskins for the beds, and trimmed them to just the right shape.

This was hers. The house, the land around it. It was the first time she had ever owned anything except her clothes and books and toys, and even those had been sold when Mum grew ill.

This was ... solid. What had her father said? *The land will still be there.*

She ran her hands over the wooden surfaces then gazed out the door again. The high cliffs seemed like protective hands clasped around her, keeping her safe not just from the winds and heat. The high cicada buzz in the trees could have been the land itself singing to her: *we are yours, we are ours, you are ours, we are yours.*

A sense of peace flowed through her. This is the first time I remember, she thought, that I have nowhere I have to go. Not to Miss Thrush's school, not to the factory, nor to find her father. She was here, forever.

And she had water to drink and a bed to sleep in. All she needed now was food.

She moved slowly over to the swag, then crouched down and untied it, rolling out the grey blanket that held the tucker bag, her spare dress, her father's trousers. There was a leather pouch too. She pulled open the drawstring and felt inside. Coins ...

A threepence, three sixpences, a couple of shillings, ten big brown pennies and a ha'penny. Four shillings and sevenpence ha'penny. More than a week's wage at the factory, and Mr Doo had sold all those vegetables for tuppence.

Or was that charity? she wondered. She didn't want charity. But maybe she'd have to accept it, for a while.

There was a lump in the tucker bag. She shook it over the floor. Two sinkers fell out, smelling faintly of fish. She'd need to wash the bag before it stank.

She picked up one of the sinkers and began to nibble it as she carried the blankets back into the bedrooms, hung the clothes on the wooden pegs on the wall. She was still wearing her father's hat, she realised. She hung it up too.

The sinker sat hard and heavy in her stomach, but she couldn't afford to waste food. You had to eat to keep on going. She turned back to get the other.

A furry shape glared up at her from the doorway. She bit back a scream. For a moment it was no animal she recognised; then she saw it was a dog, but moving like no dog she had ever seen, down on its belly so it seemed to have no legs, creeping toward the tucker bag. As she looked it grabbed the last sinker in its jaws, leaped to its feet, then bounded out the door and down the steps.

'No!' That sinker was hers. She was out the door and halfway up toward the cliffs when she realised what she was doing. She wasn't desperate enough to eat a sinker covered in dog slobber. And anyway the dog would have eaten it by now.

Plus there would be no one to help her if the dog bit her. Weren't wild dogs dangerous? But that's what they had said about Bruiser. She was good with dogs, and anyhow she didn't care, not now. This was something to do, something to keep her moving, stop her thinking. She kept on going, scrambling up toward the cliff to where the yellow streak had vanished. Maybe she was already more lonely than she had realised. Maybe it was the memory of Bruiser, still chained up at the factory, back in the city ...

She slipped between the tumbled boulders. There was a path, she realised, trodden perhaps by wallabies or other animals. Or by her father ... she remembered him saying *I'll show you where I hid the buckets*. But he hadn't. They had left the next morning.

Did this path lead to the buckets? Where had her father hidden things?

Stop it, she told herself. You'll be dreaming of buried treasure next. Which was impossible — her father's entire wealth was four shillings and sevenpence ha'penny. If he'd had more than that they wouldn't have needed to go waltzing Matilda to find work. He'd have bought rams and ewes and pipes ...

Suddenly the path ended in a small flat space about the size of a table. She peered up the cliff-face — it was too sheer to scramble up, even for a monkey. She glanced down. The house looked like a toy from here. She hadn't realised how far up she'd climbed. The dog must have slipped away from her, further down.

She turned to go back down. The path must have been an animal track, then. But why would an animal come all the way up here? There was no grass among the rocks.

Suddenly she stopped. The dog *had* come up here — there was a dog print in the loose dirt at one edge of the track. And this *was* a path. Maybe ... maybe her father had hidden things among these rocks or buried them ...

Buried a bucket? It didn't make sense. If he was going to bury something it would be easier in the soft soil down below. But nonetheless she turned back and began to search, running her eyes along the rock, every inch of it, then back again.

Nothing. Except ... she stared up the cliff-face at a ledge like a step. She looked up. There was another ledge above it, just above eye-level.

The higher ledge looked too small to hide a bucket, much less a dog. But she still put her foot on the step, then pulled herself up onto the second ledge.

A breath of cool air washed over her. It was as though the cliff itself had exhaled.

There was a gap here: the rock was grinning, the lips smooth from years of wind and rain. It was just big enough for a man to crawl into. Or a dog. And quite big enough for a girl.

She hesitated. If the dog was in there it might bite her as she crept inside. Maybe it had puppies. A mother dog with puppies would bite no matter how carefully Matilda approached her.

But she lay on her stomach, and pushed herself inside. 'Here, girl, boy, whatever you are.' She tried to make her voice as soothing as she could. 'No need to bite me, dog.'

The rock was cold under her stomach. Snakes. She hadn't thought of snakes. Was one about to strike her, its fangs raised? 'Go away,' she said more loudly. 'I'm a ferocious human. Scat!'

She was almost inside now. She reached forward. Her fingers struck stone.

A blank wall. All this way and nothing —

She twisted her head. No, there was light coming from over there. She twisted again, and suddenly her hand met open space. She hauled herself in another foot, and there it was: an opening like a big round window, not even jagged. She sat up, thrust her legs through, then pushed herself to her feet.

The cave was as big as the parlour at Drinkwater. Light speared in from holes in the cliff. The ground at her feet was littered with dried grass and twigs and tiny bones, bleached white. From birds' nests above, she thought, remembering a sea eagle's nest she and Mum had seen on the cliffs, in the last year of peace before Aunt Ann died.

Still no dog. But there was the bucket ... no, two buckets: a heavy wooden one, with polished sides and handle, and a battered tin one. Five lengths of metal piping — she supposed thieves might take them too; an old fruit box full of metal bits and pieces; and a hammer on top, shiny with what she supposed was dripping, to keep the rust away. A spade, an axe, a wood splitter, a garden fork, a shovel, a rake and an unfamiliar, long-handled tool with two prongs. They too were fat-covered, the shininess slightly dulled by dust. A wooden chest, with leather straps. She undid it carefully, watching out for spiders, then pulled open the lid.

Her heart thumped with disappointment. What had she expected? Gold coins? Rubies and diamonds?

It was a china dinner service: thin and cream, with a pattern of rosebuds around the rim. Dinner plates, bread and butter plates, soup bowls, dessert bowls, tea cups and saucers. Twelve of each, she thought, running her finger lightly up the sides of the stacked plates.

When had her father bought them? Just before her mother arrived here, a gift of daintiness for his city wife?

I'd even set the table nice for her, he had said. Or had he bought them afterward, when he still dreamed that if he filled the house with pretty things she might come back?

She would never know. In a way it didn't even matter. She just wished he could have known that his gift had at last been found, and would be loved.

She closed the lid. She'd have to take the china down piece by piece, in case she dropped it. It could stay here for a while, anyway. There was no one to serve tea to …

No, she thought. She'd take the whole set down to the house today. She'd eat from it, as her father had intended. She'd prop the plates on the dresser, where she could see them all.

Something growled behind her. The dog. She turned, slowly, so as not to spook it.

The animal lay on its stomach behind her. Now it was still she could see it was thinner than she had thought. No, not thin, just

125

sort of stringy, like a pencil with the wood shaved off. Its eyes looked almost golden in the sharp lines of sunlight from the cliff holes above.

A golden man, she thought, and golden hills. Now here was a golden dog.

The dog gave a short yip. It stood, ran a few paces down the slope into the dimness, then stopped and stared at her.

It wanted her to follow it.

Did it want to take her to its puppies? But mother dogs didn't like humans near their young. Matilda trod carefully down the slope. The rock was shiny, carved into a hundred tiny folds of stone. And then a cave opened out.

It was so vast it took a moment to accept that it could be here at all. A cold dead drip ran down her face. She looked up and saw white points of rock spearing down toward her. But these were frozen to the ceiling, too far above to even see the roof.

She had never known silence like this. It was so still ...

Or was it? Her eyes were becoming used to the dimness now. Something black slid in front of her in the darkness. It took a moment to realise it was water: a black river, here under the earth.

She shivered. She might have fallen into it by accident. How deep was it?

Did the spring come from here? Maybe, she thought, but there was a hundred, a thousand times more water than met the sunlight down below. *There's more water there, if you know where to look.*

She had forgotten the dog. It yipped again, a few feet away. And then words, so soft she hardly heard. Something she didn't understand, then, 'Help me.'

Chapter 20

The woman lay in a crumple of limbs near the wall. Even in the dim light it was obvious she was a native: the dark skin, so dark it was impossible to see her features clearly, the grey hair with a few remaining streaks of black.

For a moment Matilda wondered if she was a wild native, shot by Mr Drinkwater and his boys. But surely no wild native would wear a dress, even if her feet were bare.

What could have brought her up here? Was she hiding from the shooters?

Matilda kneeled beside her. 'What's wrong? Can you move?' The woman must have been trying to pull herself to daylight — Matilda could see drag marks along the rock — but now she clung to herself with cold. There was a smell, too, foul and stale: the woman's bowels had emptied onto her dress.

The sinker lay at the woman's feet — tough feet, with calluses thicker than boot leather. The dog is hers, she thought. It's brought her food. She felt his cold nose pressing on her arm. It whined, then gave another yap.

'Can you move if I help carry you?'

The woman nodded. Matilda felt relief that she understood English; fear that despite her offer she couldn't lift an adult; revulsion too at the stench. But in a funny way the smell made it almost familiar. It was the same smell as Mum's chamber pots, which she had after all cleaned so many times.

She put an arm under the woman's shoulders. And now she saw what was wrong. One side of the woman sagged, unusable, her left arm, her leg, even her face looked lopsided.

No, the old woman hadn't been shot. She'd had a — what was it called? An apoplexy, a stroke, like one of Aunt Ann's friends from the Women's Temperance and Suffrage League. Some people died of a stroke, but others got better — well, sort of better, for Aunt Ann's friend still needed a stick to walk and had only half a smile.

The old woman was so light, as though her bones were hollow. She was no taller than Matilda. We can make it, she thought, as they moved slowly toward the light, the woman still shivering, but using one foot to help move her along.

The dog pushed at Matilda's knees, as though wanting to help. She was afraid she would trip over it. The light grew nearer and nearer still. And then, after an awkward crawl through the grin in the rock, they were there on the small ledge outside, the afternoon light flooding across them with all its warmth.

It took less time than she had thought to get the old woman back to the house — she seemed to move better all the time, as though the heat revived her.

The steps up to the verandah were a struggle, but once inside the woman helped support herself, grasping the table and chair tops as they passed, till finally they reached Dad's bedroom. Matilda left her on the floor while she pulled the sheepskin mattress back over the bed, then hesitated. It would be easier to wash the woman on the floor.

To her relief the woman made no objection when she brought the pot of water from the spring and washed her all over with a wet rag, just as Old Mother Basket had shown her how to wash Mum.

It was strange washing black skin instead of white, but once again the familiar chore was almost a comfort. The woman accepted it, almost as though it was her due, unlike Mum's embarrassed protests.

At last she fitted one of Mum's nightdresses over her, with the pin-tucks Mum had placed so carefully in the cotton, and lifted the woman onto the bed, with a rolled-up blanket for a pillow, and another over her. Her shivering had almost passed now, but her skin still felt cold, especially after the chill of the spring water. Tea, thought Matilda. And a fire to make the tea. The matches were in the swag, the tinder still where she had left it, two nights ago. Thank goodness for the heap of firewood.

She had forgotten the dog. It lay on the verandah as she went out for more wood, its tongue lolling, as though it knew it was not allowed indoors, but had chosen the best place to view the valley. Nothing could come up the track without it seeing. Once more she felt comforted. A dog and someone to look after …

As soon as the pot boiled she went to look at the woman again. But she was asleep, a deep snoring sleep. Matilda touched the woman's hand lightly. It felt warmer, and the shivering had stopped. The woman didn't stir as she pulled the blanket up to her neck and tucked it in.

Sleep was good, wasn't it? But the woman would need food when she woke up. Soup maybe. There was nothing left to make soup with though, and another day — or was it two? — before Mr Doo would come again.

Matilda hesitated, unwilling to leave the woman alone. But she needed the buckets — she couldn't keep using the one pot for cooking, washing and carrying water — and the axe would be good for chopping kindling too.

In the end she climbed to the cave again, taking two trips to bring back the tools and bucket, and then several more for the china. Maybe it was silly to bring it. But if there was only tea and damper to eat then at least she could serve the tea in china cups, slice the damper thinly and put it on a pretty plate.

The dog accompanied her. He will need feeding too, she thought with a touch of desperation. Three of them to feed now. Dogs needed meat. How was she going to find meat here?

She washed the cups at the spring and put a damper by the coals to bake, with the pot of hot water ready to bring to the boil for tea. Still the woman slept. The shadows were growing outside. She'd need to light the lamps soon ...

The dog gave another high-pitched yip, more a howl than a bark, and then another. She ran out to the verandah.

A wagon was coming through the gap in the cliffs. For a moment she couldn't see who the driver was, and then he lifted his head.

It was Mr Drinkwater. And soon she could make out in the back of the wagon her sheep, lying on its side with its legs tied together, gazing up indignantly.

The dog glanced at her, as though asking if she needed him to keep yipping or maybe bite the horses' heels. She put her hand on his head to calm him — the first time she had touched him — and felt him settle down.

She stayed where she was as Mr Drinkwater took down the back of the cart, undid the poddy's legs, and then slid a length of wood up so he could push the sheep down. It landed in a heap of ungainly wool, muttered a baa under its breath, then immediately began to munch at the grass.

'Could you put the sheep in the pen? Please,' she added, feeling Aunt Ann, stern at her shoulder.

'It won't roam far. Not a poddy. It'll stay near water too.'

'Baa,' said the sheep. It saw Matilda and began to trot up the steps toward her.

The dog growled.

'Baa,' said the sheep reproachfully. It headed back down to the grass.

I will not cry, thought Matilda. 'Where is my father?'

'One of the men is taking him to the funeral parlour in town.' He held up a hand. 'It's the best thing to do, child.'

He was right, though she didn't want to admit it. 'My name's Matilda O'Halloran,' she said instead.

'Very well, Miss O'Halloran. May I come in?'

'Why?' Aunt Ann would have been cross at her rudeness. But she'd have been pleased that Matilda stood her ground.

He nodded toward the cart. 'I've brought you some things.'

Part of her wanted to refuse anything from him; part of her wanted to yell that there was no way he could ever give back what he had taken. Instead she just said awkwardly, 'Oh. Thank you.'

He nodded, and lifted a sack over one shoulder, with a wooden box under the other arm. They looked heavy, but he

131

seemed not to notice, despite his age. He climbed up the stairs and passed her, into the house, then put both sack and box on the table.

She followed, looking at them curiously.

'Food,' he said. 'A parcel of clothes too, from my sister. But child —'

'I told you my name.'

His lips twitched, as though he was trying not to smile. 'My dear Miss O'Halloran, you can't stay here by yourself. How old are you?'

'Fourteen.' The lie came easily again.

'Really?' he said quietly. 'I remember your father building this place, just before he was wed. Not much more than twelve years ago, I'd say.'

She shrugged, unwilling to admit anything to this man, no matter what he'd brought her.

'Come back to Drinkwater,' he said suddenly. 'This is no place for a girl, especially not one from the city.'

She had expected him to offer her a rail fare back to town. But Drinkwater ... for a moment she imagined herself there, dressed in white, on the swing.

'There is always space for another housemaid.'

'Housemaid!' She stared at him. 'You killed my father, and now you expect me to scrub for you?'

He looked puzzled. 'You'll be paid.'

'As though money makes it any different! You old ... old biscuit!'

His lips twitched again. She wanted to throw something at him, but the only things nearby were the china cups, which were too precious, and the pot, which was too heavy. She wondered if the dog would obey if she yelled, 'Bite him.'

'I'm sorry if you think it an insult.'

'It is.'

'I'm only thinking of what's best for you. I can't let you stay here alone.'

'I'm not alone.'

'A dog is scarcely enough.'

She gestured into the room beyond them. 'I'm not alone,' she said again.

He looked startled, then stepped to the door and glanced in at the grey head on the makeshift pillow. From this angle and with the blanket up it was impossible to see the figure in the nightdress.

'Who is she?' He sounded genuinely curious.

'None of your business.' She was glad that the woman's face and hands weren't visible, or her illness.

'Everything that happens in this district is my business.'

'Not here. This is my house. My land. The man who murdered my father is not welcome here.'

'It wasn't murder.' He met her stony stare. 'Very well. You can stay here. For the moment. I'll call again in a few days, in case you change your mind.'

For when you change your mind. She could hear the words even though he hadn't said them.

'As for your father … the funeral will be on Friday, in three days' time. I will pay all the expenses.'

She opened her mouth to say, 'No.' But four shillings and sevenpence ha'penny wouldn't pay for a funeral, not even for a coffin. She knew that all too well. But the man who had killed her father shouldn't pay for his funeral. She didn't want even his money to touch her father now.

'No need.'

For a second she thought she had said the words. Then she saw the man at the door.

It was the grey-bearded man from the wagon, Mr Gotobed, who had taken her to town. Bluey and Curry and Rice stood behind him. Do they always travel as a threesome? she thought irrelevantly.

Mr Drinkwater turned. 'Gotobed,' he said. 'What business is this of yours?'

'Union business. The union will bury its own.'

'Man's got a right to look after his comrades,' said Bluey.

'News travels fast,' said Mr Drinkwater.

'Fast enough. You've no call to be here, Drinkwater.'

The relaxed, almost comical men of the railway siding and cart had vanished. These men looked like rocks, unmoving on her verandah.

Mr Drinkwater looked at them, then back at Matilda, his expression once again impossible to read. 'I will be back,' he said. He brushed past them out the door, then paused at the table on the verandah and took the letter to Tommy, glancing at the address.

Matilda heard his boots clang down the steps.

'You all right, girly?' said Mr Gotobed.

She nodded.

'Of course she ain't right, you bast— you old coot. Her pa's been killed.'

She looked at them, their dirty faces so concerned. And then at last the tears came.

They clucked around her, giving her awkward pats, as she sobbed on the horsehair sofa. Mr Gotobed made tea — strong enough to melt a teaspoon — and handed it to her in a tin mug, as though he was afraid if he touched the china it would break.

'There, there,' said Curry and Rice. He'd said it several dozen times before, as though they were the only words he knew to soothe a crying female.

At last the sobs died away.

'You all right now, lassie?'

She nodded, reaching for her hanky. She blew her nose.

'Good-oh.' Mr Gotobed looked relieved. 'Like we said to the old bast—' He stopped and looked at her.

'Biscuit.'

'Er, *biscuit*, the union'll look after your pa. None o' that Friday stuff, neither. The funeral will be Saturday arvo, when those who has jobs are free to come. Whole town'll turn out for your pa.'

She wiped her nose again. 'Why?'

'Your pa started the union in these parts. He were the one who invited O'Reilly to come, an' all the other speakers we've had here too. We'd do the same for any union man. But your pa — he were the best.'

The others nodded. Mr Gotobed looked at the sack and the box on the table. 'We brought you some other stuff too. Not much — no one has a brass farthing to rub together around here just now.'

'Except for Drinkwater,' put in Curry and Rice.

'Except for the old, er, biscuit. But we'll see you right, best as we can. When things is bad you got to stick together.'

'Comrades got to stick together,' said Bluey.

'Thank you —' she began.

'Now, you want a lift in to town? Mrs Lacey offered to put you up. And the Fergusons —'

'No. I want to stay here. This was my father's place. He'd want me to stay here. It's mine now.'

To her relief they seemed to have expected it. Bluey nodded. 'Girl's got a right to stay in her own home.'

'Besides,' she added, 'I'm not alone.' She gestured into the room beyond. The woman stirred, as though she had heard their voices, and rolled over, showing her face.

Mr Gotobed stared. 'That's old Auntie Love. Ain't seen her around for a donkey's age. What's she doin' here? What's wrong with her?'

'I found her. She's had an apoplexy, a stroke, I think, but I don't think it's too bad. Whose auntie is she?'

'Sampson's, I reckon. He's one o' the natives that works for Drinkwater. But everyone used to call her Auntie. Sampson's a good bloke, almost like a white man. Knows sheep too.' The last sounded like it was one of the best compliments he could pay. Almost, she thought, as good as saying someone was a union man.

Suddenly she just wanted them to go. To leave her alone. She wanted silence and time to think. Time to make soup — if there were the right things in the sack.

Just … time.

The sun had long sunk behind the ridges. Curry and Rice looked out the door, then nudged his companions. 'Better get back while there's still light.'

And then, at last, they left.

-∰☉

Mr Gotobed had given her a dozen lamb chops. She kept four to cook tonight. The others could go in the meat safe by the spring, along with a hunk of cheese.

She looked at the things Mr Drinkwater had brought next.

More meat — a giant leg of mutton. The dog whined. It

136

crouched on the floor and gazed up at her longingly. She cut off the shank and put it out on the verandah. The dog chewed it hungrily while she unpacked the rest.

Bread — real bread, not damper, and fresh too; a heavy fruitcake; a jar of melon and ginger jam — not Mr Thrattle's, she was glad to see, but home-made. A big sack of flour, another smaller sack of sugar. No vegetables or barley to make soup, but she could cut the grilled meat up fine for Auntie Love and dip thin slices of bread and butter in the tea.

The chest held clothes. There was a dress she supposed was Florence's, white with a grass stain at the hem. Her lips curled. Of course Florence couldn't be expected to wear a stained dress. But Aunt Ann had shown her how to get out grass stains with sugar.

A nightdress, far too big for her — it must be Mrs Ellsmore's. Two handkerchiefs, edged with lace. Soap and a hairbrush. For the first time her heart softened. These weren't just cast-offs. Mrs Ellsmore must have actually tried to work out what she might need. And the hairbrush was beautiful: ivory with an inlay of silver. This was a genuine gift to a girl who had lost her father.

She'd wash her hair properly tomorrow, and then brush it before she plaited it again.

But the chops first. Her mouth watered. It had been almost a year since she'd eaten meat, except at the factory in Tommy's sandwiches.

Would Mr Drinkwater post Tommy's letters? She bet he'd read them first, if he did. She'd better write another letter, in case Tommy never got her first two. A penny was precious, but somehow a letter would make Tommy feel closer.

She had to find a way to make some money. Was town near enough to get a job, but still live here? She suspected she had come the long way round. She should have asked Mr Gotobed how long it took to get there. But probably the striking shearers or their wives and daughters had taken any jobs.

Maybe she could make money doing mending if anyone could afford to pay for it. Her sewing wasn't good enough to do dressmaking, like Aunt Ann and Mum, despite all their attempts to make her stitches neat.

She put her chin up. ('Chin up,' Aunt Ann used to say, when she'd sighed over her copy book or her sums.) Her father would want her to be happy, not sad. Proud of him and proud of Moura too.

Meanwhile there were chops and fruitcake.

Chapter 21

Dear Tommy,

I hope you are well. I am really, really sorry I cannot visit you. I hope you got my last letters too. I will find some other way to send this letter in case you did not. Mr Drinkwater took the letters to post but I do not trust him. He lives next door, except next door is about five miles down the road.

My father had a little money in his swag but I will have to make some more soon. I think I can make money mending; there are a lot more men than women here and their clothes look like they need mending. I do not like sewing much but it is better than the jam factory.

It is very beautiful near my house, I wish you could see it. It is not like a painting of the bush, there is no green except the trees. The cliffs are brown and the dust is white. There were kangaroos up at the spring this morning but Auntie Love's dog chased them. Auntie Love is a native, she stayed here last night because she had a stroke, I think, but she is getting better. It is nice to have a dog around, they made Mum sneeze.

It hurts to think of Mum and Aunt Ann and Dad, but I am trying to do what they would want me to do, and it doesn't hurt as much.

I will write again before I post this, so I only have to pay a penny for both letters.

Your loving friend,
Matilda

~❦~

Auntie Love had wakened before Matilda, and must have somehow made her own way out to the dunny. Matilda found the old woman sitting half sprawled in a chair on the verandah, the dog at her feet. Inside the fire had been freshened with a new bit of wood, and the water in the pot at the edge of the hearth was just off the boil. Auntie Love was used to kitchens, it seemed, despite her bare feet.

Matilda approached her shyly. This looked a different woman from the shapeless bundle she had washed and cleaned and dressed.

'Hello. How are you?'

Auntie Love nodded, almost regally. She waved a hand to the other chair.

Matilda sat. 'It is all right if I call you Auntie Love?' she asked hesitantly.

Auntie Love nodded.

'My name is Matilda O'Halloran.'

Auntie Love nodded again, as though she already knew. Or maybe, thought Matilda, she couldn't speak much, just like Aunt Ann's friend had lost most of her words, as well as not being able to use half her mouth. 'Are you sure you should be out of bed?'

Auntie Love stared at her, her face twitching. Matilda realised the old woman was trying to smile.

'Not sleep inside. Sleep here,' she said at last. The words were indistinct, and a touch of spittle ran down her chin. She lifted her right hand — the left one lay still in her lap, as though she had placed it there — and used the hem of her nightdress (Mum's nightdress) to wipe it away.

There was no way to argue with the certainty in those brown eyes. 'Would you like some breakfast? I could make toast and jam. Chops.'

The dog looked up at the word 'chops'. It had shared her bread last night, then her two chop bones too. The bones sat, well gnawed, between its paws.

Auntie Love seemed to consider the chops, to realise perhaps that she couldn't chew them. At last she mumbled, 'Toast.'

It was almost an order. Matilda nodded, and went to cut the bread.

~∰◯

The man arrived while they were on their second cup of tea, Matilda holding the cup — china, today, with its border of pink rosebuds — to Auntie Love's lips. The old woman had eaten two slices of toast, sodden in tea, then waved her refusal of a third.

The dog heard the horse before they did. It sat up, but didn't give its yipping bark. Matilda stood as the rider dismounted and came up the steps.

He was a native, but not a wild one, she saw in relief. Except for his dark skin he looked like all the other stockmen she had seen, from his boots to his sweat-stained hat. He was about her father's age. He tipped his hat to Matilda, then bent down to Auntie Love. 'What you doin' here, Auntie, eh? You all right?'

Auntie Love gave him a blunt nod. The man stood and took his hat off politely. 'Good day, miss. I'm Sampson,' he said.

'Pleased to meet you —' She hesitated. Did you call natives 'mister'? But this man had a job, and wore proper clothes. '— Mr Sampson,' she added.

He looked at her consideringly. Very like his aunt, she thought, the same stare, the same wrinkled eyes and hair, though his had no sign of grey.

'Thanks for looking after Auntie. How did she get here?'

'I don't know.' She didn't want to tell a stranger about the cave. 'Why wasn't anyone looking for her?' She felt a spurt of anger that an old woman could wander so far without anyone sending out a search party. But then they were natives.

'She doesn't live with me,' he said shortly. 'Auntie don't like houses much these days.'

Matilda stared at Auntie Love. 'You mean she's … she's wild?'

She thought she saw a flare of anger, well controlled. 'I mean she don't like houses.'

She bit her lip, unsure of how much she should say. 'A few days ago I heard Mr Drinkwater's son say he and his father and brother had been hunting wild natives. He said they'd shot one …'

He went still, waiting for her to say more.

'Could … could Auntie Love have been there?'

He didn't move. At last he said, 'She ain't been shot, has she?'

Matilda shook her head. 'I think it's what's called an apoplexy, stroke. But she's better today than she was yesterday when I found her. I think she needs a doctor though.'

'Doctor won't come, eh? Not to her.' His voice was matter-of-fact. He turned to the old woman again. 'Hey, Auntie … did they shoot at you?'

The woman looked from him to Matilda, then back again.

'Shot Galbumayn.'

'Who's Galbumayn?' Matilda whispered.

He didn't look at her. 'Not a name. You don't name the dead. Means younger brother. They didn't hurt you, Auntie?'

'Found him.' The effort of talking seemed too much for her.

Matilda could almost see it: the old woman, hearing the shots, running, stumbling. The man and boys on horseback already gone, perhaps, the body lying in the sand.

'Please, could you ask her why she came here?'

Mr Sampson crouched down by the chair. The old woman spoke again. At first Matilda thought the words were strange because the old woman mumbled. Then she realised this was another language, one that Mr Sampson understood.

He looked up at her. 'Auntie was coming to tell me about her brother. Heard your father died.'

'How did she hear that?'

He shrugged. 'Auntie hears everything. Heard two stockmen talking, I reckon. She came here to see you was all right.'

'I'm all right,' said Matilda slowly. The old woman must have set out here before she had left Drinkwater. Or maybe she'd travelled faster, knew a shorter way than the road.

But why would a native woman bother about a white girl? And why had she gone to the cave? Did Mr Sampson know about the cave? She didn't like to ask in case he didn't. Her father was right — hiding places were good sometimes.

The old woman banged her hand against the chair to get Matilda's attention without having to mumble. She shook her head at Matilda, as though to tell her to stop asking questions.

'I'll bring the cart over, take her home. Me wife'll nurse her, and me and the boys. My sons —'

'No.' The word was the clearest Auntie Love had spoken yet. She took a deep breath, then forced the words out clearly. 'Stayin' with the girl. Women's business.'

What was 'women's business'? Was it like having babies? But she was too young to have babies and Auntie Love too old. She waited for Mr Sampson to argue or even to just tell the old woman she was coming home. But instead he just crouched down, his face level with the old woman's. 'All right, Auntie. I'll bring your things, eh?'

Matilda stared. 'You're just going to leave her here?'

'What she wants.'

'But —' You might have asked me if I mind, she thought. It would be a lot of work caring for the old lady. Then she remembered the fire lit this morning, the kettle on to boil ... or maybe not so much.

Mr Sampson tipped his hat again. 'Miss.' He walked back down to his horse. It was almost as beautiful as the ones Mr Drinkwater and his sons had ridden, the same shiny brown.

'Tea,' ordered Auntie Love.

Matilda went to make another pot.

She spent the morning sewing the hem of Mum's black dress more securely — she had only had time to tack it for Mum's funeral — so she could wear it on Saturday for her father, and taking in the waist so she didn't have to tie it with a belt.

She thought that Auntie Love was sleeping in the chair on the verandah, but when she looked up the wrinkled eyes were open. She looked at Matilda for a moment, then seemed to come to a decision. She gestured for her to come closer, and then to help her down the stairs.

Did Auntie Love want to go to the dunny? She put her arm under the old woman's shoulders. Once more Matilda was aware of how small she was, how thin and light. She helped her down the stairs, the dog following them, but when she tried to head over to the dunny the woman shook her head, and moved in the opposite direction.

Why on earth does she want to go over there? thought Matilda. It was just a patch of dirt and tussocks. But she moved that way obediently.

'Baa.' It was the sheep, nudging at her.

'Go away,' said Matilda crossly. This was hard enough without a sheep.

The dog growled, long and low, then made a lunge at the sheep's back leg. The sheep skittered out of the way.

'Baa,' it said, reproachful again. It headed off to eat near the spring.

Auntie Love looked around, then let herself slide down onto a bit of ground seemingly just like all the rest of the ground around. The dog lay down next to her. She picked up a bit of branch and held it out to Matilda.

'What should I do with this?'

The old woman made digging motions. At last, because it was easier, Matilda obeyed, scratching at the hard baked soil. She had only got a few inches down when she saw a round shape, almost like a potato, but longer. She held it up, glancing back at Auntie Love.

Half of the dark face smiled. The old woman nodded, and pointed to another place. Matilda began to dig again.

There were about twenty of the potato things by the time Auntie Love seemed to think they had enough. Or perhaps, Matilda realised, she was too tired to sit there any longer. But she had the strength to reach over and pull at a sheet of thin white bark lying in the leaf litter. As Matilda watched she twisted it, this way and that, till suddenly a basket appeared in her hands.

'Can you teach me to do that?'

The old woman gave the twisted half-smile again. It was as though Matilda had passed a test. Of course, thought Matilda. She's teaching me. Women's business ...

She wondered how these strange roots would taste like. Could you use them to make soup? She put them in the basket, then leaned down to help Auntie Love to her feet.

－⁓⁓◎

Mr Sampson was back that afternoon with a few clothes and two blankets in a hessian bag, and another hessian bag clustered with flies.

'Meat,' he said as he dumped it on the table. 'Flour too, an' sugar.' He paused. 'Drinkwater don't pay wages, not to me and the boys. Just rations. But I can bring you those.'

'But ... but everyone gets paid wages.'

A sharp look, this time. 'Not natives. You all right, eh, Auntie?'

Auntie Love nodded. She'd slept for an hour, then hobbled in to take the damper dough from Matilda's hands and show her how to mix it more lightly before she sat on the verandah chair again.

'Mr Sampson?' He waited for her to speak.

'Do you have any daughters?'

'Why?'

'I just thought ... your auntie ... she keeps showing me things.'

He nodded. 'She's like that. No, I don't have daughters. Good thing too. Drinkwater only wants blacks for stockmen. Wants white women in his kitchen, these days at any rate. Don't want daughters of mine sent to the reservation.'

She had thought that reservations were good places, where natives learned to speak English and live in houses. There were collections at church to buy Bibles for the natives on reservations. But something in Mr Sampson's voice said that maybe they weren't like that at all.

'Would Mr Drinkwater send Auntie Love to the reservation?'

Mr Sampson looked at her impassively, as though this was an answer he didn't want to give.

There was too much here she didn't understand. It's because they think I'm a child, she thought. Mr Drinkwater, Auntie Love, even Mr Sampson. There are things they aren't telling me. Another thought came to her. 'Mr Sampson, are you in the union?'

For a second she thought she had offended him. Perhaps native men weren't allowed in the union.

He shook his head. 'No.' He paused and added, 'Not yet.'

Chapter 22

Dear Tommy,

I hope you are well.

Mr Doo has just been and taken the last letters. I hope you get them soon. Mr Doo was very kind. He had heard that my father died. I think everyone around here knows now, it is like the cockatoos fly from tree to tree and yell out all the news.

I will be able to give this letter to someone to post when I go to town. It is my father's funeral today. I am glad I have Mum's black dress to wear. I want to look right for Dad.

Mr Doo gave me more vegetables. He would not even let me pay tuppence for them. It is a whole sack of potatoes, and a string of onions and two big cabbages, they will last for ages with just the two of us.

You will be glad to hear I am not living here alone. Auntie Love is still with me. She is not my auntie but that is what everyone calls her. She is a native but not like a native in the books, she is very nice. She does not carry a spear or anything and she wears clothes.

Mr Doo said something about my teaching someone English. I am not sure what he means, but it may mean I earn some money or maybe he will pay me in vegetables which will be as good. He looked all around the spring and showed me where it would be a good place for a vegetable garden and fruit trees. I think he and his brother mean to help me plant them.

I do hope your arm is getting better. If you get a chance could you write to me, or ask someone else to write if you cannot write yet, to tell me how you are? Mr Drinkwater who lives next door stopped my letters getting to my father but I am going to tell him that he has to give me my letters or else.

Your loving friend,
Matilda

PS I do not know what 'else' is yet but I will think of something.

No one had told her when they would pick her up for the funeral on Saturday. So she dressed at dawn, and got Auntie Love settled with more tea and toast on the verandah, and fed the dog the meat they hadn't eaten — it was going off fast in this heat, even though she'd cooked it.

Auntie Love seemed stronger. She could lift her left hand now, and only dragged her foot a bit as she walked. But she had made no sign that she wanted to go home, wherever home was. Matilda had a slightly uncomfortable feeling that 'home' was here now.

She didn't know if she minded or not. She had never had a chance to 'mind' things before — adults or fate decided, not her. But at least with Auntie Love here no one could say she was too young to stay on Moura alone.

The morning passed. Auntie Love limped out of the house, waving Matilda back when she started to follow. She came back with an armful of dried grass stems. She sat in 'her' chair on the verandah again, and began to plait them, weaving one layer of grass into another, then handing it to Matilda to continue.

It was peaceful, sitting twisting grass stems, watching a sort of netted cloth slowly appear under her fingers. Auntie Love took it back now and then, to twist it in different ways. By the time Mr Gotobed's wagon clattered through the cliffs there was a basket, in stripes of gold and white and faded green, big enough to keep vegetables in, the colours of the landscape strangely captured in its fabric.

Matilda had half expected Auntie Love to want to come to the funeral. But she and the dog just watched from the verandah as Mr Gotobed helped her into the wagon, then rattled the reins to get the horse moving. There was no sign of Bluey or Curry and Rice today. Nor was there any conversation beyond the initial, 'You all right, girly?' when they started out.

She was glad. There was too much to think about to talk. Too much to feel too. Grief, but mostly anger, a sense of loss not so much for the man she had so briefly known, but for all the years they'd never have together. Mr Drinkwater had taken those, but there was a lingering deeper feeling that her mother too might have stolen time she could have spent with her father.

But the years by the sea had been good ones. Would she really have wanted to swap her memories of Aunt Ann for ones of her father?

No, there was too much to think about to want to talk now.

It was a shorter ride back to town than she had thought, hardly two hours, even at the slow walking pace of the horse. Town seemed deserted; the houses had a strange blank look. It was only when they were almost at the Town Hall that she realised that every door was shut and every window had its curtains pulled.

The combined funeral parlour–saddlery was around the corner from the Town Hall. The coffin was already outside on the hearse, a long narrow cart of dark wood; and there were black plumes on the heads of the two black horses. A man in black lifted his top hat to her. 'My condolences.'

She nodded, unsure what she was supposed to say. Tears pricked her eyes suddenly. Were she and Mr Gotobed to be the only mourners? She had expected at least Bluey and Curry and Rice to be here. Surely her father had other friends? Mr Gotobed had said the whole town would be at the funeral.

Perhaps, she thought, they were afraid of Mr Drinkwater's anger; maybe they'd lose their jobs if they were at the funeral of a union organiser. The union was paying for this funeral, but it seemed its members would stay away.

The hearse began a slow pace along the road. Mr Gotobed's wagon followed it. Along another street, then up a hill. Once more, each road seemed deserted.

And then she saw them — a line, all the way along the street, men, women and children, some dressed in black, others with black armbands, standing silent, heads bowed as the hearse passed.

The crowds continued as they drove into the graveyard, not just lining the road now but standing among the graves. The only sounds were the clopping of the hooves and the cry of a baby, abruptly hushed.

The hearse stopped at the top of the hill, next to a freshly dug grave. Mr Gotobed helped Matilda out, then reached under the seat for another dusty hat, ragged at the edges but still black. He led her to the far end of the grave as twelve men marched forward. Their hats too were black — freshly dyed, thought

Matilda — and each wore a coat, despite the heat, with a black tie, and black band on his left arm. The first two slid the coffin to the edge of the hearse. The others helped pick it up, then marched slowly to the graveside, and put the coffin down.

There was no preacher. Instead Mr O'Reilly, also wearing an armband, stepped forward out of the crowd. He took off his hat, and held it across his chest. Once again he looked insignificant in his rusty suit until he began to speak.

'Friends, we have come here to bid our last respects to Jim O'Halloran, a good man, a good friend, a good father, a good union man, brought down by the oppressors.'

''Ere, 'ere,' muttered someone. There was a chorus of 'hush'.

'I won't go on about O'Halloran. You all knew him. You remember the time he swore he could shear anything, and the blokes bought him a camel? Took him more 'n an hour but he did it.

'Remember how he'd give you the shirt off his back or his last crust to a mangy dingo? Remember how he started the union here, shouting down Drinkwater when we had that first meeting in the shed?

'We all knew Jim O'Halloran. We won't ever forget him.'

He raised his voice till he was shouting across the hill. 'You don't kill a man like Jim O'Halloran. His body may lie here today, but the things he fought for live forever. His ghost will be heard as you pass by that billabong. It will be heard wherever men strike for the rights they are denied. It will be heard wherever those starved and beaten cry, "No more! No more!" and start to organise. It will be heard as we stand together, arm in arm, and forge a new nation, where every man is equal. A man like Jim O'Halloran never truly dies.'

He stepped aside. A woman hissed: 'Billy! It's you now.'

A boy was pushed from the crowd. He was about Matilda's age, dressed in too-big man's trousers rolled up at the cuff and shoes that flapped on his feet, also borrowed for the day from an older brother or father. He too wore a black armband, ragged cloth cut from someone's petticoat, perhaps. He cleared his throat and gazed across the crowd nervously. Then he began to sing.

'Come let us be banded together
And place in each other our trust
And may we in heart never sever
Or flinch from a cause that is just.'

The boy's voice soared above the graveyard. It was one of the sweetest, most beautiful sounds Matilda had ever heard. Tears sat hot on her cold cheeks. But people were looking at her, as well as the boy. I will not sob, she thought. I will be strong, for Dad.

The boy's song rose louder as he grew more confident.

'Come give me your hand while we're singing
It will make it sound sweeter and then
Our song through the world will be ringing
With cheers for the Union men.'

One by one the crowd held hands. Soon they were all singing too, except Matilda, who was trying to make out the words.

'Three cheers for the Union men
Three cheers for the Union men
The place will resound with our singing
Three cheers for the Union men.

'So let us be true to each other
Our rights we are sure to obtain
For small is the loss and the bother
Compared to the prize we shall gain.

'When gone to our last cold oblivion
And all earthly duties are done
Three cheers by our sons will be given
When told how the victory was won.

'Three cheers for the Union men
Three cheers for the Union men
The place will resound with our singing
Three cheers for the Union men.'

Then it was finished. The boy shuffled his too-big shoes back to his mother. Four men slipped ropes around the coffin, and they and the eight others lowered it into the hole.

She almost told them to stop, to let her see her father's face one last time. But it wouldn't be right, not here in public. Not when he had been dead for days. She shut her mind to what might have happened to his body in this heat.

One by one each man threw in a handful of dirt. Mr Gotobed took Matilda's arm, and led her to the grave. She bent, and threw in a handful of soil too. A pebble clicked onto the coffin.

A sob escaped. She bit her lips, hard. The boy's mother moved over and put her arm around her. Her black jacket smelled of mothballs as she led Matilda back to the edge of the crowd. People were already heading down the hill.

The funeral was over.

She made Mr Gotobed wait till the grave was filled. She didn't want to leave her father till the task was done. Mr Gotobed seemed in a hurry, shifting from one foot to another.

'Right,' he said, as the last spadeful was tamped down, 'let's go.'

She didn't know what the hurry was — no one had been in a hurry at her mother's or Aunt Ann's funeral. Maybe, she thought, Mr Gotobed just wanted to get it over. She sat quietly in the wagon as the horse clopped down the hill again, then into the main street. The small town of Gibber's Creek looked as crowded now as when she had first seen it, with horses and wagons tied to every hitching rail.

Mr Gotobed stopped by the Town Hall. There was a space left, as though for them.

'Come on!' he urged. 'I'm as dry as a dingo's armpit.'

She shook her head, bewildered. 'What's happening?'

'The wake!' he said impatiently. 'Got six barrels of beer. The bast— *blighters* will have drunk 'em half dry already.'

'You were in a hurry for … for spirituous liquor? At my father's funeral?'

Mr Gotobed grinned. 'Nothing but the best for your pa.' He ran up the steps before her, and vanished into the crowd.

Matilda followed more slowly.

The Town Hall was as full as before. Once again, men clustered down near the stage — where the beer barrels were, she supposed. This time though there were tables along the edge of the hall, topped with an assortment of shabby tablecloths and what she suspected were sheets too — and plate after plate of food.

She wasn't hungry, but at least walking along the tables gave her something to do. Most of the food seemed to be some variation on flour and lard or sheep: lardy cake without currants, scones, mutton sandwiches, jam tart, more tart than jam. A woman gave her a hug, then put a cup of tea into her hand — she was glad not everyone was drinking spirituous liquor. Another woman kissed her cheek, and handed her a plate with a scone, topped with melon jam, and a mutton sandwich spread with yellow pickle.

All at once the crowd by the door grew silent. The silence spread across the room. Matilda peered through the crowd.

It was Mr Drinkwater. He wore a black jacket, black boots and a black top hat, as if he had been at the funeral too, though she was sure she would have seen him if he had been.

Mr Gotobed pushed his way through the crowd, a mug of beer in his hand. 'What are you here for?'

'To pay my respects. Like all of you.'

'Well, you ain't welcome.'

He's *my* father, thought Matilda. I should be the one saying that. She pressed closer till she was standing next to them.

Mr Drinkwater glanced at her, then back at the crowd. 'I have also come to say this: from now on Drinkwater will be a union shed. As Jim O'Halloran demanded, "The sheep will be shorn union or they won't be shorn at all."'

There was silence, as though no one knew how to react. Mr Gotobed glared pugnaciously. 'What about your stockmen? You let them join a union too?'

'Yes.'

Someone at the back cheered, but then was silent when no one joined in. This was a funeral, after all.

Mr Drinkwater turned. Matilda watched the man who'd killed her father walk away.

Chapter 23

Dear Tommy,

I hope you are well.

It was a wonderful funeral. I cried but it was good to see that so many loved my father, or maybe loved what he worked for. In a way it was as though I know him better now from seeing the people that he knew.

It almost seems like I have been here for years. I woke up when the kookaburras called this morning and it was as though they had been waking me up all my life. Auntie Love had lit the fire and made a billy of tea and some damper. She does this every morning before I get up. I think she has worked in kitchens before because she knows how to wash up and everything. I do not think that natives wash up cups and plates in the bush. I have not seen any do that in the paintings.

I try to tell Auntie Love to go back to bed and rest, like Aunt Ann's friend did, because one side of her face still hangs down sort of funny and she can't use her left hand properly either, and she shuffles like one leg does not work well too. I think she

157

understands what I say but she does not take any notice. She calls
the dog 'Hey You' so I do too.

I do not know when this will get posted, but I wanted to tell
you what happened anyway.

Your loving friend,
Matilda

The visitors started to arrive the day after the funeral: men on horseback, women in sulkies. Each brought a gift 'for Jim O'Halloran's girl'; each stayed for a cup of tea, then left. Matilda had to brew the tea leaves many times over, till the last brew was just a pale tan, but at least, she thought, I've had something to offer them.

Auntie Love kept the pot boiling and the teapot filled. No one spoke to her, but no one seemed surprised to see her, either. Nor did they speak to Matilda much. She lost count of the number of times someone said 'he was a good man' and 'he'll be missed'. What else was there to say?

Except one woman, her skin dried to leathery folds from age and sun. She looked at Matilda with faded eyes, and lifted up the young hand in her own brown spotted one. She grinned. 'You'll stay, girl.'

'How do you know?'

'Calluses on your hands. No one with dainty hands has got a life out here.' Then she was gone too, in another flurry of dust and hoofbeats.

The gifts covered the table in the house, then spilled out onto the verandah: a cake, smelling of slightly rancid dripping; a battered 'spider' frying pan with long thin legs to sit over the fire;

three hens and a bewildered rooster, their legs untied, then left to cluck around the house, and a 'my Joe'll be over this afternoon to build a coop. Got wire netting an' all.'

'Netting?'

'To keep the dingos out, love.' The woman sounded patient. Then she too patted Matilda's hand and left.

A tin bath, with a hole in one end. 'You'll find a use for it, lovey. Good to keep the kindlin' in.' A feather quilt, stained but clean. Two saucepans, a wooden spoon, a dozen big blue pumpkins. 'Last season's, love, so use 'em fast before they rot.' It was as though everyone around had heard that she was staying here; as though each felt the need to give something to her father's daughter, anchor her to his plot of land.

She had never had so much — not just the things, but the feeling that there were people around who had loved her father, and who were there for her too.

And then she saw the Heenans' cow.

It wandered up between the cliffs, its head down, as though it had no hope of greenery in this world of heat, seemingly unrelated to the barefoot boy who walked behind it with a stick.

Suddenly the cow lifted its head. It stared around at the shadowed grass, then took a few swift paces forward and bent to eat, crunching each inch of the blades at its feet.

The boy kept walking till he was on the verandah. 'Present from Ma,' he said. He turned to go again.

'Wait!' Matilda ran down the steps. 'You can't give me your cow! Don't you need the milk?'

Billy looked at her scornfully. 'She ain't in milk. Not till her calf is born. We ain't got the grass for her, down our way.'

'Maybe she could ... could visit here. You can have her back when it rains.'

'Ain't never gunna rain again. Not proper like. I want ter go to the city. Ma says there's water comes outta taps there.' He spoke as though it was an almost unbelievable wonder.

'But it's better here —' She stopped. What was right for her mightn't be right for him. Besides, he was no longer listening, just loping back down the track.

The cow didn't even look up as he left.

Chapter 24

Dear Tommy,

I have a sheep and a cow and calf and two hens and a rooster and chickens and a dog! The dog is still really Auntie Love's, but the others are all mine.

Another girl stayed here for two weeks. She is Chinese, but she was born in Melbourne. Her name is Patricia. She is going to be Mr Doo's wife. Mr Doo is going to open a shop selling seeds and farm machinery and things, and he wanted me to teach her some more English, especially writing and our numbers.

Mr Doo and his brother dug the vegetable garden for me and planted it and dug a channel from the spring. I have to move the stones every morning so the different gutters between the vegetables fill with water. It is much easier than watering the vegetables with a bucket.

Patricia went back with Mr Doo yesterday. I miss her. She did not speak English much but she learned very quickly and she was only a few years older than me, which was good. Auntie Love does not talk much.

I do not know if Patricia really wants to marry Mr Doo. He is much older than her. But every time I asked she nodded. He is a nice man though and I think he will be good to her. I will miss his visits here when he has his shop, but we will have lots of vegetables in the garden. The radishes will be ready to eat next week I think and the lettuce and the spinach are as tall as my finger already. There are carrots too, and funny cabbages that Chinese people eat and proper cabbages and spinach and onions and pumpkins and corn, but they are not ready to eat yet.

Mr Doo says I have to plant potatoes, but Mr Sampson says he will do it. He comes over on Sunday afternoons to see his aunt and bring us flour and tea and sugar and meat. Did I tell you he is a native? But he is not the wild kind, he is very nice.

He and Auntie Love talk in their own language sometimes. I did not know that natives had a proper language. Mr Sampson does not have a spear or a boomerang, either, so it is not at all like the paintings or the books at school. He has built a fence around the vegetables so Mrs Dawkins can't get in.

Mrs Dawkins is my sheep. I know it is rude but the sheep has whiskers just like Mrs Dawkins and the same expression sometimes too. I have called the cow Daisy and the calf Buttercup and the hens Fluffy and Feathers and the rooster is Old Biscuit because he tries to tell them what to do. I am glad we have enough water for them all.

Matilda paused again to nibble her pencil. Auntie Love was funny about the spring. She made Matilda sweep the sheep and cow dung and wallaby droppings away from the pool every evening with the big straw broom, and she wouldn't let Matilda dip the bucket in either, making her flick the water out into the bucket with her hand instead.

It took much longer to fill a bucket that way, but Matilda didn't dare disobey, not when the old woman stared from the verandah.

She had got upset too when Mr Doo first started to dig the channel from the spring: she squatted in the shade of a tree and glared at the brothers as they worked. By the second day she seemed to accept the pool wasn't being hurt.

Sometimes Matilda wondered if Auntie Love realised that Matilda owned the farm. She had tried to explain the land was hers now, but Auntie had just nodded, as though it didn't matter at all.

One of the union men built a chook run so the dingos can't eat the chickens. I think Hey You would like to eat them too. I have heard the dingos cry at night. They do not sound like dogs. It is a high cry and strange and makes me glad Auntie Love is here, and Hey You.

There is a lot of work to do here, but I like it, it is not like working in the factory. I have to weed the garden every day and in the afternoon I go to gather firewood, just branches, not the big hunks Mr Sampson cuts for us. It takes a long time.

I am making a fence and a gate for a sheep pen. Mr Sampson showed me how. He says he will get more poddy lambs next spring and will give me some to look after, now I have a cow with milk to feed them, and I do not want them to run away. I would like to have many sheep here, good ones, because that is what my father wanted.

The fence is half done, it looks good, but the gate looks lopsided and I do not know how to make it swing or what to use, but I expect Mr Sampson will know. Mr Sampson says if I have some sheep I can sell wool and lambs and make some money, not a lot but maybe I will not have to look for any sewing as it does not cost anything to live like this, so maybe my money will last till I can get some sheep next year and cut off their wool.

Do you know what I did yesterday? You will never guess. Auntie Love showed me how to track a goanna. They make a big swish in the dirt. This goanna must have tried to get into my meat safe, as there were tracks all around. Goannas eat meat, did you know that?

It was easy to track. It was in a crevice in the cliff, I could just see its tail. Goannas sleep all winter, I did not know that either, but it was warm enough for it to wake up awhile yesterday. But when I pulled it out it did not move, it was like it was dead.

I was glad about that because it was very big, almost as long as I am. Auntie Love killed it with a rock, then showed me how to clean the insides out of it. I did not think that I could eat it, but it is like kangaroo, it is all right if you add enough potatoes. The skin is nailed up on the side of the house. It was pretty at first, all yellow and grey, but now it is going brown and curly at the edges.

I am learning lots of things, but think of you often.

Your friend,
Matilda

Matilda put the pencil down. She'd have to sharpen it with a knife before she used it again.

Should she have mentioned eating goanna to Tommy? Maybe he'd think she had gone bonkers. She'd never have eaten goanna even a few months ago. But once you had learned that potato-like things sat under what looked like dead bare ground, once you had picked tiny native cherries from shaggy, dry-looking trees, or the little dark fruit on the wiry bushes at the edges of the gullies that Auntie didn't give a name to, once you'd seen how live sheep got turned into chops and legs of lamb or mutton and chutney sandwiches, you sort of forgot that 'real' food was bought from the corner shop.

There were other things she'd have liked to tell Tommy too. How she'd tried to make a rice pudding using Aunt Ann's recipe with the rice Patricia had brought and how she and Auntie Love had tried a spoonful each then laughed, as though sweet, not-quite-cooked rice was the funniest thing they'd ever eaten.

How Mr Doo showed her how to use the hen droppings and the manure sweepings from the spring to scatter on the vegetables — she'd *never* have eaten a vegetable back in the city if she'd known what they were grown with.

But how could she explain to Tommy the peace of sitting on the verandah in the dusk with a woman who rarely spoke, twisting at grasses to make the striped containers that now held everything from their daily damper to her sewing?

It was so different from her life before, even more different from the life she had dreamed of with her father, the one with a white farm house and pink pigs.

Grief for Mum and Aunt Ann sometimes stabbed like a knife. The sadness for what she'd never have with her father was always there. But she was happy — free in a way she had never been before. Auntie Love might make whooshing gestures at her till she swept the pool each dusk, but she didn't expect her to get up at the same time every morning; she didn't even tell her when to go to bed or what to cook for dinner.

Matilda looked down at herself and grinned. What would Tommy think of a girl who wore her father's trousers, tied up above the knee to make them shorter, and her father's shirt and hat? It was impossible to collect wood and weed the vegetables in a skirt ... well, not impossible, she supposed, as other women seemed to do it. But Auntie Love hadn't even looked surprised when Matilda came out one morning dressed in the trousers.

She folded another piece of paper up to make an envelope, and sealed it with flour and water paste. She'd give it and a penny to Mr Sampson next Sunday, and he could give it to one of the men to take to town to post.

The letters to Tommy were the only things she had spent money on, except a reel of cotton from Ahmed the peddler who took his wagon from house to house every year. The cow was giving milk now, and Auntie Love had showed her how to milk it — her left hand still wasn't strong enough to do it herself. Auntie Love showed her how to let the cream rise and whip it to make butter too.

One of the hens had gone broody soon after it arrived. Now there were five tiny yellow chickens running out in the chookyard. The other hen gave an egg almost every day. With the free vegetables and fruit from Mr Doo, and the meat and flour and sugar from Mr Sampson, they had more to eat than they needed.

Even the fences were made without nails: they just cut a square out for the next bit of wood to fit into.

She walked outside, and sat on a chair on the verandah, next to the sleeping Auntie Love. It was too hot to weed yet. She looked down the track toward the break in the cliffs.

It would be nice if someone suddenly came to visit them ... Mr Doo and Patricia, maybe, or Mr Gotobed, or even Mrs

Ellsmore, who had been so kind. But Mrs Ellsmore might be shocked at the unpainted, wood-shingled house, and anyway she suspected that Mrs Ellsmore and Florence had already gone back to town, and that the boys had gone back to their boarding school.

She was glad the boys had gone. Perhaps there would be no more shooting parties now. Despite what Gotobed had said about wild blacks she didn't think they could be so dangerous, not if Auntie Love had lived with them.

She drew in a deep breath. All right, she was a little bit bored. But she was proud too. The new garden, the fruit trees brought carefully wrapped in old newspaper, and already showing new shoots. She even had a sheep.

Matilda looked over at Mrs Dawkins, then ran over to the railing. 'Auntie! Auntie! Look!'

Auntie Love opened her eyes. Matilda heard the old woman chuckle as she ran down the steps, Hey You at her heels.

Mrs Dawkins stood munching at a tussock. Two small white heads nudged their noses beneath her, wriggling their tails in the air. 'She's had lambs!'

Soft and snowy, the first things she had ever seen out here that were exactly like her book. 'Real lambs!'

Hey You barked, then dropped onto his stomach, as though checking that the lambs weren't about to invade the house and his territory.

Auntie laughed again, sharing the joy or amused at Matilda's enthusiasm. Matilda danced back up the steps. 'We should do something to celebrate! Make pikelets ... except we don't have any jam left.'

Auntie Love pushed herself to her feet. They were still bare — Matilda had offered her Mum's other pair of shoes, but though

Auntie Love had taken them, she had never worn them. Matilda had found Hey You chewing one beneath Auntie's chair. It had hurt seeing Mum's shoe in bits, but she hadn't taken it from the dog. She had given the shoes to Auntie Love, after all. And besides, the one shoe left was no good to anyone.

Now Auntie limped inside, and took a bucket from its hook on the wall and a long-handled wooden spoon. She gestured to Matilda to help her down the steps. She used a stick when she got around by herself now, but when she walked with Matilda she expected to have a shoulder as a crutch.

Matilda put an arm around her. The old woman was as thin and light as before, seemingly existing on tea and damper. Even on their 'fresh meat' days she waved away the offer of chops or mutton roast from above the fire.

Down the steps, one at a time, so Auntie could favour her good leg, then up behind the house, following Auntie's gestures.

'Baa!' Matilda glanced round as Mrs Dawkins decided to join them, her twin lambs trotting at her side.

Auntie stopped, which meant Matilda stopped too. 'What's wrong?'

The old woman shook her head. She put a hand behind her ears, then touched her eyes. 'You want me to listen? Look?'

Auntie nodded.

Matilda shrugged. There was nothing to hear, except the wind, high up above the ridges, a low moan like someone was crying in the sky. Nothing to see ... or rather a lot to see: the cliffs, the gum trees waving up on top, an eagle trying to balance on the wind. But somehow she didn't think Auntie meant any of those.

Then she saw it — a flicker past her nose. And then another. And another ...

Bees.

She glanced up to see Auntie look at her with approval, before sliding down to sit on the ground. She flapped her hand in the direction the bees were going.

Matilda looked at her incredulously. 'You want me to follow the bees?'

Auntie nodded, then shut her eyes for a brief doze. She seemed to have the capacity to sleep sitting in any position.

There was no arguing when Auntie just shut her eyes like that. Matilda advanced cautiously in the direction the bees had taken. Bees lived in hives, didn't they? And they stung you. She had sat on a bee when she was small, and Aunt Ann had pulled out the sting. It had hurt.

She stopped. There were no bees to be seen.

She looked back at Auntie Love. The old woman opened her eyes, then pointed at an anthill. It was as tall as Matilda, somehow redder than the surrounding dirt, as if the ants had painted it.

'That's an anthill, Auntie. Bees live in hives.'

Auntie held up her hand impassively. Matilda helped her up again, then put her arm under the old woman's shoulder so Auntie could limp toward the anthill. She stopped a couple of yards away.

And then Matilda heard it. A humming sound, more a vibration in the air than noise. And suddenly there were bees ... long dark ones, hovering for a few seconds on the other side of the anthill, then vanishing inside.

Auntie gestured for Matilda to move away. Matilda hesitated. What if Auntie got badly stung?

But she had known where the bees were. Somehow she was sure that the native woman knew exactly what to do now too. What bee would dare sting Auntie?

Auntie Love limped forward, the spoon and bucket in her good hand. She crouched by the anthill, then thrust the handle of the spoon into the structure and wriggled it for a couple of seconds, then balanced the other end on the rim of the bucket. She stepped back surprisingly quickly, making shooing motions to get Matilda to move too. They stood about ten yards from the anthill.

Matilda stared. What was the spoon supposed to do? But even as she watched the handle began to darken. The blackness slid down the spoon then dripped into the bucket. *Drip, drip, drip*.

Honey.

Auntie looked satisfied. She leaned on Matilda's shoulder again and limped toward the house.

The sun was high when Auntie waved her hand toward the anthill.

'You want me to get the honey?'

Auntie nodded.

What if the bees stung her? But Matilda nodded. You couldn't argue with someone who used so few words, not when you never knew if they understood your words or not. And the bees hadn't stung Auntie earlier.

She stopped a few yards from the hive, then made a sudden dash, pulling out the spoon and grabbing the handle of the bucket in one go. A bee danced in front of her face as she ran back, and then another. She ducked, then glanced at the bucket. Half a dozen bees clustered on the lip, but even as she watched they flew back toward the hive. She kept on running, stopping only when she was inside, out of breath.

Auntie laughed. She picked up the bucket and looked inside,

then nodded in approval. Matilda peered down too. About an inch of honey rested in the bottom of the bucket. Two jars' worth, she thought, or even three, all for a minute spent jiggling a wooden spoon.

She looked up to find Auntie watching her. 'Thank you,' she said.

It was more than thanks for the honey. She suspected that Auntie knew that too. The old woman simply nodded.

The scent of honey had filled the house. It had been more than a year since Matilda had eaten it. Even at Aunt Ann's it had been a treat. Pikelets, she thought. She had an egg, and lots of milk and flour and butter, and now they had honey too.

Definitely pikelets.

~※◎

The house smelled of hot butter as well as honey now. Matilda watched as Auntie Love flipped out another pikelet.

Auntie had taken over making them when the batter turned lumpy. They were the best thing Matilda had eaten for over a year: hot from the pan, the butter and honey soaked in, rich and sweet and savoury. She spread honey on another, then slipped one — without honey this time — down to Hey You. The dog gulped it as swiftly as he had eaten the last four, then sat, waiting for another.

All at once he cocked his ears. He gave his yelping bark, then looked from Auntie Love to Matilda and barked again as though to say: 'Come on. I've told you someone is there. Now what are you going to do about it?'

Matilda walked over to the door as Mr Drinkwater tied his horse's reins to the rail of the verandah. Behind her Auntie Love got to her feet and shuffled into the bedroom as Mr Drinkwater climbed the steps.

'May I come in?'

She considered saying no but she doubted he would go away without saying what he wanted. All she'd achieve would be a conversation in the doorway. She stood back politely (Aunt Ann was whispering to her again). 'Would you like a cup of tea?'

He seemed startled. 'Yes. Thank you.'

She took one of the pretty cups from the dresser, poured out tea and added hot water from the pot, then — reluctantly — passed him the plate of pikelets. Still standing up, he took the cup and a pikelet, and bit. 'It's good.'

'Thank you.'

He looked around. 'You seem to be managing.'

She smiled, suddenly proud of it all. 'Yes.'

He looked around again, then saw Auntie Love's abandoned cup. He met her eyes sharply. 'People are saying that you have a native woman living with you.'

Matilda looked at him warily, suddenly afraid that it might be against the law. She wasn't going to let anyone take Auntie Love to a reservation. She said cautiously, 'Does it matter?'

'Who is she?' The voice was abrupt.

If he hadn't sounded so demanding she might have told him. 'It's not your business.'

'Everything that happens here is my business.' He sounded as though it was so obvious she almost laughed.

'This is my land.' A thrill still went through her at the words. She said them again, just for the pleasure of it. 'This is my land. I can ask anyone I want to stay here.'

'You are a child who has no idea of what she is getting into.'

She met his eyes defiantly. He gave a brief nod. 'Very well

then. Not a complete child. Mature enough, I hope, to take the advice of a neighbour who is concerned about you.'

She was wary now. 'What advice?'

'Don't go listening to gossip from natives.'

'They haven't told me any gossip —' She stopped, aware of what she had revealed.

'So there is a native woman here. I heard she was ill too.' She could see the exasperation in his eyes, and something she didn't understand too.

'If she's ill she needs help. A doctor.'

Was it a trick? Would a white doctor help a native woman? She didn't have enough money to pay a doctor to come all the way out here. Auntie Love was getting better, wasn't she?

For a moment she wanted to do what this man asked: hand the whole problem over to him. But what if the only way to get Auntie Love to a doctor was to take her to a reservation?

No, she thought. She shut her mouth tight, in case any more confessions escaped, and sat down on one of the chairs. It was rude to sit down in front of a grown-up; rude to cross her arms like this too. But somehow she had the feeling that Aunt Ann was patting her shoulder and saying, 'Good girl.'

He looked at her without expression, then stared around the room again. If you start hunting through my house, thought Matilda, I'm going to kick you.

Instead he sat on the chair next to her. At last he said, 'I'll give you fifty pounds for this place.'

'What? No!'

'A hundred.'

She had no idea how much the land was worth, and the house. Was he trying to cheat her?

He looked at her expression. 'Two hundred then.'

So he had been trying to cheat her when he offered fifty. 'No. No matter how much you offer. This land is mine.'

Hey You ran to the door again, but this time he didn't bark. Mr Drinkwater got to his feet. 'What is Sampson doing riding up this way?' He stepped out on the verandah, waiting, as the other man tethered his horse, then stood, embarrassed.

'Boss.'

'Sampson. Got business here?'

'Yes, Boss.'

'May I ask exactly what that might be?'

Matilda brushed past him. 'Mr Sampson was a friend of my father's. He's come to visit me.'

'He wasn't that close a friend,' said Mr Drinkwater slowly. 'Your father had better friends than him. His union mates, for one.'

Matilda saw Mr Sampson stiffen. Mr Drinkwater turned to Matilda. 'Answer me, girl! Who is the woman staying with you? I demand to see her. Now!'

Why did it matter? she thought. But the very fact that he wanted to know so much made her want to hide the truth. 'I want you to leave —' she began, then stopped, as Auntie Love shuffled out behind them.

Chapter 25

Her dress was gone. Matilda dropped her gaze, then lifted it again, unable to look away. It was the first time she had ever seen a naked woman — a naked anyone. She had never even seen herself in the mirror without clothes.

Did all old women look like this when they were naked or only native ones?

Though Auntie Love wasn't quite naked. A string of red-brown beads hung round her waist. Even more extraordinarily, she wore a ring on her left hand — a gold one, set with a small red stone. Matilda had never seen it before. Auntie must have carried it under her clothes.

She expected the men to say something, anything, about a naked woman on her verandah. But both were silent. Mr Drinkwater's hands clenched into fists, so tight the knuckles were white. He and Auntie Love stared at each other, neither saying a word.

Mr Drinkwater spoke first. 'Why are you here?'

Auntie shrugged. The shrug could have meant anything, thought Matilda, from 'I don't know' to 'I do not want to say'.

Mr Drinkwater tore his gaze away. 'Take her away from here,' he said to Mr Sampson.

'How, Boss?'

'I don't care. Just get her off this land —'

'This is my land,' said Matilda clearly.

Mr Drinkwater turned on her. 'You have no idea who this woman is.'

'She is my friend.'

'Friend! She's ten times your age.'

'One hundred and twenty?'

He snorted. She had never heard a man snort before. 'Six times then. She doesn't belong here.'

Matilda glanced back at Auntie Love. She had no idea what was happening, why the woman had so suddenly decided to look like a wild native. Why she stood there without speaking, why Mr Drinkwater had looked like his world had shattered as he stared at her.

'I think you need to go,' she said to Mr Drinkwater.

Mr Drinkwater pointed at Mr Sampson. 'Bring her to Drinkwater. Now.'

'No, Boss,' said Mr Sampson.

Mr Drinkwater's face flushed red under his white eyebrows. 'You will do what I tell you.'

'No, Boss.'

Mr Drinkwater moved toward Auntie Love. Matilda stepped between them, pushing Auntie Love back toward the door. 'If you touch her,' she said, 'I'll ...'

She darted into the house and grabbed the frying pan, and came back out, holding it over her head. The last pikelet fell on the floor. She was dimly aware of Hey You gulping it down, then sitting at her feet, looking up for more, the love of pikelets more important than the surrounding tension.

Mr Drinkwater unclenched his fists. He stared down at Matilda with her frying pan, then at the woman behind her, unmoving in the doorway. Then he turned again to Mr Sampson. 'You're fired. I want you off Drinkwater tomorrow morning.'

'But Boss —'

'You can leave your horse too.'.

For a second a look of anguish shone in Mr Sampson's eyes. 'I broke that horse.'

'I don't care who broke it. It's mine. If you're not gone by tomorrow I'm calling the troopers.'

Mr Drinkwater lifted his hat to Matilda. 'You're making a mistake having that woman here. Good day.'

She watched him climb up onto his horse, and ride back between the cliffs.

After a moment Auntie Love limped back through the doorway. Matilda followed, and put the frying pan down. Mr Sampson brought up the rear, sinking down onto a chair.

'What's going on?' she demanded. 'Why was he so upset?' (And why was there a naked woman standing in her house? But she couldn't say that.)

Neither Auntie Love nor Mr Sampson replied. Auntie limped back into the bedroom and closed the door, Matilda hoped to get dressed again.

She didn't understand what had happened. She didn't know why it had happened either. Only one thing was clear: Mr Sampson had lost his job, his home and his horse.

He stood up, nodded to her and turned to go.

'No, please: wait.'

He turned.

'What will you do now?'

'Like he said. I got to go.'

'Where? Can you get a job on one of the other properties?'

He seemed reluctant to talk. 'Other bosses won't hire me now. The boys should be right, but.'

'Your sons? You think he's fired them too?'

'Maybe. Best they go, now, eh? Best they go.'

It isn't fair for one man to have so much power, she thought. Not to take one man's life, and then another's house and job and horse.

Mr Sampson looked away, speaking almost to himself. 'My dad built my house. Cut the wood. Put a new roof on myself. Sold possum skins to buy the iron.'

'Then it's *your* house?'

Mr Sampson looked back at her, his face still impassive. 'House is on his land.'

She spoke without thinking. 'Move the house then!'

A few months ago she had lived in a world where houses just — were. You rented or if you were lucky bought them, you lived or died in them. Not now. 'You and your boys — take the wood and the iron.'

Auntie Love appeared in the doorway, her old dress hanging on her thin frame. She looked at Matilda without speaking.

Suddenly she laughed. It was the first time Matilda had heard her laugh like that. And then Mr Sampson was laughing too. It seemed such a natural sound, so much a part of who they were. It was as though ropes had fallen off them.

'Move the house!' chanted Auntie Love.

'Move the house!' Mr Sampson slapped his hat against his side and laughed again. 'There's a spot other side of Dhirrayn.'

'Dhirrayn?'

He gestured to the cliffs and the hill above. 'Dhirrayn.'

'But that's —' She stopped. That was Moura land. Her land.

But where else are Mr Sampson and his wife to go? she thought. All land was owned by someone. Wasn't it?

Mr Sampson seemed not to have even realised he should have asked her first. 'Boys and I can take the place apart after dark. Boss won't know what's hit him, eh? Get the boys to drive the sheep over now, afore it gets dark.'

'Sheep?'

'Poddies. Elsie's been feedin' them.'

'They'd be your sheep but on my land,' she said slowly.

The laughter stopped. He stared at her. Auntie Love stared too. She was aware that there was so much unsaid, so much she didn't understand.

'It's all right,' she added quickly.

But the words had been spoken. The laughter had vanished. Mr Sampson said at last, 'You get half of what the poddies bring. Half for the wool, half of the meat. That's the way the boss does it.' He paused and added, 'I'd be workin' for you, eh?'

It wasn't quite a question or a statement. She wished she knew what her father would have said, even Aunt Ann. 'I'd have to give you rations? I … I haven't got enough money.'

He shrugged. 'Don't need rations. Plenty roos, other tucker.'

It wasn't right. But she didn't know what right was. She thought of the crowded hall of unionists. Did any of them know, either? Or were they also trying to work out something that might be truly fair?

'How about everything we make we share?' she said slowly. 'Not just from your poddies. Always, whatever we make from sheep on Moura. Half for you. Half for me.'

It still didn't seem fair. They were his sheep and his skill. But it was her land. That had to count for something.

To her surprise he smiled again, as if she *had* got something right. He nodded, then headed out the door and down the steps, as though there was nothing more to say.

Chapter 26

Dear Miss O'Halloran,

I recently heard from my nephews that you are still at your father's house, and that one of Drinkwater's former stockmen is working for you. I gather that my half-brother is not impressed. My nephews too appear to feel that you have transgressed by being female, young and somehow escaping their father's control. Their tales certainly enlivened the last weekend they spent with me. I wish you every success with your endeavour.

You mentioned an 'Aunt Ann' and my brother says he believes your mother's maiden name was 'Hills'. It only occurred to me when I returned here that it is possible that you may be related to a late acquaintance of mine from the Women's Temperance and Suffrage League, Miss Ann Hills. She and I first met when we worked together gathering signatures for the petition to give women the vote their husbands have enjoyed for decades.

She several times mentioned her niece, Matilda O'Halloran, who lived with her, and although it is not an uncommon name

I suspect the determination such as you and Miss Hills have both displayed is rare.

If you are Miss Hills's niece, please accept my apologies for not realising the connection earlier. Please, now, accept my deepest condolences on her death, as well as once again for your father's and, I suspect, your mother's too. It is indeed a lot to bear for someone so young. Miss Hills's death was a loss to many, and not least to the cause for which we women of all classes and backgrounds are working.

I hope you will excuse the presumption of the accompanying parcel. It contains some of my late husband's garments that your workman may find useful, and others perhaps for yourself as well. Please also accept my assurances, too, that if you ever decide that the bush life is not for you — as it certainly is not for me — that I and your aunt's friends will make sure you have both comfort and security.

Yours, most sincerely,
Mrs George Ellsmore

Matilda put the letter down, and stared out the window. The sheep were grazing below the spring, and an eagle soared high above her valley.

So the remote, fashionable woman and her daughter at the railway siding had been part of the lost world of Aunt Ann and their cottage. It seemed so impossible, but it made sense too. The Women's Temperance and Suffrage League brought together so many women — capable, determined women like Mrs Ellsmore and Aunt Ann. She smiled, imagining Mr Drinkwater trying to boss his half-sister.

Would things have been different if she had gone to Mrs Ellsmore that first day, instead of to Mr Gotobed and his friends? If she had said, 'Excuse me, I am Matilda O'Halloran, can you help me please?' Would Mrs Ellsmore have convinced Mr Drinkwater not to try to trap her father with the poddy sheep?

There was no way to know. But it was strangely good to know that somehow Aunt Ann was still helping to take care of her, even now. If she had known her aunt's friends might help her she would never have left the city. But leave Moura now? She shook her head.

Why hadn't Mum let Aunt Ann's friends know how bad things were? Pride, she supposed, not wanting anyone to know the bailiffs had taken their furniture, even Aunt Ann's gold locket.

Mr Gotobed had brought the letter and the big parcel out that morning, on his way to do some work at Drinkwater. It had been sent to the pub 'to be collected'. Mrs Ellsmore might be Temperance, like Aunt Ann and Mum, but she knew that the hotel was the one sure place to find Mr Gotobed or someone from the union who knew her. Matilda supposed that Mrs Ellsmore too doubted that Mr Drinkwater would pass on the mail to Moura.

She worked at the knot around the brown paper. It would be easier to cut it, but string was precious. Auntie Love made string from bark and what Matilda suspected was her own hair, but it wasn't as strong as proper string, though it was good for tying her hair back.

She opened the brown paper and stared. She wouldn't need to use string for her plaits now. A cluster of hair ribbons, white and yellow and pale green. A new white dress — she fingered the lace on it wistfully. She had worn the other white dress only once, when Mr Gotobed and his mates had arrived to take her in to the opening of the Workers' Institute in town, with its library and reading room.

By the time she'd got home the dress had dust stains on the hem and perspiration stains under the arms. The stains had vanished by the time she'd boiled the dress in the cooking pot, then dried it on a clothesline of plaited string stretched between the trees, using the pegs her father must have carved years ago. Now the dress was too crumpled to wear, and she had no iron.

She lifted the new dress, folded it carefully in the brown paper again and put it in the chest in her room, wrapped in a blanket to keep away the dust that seeped into every crevice, and then looked at the other garments. Six pairs of flannel trousers, a tweed jacket, six collarless shirts, a pair of boots.

She hoped the boots fitted Mr Sampson. The shirts and trousers looked like they might be a bit too big, but nothing that a belt or braces couldn't fix, or a bit of needlework.

She lifted up a pair of flannels thoughtfully. A few hours' sewing would make them fit her too. It was so much easier wearing trousers, and there was no one who minded to see her. She could always run and change if Hey You warned of visitors, although she suspected that neither Mr Doo nor Mr Gotobed and his mates would worry.

Mr Drinkwater probably would. She grinned at the thought of shocking Mr Drinkwater. But he hadn't ridden by again, not even when Mr Sampson's house had vanished in the night, and his mob of poddies too. There had been more sheep than she'd expected, eighteen of them, not just this year's poddies but some older ones, as well.

Mr Sampson's house was finished now, though she gathered it was smaller than it had been, for there was a pile of corrugated iron left over. Perhaps neither he nor Elsie needed more than a single room now their boys were working on other properties.

She saw something move out of the corner of her eye. She froze, then slowly turned her head.

It was a snake, a red-bellied black one, its tiny head peering into the dish where she kept her water. It stopped too, as soon as it sensed her movement, lying there as though to say, 'I am a stick.'

She almost grinned. The two of them, both too scared to move. If she moved it might strike her, kill her. If it moved she might kill it — if she knew how to kill a snake, which she didn't. But the snake didn't know that.

Suddenly she heard steps shuffle up the steps, and breathed in relief. Hey You padded into the room, followed by Auntie Love, carrying an armful of dead branches for the fire.

'Stop.' Matilda nodded over to the water dish. 'Snake.'

Hey You dropped to his stomach, staring at the reptile. Auntie Love smiled. She put down the wood, then made a short lunge. Suddenly the snake's tail was in her hands, and the head cracked once, twice, against the floor.

The snake writhed, but Matilda could see that it was dead, its head smashed. It had taken about five seconds.

For a moment she felt like crying at the loss of its beauty. Because it had been beautiful, even though deadly — the shiny black, the flash of red like a flower, the silent grace of it. And then the loss faded, and she was just glad that her house was snake-free.

She'd check the bed, though, tonight.

'Good tucker.' Auntie Love grinned.

'Errk! Not snake!'

Auntie Love laughed. 'You got carrots, potatoes, big pot. Stew 'em up.'

She couldn't eat snake. But Aunt Ann had made breaded eel. Maybe if she pretended the snake was eel …

'It won't poison us?'

Auntie laughed again. She pantomimed horror, clutching her throat like she'd been poisoned, then shook her head. She took the snake to the table and grabbed a knife. She sliced off the head, then began to pull off the skin, her left hand still clumsy.

Matilda glanced away. Next time, she thought. I'll watch how she does it next time. I'll never eat it if I see how she cleans it now, and if I don't eat it she'll be hurt.

At least Auntie Love was wearing a dress again today. Matilda hoped she wouldn't appear without her clothes again. It was embarrassing.

But why had she done it? It was almost a taunt to Mr Drinkwater, as though to say: 'I am a wild native, and there is nothing you can do about it.'

And there isn't, thought Matilda stubbornly. No one was going to shoot natives on Moura land — or Drinkwater, if she could help it. And there was no way Mr and Mrs Sampson or Auntie Love were going to be sent to a reserve, either.

Hey You gave a sudden yap, then trotted out the door. Matilda followed him, glad to have an excuse to leave the kitchen while Auntie Love dealt with the snake.

It was Mr Sampson and his two dogs, pushing the mob of sheep — now containing Mrs Dawkins and her two lambs — toward the open gate of the stockyards. The dogs worked either side of him, yapping and snapping to keep the sheep headed toward the gate.

Matilda ran down to him. 'What are you doing?'

'Checkin' for fly strike.'

'What's that?'

He shook his head. 'Don't worry, missy. I do it.'

'But they're my sheep too now, aren't they? I should help you.'

Mr Sampson looked even more shocked than she had been at the idea of eating snake. 'Not right. Dirty work, missy.'

'Call me Matilda. Please, Mr Sampson.'

He stared at her, then nodded. The sheep were inside now. He shut the gate, then picked up a pair of hand shears and a bucket of something dark and evil smelling. There was a strange-looking brush sticking out of the gloopy stuff.

'What's that?'

'Bit o' wattle bark, turps, tobacco. Kill the strike.'

At least he didn't call her 'missy' this time, even if he hadn't said 'Matilda', either. 'What's strike?'

He looked at her consideringly, then slipped between the slats of the gate into the yards. She followed him. His dogs stayed outside, lying on their bellies, looking cautiously at Hey You, seated imperiously now up on the verandah as though to say to the other dogs, 'Just remember all this is mine.'

Mr Sampson lunged, grabbing one of the ewes by the neck. A sudden movement and it was seated on its bottom, looking stupid. Mr Sampson ran his hand through its fleece, then pointed at a damp-looking patch. 'Strike.'

Matilda peered closer, then drew back. 'Ohh.'

The damp patch was rotten wool, stinking and yellowish. But worse was underneath — raw flesh, filled with tiny maggots, burrowing and crawling. She patted the sheep's nose, startling the animal still more. How did it bear the pain?

Mr Sampson nodded at the bucket. She picked up the brush, and saw it was a big grass tussock, trimmed to bristle length. Liquid dripped from it.

'Put it on thick,' said Mr Sampson.

She gritted her teeth, dipped the brush one last time, then thrust it into the sheep's side. The animal struggled in obvious agony.

'Again,' said Mr Sampson.

Once again she dipped and thrust. Mr Sampson let the sheep go.

'It's … it's horrible.'

'Worse if we don't, eh?' said Mr Sampson gently.

Matilda nodded. She thought she would be sick — sick from the pain in the sheep's eyes, sick at the red flesh, sick from the smell of the stuff in the bucket.

But these were her sheep. Half hers, anyway. If this wasn't done they would die — in even worse pain than they felt now, eaten at by the strike.

She took a deep breath. 'Easier to do this with two.'

Mr Sampson nodded.

'You hold them. I'll splash on the wash.'

He looked at her for a moment. 'We got to take the tails off of them lambs too.'

'Why?'

'Stop the fly strike on their bums.'

'But … but won't they bleed to death?'

'No,' said Mr Sampson.

Matilda glanced at the two lambs, butting Mrs Dawkins's sides, their tiny tails wriggling in the air. It seemed impossibly cruel to hurt them. But she had never seen a grown-up sheep with a tail, she realised. Mr Sampson must know what he was doing.

She nodded slowly. 'I'll help with that too.'

'You sure?'

'I'm sure.'

He smiled. 'Good-oh,' he said, then added, 'Matilda.'

Chapter 27

Dear Mrs Ellsmore,

I hope you are well.

Thank you very, very much for the clothes. Mr Sampson liked them, and so did I. I had to take in the trousers. I think your husband must have been ~~fatter~~ bigger than Mr Sampson. I am keeping the beautiful dress in my chest for the next time I go to town.

Yes, Miss Hills was my Aunt Ann. I am very grateful for your offer of help, but this is my farm now, and I do not want to leave it.

I am learning a lot about sheep. There were lambs in my picture book when I was small. Real ones are even funnier. They jump up and down playing 'king of the rock', trying to catch butterflies and darting about with the wind. I love the mother sheep too, their patience as the lambs butt under them for milk, and how they stand with their backs to the wind, looking like grey rocks.

We have twenty-two sheep now, after lambing. We have one ram too. He has a long nose and looks down it at us as though he disapproves of us.

The sheep come back to the valley where my house is every night, so they can drink, then go out every morning to see what they can find beyond the cliffs.

The sheep keep trying to get into my vegetables, but Mr Sampson and I have finished a fence to keep them out, and Hey You barks when the wallabies get under the railings. Hey You is a dog. I think he might be part dingo, but he is very well behaved.

Thank you again for the clothes, and your good wishes. I am looking forward to wearing the dress with lace.

Yours respectfully,
Matilda O'Halloran

Matilda finished her letter then glanced out the door at the shadows. It would be midday soon. She should go and weed the vegetables, dig up new plots for the seeds Mr Doo had given her, each kind wrapped in white paper, with a drawing of the vegetable on the front — useful, she suspected, for his customers who couldn't read. Lettuce, cabbage, carrots, beetroot, leeks, radish, a big bag of corn seed, so she could grow extra for the hens as well.

She glanced at her hands. There was dirt ingrained in the fingernails, and different calluses from the ones she'd had in the factory. They weren't the hands of someone who wore a lace-trimmed dress. They were hands that cut the smelly dags off sheep, that hoed the ground for vegetables, that tipped mutton fat into old treacle tins and dipped wicks into saltpetre bought from Mr Doo, to make slush lamps instead of buying candles.

Why was she lingering when there was work to do? Dreaming of a white-dress life?

I'm lonely, she realised. Not alone, but with no one really to talk to, no one who knew the world she had grown up with or who was even close to her own age. Auntie Love and Mr Sampson sometimes talked to each other in a language she didn't understand, even when she recognised English words like 'sheep'. Even Hey You was really Auntie Love's dog.

As though it had heard her thought the dog gave a high howl from the rocks below the cliffs behind the house. Auntie Love spent more of her time outside now that she was so much better, though she still slept in the house — or on the verandah — each night. This morning when Matilda woke up there had been a bucket of gum blossom soaking in water: it made a cordial, sweet and slightly bitter too, a bit like lemonade.

Hey You howled again then ran down toward the track, the sheep scattering with indignant baas.

Matilda grabbed her hat. Hey You had never behaved like this with visitors. What was wrong? She reached the bottom of the stairs just as two men ambled between the cliffs.

They were no age, their beards were dirt coloured, their faces too. Even their clothes and swags were the colour of the dust. Only their eyes showed blue and white. The tallest held up a hand in greeting. 'Hello, missy. Lovely place you got here. You made it real nice. Your ma or pa around?'

They know, she thought, as Hey You ran to her heels. They know it's only me and Auntie Love.

'You got any work for a pair o' swaggies down on their luck? I'm that hungry I could eat a hollow log full of green ants. Chop you a whole woodpile for a bit o' dinner.'

The dog sank to its belly and growled.

Matilda didn't quite trust them either. They were too innocent, too friendly. But she hated asking Mr Sampson to chop wood for her — he had enough to do already. The axe was sharp, and there were the ringbarked trees up by the cliffs ready to be felled. And she could cook them dinner.

The taller one shook his head mournfully. 'Ain't had a crust to eat since day before yesterday.'

This could have been her and Dad, begging for work to fill their bellies. Suddenly she felt ashamed of her suspicion.

'Wait here. I'll bring you some damper and cold meat before you start work — that all right? And the axe.'

'Ah, you're a good girl. Yes, a real good girl. You got a wood splitter and wedges too?'

She nodded.

'We'll do you a right good wood heap.'

His mate grinned, showing three long yellow teeth in a mouthful of gums. She could smell the stink of his breath. 'Too right,' he said.

~❦~

The sounds of axe blows rang around the cliffs while she mixed up a fresh damper, put the haunch of roo Mr Sampson had brought her the day before on to boil with precious onions and potatoes. If the only way she could repay their work was with dinner, she'd make it the best she could.

A whole pile of properly chopped wood, instead of twigs and sticks and branches. She could make it last for weeks, months maybe …

Hey You gave a woof. Auntie Love appeared, silent as always. She gestured out toward the sound of chopping.

'It's two swaggies.' She realised she didn't even know their names. 'They said they'd chop wood in return for dinner.'

Auntie Love's lips grew thin. She stared outside for a moment, then shook her head.

'It's all right. Really …'

Suddenly Matilda realised the sound of the axe had stopped. 'They must be stacking the wood,' she said uncertainly. They weren't stealing the axe, were they? And the wedges and wood splitter?

'I'll just run down and check on them — no, Auntie,' as the old woman made to come too. 'I'll be faster by myself.'

She was glad she was in trousers, not a skirt. Impossible to run in a skirt. Hey You followed at her heels, for once staying with her and not his mistress. She stopped, a giant pile of wood in front of her.

How had they managed to chop all this in such a short time? She had misjudged them. They were just what they had said — two swaggies down on their luck, and hard workers too.

She looked around. 'Hello?' she called.

No answer. They must have headed up to the spring for a drink. But then she'd have met them on the road. She stared around again, then on impulse looked down at the ground.

Suddenly it was just like tracking the goanna with Auntie Love. There were their boot marks — two different sorts of boots, one with a hole in the heel. A whole mass of prints around the wood heap, then two sets heading back toward the house and spring, but around the cliffs, not toward the track.

They must have decided it was shorter that way, she thought. Or shadier. She'd catch them up, offer them a cup of tea, more damper, before they started work again. She reached for some wood to carry back for the fire.

The heap collapsed. She stared at it, a stick of wood in her hand. They had built it hollow. How many farm women had they conned, she wondered, to get so skilled in building hollow stacks?

And where were they now?

She dropped the wood then began to run again, back toward the house. No time to find Mr Sampson. Hey You was silent at her heels.

The house was quiet. Too quiet, no sound of Auntie stirring the pot. She peered inside the door.

'Wondered where you were, missy.' The smaller man grinned his gap teeth at her. He held a bulging sack. A piece of cloth poked out from the top. Her sheets ...

'How dare you —' She stopped, as the other swaggie held up the axe.

'Cunning as a dunny rat, that's me. Now you be a good little missy, and maybe we'll leave you and the old darkie in one piece.'

Matilda stared around at Auntie Love, sitting silent in the corner. Auntie met her gaze as though to say: be quiet. Don't anger them.

Matilda edged toward her. Auntie was right. What could an old woman and a girl do against two men? Especially when one man held an axe. If only she had gone to find Mr Sampson. If she had screamed for help down at the fake woodpile he might have heard her.

And maybe they'd have used the axe against him too.

Her axe. Her sheets. Even the hessian sack was hers.

No, she thought. I have lost too much. Lost Dad and Mum, Aunt Ann. This place is mine ...

It was as though the land itself sent strength up through her boots. She had fought bullies before, and she had won. She could win now too.

She clicked her fingers. Hey You sat up, still staring at the strangers.

'You see this dog?'

'I see him, missy. So what?'

'If I click my fingers again he'll tear out your throat.'

It was a lie. The dog obeyed Auntie Love, not her, if it obeyed anyone. But the man looked at the dog uncertainly. 'Don't look savage.'

'He isn't. Just well trained.'

The man held up his axe. 'Just let him try it then.' But his voice held fear.

Matilda forced her lips into the smile she had used on the Push. 'Will we see what happens then? I'll click my fingers and one of you will be dead. You or the dog.'

'Let's get out of it.' The taller man used a rag to grab the handle of the pot from the fire. 'We're going, missy.'

'Put my pot down before you go. And the sack.'

'Don't listen to her —'

Hey You growled.

It was a low rumble, almost too soft to hear. The man hesitated, then slowly put the pot down.

'Now the sack. Where's my wood splitter?'

The taller man pointed to the tools on the table.

'Get going then. And don't come back. The dog and I will track you off this place. And if I see you again anywhere near my land,' she put the smile back in place, 'I'll click my fingers. And you know what?'

'What?'

'I'm not a good little missy.' She let the anger take her. It felt wonderful. 'I'll see your throat ripped out and I'll enjoy it.'

She could hear their feet pound down the track as they ran.

Chapter 28

Auntie Love made tea. Matilda felt that the cliffs could shake into tiny pebbles and Auntie Love would make tea. She watched the old woman put out the thin china cups, the saucers, pour hot water into the pot, then add two spoons of sugar to both their cups.

Matilda's hand shook as she lifted the cup from its saucer. But the tea steadied her with its warmth and sweetness.

Auntie gave a short laugh over the table. 'You scared 'em proper.'

Claws clicked on the steps. Hey You reappeared. Somehow Matilda was sure he had been following the men down to the road.

She looked at Auntie Love, calmly sipping her tea. Had her words really been a bluff? Would the dog have defended them if Auntie had given the command?

She was glad she hadn't had to find out. 'Good dog.' She reached down and rubbed Hey You's ears. The dog accepted it.

She grinned, the strength coming back to her, and buttered a hunk of damper, and put it on the floor for the dog. Hey You gulped it, sniffed for crumbs, then lay down next to Auntie, his nose across her feet. Suddenly his ears pricked up again. He gave a growl, then raced out the door again.

The swaggies were coming back! Matilda glanced at Auntie Love, then picked up the axe. This time it would be in her hands, not theirs. She saw Auntie reach for the wood splitter as she ran outside.

Something was climbing through the cliffs … two thin wheels, spinning almost too fast to see, Hey You running beside them, barking. A young man in a broad-brimmed hat, crouching over the handlebars.

A bicycle, she thought, though much smaller and faster than any she had seen before.

The young man saw her. He lifted up a hand, scarred red and almost claw like.

It was Tommy.

She ran down to meet him, her face breaking into a vast smile as he skidded the bicycle to a stop. Taller than when she'd seen him last, his wrists and ankles poking out of his trousers and shirt, the scar on his face flushed red from the sun, his left hand — she tried not to stare — almost a skeleton's hand.

'What do you think of her?' His feet raised two small clouds of dust. He stood astride the machine proudly.

'Er … it's very nice.' Trust Tommy! The last time she'd seen him he'd been in a hospital bed, and the first thing he said was about a machine.

'Nice! It's a Remington sports,' he said reproachfully. 'It's a free wheeler, got pneumatic tyres and a curved front fork and the new stirrup brakes. Think I need to work on those though … I got an idea to —'

'Tommy!' She wanted to hug him or at least stop him talking about bicycles. 'What are you doing here? How is your arm?'

He held it up, answering the second question first. 'Ugly, ain't it?'

'No.'

'Liar. But it works all right, most of the time. It's getting stronger too. Don't think my face'll get any better but.' He took his hat off, turning the scarred side of his face to the sun. 'Pretty horrible, I know.'

The scar reached from the corner of his mouth almost to his eye. It was plum red, red like jam, she thought, and forced herself not to shudder. But the worst was the way it pulled his mouth out of shape, making it look like he was sneering.

'It's not so bad,' she lied.

He grinned at her, putting his hat back on. 'It's all right. I don't mind.'

He did. She could see that he did. 'I'm glad to see you.' More than glad, she thought. Impossible to say how glad. 'But how did you get here?'

'Train, of course.'

She punched his arm — his good arm, just in case. 'Not that sort of how, you coot.'

'You asked me to visit.'

'Yes but …' She watched as he gazed around at the cliffs, the garden and the sheep. She smiled, proud of it all, waiting for his delight.

He looked back at her, his face suddenly serious. 'I came to save you,' he said.

Chapter 29

'Save me from what?' How could he have known about the swaggies? she thought.

He flushed, a different red from the scar. 'From this place, of course. I read your letters.'

All the lingering thoughts of the swaggies vanished. 'What's wrong with this place?' she said hotly.

He shrugged. 'It ain't as bad as I thought,' he admitted.

'It's beautiful!'

'Well, yes.' He shifted uncomfortably. 'It's pretty. The house looks nice enough. And I like your garden. But you shouldn't be here like this.'

'Why not?'

He looked even more uncomfortable. 'You ain't got no one to tell you, except me. But it just ain't proper. My mum says so too,' he added, as though that clinched it.

'What isn't proper? Look, come out of the sun. You'll melt.'

'I'm all right.' But he followed her up the steps and sat on one of the verandah chairs. She saw him trace its shape with his hands, and felt a burst of angry pride at her father's handiwork. Tommy of all people should appreciate what her father had built, what she had already achieved here.

'Come on,' she demanded. 'What isn't proper?'

This time he met her gaze. 'A white girl living with blacks. That's what ain't proper. Look at you,' he added.

She had forgotten he had never seen her in trousers before. She stared at him, so dear, so impossibly stupid. 'That's who you're saving me from? Auntie Love? Mr Sampson?' She would have laughed if she hadn't been angry.

'You can't go round calling natives "auntie",' he said earnestly. 'It ain't done.'

'Who doesn't do it?'

'Everyone! People will get the wrong idea! Look, Mum told me I should come here. It ain't just me —'

'Stop using your mum as an excuse.'

'I ain't. But you can't stay here.'

She glared at him. 'You expect me to go back to the city? Leave my farm?'

'Not if you don't want. Look,' he said eagerly. 'I got a job already. Called in to the Chinese bloke you wrote about. Well, I had to, hadn't I, to see how to get here? He's all right for a Chinaman. Offered me a quid for every machine I repair, more maybe, if it takes a lot of time. I got a room at the boarding house too. They got a spare room for you, as well. The landlady says you can do the scullery work in return for your board.'

If one more person suggested she work as a maid she was going to — she tried to think of the worst crime in Aunt Ann's view of the world — to spit.

'You don't have to sell this place either. The bloke next door, Mr Drinkwater, he'll run it for you.'

Suddenly she felt cold, despite the heat. 'How do you know he'll run the farm for me?'

He shifted uncomfortably in his seat. 'He wrote to me.'

She felt hot now, not cold. Spitting wasn't enough. She wanted to throw Mr Drinkwater down in the dunny pit. She wanted to shake Tommy ... She looked at him again, staring at her so anxiously.

Sweet Tommy, who had brought her sandwiches and looked after her, who had come all this way to save her, even if she didn't need saving.

Her anger grew again, but not at Tommy. This wasn't Tommy's fault.

'The bloody old ... old biscuit!' she swore.

He blinked, then began to laugh. 'I never heard you swear before.'

She blushed. 'The men out here all say "bloody".'

'Not when you can hear it, I bet.'

'Well, not when they think I can hear it.' It felt so good to talk to him, she realised, even if it was a wasted journey.

He regarded her steadily. 'I still got money saved from when I worked at the factory. I was saving for a workshop of my own. You can use it to pay your land tax.'

'My what?'

'You don't know about land tax?' Tommy nodded. 'Thought you mightn't. You got to pay it every year to the government.'

She sat still, staring. 'Did Mr Drinkwater tell you about that?' Her father would have known about land tax, she thought. But Mr Sampson had never run a farm, nor had Auntie Love.

'That's one o' the reasons he wrote to me. He said he'd pay the tax for you, in place of rent.'

And get my farm for nothing, she thought. But Tommy was still speaking. 'Don't you worry about the tax though. I got enough money to pay it for you. It's all going to be fine, you'll see.'

He stopped as Auntie Love stepped out of the house.

She must have been listening, thought Matilda. Because for the first time the old woman wore Mum's big white apron — startlingly white over her dark skin. She wore Mum's best dress too — long enough to disguise her bare feet, for Matilda was sure that even now Auntie Love wouldn't put on shoes. Her right hand balanced the painted tin tray with two fresh china cups and saucers, the teapot, the sugar bowl and a plate of damper, thinly sliced and spread with honey.

'Tea, Miss Matilda?' she said.

Matilda had never heard her speak like that. It was almost Mrs Ellsmore's voice, with her sharp-edged accent. She wondered how much effort the old woman was making not to drag her left foot or mumble. And she didn't even seem to glance at Tommy's scars.

She's doing this for me, she thought. It's not ... respectable ... to have a black woman as a friend. But it's all right to have one as a servant.

Tears stung her eyes. She stood, and took the tray and put it down on the table. She wasn't going to pretend. Not with Tommy. Not with anyone. She still wasn't sure why Auntie Love had decided this was her home, but she knew that she was glad.

'Auntie Love, I'd like you to meet Tommy,' she said gently. 'Sit down, Auntie, and I'll get another cup. Try the honey,' she added to Tommy. 'It's wonderful. It's bush honey. Auntie Love showed me how to find it. She's showing me all sorts of things.'

Tommy stared at her, then back at Auntie Love, sitting

impassively on the chair beside him, spreading her skirts. Auntie Love handed him his cup of tea, using her good hand. He took it in his own good hand, dazed.

Auntie Love passed him the sugar bowl.

Tommy still hadn't spoken when Matilda came back with another cup. She poured the tea for Auntie Love, and placed it on the table where she could take it with her right hand.

Hey You stood up again, looking down toward the cliffs. But this time he didn't bark.

A few seconds later Mr Sampson appeared, walking with his easy stride, with what looked like a quarter of a dead roo over his shoulder. He had given up his boots since he had left Drinkwater — Matilda supposed he was keeping them for going to town. He was bare-chested today too to keep the roo blood off his shirt, but he wore his tattered hat.

He glanced at the bicycle leaning against the horse rail, then at the three seated on the verandah. He lifted his hat politely to Matilda and Auntie Love, then crossed behind the vegetable garden to the meat safe above the spring.

'That's Mr Sampson,' said Matilda.

Tommy nodded. He looked thoughtful, as though he had expected a naked man with a spear. Despite the bare chest and feet Mr Sampson looked like the stockman he was.

Matilda passed him more damper. He bit into it as Mr Sampson appeared again, freshly washed. He lifted once more his hat to Matilda, then stood by the steps, silent, examining Tommy from hat to boots, not lingering on his scars, but looking at him like he might inspect a horse or ram, to tell its temper.

'Mr Sampson, this is my friend Tommy, from the city.'

Another nod. Tommy nodded back.

'Would you like some tea? I can get another cup.'

Mr Sampson shook his head. He still stood without speaking.

The silence grew uncomfortable, then to Matilda's relief he said, 'Goin' to make a pen for the sheep. Shearin' next week. Wondered if you'd like to see where we can put it. Up near the spring, I was thinking. Easier to herd the sheep to water.'

'A sheep pen?' Tommy stared at him, sudden interest sparking in his eyes, then back to Matilda. 'I started thinking about a design for a stock gate when you said you had sheep. Look.' He kneeled down and undid his bag, then pulled out a thick drawing pad. He flipped over the pages, sketches of various machines and structures flipping past till he found the diagram he wanted.

'Here it is. See, the gate only swings one way. The sheep can get in but can't get out, unless you pull the toggle. A bloke in England invented it for cows, but it'd work for sheep too.'

Mr Sampson climbed up the steps, then crouched down, staring at the drawing. 'Yep, reckon it'd work.'

Tommy sat back on his heels. 'I bet it will. You going to make runs too?'

What were runs? wondered Matilda.

'Yep. Got some corrugated iron left from my roof. Corrugated sheep runs is good. Sheep can't see what they're gettin' into.'

'I saw Mr Doo had some old corrugated iron. Maybe he'd let me have it cheap.'

Mr Sampson looked at him cautiously. 'Enough for a shearing shed roof too, maybe? How much would he want for it?'

'How big do you need the shed?' Tommy made a quick sketch on the pad. Mr Sampson gazed at it thoughtfully.

Five minutes before they'd been like dogs sizing each other up. Now they were ignoring her.

Matilda felt her temper flare again. This was *her* farm!

Mr Sampson might know more about sheep and Tommy about machinery and Auntie Love about, well, probably about almost everything. But this place was still hers.

'It'd be my shearing shed, remember. It's my land.'

Boy and man looked up at her, as though surprised she was still there. Tommy frowned. 'You want to make the shed different?'

'No. I just ...'

She didn't know what she wanted. Didn't know how she felt, either. She didn't need anyone riding their bicycle up to rescue her. She didn't even need Mr Sampson or Auntie Love. She'd have managed on her own ...

Wouldn't she? Suddenly she realised she was glad she had never had to find out. You fool, Matilda, she thought. They were here. A family, in a funny way. And Tommy made it complete.

'Tommy,' she said.

He looked up again from his plans. 'What?'

'I'm glad you're here.'

He flushed again, embarrassed. 'It's going to be a swell shearing shed.'

'I know it is,' she said.

⁓✺

Mr Sampson left, at last. Auntie Love went to poke up the fire in the stone fireplace behind the house — now that the weather was so hot they mostly cooked outside. Matilda supposed she was going to put the haunch of roo on to roast. She and Tommy sat on the verandah together.

'Do you really think this place is so bad?' she asked at last.

'No.'

'Go on. Say it.'

He grinned. She could hardly see the scar on his face from this side. 'All right. Maybe I was wrong.'

'Say: "This is the best farm in the world".'

'This is the best farm in the world. No, really,' he added quietly, 'it's slap up. The way you got the house an' all, the veggies growin'. I'm sorry I said what I did.'

'About the natives?'

'Them too.' He was silent a moment. 'They ain't what I expected. They're ... like white people.'

'No, they're not.'

'All right. They're not. But it ain't like what Mum thought, neither.' He gazed out at the shadowed cliffs again. A kookaburra yelled, up where a slender shaft of light still lit a cliff top. 'She didn't send me out here just to look after you, you know.'

Matilda waited for him to say the rest.

'She ... she cries when she sees my hand, my face. People stare.'

'They'll stare here too,' she said honestly. 'Till they get to know you.'

'I know. But there ain't as many people out here. I won't be meeting new ones all the time. They'll get used to me. Besides ...' He shrugged. 'Old Thrattle gave my job away while I was in hospital. Couldn't get no other job, neither, not looking like this. I reckoned there'd be more call for a bloke who was good with his hands out here.' He looked down. 'Good with one hand, anyhow.'

'Tommy ...' She tried to find the words, then suddenly they were there. It was so simple, she thought.

'I'm glad you're here. Gladder than I've ever been. I ... was lonely. I didn't know how much, till I saw you. And I didn't know about the land tax, and probably a hundred other things. I do need you. And Auntie Love and Mr Sampson too.'

He held out his hand, his good one. 'Friends again then?'

She took it. 'Friends.'

He stood up. 'I better go or it'll be dark afore I get back to town.'

'You could stay for dinner. It's roast roo,' she added mischievously.

He looked at her cautiously. 'What's it like?'

'Tough,' she said. 'Sort of strong tasting. I'm getting used to it. We can't afford to eat any of the sheep.'

He shook his head. 'There's Irish stew back at the boarding house. People will talk if I stay here.'

People are talking about me already, she thought. About Jim O'Halloran's daughter who'd seen her pa die in the billabong, and refused to leave his land.

Tommy was right, though. Mostly they were only saying good things now, but she didn't want to get a 'reputation'. She could almost hear Aunt Ann say the word with a sniff.

'When will you be back?'

'Day after tomorrow? Got a bit of work to do for Mr Doo first, then I'll bring the iron out for the shearing shed if he'll sell it to me cheap. Think he'll lend me his cart?'

'I'm pretty sure of it.'

She watched him ride away along the track, even faster now downhill. How long would it take him to get to town? Less than an hour, she thought, but she'd rather have a nice solid horse than balance on two wheels.

She could smell roasting meat. Hey You had left to stand guard on the fire in case the sheep suddenly developed a taste for roast kangaroo. She'd need to put some cabbage and carrots on to boil. Auntie Love never bothered with vegetables.

The sheep were slowly making their way up to the spring. Later, after they'd drunk, the other animals would come, more secretly: the wallabies from up among the rocks; the wombat who snuffled under the house each night, ignoring Hey You's growls; and the possum who clambered across the roof. All of them part of her life. Her farm. Her home.

And Tommy would be back, the day after tomorrow.

Chapter 30

DECEMBER 1894

Dear Mrs Ellsmore,

I hope you are well.

Last Sunday I wore the dress you sent. A preacher comes every two months to the church in town. My friend Tommy took me on the back of his bicycle. I had to be careful not to tear my dress. It got dusty but Tommy has made me an iron so I can wash and iron and wear it as often as I want.

The iron is Tommy's invention, it is hollow with a wood handle welded on top. You put hot coals in it, so you do not have to heat it up on the stove like other irons, because I do not have my stove yet. If your housekeeper would like one, Tommy could make you one. You can write to him care of Mrs Lacey's Boarding House, Gibber's Creek. He is a very good workman.

He has made me a stove for Christmas too! He is going to bring it out in Mr Doo's cart tomorrow. I have not seen it yet. He says it is a new invention as well, as it is made of two layers of metal with air in between them so the room does not get so hot.

I do not see how air can stop a room getting hot, but Tommy says it does and his inventions work nearly all of the time.

I wish my father could have met Tommy. My father made things from wood and Tommy makes them from metal, but I think they would have liked each other.

It hasn't rained yet, not since I have been here. Everyone at church said the drought is getting worse. Tommy and Mr Sampson and I have put pipes from the spring here down to a trough for the sheep. They do not stand in the water now, so the spring stays clean. We have put more pipes down to the cornfield too. It is a big cornfield, so we can feed the sheep corn too. I move the pipe twice a day so in a week the whole field gets wet.

Mr Gotobed, who was a friend of my father, says he has never seen corn grow so fast. He brought me a cartload of sheep droppings from Mr Drinkwater's shearing shed to feed the corn, but perhaps Mr Drinkwater does not know where his sheep droppings were going, so please do not tell him.

I have my own shearing shed now. It has a wood floor so the clean side of the wool does not get dirty, and a corrugated roof, but no walls as we did not have enough iron. There is also a corrugated iron dip for the sheep to get them clean under and ~~kill maggots~~ treat them for parasites.

We sheared over a hundred sheep. I bought more sheep cheap because we have grass and water and other places do not. Tommy lent me the money but I have paid him back now that we have sold the wool and some ram lambs.

Mr Gotobed and his friends came to shear, they would not let me pay them because of my father, but I think my father would have wanted them to be paid properly, so I gave the Workers'

Institute in town money to buy books instead. I now think maybe that was not the right thing to do though, because I will borrow the books and I fear that Mr Gotobed and his friends will not. They would rather have spirituous liquor, but that would not be good for them so perhaps I was right to get the books. It is very difficult.

Thank you again for the parcel. I am very grateful indeed. I hope you and Florence have a very merry Christmas.

Yours respectfully,
Matilda O'Halloran

PS I know I wrote a lot about my friend Tommy but he lives in town, he only visits here so there is nothing improper.

PPS I hope I am not being rude, but if Mr Drinkwater's sons visit you again could you tell them it is not Christian to shoot natives?

There are not many natives here as nearly all have been taken away to the reserve except those who work on the stations, but sometimes they might look like wild natives so the boys may make a mistake, and even if it is a mistake it is still not Christian. I know my Aunt Ann would have said so. I hope you agree, Mrs Ellsmore, and that I am not being forward in asking you this.

Sometimes it is hard to know what is good manners. There is no one I can ask here, Tommy is a boy so he does not understand about manners like women do.

Yours respectfully again,
Matilda O'Halloran

A scream woke Matilda early on Christmas morning. For a moment she blinked in the darkness.

The hut was silent. Matilda lay back. She must have dreamed the scream. Through the window the moonlight made tree shadows on the ground. She wondered if the cross had turned over yet. It must be hours till morning. She shut her eyes ...

'Graaaarrhk!' It was as much a snarl as a scream.

Matilda flung herself out of bed. 'Auntie Love?' Why hadn't the old woman woken? Why hadn't Hey You barked?

She stumbled out to the living area, suddenly aware of one problem with the new stove. Tommy had been right: it didn't heat up the room as much, and it stayed alight all night more easily. But the fire was hidden in its metal box, which meant there was no red glow to see by.

She fumbled for a slush lamp and a match.

The shriek came again. Something swung toward her. Her eyes were growing used to the moonlight now. She ducked as it swished above her head.

'Ghhhghhhh!' Something small and furry thudded onto the floor, then scampered out the door. The possum! It must have been trying to tear the cloth to get into the pudding.

She reached up and felt the pudding carefully, but could find no sign of a tear. She smelled it too in case the possum had left a damp spot. But it just smelled of raisins and treacle — good Christmas smells.

Hey You padded out of Auntie Love's bedroom. He gave a small woof, then sat and gazed at her.

'Fat lot of good you are,' said Matilda. 'Can't even scare off a possum.'

'Woof,' said Hey You. He yawned, then trotted back into the bedroom.

Matilda untied the rope from around the pudding. Best to take it to bed with her, in case the possum tried again. The raisins and treacle had been expensive. It had taken her hours to pick out the seeds from the raisins, more hours to collect the firewood to keep the pot on a rolling boil, so the pudding wouldn't get heavy. Auntie Love knew how to make a good damper, but she didn't know about puddings. Besides, Tommy was coming to dinner, and the pudding was the only real Christmas food they had.

She cuddled it to her, then smiled at herself, hugging a Christmas pudding. She slept.

It was late when she woke again, long past dawn, six o'clock maybe or even seven. But she wasn't even going to milk the cow today — its calf could have all the milk — or water the vegetables. Today was going to be a holiday.

She stepped out in the cool morning air to wash by the spring. Auntie Love was already on the verandah when she came back.

'Merry Christmas!'

Auntie Love laughed. Matilda had learned to distinguish the laugh that said Auntie Love was happy from the one which meant she didn't know what to say, or one that indicated she thought something was funny. This laugh seemed to mean: 'Well, if it pleases you to think of a day as Christmas, I'll go along with it.'

Matilda went into her room and began to dress. No trousers today. She put on the first dress Mrs Ellsmore had given her, which she thought of as her second-best dress, but left off petticoats and stockings — it was far too hot. Too hot for shoes too. She only wore boots now when she was working, and her feet were growing tougher. She hesitated, then put her city shoes on. It would spoil the look of her dress to have bare feet.

She wished there was something other than shoulder of roo to roast. But the sheep were too precious, and too familiar too. At least she didn't know the roos that Mr Sampson shot.

She stirred up the fire, made a pot of tea and toasted damper for herself and Auntie Love, then spread a tablecloth over the verandah table. It was made from one of her petticoats. She hoped no one would see where she had joined the fabric at one end. But it looked good with the china plates and cups and some twigs of gum leaves in an old ginger-beer bottle. She had just finished when she heard singing.

It was Mr Gotobed in the cart, with Bluey and Curry and Rice next to him. Mr Gotobed raised his jug to her. 'Merry Christmas!'

She stared. 'Merry Christmas.'

Did they expect to have Christmas dinner here too? She calculated quickly. She could put on more potatoes and pull up more carrots, but the meat wouldn't stretch to six.

She watched as Mr Gotobed pulled a hessian sack from the wagon. The three of them staggered up the steps toward her.

'*We three kings of thingummie are,*' bellowed Bluey. '*Dum de dum we travel afar …*'

He gave her a clumsy hug and a kiss on the cheek. His breath stank. Mr Gotobed thrust the sack at her. 'Merry Christmas!' he yelled again.

They must have been drinking spirituous liquor all the way here — maybe all night too. She watched as they plumped themselves down in her verandah chairs. Aunt Ann would have shown them the door.

But they had shorn her sheep. They were her father's friends. Her friends too, she realised. Besides, they looked too drunk to find their way back to town, unless the horse knew where it was expected to go.

The horse … it couldn't stay there in the sun. She dumped their sack on the table, then unharnessed the animal — it knew where the water trough was and wouldn't wander far — and went back and looked in the sack.

It was a bird, the biggest she had ever seen, already plucked. 'A turkey!'

Curry and Rice looked uncomfortable. 'Not exactly a turkey,' he said.

'Near enough but,' said Bluey. 'Man's got a right to a bird at Christmas.'

Matilda gazed at the bird again. 'What is it then?'

'A swan,' admitted Mr Gotobed, helping himself to damper as Auntie Love came out with another pot of tea. 'Shot it down the river last night.'

Matilda blinked. She had never heard of anyone eating swan, but she had after all eaten weirder things in the previous couple of months. It still hurt, though, to think of all the beauty of a swan turned into a big hunk of meat.

'There's good eating on a swan,' Curry and Rice assured her. 'Just put plenty of stuffing in it and it'll be fine.'

Plenty of stuffing … She supposed you could use the same stuffing in a swan as in a chicken, damper instead of breadcrumbs, and the onions she kept hanging up inside. There was even sage growing in the garden now, to season it, and last week's butter in the cold safe.

She inspected the swan carefully, in case the flies had got it, then washed it inside and out just in case. But no crawlies floated in the water. Impossible to think of it big and majestic on the water.

215

She made the stuffing, put the swan in the oven in the big oven dish Tommy had bought for her, then pulled up more carrots and new potatoes and a few turnips too. Her dress was grubby at the hem now, and there were red spots on it from the swan. She washed them off quickly, hoping they wouldn't stain, then rinsed the hem of her dress. Luckily it'd be dry in a few minutes in the heat.

She looked out the door. The men were asleep, their mouths open, their snoring louder than the yelling of the cicadas. She hoped they'd wake up sober. There was no sign of Auntie Love.

She turned to peel the potatoes as Auntie Love came out of her room, wearing the big white apron over her dress, carrying a bark container. She gestured to the sleeping men outside and wrinkled her nose.

Matilda laughed, then looked down at the bark container. It was shaped like a pot, with a bark lid tied down with home-made string. She untied it and looked inside.

It was a necklace of red and black seeds, strung onto hair, she suspected. The seeds were shiny, like tiny jewels against the bark.

'Oh, Auntie.' So Auntie Love did know what Christmas was. She bent and kissed Auntie Love's cheek, then slipped the necklace on. Auntie nodded, then went over and began to peel the carrots.

'Auntie, this is for you.'

Auntie Love unwrapped the brown paper — the only paper in the house — then smiled. It was a hanky, made from a bit of another petticoat, carefully hemmed in secret and embroidered with daisies at the corners. She tucked it into the belt of her apron, then kept on peeling.

⟶⫘◦

Six hours later Hey You was chewing the leftovers. Auntie Love, Mrs Sampson and Matilda sat on chairs on the verandah, while Tommy and the men leaned against the wall, their legs out, finishing the last of the pudding.

Matilda hadn't expected Mr and Mrs Sampson. She had only met Elsie a few times. She was as tall as her husband and much fatter, a strong woman but shy with people she didn't know. She'd hardly spoken throughout the meal, just smiled and laughed when everyone else did.

But somehow it seemed right that Mr and Mrs Sampson should be there. She'd made handkerchiefs for them anyway, and for Tommy, and had hastily wrapped up three of her own for the union men.

The pudding had been voted delicious, in spite of the lumps; the swan hadn't been as tough as it might have been; and the taste of soap in the gravy was hardly noticeable at all. A giant Christmas cake, a present from Tommy's landlady, sat under a fly net, next to the basket from the Doos, with its squat jar of preserved ginger, its red-blushed peaches and a box of dates.

'Well, I'm full as a goog after that. Who's for a song?' Bluey pulled out a mouth organ. Curry and Rice took out a pair of gum leaves from his pocket. As Matilda stared he held them to his lips, and hummed a tune she almost recognised.

'*Silent night,*' roared Mr Gotobed. '*Da de dum night …*'

The last time she had sung this it had been at Aunt Ann's, three Christmases ago, those easy days she thought would last forever.

'*All is calm, all is bright …*' Tommy's singing voice was deeper than she'd expected.

'*Round yon virgin mother and child …*'

'*Dum dee dum dum, dee dee dum, dee deee.*'

'*Sleep in heavenly peace,*' Matilda stared as Auntie Love joined in, her voice pure and clear. '*Sleep in heavenly peace.*'

How had the old woman learned the song? Where? Had she worked for Mr Drinkwater or some other squatter, years ago? Had Mr Drinkwater fired her, like he had sacked Mr Sampson? Was that why he was so angry she was here?

But it still didn't explain why the old lady had stood in front of him, almost naked. She was sure that anyone working in the Drinkwater house would have to wear proper clothes.

Mr Gotobed swung into 'Jingle Bells'. Curry and Rice followed him on his gum leaves, sounding like a mob of almost tuneful bees.

The sun was below the tree tops when they left. Tommy loaded his bike onto the wagon; Matilda hoped the men's horse knew its way back in the dark. Auntie Love vanished into the bedroom. Hey You grabbed the swan carcass in his jaws and took it down to the deeper shade under the steps. The Sampsons left, with his laconic: 'I'll check for fly strike in the mornin', Boss.'

It was the first time he had called her 'Boss'. She wanted to protest. But it was true that when he called her 'Matilda' it made it sound like he was talking to a little girl. She *was* thirteen …

She stopped gathering up the dishes, and looked down at her hands. Work-stained, tough hands.

She had missed her birthday, hadn't even known what date it was till Tommy had asked too carelessly what she was doing for Christmas dinner. No one else in the world, she thought, knows when my birthday is now.

She washed the dishes in a bucket by the water trough, then threw the dishwater onto the corn. She was just putting the plates carefully in the dresser when Hey You barked again.

She looked up. Was Mr Gotobed so fuddled with spirituous liquor that he'd come back by mistake? But Tommy would have taken the reins …

Two horses cantered between the cliffs. She recognised the horses first — those giant shiny brown animals — before she knew the riders. The Drinkwater boys, James and Bertram.

It had been too good a day to be angry with anyone, even the Drinkwaters. 'Merry Christmas!' she called.

The boys pulled the horses to a stop by the house. They didn't dismount. James reached down to his saddlebags and took out a parcel. He threw it down into the dust. 'For you,' he said abruptly.

She looked at the brown paper in the dust. 'I don't understand.'

'Our aunt has decided that you're a worthy recipient of her charity.' The words bit like cold water. 'We're delivering it.'

She made no move to grovel by the horses' hooves to get the package. 'Please thank your aunt,' she said quietly. 'Or I will write and thank her.'

'You're good with a pencil, aren't you?' James was white-faced with fury now. 'Aunt passed on your message about hunting natives. We don't appreciate grubby little bush girls giving their betters lessons in behaviour. Do we, Bertram?'

The younger boy shook his head. He was grinning, as though this was simply fun. His brother's horse rolled its eyes, as if it could sense its rider's anger.

'Just so you know. If you mention us again, to anyone, you are going to regret it. You understand?'

She wanted to yell at them that she'd say what she liked. But despite Hey You growling at her heels she knew she was helpless. They had whips. They had firearms, longer and shinier than the blunt weapon Mr Sampson used against the roos. She had no doubt that the older boy at least would use them both, if not against her, then certainly against the dog or Auntie Love.

Who was to stop them? Their father ruled this world. These boys believed that they did too.

This is what made my father angry, she thought.

She prayed that Auntie Love was sound asleep and couldn't hear what was happening.

'I understand.' She spoke as calmly as she could. She stood immobile, hoping that if she showed no other reaction they would go.

The older boy, James, spat. She could see the spittle frothy in the dust by his horse's hooves. His brother copied him. James yanked the reins; his horse turned. In seconds they had cantered back between the cliffs, toward the setting sun.

She was shaking, from fear as well as anger. She sat on the steps, and pulled Hey You into a hot and doggy-smelling embrace till her heart stopped pounding. At last she let him go, picked up the parcel and took it back to the verandah.

It had been untied and roughly wrapped again. The string was so badly knotted she finally had to get the knife to cut it. She pulled the paper away slowly.

The smell hit her first. Dog's droppings, rubbed into the fabric of the dark blue dress. A new dress, she thought. Not Florence's cast-off. A new dress for her. Silk stockings, slashed with a knife. A bar of soap, cut into pieces, its scent of violets almost as strong as the stench of muck.

It didn't matter, she told herself. Nothing the boys had done had touched her really. She would wash the dress and iron it — the stain was fresh at least, so would come out. She could mend the stockings — no one would see the mends under her skirt.

Even the soap could be used in pieces. It would last longer that way.

She wasn't going to let James Drinkwater destroy her Christmas present.

She fetched a bucket and carried everything to the trough in the last of the light. Best get it done now, so the stench would be gone, the smell of hatred banished from this Christmas Day.

It was dark when she'd hung it all on the line. She trudged slowly up the steps again, then caught sight of her skirt. Damp, stained with gravy and paw prints. There would be stains under her arms too, she thought, and probably smudges on her face. She felt her hair, escaped from its plaits.

So that was how the boys saw her, a bush girl in a dirty dress, with a grubby face and callused hands. A busybody, who interfered with their right to call everything on this land theirs.

Let them, she told herself fiercely. She was the one who had a farm of her own. And a house, and a half share in 116 sheep, a cow and calf, eight hens. She looked down, and smiled at herself. And a small share in a dog too.

They were still schoolboys, despite their wealth. No, not their wealth. Their father's. She was older than them in more than years.

She got herself a cup of water and a peach then sat on a chair back on the verandah. The peach smelled like a honey tree, driving out the last scent of muck. The moon wouldn't rise for an hour at least, but the stars were bright.

She looked for the three brightest — two on one side of the black sky lake, a reddish one on the horizon. She raised her cup to them. Mum, Dad and Aunt Ann.

'Merry Christmas,' she whispered. She hoped they would be proud.

Chapter 31

Dear Mrs Ellsmore,

I hope you are well.

I am glad you had such a good Christmas too. I wore the dress you gave me into town last week. Mr Gotobed drove me to the library.

I took out six books. You are only supposed to take out two but the librarian used to work with my father so he lets me take out more, because I don't get in to town often. Most of the books are not very interesting, but there is one on diseases of sheep that will be most useful. I will study it hard before I take it back. Two of the books are novels. My aunt did not approve of novels but my mother read them. What do you feel about novels?

I have been worried too about what Mr Sampson should call me. He calls me Boss now. Do you think that is all right? Also, should I call Mr Gotobed's friends Mr Curry and Rice and Mr Bluey? They do not seem to have any last names, and when I asked, Mr Gotobed said, 'Just call him Bluey, girl.' But should it be Mr Bluey?

Also there is a Women's Temperance and Suffrage League dance in town. There will be no spirituous liquor in the hall, though some of the men will imbibe outside. Tommy will not go, he says he does not want to go to a dance, but Mr Gotobed and his friends have said they'll take me. Would it be improper?

Now that I write this I see that it probably would be. You would not let Florence go to an evening dance with three men. It is very good to be able to write and ask your advice like this.

Yours gratefully,
Matilda O'Halloran

'Fire coming,' said Auntie Love.

Matilda put down the pencil. She was trying to do the accounts today, working out how much they had spent on the farm compared with how much the wool had brought.

Patricia Doo had shown her how to balance 'income' and 'expenses', and Mr Gotobed had taken her to the bank to open an account, and one for Mr Sampson too (in her name, as it seemed that natives had to give their wages to the Native Protectorate's Trust Fund). But the bank manager assured Matilda that if she and Mr Sampson signed the withdrawal slip and he brought in the bankbook, Mr Sampson could take money out.

She glanced outside. The day was still, the trees hanging silent above the breathless ground. The shadows, too, were still. The sky was an untouched blue, without even a smudge of smoke from their own fire. It would be cold meat and cold damper today, with apricots that Tommy had brought yesterday from Mr Doo. 'I can't see any smoke.'

223

Auntie Love heaved herself to her feet and reached for her stick. The weakness of her left side had almost vanished, but the old woman was growing thinner and more fragile, like a gum leaf that would crumble if you pressed too hard. She made her way outside. Matilda followed her down the steps.

She expected Auntie Love to point up at the sky, to show her a shimmer of smoke she hadn't noticed. But instead she lifted her stick up to the wattles. 'See. Seeds.'

Matilda peered at the brown clusters, like knobbly hands clinging to the branches. 'What about them?'

'Tree knows when fire comes. Makes many seeds for new trees after fire.'

It was the longest explanation Auntie Love had ever given. She waved her hand at one of the shrubby bushes at the edge of the rock tumble. Its flowers had blazed like purple fire last spring, Matilda remembered. Like fire.

'You mean … sometime next year there'll be a bushfire?' She had read about bushfires. She hadn't understood why everyone just didn't put them out.

Auntie Love stared at her, her expression as always impossible to read. 'Trees say this year,' she said at last. 'Wallabies say now.'

'The wallabies? But there aren't any wallabies around.'

She stopped, suddenly understanding. 'You mean the wallabies weren't at the pool last night,' she said slowly.

Auntie Love nodded.

'But if there was fire we'd see the smoke. Smell it. Wouldn't we?' There'd been lots of smoke when a house down the road had caught fire when she was small. Didn't fires always have lots of smoke?

'Smoke come,' said Auntie Love.

The smoke came the next morning, a haze of white first, then billows, till at last the whole sky was pale grey. Matilda went out with Mr Sampson and Elsie, herding the sheep up into the valley between the cliffs around the house.

'Safer here,' said Mr Sampson.

The valley was a sea of sheep. The animals stumbled and complained, as Elsie pulled a rough wire fence between the cliffs so the sheep couldn't get back out.

'You mean the bushfire won't burn in here?' asked Matilda hopefully. Perhaps the cliffs would protect them.

Mr Sampson shrugged. 'Fire's coming that way.' He pointed to the north-west. 'Means it comes up the slope, fast.'

Then it could come between the cliffs, thought Matilda. 'Can't we put it out?'

He stared at her then shook his head. 'Stop it coming here, maybe.'

'How?'

He seemed to be considering. 'You go up to the cave with Auntie. She'll look after you. Elsie and me'll stop here.'

'I don't need to be looked after!'

He said nothing, just nodded, then walked down the road, wriggling his way out past the fence.

For a horrible moment she thought she had offended him, that he was leaving. But he just looked back at her. 'Don't want to lose my swag if the house burns.'

She shivered as she watched him and Elsie hurry down the road to their house. Of course, their house was more exposed than hers. I should have told him to build it up here in the valley, she thought guiltily. But she had never even thought of fire. He must have known they would be vulnerable. But he would never have said.

She glanced around at the sheep, their heads down, hunting for the last shreds of grass, then at her house. She should take her own valuables up to the cave: not just valuables, but necessities too.

She had made two trips before she realised that Auntie Love was helping her, lugging one of the chairs her father had made down the steps. She put her hand on the old woman's arm. 'Leave it. It's too heavy.'

Auntie Love shrugged, then looked at the blankets in Matilda's arms, and shook her head.

'I shouldn't take the blankets?'

'Wool don't burn. You wet the blankets, wrap yourself up if fire comes.'

'Then the sheep won't burn either?'

Auntie's eyes were soft with compassion. 'They burn,' she said.

The day grew darker, though the smoke seemed no thicker in the sky. The shadows vanished, and the sun. The light seemed to come from everywhere, a strange unearthly glow.

She changed into her thickest trousers, shirt, boots and hat (her girl's clothes bundled up in her shawl, safe within the cave). Nothing more remained in the house except the things too big to move: the table, the beds, chests and stove. She imagined again her father, month after month, chopping trees and splitting logs, smoothing and shaping the wood, dreaming of his family living here, sharing his world.

Living here had helped her to bear his death. The fire could eat, in one afternoon, all he built, she thought.

It wasn't right. It shouldn't be like this, that so many years of work and love could vanish.

Love … She had never thought of it before. I've loved you, she thought to the valley around her. It wasn't love at first, just nowhere else to go. But I love you now. Don't let me down. Please. Don't let me down.

Stupid. As though the land had a mind or heart. She sat on the hot ground suddenly, disturbing the sheep, who baaed and moved away, and spread her hands on the soil. It felt hot and dry, but there was something else, almost a vibration in her hands.

A heartbeat? Or just a shudder from the footsteps of the sheep? Or was it her own heart she felt? It doesn't matter, she thought. We're all in this together now.

She looked up to find Mr Sampson staring at her. She stood and dusted her trousers, embarrassed. He handed her a green wattle branch, thick with leaves.

'What do I do with this?'

He shrugged, as though she would know when the time came. They made their way back down from the cliffs, through the mob of sheep shuffling and bleating uneasily, to join the others in front of the house.

She could smell the fire now.

She had expected it to smell like a cooking fire. It didn't. It wasn't just the lack of hot meat or flour. This was another smell, as though more than wood was burning. The earth? she thought.

A sound crashed behind her. She turned, thinking a rock had fallen from the cliffs. But it was the wind.

It had been still before. Now the air tumbled about the cliffs, a growling howl like a giant dingo had swallowed the wind and was roaring it out. The smoke whirled in strange soft patterns, almost too fast to follow.

Mr Sampson and Elsie drew close to her, branches in their hands. Auntie Love was calmly dipping the blankets into buckets of water on the verandah, Hey You standing close to her, his tail between his legs, hardly even glancing up at the cliffs where the sheep called nervously.

If only we had a thousand buckets, thought Matilda. A million. A million hands to carry them.

How could wattle branches fight a fire?

'How long before it comes?' She hadn't meant to whisper. The words were whirled into the wind. She tried again, and found her voice hoarse with smoke.

'Not yet,' said Mr Sampson. He nodded up to the spring. 'We wait there.'

She followed him, then stopped. Someone was coming through the smoke between the cliffs.

For a moment she hoped it was Mr Gotobed, with a hundred men from town. But Mr Gotobed and his mates were shearing down toward the Murray. It would be autumn before they were back here. The object came closer, and she saw it was the bicycle, with Tommy sweating as he rode.

She ran down to him. 'There's a fire coming.'

'I know,' he said shortly. 'Why do you think I'm here? They said it was headed this way. Going to miss town, they think, but the men are burning a firebreak in case.'

'What about the other farms along the river? And Drinkwater?'

'They say it'll miss Drinkwater, unless the wind changes.' He looked troubled. 'The only other place in its path is Heenans'.

It'll burn before the fire gets here. I told Mrs Heenan to take the children to town. She said she would.'

'But you don't think she will?'

'I don't know. You know what she's like.'

Past caring, thought Matilda. But surely she wasn't past *all* care for her children.

He began to wheel the bicycle up to the house.

She didn't question what had brought him here. 'Better take it up to the cave.'

'What cave?'

She realised she had never showed it to him or told him how she had met Auntie Love either. No time to explain now. 'Follow me.'

It was black within the cave, the world around too dark to shine any light within. They pushed the bicycle roughly through the lip in the rock, then headed down again. A leaf whirled and fluttered down from the cliffs. Matilda stared. It was charred, a shred of green, then black.

The wind was even louder now. Or is it the fire? thought Matilda. It was almost impossible to see the figures standing by the spring.

Mr Sampson's clothes looked wet with sweat, and then she realised: he had dampened them in the spring. She did the same, scooping up water in her hands. Beside her Tommy followed her actions.

She wished he hadn't come. He was already so scarred. He could have been safe, back in town. This was her fight, not his. She glanced at him. It probably wasn't safe for him to head back now. And every fight of hers, she acknowledged, he had made his own.

It seemed a long way from Mr Thrattle's factory.

She glanced up at the sky. A red haze shone against the black. And then the fire came.

She had thought the wind already too strong to bear. She had been wrong.

The fire's voice was lower, higher, a sound that had no name. She saw the fire bite the air above the cliffs, the trees become a ring of flame, dancing red and black. The redness moved, circling above them now.

She waited for the flames to drop on top of them. Should they run for the cave now, and save their lives, at least? Surely there was no way five people — one a frail old woman — could fight a ring of fire.

But they couldn't abandon the sheep yet — nor the house her father had made with so much love and hope.

The heat and glare hurt her eyes. She shaded them with her hands, staring upward.

The air was filled with tiny embers and ash that made it almost impossible to see. Only the red of flame was visible. At once she realised — the blaze had jumped across the valley. Both ridge-tops were alight now, but the fire wasn't heading down the cliffs.

She felt a shiver, almost as though her father had whispered to her. This place he had chosen was protected against fire as well as drought — as long as they could fight the fire-front coming up between the cliffs, and put out spot fires from the embers raining down.

They were a long way from safe. But now they had a chance, not just to survive, but to protect the valley from the flames.

She was aware of Mr Sampson moving in the thick ash-dark.

'Boss? Got to get down to the cliffs. That's where it's comin' from now.'

'I'm coming!' She stumbled after him, trying to keep up, the sheep milling and crying around them, circling in a blind panic looking for safety. For a second she lost her footing, but felt Tommy's hands — the good one and the scarred — help her up.

It's the first time I've touched his scar, she thought. Was that why he wouldn't go to a dance with her? So she didn't have to touch his scar?

Auntie Love forged through the frightened beasts, upright despite her frailty. It was almost as though she knew how to move between them.

The wind buffeted Matilda again, coming in a great wave of heat and burning leaves up the track. Once again she almost fell. By the time she was steady the air had cleared.

She blinked, not quite believing it. Beside her Tommy stared upward, his face intent, so fascinated it was almost as though he had forgotten the danger. 'The updraught,' he yelled. 'It's taking the smoke away. Isn't it incredible?'

She nudged him, and pointed, down toward the road. Mr Sampson was right. The fire was coming up through the cliffs now, running fast uphill. Trees burst into flame even before the wall of fire reached them. Even the ground seemed to burn.

Already Mr Sampson and Elsie were running toward the flames. As she watched they began to beat the ground with their branches, and beat out the burning bark on the trunks of trees as well. To her surprise the flames vanished where the green branches lashed them.

Impossibly the sheep had pushed further up into the gorge behind the house. Their bleats of terror were part of the shriek of the wind, the deeper roar of the fire. Hey You ran along the rough fence in front of them, yapping and nipping, keeping them bunched up and out of everyone's way.

Someone touched her shoulder, briefly. She glanced at Tommy, his scar flame-red in the glare of fire. He gestured to the house, as though to say he would help Auntie Love put out the spot fires there. She nodded. There was no time to talk; almost no air to breathe.

Matilda ran toward the Sampsons, and began to beat the ground too.

꧁

Time lost meaning. Her body seemed to vanish. There was only the fire, snickering through the grass, leaping into the trees, flaring from branch to branch. If you could kill the fire around the tree you could leave the top to burn itself out.

Dimly she was aware of Tommy yelling from the house, of Auntie Love lugging buckets through the smoke. It was thicker again now, the burning grass and trees here in the valley filling the world with grey.

Was the house alight? There was no red glare up there, just the trees like giant candles, flaring above the screaming sheep. But at least the fire had only spread a few yards into the gorge. So far, at least, they had kept it back.

How long could they hold it? She didn't know, couldn't think, not in this heat, this glare. All she could do was lash with her branch, over and over, one tussock out and then another, one tree after another ...

Her body longed for air, for water, for a time of cool and peace. But there was only heat and flame, the trees like wild torches in the air, smoke so thick it was almost like breathing ash, the wind strong enough to keep you upright if you leaned against it.

Then it was gone. The wind was gone. She waited for it to

eddy back. But slowly the valley began to fill with air again —
real air that you could see through. Air that you could breathe.

The wind had changed direction. She leaned on her branch,
gasping at the fresh air, feeling it seep into her body. The grass in
front was black, but it no longer burned. The tops of a few trees
still glowed, but that was all.

She glanced up at the cliffs. Trees shone there too, like strange
red skeletons against a black sky. Beside her Mr Sampson leaned
over, gasping for breath. Elsie stood next to him, her chest
heaving.

She turned herself around again, and ran panting back up to
the house. It was still standing. Tommy's face peered from the
door, his eyes strangely white in an ash-grey face.

'It's all right,' he gasped. 'The shingles caught alight. But we
got them. Auntie Love an' me. We got them out.'

She looked up. Perhaps a quarter of the roof was gone, the
edges blackened. Another hole sagged further along.

But the main frame of the house was safe. The sheep were safe.
And Tommy, Auntie Love, the Sampsons and she were alive.

She staggered toward one of the buckets. They were empty.
Of course they would be empty. She wondered if she had the
strength to get to the spring; she felt Tommy press a mug of
water into her hands. She drank, and felt the water soothe her
mouth and throat.

She leaned against the wall, gradually feeling her energy come
back. Vaguely, she was aware of Tommy, lugging a bucket from
the spring; of Mr Sampson and Elsie, drinking beside her; and of
Auntie Love incongruously sitting in her accustomed chair on
the verandah, as though none of it had happened.

But it had. She looked around at her house, her poor dear
house, with its sagging, blackened roof; at the sheep now out of

their rough pen and milling, terrified and baaing; at the scar of black across her valley; and at the fire trees still flaming up on the ridges.

But the sky showed a thread of blue now. She sniffed the wind. It smelled moister, softer: a wind from the southern snows.

She looked down at Auntie, saw her nod, agreeing with the question she hadn't asked.

'It'll blow the fire the other way,' said Tommy hoarsely. 'We're safe now, ain't we?'

Mr Sampson nodded. He looked at Matilda, his expression as always impenetrable.

'What's wrong? There's something wrong, isn't there?'

'Fire's heading to Drinkwater now.'

She stared at him. He had spent his life at Drinkwater, tending their sheep, knowing its land. 'They have enough men to stop it, don't they?'

He shook his head. 'Fire-front will be too big to stop in open country. They'll burn a firebreak around the house to keep it and the buildings safe. That's what we did last time.'

'What about the sheep?'

His face twisted. 'They won't have expected the wind change. They'll bring in what they can. No time to get the rest, not the ones up this far. They'll —' He stopped, as though unable or unwilling to say the rest.

The sheep. The stupid, impossible, trusting sheep. The sheep who followed you, who'd die wool-blind if they weren't shorn, who'd die if they weren't dagged and dipped.

She looked out at her own sheep still huddled together, aware that there had been danger, but not understanding what. Hey You still crouched nearby, keeping them clustered as far up the valley as possible.

What happened to a sheep in a fire? Did they die of heat or smoke? Or did they burn? She felt weak at what she didn't know, at what hadn't happened here.

'We have to help the Drinkwater sheep.' She looked urgently at Mr Sampson, then at Auntie Love. 'Could we herd them up here?'

Mr Sampson shook his head. 'They've never been up here. Reckon they won't go now, when they're scared. Have to push them down toward the homestead.'

Elsie nodded. Matilda looked over at Auntie Love.

The old woman stared out at the fire-blackened ground. 'Fire won't have reached the river yet. Can push 'em down that way.'

Tommy stared. 'Matilda, you can't face that again. You owe Drinkwater nothing.'

She took his scarred hand in hers, felt the shock run through his body. 'Tommy, it's the sheep. We can't just let them die.'

'You'll risk yourself for a mob of sheep?'

'Yes,' she said.

Chapter 32

The land was black. Her feet would hurt, if she let herself feel pain.

She suspected the moistness in her boots was blood or broken blisters, not perspiration. Above her the burning trees still flickered; the leaves had vanished, only the bark and branches were left to burn. But the trunks were strangely solid — marked by fire, but standing.

The wind brushed hot again against her face, and once she had to bat away a burning leaf. The fire was a wall of flame and smoke behind them. But this time she had put herself in its path.

She refused to feel the pain on her face either. Tommy walked on one side of her, Mr Sampson, Elsie and Auntie Love on the other. Somehow Auntie Love had made Hey You stay behind, keeping the sheep penned in the gorge. They should be safe even if the fire swung back, thought Matilda. It had left its own firebreak behind it.

They were off Moura land now. All of Moura except the

valley had burned; Heenans' too, she supposed. This part of Drinkwater had burned as well.

But down toward the river the trees were still green. There would be sheep down there; sheep who would be trapped between the fire and the river if a human didn't tell them what to do.

Suddenly she saw what happened when sheep burned. This mob must have run together in their panic. Now they lay in a curious clump, most of the wool intact. Only the flesh had burned — the fat, the bones. A single sheep a little way away had done the opposite: the wool had burned, leaving the skin stretched and black and bare, the teeth revealed, yellow and white. A two-tooth, she thought automatically, then forced her mind away.

Were they insane, trying to beat the flames behind them? The heat has turned my brains, she thought. I should be back home, with my own flock. What if the wind turns again?

Something moved. For a moment Matilda thought part of the black earth had come to life again, then she realised they were live sheep, their fleeces dark with soot, the only colour the red of their eyes. About six of them clustered together, panting, so dazed they moved obediently as one when Elsie shoved her branch at them, driving them down toward the river.

Had the sheep outrun the fire? Impossible to tell.

It was strange, crossing from the land claimed by the fire into the unburned country; it looked as though a giant had drawn a line across the land, and coloured the world black on one side of it. Below them the river twisted, glinting between the trees. Matilda hesitated. The Drinkwater sheep could be anywhere between here and the river.

'We'd better split up. We can round up more of them that way.'

Mr Sampson nodded. 'You and the boy go down to the river. We go up this way.' He gestured into the land of smoke and blackness. 'Sheep get scared, they can run all over the place.'

Even as he said it, Matilda realised Mr Sampson was giving her the safest route to Drinkwater. If the flames hit them she and Tommy could wade out into the water. But it made sense too. He and Elsie and Auntie Love knew this land, could find their way even in the smoke.

She glanced at Tommy. He had come out to help her. Now she was asking him to risk his life just for some sheep. He didn't even like sheep. He smiled at her.

It was a smile that said: 'I know what this means to you. I am here.'

She wished she had something to say in return. Or perhaps, she thought, Tommy knows just by looking at me too.

Then suddenly the others were gone, invisible in the haze. She prayed Auntie Love was all right. Surely the native woman, of all people, could find safety if she was unable to keep going.

Matilda ran down toward the river, Tommy at her side. The smoke gusted and eddied about her. Suddenly she saw the first lot of sheep, a dozen at least, standing dazed and terrified under one of the big gums; the blackened sheep they were already leading trotted toward their companions.

'Come on! Get on with you! Harrup!'

The sheep gazed at her, bewildered by the familiar human yells from someone who wasn't on horseback. They were used to being herded, but not by her.

'You go behind them,' she yelled to Tommy. 'I'll stop them breaking back uphill.' The stupid creatures were as likely as anything to head right into the fire.

She spread out her arms and the singed branch. 'Go on! Garrrrnnn!'

The sheep began to run. They're not running just from me, she thought. They were spooked by the wind and smoke, and happy for an excuse to run from it.

More sheep joined the mob. She trotted on one side of them, Tommy bringing up the rear, yelling and waving their arms each time the terrified animals tried to scatter. Now and then the sheep tried to break toward the river, panting.

She was afraid they would collapse if they didn't drink — but even more afraid of the flames surging across the land toward them if she let them stop.

She peered up the slope, hoping to see a glimpse of Auntie Love or the Sampsons. But even the slight hill up from the river hid them from view. She looked back at Tommy. He gave her his twisted grin and a thumbs-up sign.

The wind was roaring again. It had shifted once more and was no longer just from the south: gusts like blows now came from one direction then another. A fire wind, she thought.

Where were the flames now? She tried to think. They had been behind her when they started out. But with the changing winds the fire could be uphill from them or even in front ... She shut her mind to that. Going forward was their only hope.

About a hundred sheep bleated and stumbled in front of them now, some black, others still dusty grey. They ran almost like one animal, their woolly backs rippling over the ground. Now and then one would break away, then come running back to be with the mob. It was as though the herd had one mind only and one thought too: *stay together, stay together*. They would follow whatever she and Tommy signalled now.

239

Once again time vanished. There was just the ground, the gusts of wind, the rolling formless mob, her feet, one step after another. Her world was sheep and gasping breaths. Got to keep going, going, going …

The wind battered her, feeding on the fire's heat, growing stronger and stronger still. For a moment she thought she might fall, then Tommy's arm was around her waist, helping her stay upright. They staggered together, supporting each other, the strength of two against the wind. The sheep would keep running now till someone — or something — stopped them.

She heard the first call but didn't take it in. It was only when the shout came again that she looked up.

There above her were the homestead, the cottages, the garden, the dairy and a stretch of dust filled with sheep, a thousand sheep at least, behind a ring of black. A firebreak, just as Mr Sampson had said that they would make.

Their mob of sheep was racing ahead. She looked at the animals blankly. There was no way she could make them change direction now.

There was no need. As she stood there swaying, two men on horseback rode down, yelling, cracking their whips. The sheep swerved up the hill, instinctively heading toward the larger mob, staggering over the ring of black to the others.

'You all right?'

It was Mr Drinkwater. She blinked, unable to answer. He swung his arm down and helped her scramble up onto the horse's back in front of him.

'Tommy!' she called, then saw the other rider — James — help him up. She felt the horse move below her, and Mr Drinkwater's strong arm around her, as they cantered up the hill.

He reined the horse up in the garden. She slithered off

unsteadily. A woman ran over as man and horse vanished back toward the milling sheep. She felt herself shepherded across the gravel yard, through a scullery, then into a kitchen. She sat, and drank water, glass after glass, then stood again. 'I have to go.'

The woman stared at her. 'Leave it to the men.'

'No! My friends are out there. I have to see if they've got here too.'

She was gone before the woman could protest again.

Chapter 33

She found Tommy in the courtyard, shoving his way through the milling sheep, his hat gone, burned leaves in his hair, his eyes concerned as he examined her. Tommy. She felt like crying with gratitude. But it was as though her body couldn't spare the moisture.

'Matilda! Are you hurt?' Impossible to hear with the bleat of sheep, the batter of the wind, but she guessed the words.

He hovered anxiously, holding his scarred wrist with his left hand, as though afraid it might inadvertently touch her. She shook her head, looking out past the homestead. Only the land behind them was unburned.

The flames had passed the treed land now, and were onto what should be bare ground, half a mile away perhaps. But they still looked like a wall, pushed by the wind.

Could dirt burn?

'There's water in the kitchen.'

'One of the men gave me a drink.'

'Are the others here yet?' She had to yell, and even then the words were eaten by the wind.

He shook his head. 'Haven't seen them.' He nodded over to the ring of men at the edge of the firebreak. The flames were travelling so fast the fire was nearly on them. 'I'm going over there.'

She nodded to show she had understood, then began to follow him. They pushed their way through the sheep to the line of men standing at the edge of the firebreak.

Most held rakes, others green branches. A pile of more green branches lay on the ground.

She picked one up, then found Mr Drinkwater beside her. James stood on the other side of him, staring at Matilda as though he had never seen her before. She suddenly realised what she must look like: as black as Tommy, in men's clothes and filthy at that. Even her hair was probably black. 'Don't tell me to go back to the house.'

Mr Drinkwater hardly looked at her, his eyes on the approaching flames. 'I wasn't going to.'

'It's nearly here.' James's eyes were on the flames again.

Matilda pulled at Mr Drinkwater's arm. 'Mr Sampson, Elsie, Auntie Love — I think they're all still out there with your sheep. We separated so we could find as many as we could.'

Mr Drinkwater did look at her then. 'In God's name, girl, why?'

In God's name, she thought, remembering the picture of Jesus and the lambs in Sunday school, so long ago. 'Because they're living creatures, not because they're yours. Please — could you send men out to look for my friends?'

'No.'

Anger flared with anguish. 'Just because they're natives!'

He bent close to her ear so she could hear above the roar of fire. 'I would if I could, girl. We'll look for them. But it's impossible now.' He strode off, a branch in his hand, leaving James beside her.

James yelled above the wind, 'Are you sure you don't want to go back to the house?'

'Yes.'

She stared at the approaching flames. Mr Drinkwater was right. There was no way anyone could search for others until the fire had passed. Beside her Tommy held his branch like a weapon, his eyes on the fire-front too. The end nearest the river was closest. How many minutes before it was on them? The flames circled more than half the homestead now.

She moved over to the other edge of the firebreak, staring out into the smoke, hoping to see figures running toward them. The men on either side glanced at her, then turned back to the flames. The leading edge of the fire hit, further down the line.

She looked that way. The men there seemed to be easily keeping the fire from crossing the firebreak as it ate the land between the homestead and the river.

Where were the Sampsons and Auntie Love?

'No,' yelled Tommy in her ear.

'What?'

'No, you can't go and look for them. They could be anywhere.'

How did he know what she'd been thinking? Perhaps because he had thought the same. Now the tears did come. She felt the salt sting her smoke-reddened eyes. Waste of water.

Rain, she thought. If we could only call up rain.

Another gust of smoke swirled down again. She stared into it, wishing so hard for shapes to appear that when they did she didn't recognise them at first. Sheep, 200 of them perhaps, panting too hard to bleat, and behind them the figures of Elsie and Mr Sampson. She hadn't known she was holding her breath. She let it out, then realised …

Auntie Love wasn't with them.

Had the old woman collapsed? But Mr Sampson would have carried her! Was she still out shepherding the sheep? She wanted to run to them, to make sure they were unhurt, to ask about Auntie Love.

But there was no time now. She watched out of the corner of her eye as Drinkwater men helped them behind the firebreak, and pushed the new lots of sheep into the milling mob. And then the flames arrived in force.

They were shorter than they had appeared before. Knee high perhaps. Just the dirt to burn, she thought, then saw the sheep droppings were flaring too: tiny red nuggets on the dirt. She lashed at them with her branch, saw the red turn into black. All along the line the men were flailing at the flames as well.

Fire was almost all around them now, the vagrant gusts pushing the beaters this way and that. Burning embers flew above their heads. She hoped that there were enough men stationed to put out any fires around the house. But this was Drinkwater. Of course there were.

Tommy thrashed his branch on the ground next to her. She was dimly aware of James, his body strong, his face alive and concentrated, working steadily beside her. Where was Bertram? Sheltering closer to the house? She didn't care.

Small flames burned around her feet. The firebreak hadn't stopped the fire, but it made it easier to fight. She stamped on the red tongues with her boots, watched the flames die, then beat down again with her wattle branch. Incredibly it was hardly singed, still able to easily extinguish the tongues of fire.

Then all at once there were no more flames around her. She looked up, met James's eyes. Despite his exhaustion he grinned at her, as though defeating the flames had been a triumph. A couple of the men let out a cheer.

She had no breath for cheering. No strength, no will. The land all around them was burning now. And Auntie Love was out there ...

It was her fault. If Auntie Love was dead it was all her fault ...

Mr Drinkwater strode across the ashy ground. 'Which way was the old lady going? I'll take a couple of men out now. James, can you take charge here?'

The young man nodded. 'I'll get the men to rake a path down to the river. Sooner we can get the animals to water the better.' He vanished into the smoke.

Matilda tried to visualise which way Auntie Love might have gone. She shook her head. 'She was with the Sampsons when I last saw her. They might know ...' She broke off.

Something moved in the smoke. Black animals, screaming in pain and fear, burst through into the relatively clear air of the homestead. Behind them a burned tree walked across the dead ground.

Matilda rubbed her eyes, making them sting more. Then her vision cleared. It was no tree. A blanket — a wet blanket — and at its base, a pair of boots.

When had Auntie put on boots?

She ran forward, but Mr Drinkwater was there before her. He scooped the old woman up, despite his age, pushed the blanket from her face, carried her up to the verandah. Matilda ran after him, and kneeled beside him as he laid the old woman down.

'Auntie Love!'

The old woman blinked at her, then sat up. Her breathing was laboured and her hands shook till she laid them in her lap, but otherwise she seemed unharmed. Matilda hugged her — gently, in case she was burned somewhere after all.

'I was so worried.' She looked up at Mr Drinkwater. 'Please, could you take her inside? She needs to be looked after.'

'No.'

She almost hit him with her fists. 'You … you biscuit! She saved your sheep!'

'Matilda …' For the first time he sounded helpless. 'She won't go inside. Will you?'

The old woman didn't look at him, but she shook her head.

Mr Drinkwater stood. 'I'll get Mrs Murphy to bring out wet towels. Water.'

'I — I don't understand.'

'No, I don't suppose you do.' He strode quickly into the house.

Auntie Love gestured to Matilda to help her up. Matilda hesitated, then put her shoulder under the native's arm and helped her rise. The old woman made a movement toward the far end of the garden.

'You need to have a drink —' She stopped. There was no denying Auntie Love now.

They stumbled together through the smoky garden — more smoky now than when the flames were close, as though the fire was reluctant to give up its hold. Past the swing, rocking slightly in the wind, over the grass, past the shrubs, wilted now, their flowers gone. A small fenced space stood behind the dairy, with shapes among the milling sheep. Matilda blinked; the shapes shimmered and turned into gravestones.

A cemetery … for people who worked here, she supposed. In fifty years many must have died. Their families too, perhaps.

Auntie Love forced her forward. Down, to the far edge, where a small stone was fenced in its own tiny plot. Auntie Love let herself drop onto the ground. The sheep bleated, indignant now, and edged away. Matilda kneeled beside her and peered at the tiny stone. *Dorothy Love* and then a single date. *3 September 1848*. No other words.

'Who was she?'

Her voice was too hoarse to yell, and the wind was still a roar. But there was really no need to ask. Matilda took Auntie Love's hand in hers and sat there, by the small grave of the old woman's daughter.

She didn't know how long they sat there. The smoke eddied and thinned. The wind dropped to a breeze. She shut her eyes, letting herself doze.

The rumbling woke her. She scrambled to her feet, thinking it was the fire again. Auntie Love saw her look. She pointed down toward the river.

A brown wall crashed and smashed its way across the gums, drowning the shining silver river. Tree trunks, a dead cow, the froth on the water the colour of old milk.

'What ... how ...?'

'There must have been a storm way upriver. Maybe days ago.' Mr Drinkwater was beside them again. His face too was black, with a white streak where he had wiped away the sweat. He crouched down, and handed a jug of water to Auntie Love. He watched the old woman drink it, then held out a damp towel and began to wipe her face.

The old woman stopped drinking. She put up a hand to push

the towel away. It was the briefest of touches, but Mr Drinkwater jerked away like her hands were flames.

He stood up, then spoke again to Matilda. 'The lightning might have started the fire, for all I know. We're getting the water now.'

She could feel the ground shake now, buffeted by the force of water. 'It ... it won't reach up here, will it?'

He glanced down at the surging water. 'No. We're higher than the worst flood. But it'll flood the river flats, thank goodness.'

She looked at him questioningly.

He grinned, his teeth white in his smoky face. 'It'll go down quick as it's come, I think. But you know what it'll leave behind?'

She shook her head.

'Grass,' said Auntie Love.

Chapter 34

Dear Mrs Ellsmore,

I hope you are well.

Old Jack brought out your telegram. I am quite all right, and so are the others, thank you. Auntie Love has slept a lot. Mr and Mrs Sampson are using my bedroom, as their house was burned.

It is strange to think of our fire being in the city papers. It is strange to think that you know more about it than we do. All we saw of the fire was our own little bit. It is frightening to think of thirty-six people dead, and not even know who they are yet. I am afraid some of them may be the Heenan family, who lived near us. We went there as soon as the fire had passed Drinkwater, but the only thing left was the tin bathtub. It was all black. Tommy told Mrs Heenan to leave, so I hope they are safe in town, but I do not think so. I think Mrs Heenan did not care about anything any more, even the fire.

Tommy has not gone to town yet, but he says someone has cleared the fallen trees off the road. There is a lot to do …

She put her pencil down. She didn't want to write or even think. There was too much to think about, and only her to do it.

It had been nearly dark when the Drinkwater wagon brought them back three nights before. Most of the sheep were still up behind her house, though some had ventured out as the land cooled. She had let Tommy and Mr Sampson bring the bedding down from the cave. When she woke next morning from her makeshift bed on the verandah most of her other belongings were back too.

Now ...

She shut her eyes. The Sampsons had lost almost all they had. Her roof needed repairing. But the sheep ...

One hundred and forty sheep and no food. Almost everything that could be eaten in the gorge was gone. The sheer force of bodies had broken the garden fence. The vegetables were trampled to shreds, as was the corn.

Mr and Mrs Sampson and Tommy were up on the cliffs with Hey You, chopping down branches of what Mr Sampson called 'old woman' trees for the sheep to eat.

But the trees down in the valley were mostly gums and wattles, and the leaves of the few old woman trees were dry and wrinkled from the heat. Outside the valley the world was black with twists of smoke from smouldering coals, the trees like crumpled ruins. Mr Sampson assured her it would all shoot again.

By then her sheep would be dead. By then the humans of Moura might be starving too.

No roos for Mr Sampson to hunt. They would have fled the fire. The possums would have burned in their trees. A wallaby or two, perhaps, survived up among the cliffs. Lizards ... even if Auntie Love could catch lizards there couldn't be enough to keep the four of them for long.

She would have to sell the sheep. They would be half starved by the time they drove them into town, their fleeces black with soot. No one would pay much for sheep like that.

She bit her lip. But there'd be some money. Mr Sampson would know how to make new shingles for the roof. She'd work as a maid if she had to, let the Sampsons and Auntie Love live here, bring them food from her wages, save what she could. Then, when it rained, she'd buy some more sheep … three or four lambing ewes, perhaps.

And then she'd start again.

'Matilda!' It was Tommy, peering through the door. Hey You was at his heels, glancing each way in case one of the sheep decided to climb into his territory on the verandah. 'Someone's coming. A wagon.'

Matilda stood up, wincing. Her feet hurt. The soles were still puffed with blisters from the heat — it was impossible to put shoes on. She had a burn on one arm too. The rest of her skin felt like it had been cooked, and was hot to touch under her dress. She limped out, wishing the verandah floor was smoother.

The sheep parted, bleating irritably, as the wagon made its way up the track, followed by four men on horseback: Mr Drinkwater, leading a second horse, James looking tall and straight, and two stockmen she didn't recognise. One of the stockmen led another horse too.

For a moment she felt protective fury, strong as she had felt before the fire. Were the Drinkwaters going to try to buy her land again, knowing she was desperate? But then she looked at the wagon, piled with corrugated iron and lengths of timber. You didn't bring corrugated iron to buy a farm.

Mr Drinkwater lifted his hat as she came out. 'For your roof,' he said.

'You're bringing me corrugated iron?'

His lips twitched, despite the strain on his face and the shadows under his eyes almost as dark as the land he'd ridden through. 'You brought me my sheep.'

'We look after our own,' said James. He too looked thinner, and had dark circles under his eyes. Drinkwater had been badly wounded as well as Moura. But Mr Drinkwater and James were here, not there, and they were offering help. Vaguely she wondered where Bertram was, then forgot him, gazing at the father and son sitting so confidently on their horses.

She didn't know what to say or do. Aunt Ann would have offered them tea. But Matilda would have to strain the dead leaves and sheep droppings out of the water; nor had she lit the stove — she couldn't face any flames as yet. 'I ... thank you ...'

Mr Sampson came around the side of the house and stopped when he saw the men.

Mr Drinkwater nodded. 'Sampson.' He gestured to the horse he had led. 'This is yours, I believe.'

Mr Sampson stood stock-still for a moment then strode over and took the reins, looking dazed. The horse reached down to whicker at his shoulder. 'How you goin', old boy?' said Mr Sampson softly.

Matilda felt a lump in her throat. But how were they going to feed a horse if they couldn't even feed the sheep?

'The other is for you,' said Mr Drinkwater. 'His name is Timber.'

'Me? But I don't ride.'

'Time you learned. There's a saddle for you in the wagon — not sidesaddle. Too dangerous.' His lips twitched again. 'But given your usual choice of — costume — I don't suppose you'll need it.'

She stared at the horse longingly. Tall and brown with liquid eyes, he stood steadily even with the sheep nosing around. A week ago she'd have longed for a horse like that. 'I'm sorry, I can't look after him. There's no feed.' Nor any for us, she thought, but she wasn't going to sound like she was begging.

She glanced down at James. The young man looked back at her, his gaze steady. If she had to work as a maid it wasn't going to be at Drinkwater. Then to her shock James smiled at her. 'You looked like an amazon herding those sheep through the smoke.'

Amazons were women warriors, weren't they? She vaguely remembered them from school. Was he saying she looked dirty? But the look on his face almost seemed like admiration.

James was already off his horse, helping the stockmen unload the wagon. 'Don't worry,' he added. 'We'll take care of things now.'

She wanted to tell them to shove off, despite all Aunt Ann's lessons in manners. But she had the Sampsons and Auntie Love to think of too. And that horse was so beautiful ...

Mr Drinkwater gazed at her, looking like a benevolent sultan. 'There's another cart bringing hay out from town. There'll be supplies for you too — flour, potatoes — I had the Doos add to the usual rations. Sampson, I've left Farrell and the others putting up your shearing shed again. I thought you could store the hay there. They'll work on your house next. You'd better get round there, tell them how you want things done.'

Matilda shut her eyes wearily. The old biscuit was solving all her problems. She waited for Mr Sampson's grateful, 'Yes, Boss.' It didn't come.

She opened her eyes as Mr Sampson nodded, then levered himself up onto his horse. For just a second it looked like man and horse were one creature, both more at home together than apart. For the first time in months Matilda saw him smile. He rode off, between the cliffs.

Matilda pushed her hair away from her face. She wished she'd at least brushed it, redone her plaits. She must look more of a slattern than Mrs Heenan.

'The Heenans? Did they get to town?'

James looked up at her, holding a sheet of corrugated iron. 'No,' he said quietly. 'They didn't leave.' She hadn't expected the genuine pity in his face.

'Oh.' She hadn't liked the Heenans. Had almost despised them. The land needed strength to face it, and they had given up. Perhaps, she thought vaguely, I can cry for the children and for what they might have been. She thought of the boy throwing stones at the hens, the woman with her single red geranium.

'Will someone write to Mr Heenan?'

'I already have,' said Mr Drinkwater. 'Someone will read it to him.'

So you are taking care of us all, thought Matilda. All of us around the kingdom of Drinkwater. Behind the house she could hear James ordering the men, telling them what parts of the roof needed to come down before they put up the iron.

He hasn't even asked me if I want an iron roof, she thought. But of course she did. The hard wood of the house had turned black in the fire's heat, but not burned. The shingles had blazed with a single spark.

Mr Drinkwater was watching her. 'I'm not going to thank you,' he said abruptly. 'You did what one neighbour does for another. It's about time we did the same.'

He nodded at the sheep, gathered around the pool. 'The flood's gone down already. There'll be green pick all along the river flats by tomorrow. Take your sheep down there.'

'You mean put them with your sheep?'

'The river flats will feed them all for weeks.' He glanced up at the sky. 'There's usually rain after a fire. Not much maybe, but I

255

reckon it'll be enough to get the grass growing.' His lips twisted, but Matilda didn't think it was a smile. 'The old woman will know when it's going to rain.' He hesitated. 'Is she all right?'

'Just tired.' It was too much to take in, especially with the pain in her feet, her boiled skin, the hoarseness when she breathed. Managing all this was even harder than the fire. But she had to keep going. 'How will we know which sheep are ours?'

'There's a blue raddle to mark your sheep in the wagon. Don't worry, the dye won't stain the fleece. The wagon is yours too,' he added. 'I owe you that at least.'

You owe me my father, she thought. I didn't save the sheep for you or James and Bertram. But somehow she was just too tired for enmity. And the old man was right. When a land could burn you, starve you, kill you from thirst or snakes or flood, you needed neighbours. She knew the anger this man and James were capable of. Far better to be within the protection of Drinkwater than outside it.

But words wouldn't come. They didn't teach us what to say at times like this at Miss Thrush's School for Young Ladies, she thought. James's voice rose again behind the house, laughing at something the sheep had done.

'Go and rest,' said Mr Drinkwater, and for once there was understanding in his tone. 'We'll do what's needed here.' He bit his lip. 'The old woman ... where is she?'

'She's sleeping.'

'She's all right?' he asked a second time.

Matilda nodded tiredly.

'There's a box of apples in the cart. She used to like apples. There's one of Mrs Murphy's fruitcakes in there too. Tell her —' He stopped, and shook his head, then turned his horse around.

Chapter 35

Dear Miss Thrush,

I hope you are well.

It was wonderful to get your letter. I cannot say that I miss going to school, but I am sure yours was the nicest school I could have gone to.

I did not know that you were in the Women's Temperance and Suffrage League with my aunt. I suppose that is why Aunt Ann sent me to your school. It is so good to know that you remember her. I cannot thank you enough for sending me her silverware. It was so very, very kind of you and the other members of the committee to buy some of our things for us when the bailiff sold them. I do not have words to thank you enough in spite of all the lessons you gave me on how to write letters. I remember that you told me that a woman can be judged on how she expresses herself. I promise I will try to remember all you taught me, and practise expressing myself well, even though I cannot go to school again.

I am so sorry my mother did not keep in touch with you all. She had to go to hospital soon after Aunt Ann died, and then we had to move so suddenly, and she was so ill, otherwise I am sure she would have still come to the meetings.

I wish you could have seen how nice the table looked last night set with Aunt Ann's silverware.

The other members of the committee have all been very kind. I am writing to each of them, but please tell everyone that they have sent the things that meant most, like Aunt Ann's Bible and Shakespeare's plays and the brown vase she used to put yellow dahlias in and the tablecloths embroidered by my grandmother. I have always felt surrounded by my father's love for this house that he made. Now I have the things that my mother's family loved too.

Mrs Ellsmore is very generous. She has sent me a big book on diseases of sheep. It is bigger than the book in the library. I could only keep that for two weeks.

We had a problem with liver fluke, as our sheep were feeding down near the river after the fire, but I think perhaps you would say that young ladies should not express themselves about liver fluke. I am glad our sheep are back up here now.

We have nearly 400 sheep now. It seems a great number to me, but it only takes three shearers a day and a half to shear them all, including the lambs. I was afraid I would have to sell sheep after last year's fire, but Mrs Ellsmore's brother, Mr Drinkwater, helped, and then ten days after the fire it rained. It wasn't much, but we have had tiny showers every few weeks, not enough to get the creeks or springs flowing, but enough for green grass. The sheep are so funny after rain. It's like they are shaving the ground, making sure they eat every single blade.

I have asked the shearers to do the lambs on the first day. That means the lambs can then be put back in with their mothers straight away. Some farms keep the lambs penned away for several days, and then are surprised when some of the lambs die.

I do not think men think of the comfort of the animals sometimes, which is stupid because losing lambs costs them money too. Moura has the best lambing rate in the whole district. At this rate we will have more than 800 sheep next year, but even if we keep getting a few showers Moura cannot feed so many. My father told me though that it was important to have 'good' sheep, so I separate any sheep that have problems lambing, or that get fly strike more often, or whose lambs don't thrive, and they will be the ones we sell along with the boy lambs.

I am sorry to talk about sheep so much. Mr Sampson, my foreman, knows a lot about sheep but he does not like to talk much, at least not to me, and my friend Tommy is not interested in sheep at all. But at least he listens, just like I listen when he talks about engines. An engine just sits there unless you make it do something, which seems very boring compared to sheep.

I am very much looking forward to Mrs Ellsmore's visit to her brother next week. Mr Drinkwater sent a note asking me to dinner. I will ride over by myself — Mr Sampson has taught me to ride quite well now — and I will stay the night.

I hope I have not made too many mistakes in this letter. I do try to remember all that you and Miss Elaine taught me. If I am a worthy voter when we finally get the vote, so much of it will be due to Miss Thrush's School for Young Ladies. Most men around here cannot read at all, and they indulge frequently in spirituous liquor and are not at all careful with their money. I think the

women of our district would be far more careful voters, for it is they
who have to do most of the managing.

Yours sincerely and with gratitude for all that you have done
for me,

Matilda O'Halloran

PS I am too far from town to go to the local Women's Temperance
and Suffrage League meetings, but I am an official member, and
have signed the Pledge again too.

—❦◎

The horse trod neatly along the Drinkwater road. Matilda gazed
at the land on either side. Now, more than a year after the fire,
the only signs of the hungry flames were the black scars on the
tree trunks and the bushy tufts of new gum leaves.

Even the green grass that had appeared on the river flats after
the flood had vanished now. The land had sunk back into the
world of drought: white and grey and dusty.

Little else had changed on Drinkwater, apart from more post-
and-wire fences. Matilda looked at them enviously. Fenced
paddocks meant fewer shepherds — and would mean less work
for her and Mr Sampson. Perhaps with the next wool cheque,
she thought hopefully.

She had dressed carefully for this visit — had taken so long to
do it that Auntie Love had laughed. Auntie Love kept close to the
house these days, mostly dozing in her chair. The weakness in her
left side hadn't come back, but her breathing was shallower. Yet
she smiled as she slept. She seemed happy, far more at peace than
the woman huddled in pain and shock in the cave.

It was important to look like a young lady today, not the 'grubby little bush girl' James had called her. He had never seen her in a dress or even clean. It had been impossible to wear skirts in the days after the fire, as he and the other men had repaired her house, even planted the vegetable garden again for her, and another patch of corn in time for a crop before winter. Impossible even to wash herself properly with so many people about, peering down at any time through the roof.

James and Bertram had returned to school a week after the fire — she gathered it was James's final year. Though she had called in to the Drinkwater homestead on business since then, they had never been home.

Somehow it seemed important to establish today that she wasn't a cocky farmer like the Heenans had been, but ... well, the sort of young lady Miss Thrush had tried to teach her to be.

She had carefully ironed Florence's old dress, taken off the lace and re-sewed it in a different pattern, hoping that Florence wouldn't recognise the dress as hers. She had washed her hair this morning, dried it in the sunlight, and brushed it a hundred times before she plaited it.

She wished she had lace gloves to hide her hands: callused, the nails short to keep out the dirt. Aunt Ann and Mum had never gone out without gloves. But it was silly to buy gloves instead of fencing wire.

If only her father could see Moura now, flourishing despite the fire. We'll get those 2,000 sheep one day, Dad, she thought. Only another 1,600 to go.

She gazed around, remembering. There were the hills he had told her to look at, to forget the love of green. They were gold in this afternoon's light too. She could just see the black stump in the distance, the one that he had told her marked the boundary of Drinkwater.

The horse turned its head toward the drive down to the Drinkwater homestead. Without thinking, Matilda pulled on the reins. The horse looked back at her questioningly, then obediently began to pace past the homestead gate.

Matilda glanced at the almost shadowless trees. It must only be just after noon. She was early. It still surprised her how much land a horse could cover in so short a time. But she wondered if this had been at the back of her mind all along.

She hadn't returned to the billabong since her father's death. It was too far to walk there and back in a day, though Tommy would have taken her on his bicycle. But Timber could canter there and back in an hour ...

Did she really want to see the place where her father had died? Today especially, when she would be dining with the man who'd killed him?

Yes, she thought, kneeing the horse gently so he broke into a trot. Today especially.

She heard her father's voice again, as they passed the stump. *Free*, he'd said. *We're free*.

Here was the track down to the river. She nudged the horse to the right. What would her father have thought of her riding a Drinkwater horse? But he must have ridden them often, she realised. Or had he owned his own horse? Had he sold it when money ran low during the strike?

Someone must know, but it would hurt too much to ask.

The same track, worn by swaggies' feet. The same white trunks, twisted branches dappled green and orange. The same —

She pulled on the reins, wondering if she had been mistaken. This couldn't be the right place.

The billabong had vanished.

Instead a broad sweep of sand stretched almost half a mile, the river twisting through it like a long brown snake. Even the swaggies' fireplace had gone, the stones swept downstream by the flood. There was nothing to show where ducks had once swum, where lilies had floated, where her father's body had been pulled up from the depths.

How could something that had meant so much disappear so completely? Why had she even come here at all? Had she expected her father's ghost to whisper to her in the place where he had died?

But it was still hard to leave. She stared for so long the horse became restive, pulling expectantly to one side, then taking a few paces and bending to tug at the tussocks. She waited till he had taken a few bites, then pressed her knees against his flanks. He broke into a canter, back up toward the road.

Matilda let Timber have his head. He knew where he was going now: back to the stable at Drinkwater. She felt — free, she realised. Her father was gone. Somehow it felt right that the place of his death should vanish too, leaving green grass in its place.

She was alive and happy. Her father's land was flourishing, as much as any land could under the hard skies of drought.

Rest in peace, Dad, she thought. She didn't look back.

The homestead looked as beautiful as it had the first time she saw it, its windows red from the setting sun, the oaks turning autumn red as well.

A stockman came to meet her as she cantered up the driveway, lifting his hat and calling her 'miss', then taking the reins and her saddlebag. He didn't offer his name in return, so she just said thank you. She lifted her skirts as she climbed the three front steps.

'Hello, cocky!' Even the cockatoo seemed genuinely welcoming this time.

No kitchen door for her now. She hoped she didn't look dishevelled after the ride. She had dusted the saddle and wiped the reins to make sure her dress didn't get marked, and cleaned her face and hands with a wet handkerchief too before she came in sight of the homestead. She ran her hand over her hair, checking her plaits hadn't come loose. It was even blonder out here than in the city, as though the hair had caught the colour of the sun.

'My dear, how good to see you.' Mrs Ellsmore glided forward, her green silk dress sweeping across the verandah, then reached up and kissed Matilda's cheek. I've grown tall, thought Matilda. The older woman had not been shorter than her when they had met before.

'Mrs Murphy will show you to your room so you can wash and change.'

Matilda bit her lip. It hadn't occurred to her to wear something other than her best dress.

Mrs Ellsmore saw her expression. She laughed. 'I've brought you a little something from town. Quite a few somethings. I had my dressmaker run you up a couple of dresses and some riding clothes.'

It was as though a good fairy had waved a wand. Hay and corrugated iron were wonderful gifts when you needed them, but a present she *didn't* need was almost magic. She would look exactly like a girl from the Drinkwaters' world now, the young lady Mum and Aunt Ann had hoped she'd become at Miss Thrush's school.

264

'Thank you!'

'The skirts may be a little long — just tuck some material under your sash until you can take them up. Better too long than too short ... Florence has been turning out her wardrobe too. She's in Europe, you know. I expect she's exhausting every dressmaker in London.'

'No. I didn't know.' Matilda felt guilty relief. She'd have liked to talk to a girl her age, but she was also very aware that their worlds were different. Florence wouldn't admire her sheep management, might even have condescended to her — or worse, mentioned in James's and Bertram's hearing that Matilda had arrived wearing her old clothes. 'You didn't want to go to Europe too?'

'My sister-in-law is with them. I've lost my taste for travel these days.' She laughed. 'I'd never have got Florence to come back here with me again. She hates the flies and the heat. She is to come back home in December, but the boys will stay longer.'

'The boys are in Europe too?' So James wasn't going to see her. Matilda was surprised at the pang of disappointment.

'James is studying farm management over there, with some cousins of my late husband.' She smiled, genuine happiness in her face. 'And I probably shouldn't mention it, as nothing has been announced yet, but, well, Florence and Bertram have an understanding. I know they are young, but it really has turned out so perfectly. Bertram is going to work at the London office of my late husband's bank for a year, then take over the Australian branch when he returns.'

'Congratulations,' said Matilda politely.

So James was away, for another year at least, she supposed, or even more. Europe was so far away. He might get married there. Bring home an English girl with white skin and one of those clear

English voices. An English girl would hate it here at Drinkwater, even more than Florence.

'Thank you, my dear. Oh, one last thing.' Mrs Ellsmore lowered her voice. 'I've brought you two pairs of stays. At your age — how old are you now, my dear?'

'Fourteen.'

'Quite old enough for stays. Ring the bell for Mrs Murphy if you have trouble with them.'

Matilda nodded her thanks, then followed Mrs Murphy, who had been hovering just out of earshot, down the corridor then up the stairs to her room.

It was hotter up here, but the windows were open. Glass windows! There was cool water in the basin, and a tray with a glass and a jug of lemonade under a beaded doily as well. And on the bed ...

Dress after dress was laid out on the brocade coverlet: two muslin day dresses, with frills and tucks; a plain dark blue serge skirt and two white blouses; a silk evening dress of embossed blue, so beautiful she had to stroke it; a funny baggy skirt that split into two, almost like trousers, that wouldn't look rude even if she rode in them to town; stockings; four pairs of white cotton pantaloons with lace at the ankle; two pairs of lace gloves and one pair of leather; a straw hat, like a man's boater; and three pairs of shoes — too small, she thought, but she could wet them, then stretch them. And the stays.

She took off her dress, used the cloth and basin to wash herself, slipped on a pair of pantaloons and then the stays. They were made of what felt like steel or whalebone, covered in silk, with cups for her breasts. They tied behind — awkward to reach but not impossible. A memory flooded back: lacing Mum's stays for her, before she grew too ill to wear them.

Now the stockings, with garters to hold them up, and the evening dress, with a lower neck than she was used to, and shorter sleeves. Hard to reach the hooks and eyes, but she managed that too. She loved the feel of silk swirling about her, the whisper of the fabric. Lace gloves to hide her calluses. New shoes — never mind pinched feet for now.

She turned and stared at herself in the mirror.

She hadn't looked in a mirror for … was it three years now? Not since Aunt Ann's. She had — changed.

It wasn't just that she was taller. A young woman looked back at her from the glass. It was a shock to see her father's eyes in her half-familiar face. Her hair almost glowed even more brightly than Mum's or Aunt Ann's, or maybe it just looked more golden against her tanned skin — impossible to keep her skin a ladylike white out here.

She looked — good, she decided. Very good. She wished that James was here to see her like this, instead of stained and bedraggled. Or Tommy. But Tommy would just make some remark about skinny arms. She looked at her silk sleeves admiringly again.

Mr Drinkwater stood up when she entered the drawing room. He had changed for dinner too, a white shirt and short straggle of a tie, which she supposed was fashionable. 'Good evening, Miss O'Halloran. You look lovely.'

'Thank you,' she said uncomfortably.

'My sister isn't down yet. Can I get you a sherry?'

'A sherry?' She looked at the straw-coloured liquid in the decanter. 'That's spirituous liquor, isn't it?'

His lips twitched. 'I believe it is. Lemonade? Fruit punch?'

'Fruit punch, please. Mr Drinkwater …' She had realised on the way back from the river that there was something she still owed to her father.

He turned, the jug in his hand. 'Yes?'

'My father ... he didn't burn your shearing shed down.'

He looked at her sharply. At least, she thought, he is taking me seriously. 'How do you know?'

'He told me so.'

'You believed him? After all,' he added gently, 'you hadn't known him long.'

She nodded. 'I've thought about that. But he ... he told me other things. Things he didn't have to tell me. I don't think he'd have lied. I ... I think he was glad the shed had burned down,' she added honestly. 'He didn't hide that. But I don't think he'd have lied about it to me.'

'No,' he said reflectively. 'He wasn't one for lying. He told the truth. Told it too loud, too often, maybe. But not lying isn't the same as telling all of the truth.'

She looked at him, puzzled. 'How could he tell me all the truth? There wasn't time before —'

'Before I hounded him to his death? That is what you're not saying, isn't it?'

'Yes.'

He handed her the fruit punch. The water must have been recently hauled up from the well, for the glass felt cold against her fingers.

'Matilda.' She wondered if he'd noticed he used her Christian name. 'I want you to know how deeply ... how every day I regret your father's death and my part in it.'

'Then why didn't you say so? Why did you try to get rid of me?'

'Because I thought it best you leave.'

'You offered me fifty pounds,' she said bitterly.

'I wouldn't have lost track of you. I'd have helped you in some other way.'

'As a housemaid?'

He laughed, and gestured to her to sit down. 'I admit you are not housemaid material. I admire what you have done, my dear. Yes, I know you've had Sampson's help. But to do what you have done — in a drought like this ...'

He lifted his glass to her. More spirituous liquor, thought Matilda. 'You are an amazing young woman.'

'I will agree with that.' Mrs Ellsmore came through the door, and smiled at them. 'You look beautiful, my dear. Doesn't she, Cecil?'

'Very,' he agreed, standing politely as his half-sister came in.

Matilda stood too. 'Thank you so much for the clothes,' she said awkwardly.

'It was a pleasure.'

She took the glass of fruit punch from Mr Drinkwater. 'I gather my brother has a present for you too.' She wrinkled her nose. 'A sheep. A male one. Extremely smelly, I assure you. He expected me to admire it this morning.'

Matilda turned to Mr Drinkwater. 'You're giving me a jumbuck?'

Mr Drinkwater looked at his sister indulgently. He likes it that she doesn't know anything about sheep, thought Matilda. But he likes me because I do.

Mr Drinkwater took a sip of his whisky. 'Yes, a ram. And a damned — er, dashed good beast. I've had twenty brought from the United States. Bigger boned than ours, a good creamy wool but a fine texture — much finer than we have at present.'

'But I thought we were too hot here for fine wool.'

'I don't believe so.' He raised an eyebrow. 'You've been reading up on it?'

She flushed. 'Yes.'

'Good for you. Our summers are hot, but our winters are cold. I know the general view is that you can't raise fine wool in the dust and dry, but I think breeding is more important than most people imagine.'

'But if you're wrong we might lose more lambs ...' She frowned. 'Why not try half and half for a couple of years? See what the lambing percentages are?'

'Exactly what I planned to do.'

'If you are going to talk sheep all evening,' said Mrs Ellsmore, 'I will take my dinner in the kitchen.'

'I hope Miss O'Halloran will come back to talk about sheep another time then. What should we talk about now? Votes for women?'

'Why not?' said Mrs Ellsmore. She smiled at Matilda. Matilda grinned back, and drained her fruit punch. Suddenly she no longer felt awkward.

This was good.

Chapter 36

SEPTEMBER 1897

Dear Miss Thrush,

I hope you are well.

I am sorry not to have answered your letter before — it has been a busy lambing season. I think the wording on your petition to the Victorian parliament was exactly right. If they were women politicians they would see why women should have the vote, but then we wouldn't need to petition them! It is wonderful about all your new members. Please accept my very best congratulations!

I am glad to tell you that I was able to go to the annual general meeting of our local Women's Temperance and Suffrage League. Mrs Lacey is our chairwoman. I stayed the night at her boarding house. Mrs Lacey does not have stabling there, so I had to leave my horse at the hotel. There are drunken men there at any time of the day or night, drinking all they have made from shearing, but the groom seems a sober man, and looked after my horse well.

It was wonderful to see so many women at the meeting. I did not know we had so many women near enough to town. We now have 172 signatures on the petition for women's suffrage. Mrs Lacey even took the petition over to the hotel and stood outside the door!

I am afraid that many of the men were so inebriated they did not know what they were signing, but Mrs Lacey says that this just shows how badly a woman's influence is needed in our parliaments or the new federal parliament that we may get one day.

We have had a good lambing season. It was cold going out each night to see how the ewes were, and I got very tired, but it is worth it, as that is when you most likely find ewes in trouble. Some of the ewes get 'cast', which means that they are unable to get up because their wool is so heavy.

My foreman's two sons, Peter and Michael, have come to work with us now. They were only working for rations at their last station. Mr Sampson and I share the profit from the wool and lamb sales. Mr Sampson says he will divide his share with his sons, but I do not think that is fair.

I am going to ask Mr Drinkwater, Mrs Ellsmore's brother, how much he pays his white stockmen. Perhaps Mr Sampson and I can pay the men's wages out of our shares, but I do not know yet if we make enough money to do so. We are still only running just over 400 head now, as we sell most of the older male lambs of course, and the oldest ewes too. That would have seemed a great number to me when I first came here, but I know now that this is a small farm.

Stocking rates are low everywhere with the drought. Everyone calls it a drought, but I have never known anything else, so to me this is the way it has always been. The drought has gone on for over ten years now, so I do not think the weather is going to change.

At least we still have good water at Moura. My friend Tommy has welded a series of big metal water pipes that go all the way to six troughs right down the middle of the farm. Tommy says that he did not have to pay for the pipes, but I do not believe him, and he will not let me pay for the welding either. He has also made a sort of tap that floats on the water. He calls it a 'float valve'. When the water level drops the pipe opens and more water flows out. That way we do not have to have water flowing into the troughs all the time. It is a pity that sheep do not know how to turn on taps!

I wish I knew how to thank Tommy. He comes out here every week, at least, to see if we need help, and he is always working on some invention to make things easier. I knit socks for him, but one foot always ends up being bigger than the other. I am afraid that neither you nor Aunt Ann were able to turn me into a good knitter!

I tried making cakes for him too, but somehow they always seem to get burned, I think because I forget they are in the oven while I am doing something else.

Tommy is the best brother it is possible to have. I recommend his repair work of course to all at the League, but I do not think he needs the recommendation, as his work is highly thought of. He has also sold a few of his new float valves to Mr Drinkwater, but not many, as Mr Drinkwater mostly just lets his sheep drink from the river. If he pumped the water up to troughs with windmills the herd could graze more widely and he could raise his stocking rate ENORMOUSLY, but when I told him so he just smiled. On Moura the water flows down from the spring, so I do not need windmills.

I am enclosing a drawing of the new sheep yards. I am not much
of an artist, I'm afraid, but it will show you a little of the country
here. The squiggle on one side is meant to be a sheet of bark, not
a snake.

Yours sincerely,
Matilda O'Halloran

Matilda stared at the figures in her exercise book and chewed the end of her pencil. It was so hard to work out exactly how much money she and Mr Sampson really made.

Forty pounds paid for bags of oats last March to see the horses, cows, sheep and the hens through the dry winter — Mr Sampson and the boys had cut down more kurrajong branches for feed (Mr Drinkwater had told her the real name of the old woman trees), but the sheep lost condition on scrub tucker, and lambing ewes needed something more.

Ten pounds, eight shillings and sixpence profit from the eggs and butter she sold to Mrs Lacey for her boarding house.

There was still the cheque to come in on the crutchings, the dirty wool trimmed from the sheep's rear ends in between shearing. Mr Gotobed had simply baled the crutchings up for her before, but Mr Drinkwater had suggested if she cut away the smelly dags and trimmed off the burrs she'd get twice as much or even more.

It had been smelly work, and the burrs left tiny prickles in her hands, but she hoped the new price would be worth it.

They'd used the Drinkwater shed to shear the Moura sheep this year, leaving hers as a hay shed. Mr Drinkwater even allowed her to add her wool with the Drinkwater bales, so she no longer had to sell 'mixed bales' of good long belly wool mixed with short fibres from the legs. Mixed bales always fetched a lower price.

Better still, Drinkwater wool was shipped to England and sold at auction there, something Matilda could never have afforded, even though the wool sold in England fetched almost twice as much per bale as that sold in Australia. The next cheque should be good. They could buy more pipes, fencing wire, perhaps put in a crop of wheat ...

She put her pencil down and stared out the window. Chooks were pecking under the fruit trees: the lemons she'd planted in her first month here were bearing now, and the apples, medlars and pears too. Only the persimmon tree still sulked as though it was waiting for the rain that never came. Sheep rested in the shade under the trees; the sky was as clear and cloudless as her blue skirt hanging on the clothesline. All flourishing. All ...

Lonely. She pushed back her chair and headed out to the verandah, admitting it once again.

It had been two days since she had seen anyone at all. Even Auntie Love had headed back out bush a few days ago, taking Hey You with her.

The first time Auntie Love went bush Matilda had worried about her, so frail and so tiny. But two days later Auntie Love was back, with a present of goanna eggs to bake on the fire. A few weeks later she vanished again. Now she was gone for weeks at a time, coming back for a few days to check that all was well and doze on the verandah, then one morning her bed would not have been slept in and her chair would be empty.

Matilda had only asked once where the old woman was going. Auntie Love had answered, but as it was all in what Matilda thought of as 'native language', she was none the wiser.

Were there still 'wild' natives out there? Did Auntie Love stay with them? Or was she living alone, remembering her places and her people?

Matilda hoped that she wore clothes. As far as she knew James and Bertram were still away, and there had been no more shooting parties. But Auntie Love still ran the risk of being taken to a reservation if she no longer appeared to work for a white household. Yet Mr Sampson didn't seem to be worried when Matilda told him Auntie Love had gone. 'Auntie goes when she wants, eh?' he'd said. 'She'll be right.'

Even Mr Sampson and his boys spent less time around her house now that the sheep had water further away from the valley and could range beyond the cliffs.

Matilda hesitated on the verandah. Where to now? She could call on Mrs Sampson, but Elsie's conversation was limited mostly to yes and no. She understood English, Matilda was sure, but seemed unsure about speaking it to Matilda. Once again she wished she knew another language, could talk properly to Auntie Love and the Sampsons or the Doos.

She could find an excuse to ride over to Drinkwater, perhaps to talk about when the next wool cheque was due, maybe, or even go into town, to call at the cobbler and order a new pair of riding boots. It was good to be able to buy something new, even if it was only a pair of boots. Or she could —

A shadow flickered in the heat shimmer in the gap between the trees, too fast to be a sheep. Tommy, on his bicycle.

She strode down to meet him, her heart lifting. 'How did you know I needed a visitor? I didn't expect you till Sunday. Come in, I'll put the kettle on and make some scones.'

He grinned, skidded off the bicycle and began to wheel it next to her. 'No thanks. Your last scones were too salty even for the dog.'

'I just used salt instead of sugar. I made some yesterday and they were fine.'

'I'll give them one more go then.' His grin grew wider, with its strange twist at the edge from his scar. 'Got some news.'

'What? Errk!' She reached up and grabbed a flying ant that had crawled onto her neck. 'Ooglies. It's going to rain tomorrow. Don't think there'll be much though — the other ants aren't worried. They scuttle like mad before a real storm. Come on — what's the news?'

He reached into the pocket of his shirt and pulled out a letter. It was limp with sweat, and the ink had run slightly so she had to squint at the words.

She looked up at him in amazement. 'They're paying you 300 pounds!'

'Yep. I wrote an article for *Popular Mechanics* about that float valve I made for you. This bloke wants to make them in his factory.'

'Oh, Tommy, that's wonderful! Congratulations!'

His grin grew even wider. 'I'm going to use some of the money to hire a patent attorney — someone who can register the stuff I invent. Never thought I could make money from inventions before. That ain't all either.'

'What else?'

He laughed. 'Give me a cuppa first. I'm dry enough to drink the dishwater.' He rested his bicycle against the steps, followed her up and sat at the table as she automatically moved the kettle from the side of the stove to boil it for tea, and put a cup of flour, a hunk of butter and a dash of buttermilk into the mixing bowl.

'I've rented a shop. I'll still do repairs, but I can work on my own designs. Get a boy to help me with the welding.'

'A shop? But —' She glanced over at the taut red skin of his arm, then flushed.

'It's all right,' he said gently. 'I'm used to folks staring now.'

'It's … it's not as bad as it was.'

He nodded. 'Feels better too. I can hold stuff with both hands no worries now. But mostly —' he shrugged '— people have got used to me. Anyhow, the counter is back of the shop, out of the light. Can't scare the cows there.'

'Tommy.' A lump rose in her throat. 'You never looked that bad. Even at the worst.'

'An' a flock of koalas just flew over. Anyhow, you goin' to come an' have a look at my shop? It's two doors down from Mr Doo's. Got a room at the back with a bed and a place for a stove too.'

'You can't cook.'

'Neither can you.' He ducked as she threw the dishcloth at him. 'Well, I can learn.'

'And roosters'll lay eggs. And don't you go getting your meals at the hotel either,' she added.

'No, ma'am. No imbibing.'

She looked at him warily. 'You don't imbibe, do you?'

He shook his head. 'Why waste the dosh? Anyhow, the hotel's full of strangers half the time, and they *do* stare. Forget the bally scones,' he added impatiently. 'Go get changed and come and see the shop. You won't get back afore dark if we don't start now.'

'You start off then. Bet Timber and I catch you up before you're past the boundary.'

'You're on.'

Tommy was right. It was a good little shop: two walls of shelves and a counter, and a small room at the back with a lean-to kitchen. But the shed behind the shop was three times as big — two big bays and a lock-up room as well.

'Going to put in a proper floor,' said Tommy proudly. 'Put a wall up here too, to keep out the dust. Turret lathe here, welding in the open bay. Young Billy Watson is a swell welder ...' He paused, and glanced sideways at her. 'Know what I'm goin' to make here?'

She shook her head.

'Motorcars.'

'You mean like that thing in Melbourne that blew up?'

He laughed. 'No! There're motorcars these days that work fine. But they're slow as a wet washday. I've got an idea to make 'em faster. See, they've all got big wheels, high up like a horse and carriage. Big wheels mean you don't need as much power to pull 'em, but —' He broke off. 'I ain't boring you?'

She smiled. 'No.' It was so good to see him like this. He'd been happy enough, the last few years. But this was the first time she'd seen the old Tommy, trying to reinvent the world. 'How are you going to get more power? A bigger engine?'

'Bigger engine means more weight. No, I'm going to try to keep her small. There's this bloke Ford in the United States, he's using petroleum in his engines instead of diesel. You can get more power with petrol.'

'Why doesn't everyone else use petrol then?'

'They're afraid of it exploding.'

'What?'

He grinned at her. 'Don't be a silly coot. My engines ain't gunna explode. If a car has more power it can have smaller wheels, which means it won't tip up so easily. That way it can go faster.' His face was alight now. 'Might go thirty, forty, even fifty miles an hour.'

'No one could drive a motorcar that fast!'

'Trains go that fast.'

'But they're on railway tracks. You don't have to steer them!'

He laughed again. 'Let's see if I can make a fast car, before we worry about that.' He looked at her seriously. 'Thought I'd call 'em the "Matildas". What do you think?'

She stared. 'After me?'

'And after swaggies' Matildas too,' he added hurriedly. 'You know, carrying their Matildas all over. Well, you would be able to drive my motorcars all over Australia too. You ain't laughing?'

'No,' she said slowly. 'I think if anyone in Australia can make a motorcar like that, you can.'

He grinned, relief sliding over his face. 'Thought I might have bats in me attic, even thinkin' about it. It's a long shove from fixin' pulleys at the jam factory. But I reckon I can do it.'

She listened as the words poured out of him, happy for him but a bit sad too. She wouldn't see as much of him now, she supposed, not with his own business to run and a shed to play in, following his dreams and designs.

'I'll miss you,' she said without thinking.

He blinked. 'You dozy drongo, I'll still be out at your place every Sunday. More if you need me.'

Of course, she thought. Tommy would always be there if she needed him.

'Thanks,' she said. She leaned forward and kissed his cheek, then laughed when he blushed. 'I'd better be getting back before dark.'

'I'll get the bike and come with you.'

'Then *you* won't get back by dark.'

'I've got my lantern. Don't want you on the road by yourself.'

'I'm used to being by myself. Anyhow, Timber can beat any horse on the road. Except Mr Drinkwater's,' she added.

She looked around the shed again. 'It's going to be wonderful, Tommy,' she said softly. 'Just wonderful.'

Chapter 37

NOVEMBER 1898

Dear Matilda,

I am so sorry to hear of your decision to sell so MANY of your sheep. Alas, the drought bites hard and deep. Perhaps it is for the BEST, though, my dear. I have been afraid so many were a HARD responsibility for you, being so young. However never let it be said that I doubt your COURAGE and CAPABILITY because you are female! I am sure that when the Lord sees fit to send the rain again your farm will truly PROSPER.

To answer your enquiry: yes, my dear, I think you may in all propriety put your hair up. Normally I would say that a young lady SHOULD be seventeen, but you are nearly that, and have been shouldering an adult's responsibility for so long, that I do not think that any tongues would wag.

I know you will not mind my warning you, though, my dear (for you have no mother to do so) not to make your evening necklines TOO low. A little lace at the throat not only preserves a woman's modesty, but protects against DRAUGHTS as well.

We were all saddened here by the failure of the New South Wales referendum on federation. Only TWO men in FIVE bothered to vote! It is so HARD to understand why men do not realise how important it is to have a new NATIONAL government, not just to make new, fair laws but so we can stand as one country on matters of immigration and trade. I am sure that when we WOMEN win the vote far more people will be at the ballot box!

It is cheering, though, to hear that your young friend is about to launch his new motorcar. Is 'launch' the correct word to use? There are so MANY new inventions these days it is hard to keep up with the correct terms! Who knows? Perhaps one day we may even fly like that brave Mr Hargreaves!

Perhaps we all have our own bright candle to shine to make the world a brighter place, we here in the Women's Temperance and Suffrage League and your friend with his motors. Please give him all good wishes from,

Your affectionate friend,
Alice Thrush

Matilda tied the hat ribbons under her chin and stared at herself in the mirror.

The mirror was new, bought with a little of the money from selling the sheep. The hat was new too, an elaborate confection of pale straw and white ruffles, with two big blue ribbons to match her dress. Her hair billowed out, brighter than the straw, held up by a dozen hairpins. Her dress was sky-blue muslin, narrow in the waist and wider at the black banded hem, its sleeves puffed at the shoulder then buttoned narrowly at the wrist with another tiny frill. She wore black buttoned boots.

'What do you think, Auntie?'

Auntie Love shook her head and laughed, as though the frilly hat and new dress were beyond her understanding, but still to be enjoyed. She had been back at the house for the past three weeks. Her limp was worse, and the sagging of her face too. Matilda was afraid she might have had another small apoplexy. But apart from speaking even less than before, Auntie Love seemed otherwise the same.

Wheels creaked outside just as Hey You barked. Mr Drinkwater must have arrived. Auntie Love stood up, then slowly made her way into her bedroom. Apart from the time of the fire, she had avoided Mr Drinkwater since that first, extraordinary time she had stood naked in front of him, slipping either out of the room or even up into the valley behind the house when he arrived.

Matilda no longer questioned it. And if Mr Drinkwater's eyes strayed here and there, searching for the old lady, she made no comment.

She took a final look at herself, pinched her cheeks to try to make them red, then ran outside, slowing down as she remembered she was in skirts now, and needed to move like a lady.

Mr Drinkwater tipped his hat to her. He drove the sulky today, its wood freshly polished, the leather canopy rich with beeswax too. 'Good morning, Miss O'Halloran. You look,' he raised his shaggy white eyebrows, 'beautiful.'

She blushed, then blushed even hotter when he got down to hand her up onto the seat. 'Thank you. I could have ridden to town myself —'

'And deprive me of company? Nonsense.' He hauled himself up beside her — a bit stiffly, she noticed. The last dark streaks had vanished from his whiskers, leaving them soft and white. He clicked the reins. The horses began to trot.

'You must miss the boys. Have you heard from them lately?'

He glanced over at her. 'Bertram is back in Australia. He's working in the bank already. It seems they need him so desperately that he hasn't time to visit his father. Which means his father will have to visit him. Christmas at my sister's, I think.'

'And James?' She tried to keep her voice matter-of-fact.

Mr Drinkwater smiled. 'He decided to come home via South Africa. Says they are doing breeding there that is years beyond anything here, and the climate is much like ours. At least one of my sons has the heart of a farmer.'

'I'm glad,' she said. James had his father's arrogance, but she remembered him standing next to her, the wattle branch in his hand, tall and determined as he fought the flames for his farm. A property like Drinkwater deserved to be loved. 'He's not engaged like Bertram, is he?'

'No, not James. His letters are full of sheep and troubles with Boers. He thinks the time is coming when England is going to have to make it clear that South Africa belongs to the Empire, not the Dutch. Now, do you think this machine of your young man's will work?'

She felt her face get hot again. 'He's not my young man. We're friends, that's all. Of course it'll work. Tommy says he ran the engine for three hours without stopping last week.'

'Running an engine is not the same as the engine running the motorcar,' said Mr Drinkwater dryly. 'We shall see.'

The motorcar was green, a glorious grass green in this town of dust and corrugated iron. It was smaller than any motorcar she had seen in Tommy's magazines: no longer than a horse, as wide as a kitchen table, and so close to the ground that it was like lowering yourself onto a milking stool. The seats were green leather.

It had no doors. Matilda sat gingerly, hoping that the perspiration wouldn't soak through her pantaloons, petticoat and dress and mark the leather. The wind tasted of heat and distant animals, buffeting the straw of her hat so she had to keep pushing the brim up to see.

Tommy wedged himself down beside her. He wore a grey dust-coat, its long sleeves covering both arms, and driving gloves hiding his hands. A wide-brimmed hat was pulled well down over his face.

There will be photographers out there, thought Matilda — she had seen at least one tripod on the footpath. Tommy would be happy for his car to star on the front pages of newspapers tomorrow, but not his scars.

'Ready?' she asked.

He nodded, his face pale under the hat. 'All that crowd outside. Wouldn't it rot your socks? Wish I could have tried her without all this fuss.'

'Of course there's fuss. People are proud of you,' she said gently.

'It's Billy's fault. He's never learned that a shut mouth catches no flies.' Tommy glanced over at his assistant, standing proudly with his parents by the front of the car. 'I could have taken her out at two in the morning if it hadn't been for him.'

Billy bent to the crank. 'Ready to let her go?'

Tommy nodded. Billy turned the handle: once, twice, a third

time. On the fourth the engine began to splutter, like a cat trying to cough up a fur-ball, thought Matilda. She put her hands to her ears. 'Are motorcars always this loud?'

'You get used to it!' Tommy pushed at the levers in front of them.

And suddenly they were moving, forward at first, then just as Matilda was sure they were going to crash into the shed wall Tommy pulled another lever to the right. The car swung to the left, and out past the shop onto the road.

The crowd made way for them: women with their shopping baskets and bonnets, children with bare dusty feet or buttoned boots, men in the grey faded dress of shearers or stockmen, a few shopkeepers in bowler hats and suits with white shirts tight at the collar. All watching the motorcar. All watching them ...

For a second she was glad she had put her hair up, glad she had bought a new bonnet. Then everything vanished except joy for Tommy. At last, something of his own, something that was so ... so essentially *Tommy*, this shiny motorcar with its funny rubber wheels and many levers.

It would need a Tommy to even work the thing, she thought, then looked at the fascinated faces of the men as they passed by. Dozens of potential Tommys, longing to pull the levers and speed into the distance too.

Tommy swung the lever again. They started to chug down the road. A horse whinnied from over at the hotel; another kicked up its heels. 'They'll get used to it,' yelled Tommy, echoing his earlier words.

Matilda wondered if they would. How could anyone, horse or human, get used to all this noise? The petrol smell too, with its choking smoke, so unlike the sweet grass scent of a horse.

There was no need to move the steering lever much now — the crowd along the road stayed well back, and even riders in front of them were edging well away. Tommy reached for a knob and slowly pulled it out. The motor began to move faster, and faster still. Matilda pushed her hair out of her eyes again.

'Way to go, lass!' Mr Gotobed waved his hat from over at the hotel, his mates beside him. On the other side of the road Mr Drinkwater lifted his hat too. They were flying along now, as fast as a horse could canter, but smoothly, like a train without the rails. The motor seemed quieter now at speed or maybe she *was* getting used to it.

Tommy's tight face began to relax. He pulled the knob out even further. The motorcar leaped like a sheep when the gate had been opened, its wheels bumping slightly over the ruts in the road, but it was still a smoother ride than the buggy.

The crowd was behind them now that the houses were giving way to paddocks. Matilda peered back. A mob of small boys still chased them, but from further and further behind.

'Flaming hell!'

Matilda stared as Tommy pulled one of the levers violently toward him. 'What is it?'

The motorcar swerved, almost hitting a tree, then stopped abruptly.

'Get out!'

'But —'

'Run … just *run*!'

She slid out and picked up her skirts. She had taken a few steps when a shock wave knocked her to the ground. It was only then she heard the noise. She rolled over, dust and leaves staining her dress.

'Tommy!' Flames licked the air above the motorcar and a belch of black smoke hovered.

'I'm all right.' His voice came from the other side of the motorcar.

She reached up and pulled a branch from a young wattle. 'We have to put the fire out.'

'No! Don't touch it!'

'But it'll all burn! All your work ...' Billy's work too, she thought, and the saddlers who had made the seats.

The engine gave another burst of fire and noise. Steam hissed from somewhere, then slowly the flames began to ease.

At least it hadn't exploded, thought Matilda happily.

Tommy walked around the smouldering motorcar toward her. 'You all right?'

'Yes. You?'

'Got out in time.' He gazed at the motor. The back half seemed untouched. The front was black and bubbling paint. Smoke still whispered from the engine.

'What ... what happened?'

'Don't know. Yet. Have to get her back to the workshop, hope there's enough left of her to find out what went wrong. Otherwise ...' He shrugged. 'Have to start again.'

'Tommy ... do you have enough money?'

'Not yet.'

The small boys were nearly on them, yelling with excitement as though this had been part of the show. She said urgently, 'I've money in the bank —'

'And it'll stay there.'

'Why can't I help you? You do so much for me.'

'Because it doesn't work that way,' he said shortly.

'Why not?'

'Matilda, not now ...'

The boys were pointing, laughing. Matilda realised how they must look — her stained dress, his singed coat.

'I'm sorry,' he said quietly. She took his hand in its leather glove. He squeezed it, then let it go, and walked toward the boys. 'Threepence to the first boy who can get someone to tow this back.'

She sat on a sack on an oil-stained stool, watching him work. His face was tight and white and blank, as though he refused to let emotion show.

She'd gone down to the baker's and brought back rock cakes, a billy of milk and a meat pie — he seemed to have no food in the house, except a block of stale cheese in the meat safe and a packet of tea.

She'd made the tea, and sliced a hunk of pie and put it on a plate with a rock cake. He'd taken bites absentmindedly, in between dismantling his motor. She suspected that if she hadn't been there he wouldn't have eaten at all.

He'll only let me do girl things for him, she thought. Bring him food, mend his collars. He always has to be the one who looks after me, not the other way around. That money is just sitting in the bank.

She looked out at the sun. It was dancing just above the rooftops now. Another two hours and it would be dark. She'd have to borrow Tommy's bicycle to get home, which meant she should leave soon or risk being trapped in the dark.

Tommy hunted through the pile of rags for a clean one, and wiped his hands. He held up a partially melted bit of metal.

'What's that?'

'The problem,' he said shortly. 'It's the clamp that holds the fuel line. When I opened her up this must have given way with the extra pressure. A spurt of petrol on the hot engine ...' He shrugged. 'Could have been worse.'

'How?'

'Could have blown us up with it.' He glanced at her. 'I should never have asked you to come on the test run.'

She stood up to go to him. 'But you weren't to know!'

'That's just it! I didn't know.' His voice was tight with anger, but at himself, she thought, not her. 'Don't you realise? I could have killed you! From now on the only person I risk is myself.'

The door to the shed darkened. 'I'm glad to hear it.' It was Mr Drinkwater.

Matilda looked around. 'Oh, I'm sorry. I forgot to meet you.'

'Understandable. So have you found your problem, young man?'

'Yes.'

'I suspected you would. And you can fix it?'

'Yes.'

'Good,' said Mr Drinkwater calmly. 'Then you can make me one of these motorcars. Bigger. I need room for four passengers, and suitcases in the back, and a good wide step so I can haul in a sick sheep if I need to. And a roof. I have no wish to have to hold my hat onto my head.'

Tommy stared, wiping his hands again. 'But sir ... I haven't made a working model yet.'

'I am well aware of that,' said Mr Drinkwater dryly. 'But as you said — you'll test it yourself, and when you are sure that it is safe, you will deliver it to me. Meanwhile you can charge what you need at my accounts in town.'

'Sir.' Tommy shook his head. 'I don't know how to thank you.'

'By making me a motorcar that doesn't blow up. I'm getting too old to climb onto a horse. A motorcar should be easier to manage. Assuming it doesn't explode.' He held his arm out to Matilda. 'Are you ready to go home yet?'

'Yes, of course.' She looked from one to the other, then touched Tommy's shoulder gently. 'The next one will work,' she said.

He nodded, his face a mix of emotions, from hope to the lingering horror of the day. She wished she could stay, keep him company. But Mr Drinkwater was waiting.

The shadows gathered under the trees as the horses trotted out of town. They were well muscled and glossy, so different from the drought-struck animals back in town, showing their ribs under dusty hides. These horses had been fed oats and hay, not just the poor pick in the paddocks.

'One day there'll be motorcars all along this road,' said Mr Drinkwater suddenly.

She shook her head. 'Motorcars cost too much for anyone but rich people to buy them. You can breed a horse for nothing, but motorcars don't have babies. Or eat grass. They're too hard to steer, anyhow.'

'You think?' He let the reins go slack. The horse knew its way now. 'One thing you learn as you get older, child. The world changes.' He waved his hand at the cleared grassland. 'This was all trees when I first came here. No town. No train. No sheep, except the ones I'd brought. Just roos and natives and bears in the trees.'

'Were there lots of natives?'

'Yes,' he said shortly.

'What happened to them?'

She waited for him to say that he had shot them, him and his men. But instead he shrugged. 'Most died two, three years after I got here. Influenza, I think it was. Then the measles. Wiped out whole families. Back in the eighties we moved most of the rest to the reservation. Better for them than roaming here.'

She looked at him. Was it true? She remembered what he had said about her father, that he had told her the truth but not the whole truth. Was this just part of the truth too?

'Did you shoot any?' she asked flatly.

He looked at the road ahead for a while. 'Why don't you ask if they tried to kill me?' he said at last.

She stared. 'Did they?'

'Yes. I've had a scar on my left shoulder these past fifty years. Aches when it rains. Two of my men were speared the second year I was here.'

She sucked in her breath. 'Did they die?'

'They had whacking great holes in their chests. Of course they died.'

'So you shot back.'

He didn't answer.

'Didn't you? And sometimes first.'

He raised his eyebrows at her. 'What would you do if a bunch of natives helped themselves to your sheep? Say, "How do you do, please take some more"?'

'You took their land.'

'No. I fought for it. I won.'

'Guns against spears?'

He looked at her under his eyebrows. 'Don't underestimate them. Or me.'

He waved a hand at the sheep by the road, sitting in the shade in the late-afternoon heat. 'There are 20,000 sheep here today, instead of a few mobs of roos. Do you know how many jobs that makes? There'd be no town of Gibber's Creek without Drinkwater and the other stations around here. I'm proud of what I've done, girl. And I don't see you doing any different. Your father too — why do you think he bought Moura? To grow gum trees?'

She was silent. He still hadn't answered her real question. She wondered if he ever would. She glanced at him; he was staring angrily ahead, a red flush on his cheeks. She didn't want to quarrel with him — not today.

She changed the subject. 'Were there really koala bears? I've never seen any around here.'

'Used to be so many you could hardly sleep sometimes for their snarling. Shot and trapped, mostly, back when the drought started and the banks failed. You could get ten shillings for a koala skin — good as mink or ermine, if the furrier knows what he's doing. I sold a good few skins in those first years when I was broke too.'

She stared at him. 'I thought you were always rich.'

He laughed. 'What? No. My father was an ex-convict. So was my mother. We weren't badly off. There was enough to send me to school, to have a cook in the kitchen and someone to do the scrubbing, but we weren't rich by any means. The old man made money eventually — he had a brickworks — but by then I was long gone. I wanted no part of brick-making. I headed out here when I was seventeen, with two horses, three convicts and 200 sheep to my name.'

She gazed at him. 'What did your parents think?'

'My mother died when I was nine. My father lent me the money for the sheep, pulled a few strings to get the convicts assigned, but that was as much as he could do for me. He

294

married again … oh, twenty years after that. He was rich enough by then, could afford to marry a lady and be respectable.'

'Mrs Ellsmore's mother?'

'That's it.' He smiled. 'She was a lady. But my sister gets her temper from our father.'

'Why did you ask Tommy for a car?'

He raised an eyebrow at the change of subject. 'For you.'

'Me?'

'He's your friend, isn't he?' he asked gently. His flush of anger had vanished.

'Yes.'

'Well then. I approve of him. Your young man knows how to stick at things. Knows how to dream of what he wants and make it happen too. Just like you and me, for that matter. Any more questions?' He handed her the reins. 'I'm an old man, and it's been a long day. I think I'll have a nap.'

Chapter 38

MAY 1899

Dear Mrs Ellsmore,

I hope you are well.

Please accept my best congratulations on Florence's marriage to Bertram Drinkwater. I hope they will be very happy. Mr Drinkwater says that Florence looked truly lovely. I had to ask him what colour her dress was though — men never think things like that are worth mentioning! The pink and cream must have looked beautiful with all the flowers.

Mr Drinkwater will have told you that his motorcar was ready when he returned from the wedding. I hope he really likes it. If he hasn't told you about it, it is dark blue with brown leather seats and blackwood trim.

The coachmaker here in town made most of it. Tommy only built the engine this time, and what he calls the 'suspension', which I think is the part underneath.

Mr Drinkwater drives the motorcar to town every week and it hasn't exploded yet. He seems to be able to work the levers so perhaps it isn't all that difficult. He says he likes being able to leave it as long as he wants without having to water the horses, but that it doesn't know the way home if he falls asleep. I haven't ridden in it. I think Tommy made him promise not to take me for the first few weeks in case it blows up again, which I do not think is fair.

Thank you for sending me the city newspapers. Our local paper is good but it does not have all those interesting articles by famous people. We are all thrilled about the referendum. I do so hope it passes in each state this time, so that we can truly become one country. I am going to town to watch the men vote, even if I can't vote myself. It will be most exciting!

Yours sincerely,
Matilda O'Halloran

Town looked like a mob of emus had descended upon it, tramping up the dust. But this mob was people.

Drays and sulkies lined the streets. The crowd was thickest by the Town Hall, which had been set up for voting. Men were milling round, peering at the pamphlets handed out by the union supporters; Mrs Lacey and another of the Women's Temperance and Suffrage League held up a giant banner saying *Votes for Women*; and children were rolling hoops or running under skirts. The crowd was so thick she urged Timber into a side street and went around the block, rather than try to ride through it.

Every hitching rail in town had horses tied up to it. There was no room to leave Timber anywhere near Tommy's shop. Finally she tied the horse to a fence further down the street, then knocked on the back door to see if the owner minded.

There was no one home. Gone to see the referendum too, she supposed, but they surely wouldn't mind if she watered her horse. She unstrapped the saddle, then hauled up water from their well and poured some into the canvas bag she carried for Timber. She waited till the horse had drunk, cursing all skirts and stays. But she couldn't come into town in trousers, especially not today.

She lifted her skirts in one hand, holding the saddle awkwardly under her other arm, and trod with care along the rutted footpath till she reached the shed behind the strip of shops. The ground was level here, shaded by shop verandahs and swept clean each morning by the shopkeepers.

The door to Tommy's shop was shut. He must be over at the Town Hall like everyone else. She ducked behind the shed and dumped her saddle on a bench where no one could see it. She gave a thankful sigh, then dusted her skirt and straightened her hat, and headed back to the street.

She gazed over toward the Town Hall. Mr Gotobed caught her eye, and waved his stone jug high in the air. He looked half pickled already, like most of the men here. She waved back. She would have liked to look inside, to see the men voting, but the crowd looked thicker than sheep crammed in a crush. She probably wouldn't see anything even if she did force her way through.

Well, it wasn't even as though she could vote herself. You had to be a man and over twenty-one to vote in this referendum. And white. Mr Sampson was checking the boundaries for strays today, carefully avoiding any travellers on the road to town. She wondered how much it hurt, having newcomers vote about your land, while you had no say at all.

She should have stayed at home. And yet …

These men might be helping to create a new Australia. If a

majority in every state voted yes then this time next year there might be a new nation.

She was here for her father. This was what he had dreamed of — it was part of his dream, at least. And maybe a new Australian government might even decide to give the vote to women too. As long as they were white.

Well, she had seen the referendum. When she was an old woman she could tell her great-grandchildren, 'I was there.' She probably wouldn't add, 'All I saw were crowds of men, and half of them were drunk.'

She picked up her skirts again and headed over the street to the Workers' Institute. The top floor was union offices, but the lower floor was a library, free to the family of any union member. Mr Gotobed had given Matilda her entry card when it first opened, in memory of her dad.

At least it was cool inside. The desk was vacant. The librarian — an old one-armed ex-shearer — must have been with the crowd across the road.

She looked at the new books first, and chose a novel for herself, *A Knight of the White Feather* by 'Tasma', who the book's cover said was an Australian, then picked up the latest issue of *Popular Mechanics* for Tommy.

The librarian was back at his desk now. He opened her book with a practised flick of his remaining hand, and stamped it for her, then nodded across the road. 'Wish your pa could have seen that. Don't you think folks around here have forgot him. It's 'cause of men like your pa we was voting today.'

'Did you vote yes or no?'

He looked at her sternly. 'Meant to be a secret ballot, missy. Secret ballot is important. That way no one can get back at you for how you voted.'

'Yes, of course. I'm sorry.'

He grinned, letting out the stench of decayed teeth. 'I voted yes, o' course. Tell you what; we're going to have a government of the workers within three years, or my name's not One-Arm Smith.'

Which it probably isn't, she thought, as she stepped out into the sunlight again. She knew enough by now to guess that half the men around had changed their names: ex-convicts hiding their pasts, men who'd run out on their families, had left debts or crimes behind, or just got the wanderlust.

The breeze blew eddies down the road, whirls of grass and dust. She longed for a cup of tea, or even better, a glass of lemonade, made from fresh lemons and white sugar and cool water from the spring.

Tommy's shop door was still shut. She glanced over at the Doos' Prosperity Hardware Store, but their doors were closed as well.

For a moment she wondered if Mr Doo and Patricia were in the crowd. But of course Mr Doo couldn't vote, no matter how prosperous his store. There had been more in the papers lately about the need to stop anyone from Asia coming to Australia. If the referendum was passed, the new parliament might even decide Mr Doo and his family should be sent to China, a place neither he nor Patricia had ever seen. Over my dead body, she thought, then shook her head. That too was what her father had wanted. You weren't perfect, Dad, she thought, and I don't suppose your new nation will be either.

She tried to look in the Prosperity Hardware Store windows, but the blinds were down. Mr Doo and Patricia would be out at the market garden, ignoring the hullabaloo in town. Perhaps drinking tea ...

If Tommy didn't come back soon she'd have to wait for something to drink till she got home. She didn't want to stand here waiting for him in the wind.

We need a Presbyterian Ladies' Tearoom, she thought. The only place you can get a drink here is one of the pubs.

The Pig and Whistle was on the corner opposite. A couple of drunks lounged against the hitching rails, even so early in the day. But for once the rest of the hotel looked quiet and peaceful, the words *A Clean Accommodation* neatly printed above the window by the main entrance. Another door further down bore the words *Dining Room*.

Matilda hesitated. A dining room would serve tea, wouldn't it, not spirituous liquor? And something to eat. She smiled at herself. Who would have thought a few years ago she'd have the money to eat in a dining room?

That decided her. She picked up her skirts, cursed her stays once again — she wasn't going to get into a dress again for a month, except for church — and crossed the road.

It was cool inside the dining room. The high ceiling was speckled with fly spots, but the wood floor and white tablecloths were clean. She could smell mutton roasting. From next door came the low buzz of men talking.

A woman with the leather skin of a long-time country-dweller and an almost-clean apron came out of the kitchen door, bringing a mob of attendant flies. She waved at them irritably with one hand, then smiled when she saw Matilda. 'Good afternoon, Miss O'Halloran.'

Matilda nodded, embarrassed. They all know me, she thought. Just like Mr Doo and Ahmed. I'm the girl who runs a farm. She took the menu, glad that she at least knew what a menu was.

Roast mutton; chops and eggs; chops, eggs and potatoes. It was nothing like the menu at Mum's tearoom had been — no cinnamon toast or even scones. She'd love a date scone ...

'Could I just have a pot of tea? Some bread and butter?'

The woman still stared at her curiously. 'We got apricot jam. That do you?'

'Please,' said Matilda gratefully.

'How about a nice slice of ham? Could do you a ham sandwich too.'

'Ham!' She hadn't had ham since Aunt Ann died. 'Yes, that would be lovely.'

The woman nodded. 'Be right with you, love.'

Matilda sat back and shut her eyes. Why was she so tired just from a day in town? It's the dress, she thought. This stupid mass of material weighing me down. And the stays.

The thud of someone playing piano with more enthusiasm than skill sounded from the room next door. Someone barked, 'Get off it, Joe.'

The music began again, more tunefully this time. A man began to sing, *'Once a jolly swagman ...'*

It was a good melody, wistful and jolly at the same time. She smiled as other voices joined in the chorus: *'Waltzing Matilda, Waltzing Matilda ...'*

The memory of that one perfect day with her father rose up before her, and the picture of them waltzing their Matilda together. At least she'd had that —

'Up rode the squatter —'

She froze, then stood and ran to the door. Men clustered around the piano, still with their battered hats on, singing.

'Up rode the troopers, one, two, three ...'

It was her. Her and her father. She stood immobile and unnoticed in the doorway, staring.

'And his ghost may be heard as you pass by that billabong, You'll come a-waltzing Matilda with me.'

The whole bar was singing the chorus now. She stumbled back to her chair and sat.

They'd stolen her most painful, most precious memory and made it theirs. The billabong, the sheep. Her father's unspoken challenge as he sprang into the water.

But they haven't got it right, she thought. He didn't say, 'You'll never catch me alive.' He was challenging their power, not giving up his life. Her father had too much to live for. It wasn't a jumbuck, either ... no swaggie could ever force a ram into his tucker bag, or even catch it unless it was lame or a poddy.

They didn't say his daughter was there, either. But a girl isn't important enough to put in a song, she thought. And his ghost ...

The billabong didn't even exist any more. If her father's ghost lingered anywhere, it would be at Moura, the land he had worked so hard to own, or with the union, or even at the Town Hall, where the men voted today ...

Maybe his ghost *is* heard, she thought. How many voting today still heard his words? Wherever men stand side by side, Dad's ghost stands with them too.

'Here you are, love.'

The tea came in a big pot with a knitted cosy, a pot of hot water and a flowered plate of thin-cut bread and butter, half with ham and half with oozing apricot jam. The Presbyterian Ladies' Tearoom couldn't have done it better, except maybe for a doily and fewer flies. She brushed them away from her food automatically. 'Please ... that song they were singing ...'

'"Waltzing Matilda"? It's good, ain't it? Some bloke sang it last week an' now the whole town's crazy for it.'

'Who wrote it?'

She shrugged. 'Search me, love. You wantin' anythin' more?'

'No, thank you. This is lovely.'

The music was playing again, more softly now. A single voice rose.

'You'll come a-waltzing Matilda with me.'

She shut her eyes, remembering the man and the billabong, how he had made her house with so much love and pride. I'm doing what you wanted, Dad, she thought. I've got the sheep, the best rams in the district.

The chorus of the song played again. She gazed at the door to the bar, hoping to see the expressions of the men singing. Was it a song of protest to them, of a man who refused to do the boss's bidding? Or did they just like the tune?

She hoped it was no coincidence they were singing it today — the start, perhaps, of the nation of justice her father had dreamed of …

'Excuse me?'

She jumped. She had been so intent on the song she hadn't even noticed him approach. He must have just come in from the street. *Up rode the squatter*, she thought, *mounted on his thoroughbred* … 'I'm sorry. I was miles away.'

He laughed. 'Miss O'Halloran, isn't it? I'm sorry to startle you. I'm James Drinkwater.' His smile deepened. 'We have met, you know. I hope you remember me.'

The young man she remembered had been arrogant. This man was certainly that, striding up to her in a hotel dining room. But he also looked surprisingly friendly and strangely familiar, as though she had known him most of her life.

Well, I have, in a way, she thought. She wondered if his father had looked like this when he was young, and gave a wry smile. She suspected Mr Drinkwater had mellowed in his old age, and he was bad enough now. 'Of course I remember you, Mr Drinkwater.'

He grinned at her expression. 'Oh dear. Perhaps I should have said, "I hope you *don't* remember me".'

She liked his grin. It was hard to think of Mr Drinkwater, Senior mocking himself like this, even ever so slightly. She held up her hand, glad she was wearing gloves that covered her calluses and split fingernails. 'Don't worry. I think the last time we met you were mending my roof.'

He bowed over her hand. 'And the time before that we were fighting a fire side by side. Is that the same as a formal introduction?'

Catch Tommy bowing over my hand, she thought. 'I'm not sure. I'd have to ask your aunt — she always knows the right way to behave.'

She half expected him to look angry at the reference to his aunt, remembering her letter accusing him of shooting natives. But the grin didn't falter. 'My aunt would say that a young lady should always be accompanied in a public dining room.'

Impossible not to smile back. 'I'd better do as she says then. Please, do sit down.'

He sat, placing his hat on the spare chair. 'Thank you. You know, I hardly recognised you.'

'Why not?' She flushed. The words had slipped out without thinking.

He grinned again. 'No soot, of course. No dirt. This is the first time I've seen you with a clean face.'

305

He must have seen that his remark stung. 'You looked beautiful even when you were sooty. And now you are the loveliest girl I have seen since I've been back in Australia.'

Her blush deepened. She shook her head, unsure how to respond. No one had ever spoken to her like that before.

'Now I've embarrassed you even more. Truthfully, Miss O'Halloran, I didn't mean to. Will you forgive me?'

At least there was an answer to that. 'Of course.'

'Prove it. Come to the dance with me tonight.'

'Tonight?' She flushed again. 'I can't.'

'Why not?'

She didn't want to say that she hadn't danced since she was ten years old, and Aunt Ann was playing piano in the parlour. 'I can't go to a dance in this dress. I'd have to arrange to stay the night in town too.'

He laughed. 'Not good enough. I have my father's motorcar. I can drive you home, drive you back here, then have you back by midnight.' He raised an eyebrow. 'Or later. There's no one to check when you get home, is there?'

She bit her lip. What did he mean by that? Some of her novels had hinted at men having — what was the phrase? — *designs* on young women.

This man took too much for granted. No, she would be a fool to risk her reputation — or worse — by riding in his car by herself at night.

He was watching her expression. 'Come to next Friday's dance then. I'll pick you up, all dressed and ready, then you can stay at Mrs Lacey's boarding house.'

Matilda began to nod, then realised what she'd be agreeing to. A dance. And with James Drinkwater.

The whole district would be talking about them. Not that she cared if they talked about her generally. But she'd need to know James a lot better than she did now to want their names coupled.

It's that bally song, she thought. If the men hadn't been singing it she'd have been more in control.

'Not next Friday.' She smiled, to make the refusal less pointed. 'There's a dance every Friday night, isn't there?'

'So you'll come to one with me some Friday soon?'

This was a man who didn't give up. 'Perhaps. When we know each other better.'

She expected him to be angry at being crossed. But he looked at her seriously now. 'Don't we know each other? I know that you are courageous, resourceful and beautiful. And you know that I'm ...'

He raised an eyebrow, looking disconcertingly like his father. 'Ah, there's the trouble.'

That was exactly the trouble. He knew to change the subject too.

'I was admiring your stock on the way in. Even better than ours, I think.'

She smiled. 'It's easier to selectively breed a small flock. Bad times mean stricter culling too. I make sure I cull the ones I don't want to keep.'

His grin was back. 'You're the first person I've heard taking sheep-breeding seriously since I came back to Australia. And the only girl anywhere.'

'I go on too much about sheep.'

'Never. Most landowners assume that they can keep doing the same old things, year after year. But they can't. The land gets worn out if you don't manage it properly.'

She leaned forward eagerly. 'That's just what I've thought. We've been moving the water troughs at Moura to get the land grazed evenly, otherwise the sheep camp near the water and soon as there's a sprinkle of rain it all comes up in thistles. I sometimes curse the man who brought thistles to Australia. We keep grubbing them up, but your father doesn't do a thing about them. Every time the wind blows it brings thistle seeds from Drinkwater.'

'You've told him that?'

'Of course.'

'What did he say?'

'He laughed. Said there was nothing he could do. But if the thistles are slashed before they set seed you can get rid of them.'

'Trespassing thistles. I'll have to see what I can do.' He looked at her consideringly. 'You know,' he said abruptly, 'I envy you.'

'Me? Why?'

'You do it all yourself — yes, I know you have good help, but the breeding, the management is yours. I'm just inheriting what my father has achieved.' He shrugged. 'I used to resent it when I was younger.' He met her eyes. 'Made myself act like the king of the castle, because I knew I was only the prince.'

'But you'll make Drinkwater better still.'

He grinned again. 'Never fear. I'll do that all right.'

'Matilda! Mrs O'Connor said she saw you come in here.' It was Tommy, wending his way through the tables. He stopped, staring at James.

James rose and held out his hand. 'You must be Thompson, who made my father's motor.'

Tommy shook the hand, pretending not to notice as James glanced a second too long at the purple, wizened fingers. He shoved his hand back into his pocket.

'Sorry I wasn't at the shop,' he said to Matilda. 'Got stuck helping at the hall. Some of the blokes can't even sign their names, much less read the questions.'

Matilda gestured to a seat. 'Sit down. Do you want some tea?'

James stood up. 'Take mine. I need to pick up my father.' He gave his grin again. 'And show him that I won't scratch his precious motor on the way home so he'll let me drive it again. It's a good machine,' he added to Tommy. 'I drove one out country from Cape Town, but yours rides smoother. More power too.'

'It's the petrol engine,' said Matilda wisely. 'Instead of diesel or kerosene.'

His grin grew wider. 'Is that it? You know everything, Miss O'Halloran. Good day, then. I'll look forward to our dance.' He bowed. 'It was good to meet you, Mr Thompson.'

Matilda watched him stride across the dining room and out into the sunlight, then became aware that Tommy was staring at her now.

'What's all that "petrol engine" stuff? You don't know a petrol engine from a galah.'

'I do so. I've listened to you talk about them long enough. Like a ham sandwich?'

'No, I don't want a bally ham sandwich!'

'Tommy!'

He scowled at her. 'What does he mean, "I'll look forward to our dance"?'

'He asked me to one of the dances at the Town Hall, that's all.'

'And you accepted! What the flaming hell were you thinking?'

'You watch your language with me, Tommy Thompson. Why shouldn't I go to a dance with him?'

Suddenly the day had been too much for her. The breathlessness of stays, the friends who were so much part of this land and couldn't vote today, the song and all its memories. How dare they take her life and make a song of it? How dare they take her father's memory and make it theirs? How dare Tommy tell her what to do?

She clenched her fists. 'Why shouldn't I go with anyone I like? It's not like you've ever asked me to a dance.'

'I don't dance! And anyway, you're too young.'

'Even children go to the dances here!'

'Not with a man taking them, they don't. You're too young for all that.'

'I am not! I'm seventeen.'

'Seventeen is still too young. You can't make proper choices about, well, men and stuff at seventeen.'

'Says the old man of twenty.' She flushed. 'It's a dance, that's all. And I've been running my own farm for nearly five years — don't you dare say I'm too young to make my own decisions.'

'Not on your own you haven't. You've had Mr Sampson and me.'

There was enough truth in it to make her angrier. 'I'd have managed. And I'll dance with whoever I like.'

'Then you're a fool. He only wants one thing, and you're too green to see it.'

She glared at him. What had got into him? 'You know nothing about it. He suggested I spend the night at Mrs Lacey's. I can't see Mrs Lacey allowing any funny business.'

She could see the truth of *that* hit him, and see that it was making him even more angry too.

'Don't go.' He was furious, but there was something else there too, something that she didn't understand.

Impossible to tell him that she hadn't even agreed to go yet. 'Why? Give me one good reason.'

'Because I don't want you to!'

'That isn't good enough.'

'Isn't it?' He stood up.

Suddenly Matilda was aware of the silence in the dining room, the stares through the door from the bar.

Tommy looked down at her with an expression she had never seen before. 'Sounds like I've been wasting the last four years. Sticking in this dump just to keep an eye on you.'

'I don't need keeping an eye on!'

'You need it,' he said bitterly. 'You just don't want it.'

'I didn't ask you to come to Gibber's Creek,' she said uncertainly. 'You wanted to come —'

'Have you any idea what's happening outside the back of beyond? There's people making motion pictures out there. Radios sending messages across the world. Blokes flying aeroplanes, while I'm stuck here repairing blinkin' stump jump ploughs and making float valves.'

She stared up at him. 'I didn't know ... I didn't think —'

'No, you didn't, did you? An' you're still going to that dance with that toffy-nosed git?'

'Well, you're not going to take me, are you?'

He glowered at her, then shoved himself away from the table. 'I hope you enjoy it then.' He strode out the door.

Chapter 39

The leaves hung limp and heavy between the ridges. Matilda leaned on her hoe and wiped the perspiration from her forehead.

Ladies didn't perspire — they 'glowed' — but just now she wasn't feeling like a lady, not in trousers and boots and a man's shirt, with Dad's old hat on her head and dirt under her fingernails. But it was important to keep the weeds down in the corn. It had been nearly a year since there had been any rain, even the smallest shower. The grass had shrunk from the hot soil; now the earth lay so hard-baked it was cracked.

But here at least with the shelter of the cliffs she could grow corn to help keep the sheep alive, with the water from beneath the earth trickling through Tommy's pipes.

Tommy! Every time the wind blew she thought it would be Tommy, riding out on his bicycle to make up. There hadn't been a week without him appearing before.

Impossible that he wouldn't come. Impossible for him not to apologise! Why shouldn't she go to a dance — just one dance —

with whoever she wanted? It wasn't as though he had ever asked her.

She had begun to realise why he might have been so upset about her proposed outing. Why hadn't she realised that he might be jealous? Because he had only acted toward her like a brother? She had thought he only felt protective of her. Had he been waiting till she was older, just taking it for granted they'd marry one day?

Her anger flared again. She didn't belong to anyone. If Tommy wanted her like ... like that, he'd have to court her. Tommy had never even said that she looked pretty! Going on about her skinny arms!

She bashed at the weeds with her hoe till another thought struck her.

Was he too ashamed of his scars ever to touch her? Was he afraid that she — that any woman — might be repulsed?

But that was silly. The scars had mostly faded, and anyway, when you looked at Tommy you saw his intelligence, his kindness, not his scars.

It had never occurred to her either that he stayed in Gibber's Creek only for her. Had he really given up so much to stay in her life? She had assumed that because it suited him so well to come here after his accident, he was happy to remain here forever. He'd never mentioned anything about wanting to go back to the city.

Ridiculous to think she needed him to watch over her. She was seventeen! Yelling at her just because she was going to one dance with another man ...

She stared down the track again, willing him to appear between the cliffs. At times like this she longed for another human voice. It had been weeks since she had seen Auntie Love.

She looked at her hands, their calluses and ingrained dirt. She needed some young man to tell her she was beautiful.

And Tommy ...

Tommy was her friend. It was impossible to imagine a life without him. She'd have followed to make up after the quarrel if she hadn't been so upset by that song. And when he came to apologise, she'd say ...

What?

She took a breath, and picked up her hoe. She'd work out what she would say when he turned up.

Chapter 40

He arrived just as she was carrying the milk bucket up to the house. I need a dog to warn me, she thought, as she saw his horse tied to her verandah post, saw him sitting comfortably on Auntie Love's chair.

'James!'

He stood up, and lifted his hat. 'I hope you don't mind my making myself at home.'

'No, of course not.' She flushed, aware that her trousers were stained, her boots cracked and the ribbons on one of her plaits untied. She probably had dirt on her face again too.

'I knocked, but no one answered. Dad said you have a native housekeeper.'

She lugged the bucket up the steps. He took it from her automatically. 'Auntie Love isn't a housekeeper. She's a — a friend.' She met his eyes in challenge. 'I don't suppose you'd ever have a native as a friend.'

'Of course I do. Old Napoleon used to be like an uncle to me.'

'Napoleon?'

'I think Dad gave him his name. Napoleon still draws his rations, too, even if he hasn't done a day's work for ten years.' James smiled in memory. 'He showed me and Bertram how to make a bark canoe down on the river. Bertram kept overbalancing in it. Looked like a drowned rat.'

'But you still went shooting natives?'

He had known she was going to ask this too. 'I protect what is mine.'

She could see when he realised it was the wrong answer. And what did Napoleon think? she thought. Had James ever even wondered? James held up the metal milk pail. 'Should I put this inside?'

'Please. On the edge of the stove. I'll scoop off the cream tonight.'

She watched him look around the house. It had changed since he had seen it last, a few days after the fire. There was glass in the windows now, and curtains, and a rug by the horsehair sofa. She had cushions, and two of her sketches roughly framed on the walls, as well as a painting Miss Thrush had given her two Christmases ago, the china in her dresser, and a vase of dried everlastings on the table. It was comfortable, but a far cry from Drinkwater.

To her surprise, though, he ran his fingers over one of the chairs. 'Someone who knew wood made this.'

'My father.'

He nodded. 'He was the best manager Dad ever had.'

'My father managed Drinkwater?'

'Gave it up to work this place when I was, oh, ten maybe. You didn't know?'

She shook her head. 'I thought he was a shearer.' *Did your father tell you the whole truth?* Mr Drinkwater had asked. But their time together had been too short. She hadn't realised that the Drinkwater boys might have known him.

He looked at her with sudden sympathy. 'Your father went back to shearing when the drought grew bad.'

'What was he like?'

'Clever. Proud.' He grinned. 'Wouldn't call me or Bertram "Master" like the other men. Bertram threw a tantrum but your dad told him to grow up. Only stockman I knew who was always reading. Argued with Dad all the time too. Not just about the union. Wanted him to improve the stock, things like that. Good thing too. Dad needs a kick up the … er, a good argument. He gets stuck in his ways. Look, I wondered if you'd like to come for a ride.'

'With you?'

'No, I'll stay and watch the cream rise. Of course with me.'

It had been weeks since she had simply taken a day off, her and the horse and the land. Suddenly, somehow, James was no longer threatening.

'Yes,' she said.

She changed into the divided skirt his aunt had given her, brushed her hair and put it up properly, secured her best straw hat over the top. She liked it that he went out onto the verandah when she changed, so as not even to hear the intimate rustlings.

He stood up as she came out. 'Beautiful.'

'Thank you.' I could get used to compliments, she thought.

Once they were mounted she let his horse lead the way, out of the valley and past the cliffs, then out onto the back of

Drinkwater land, far from the river. Even though it was close she had never been here.

The trees hadn't been ringbarked; nor had the sheep grazed here for years — it was too far from water. She looked up into the branches, half expecting to see koalas. But of course this land too would have been shot over, even if it looked untouched.

Is this where Auntie Love comes? she wondered suddenly. Was this why she had never seen her, not even her bare footprints, when she was rounding up the sheep?

What would James do if they came upon the old woman now?

Stupid to be worried, she told herself, her eyes fixed nonetheless on the rifle by his saddle. All stockmen carried rifles, even Mr Sampson. But she found herself calling: 'James?'

He reined in, and cantered back to her. 'Like a break? There's fruitcake in the saddlebag. Mrs Murphy makes a good one. A flask of tea too.'

'Cake! You were so sure I'd come with you?'

'No such thing. The cake was consolation if you didn't.'

They sat under the thin shade of one of the white-trunked trees. He was right. The cake was good. He held out another piece to her. She took it, then flushed when she saw him look at her hands.

'Grubby nails,' she said. 'And calluses.'

He looked at her steadily. 'I love your hands. Most women I meet have hands that have never done anything. Yours have made a farm.'

Matilda's blush grew hotter. She hunted for another subject. 'Look — there's a beehive over there.'

'Where?'

'In that tree. You can see them going in and out.'

'You are extraordinary. Did you know that?'

She bit into the cake, grateful he didn't expect a reply. Mrs Murphy must have added dates to make it so dark, she thought. There were lumps of crystallised pineapple, too, and big crystallised cherries.

'Gosh, it's good to be home.' James stretched, and put his hands behind his head. He looks beautiful too, thought Matilda. Only women were supposed to be beautiful, but that was exactly what James was.

'This *is* home, you know. I wondered when I went to England if I'd find it so much more lovely than here. Was almost afraid I would. Everyone refers to England as home. But it wasn't. Too —' He hunted for the word. 'Too water-soft. You can't see the bones of the land, like here.'

It could almost have been her father talking. And she felt that James was right. In a way they did know each other. Moura might be a postage stamp compared to the vastness of Drinkwater, but she and James watched the same clouds, walked on the same soil.

She found he was grinning at her again. 'Well, do I pass?'

'What do you mean?'

'Have I proved reliable enough to take you to Friday's dance?'

She nodded slowly. 'Yes. I think you have.'

'Good.' He sounded as if it hadn't really been in doubt. 'It's Dad's birthday on Saturday. Will you come to lunch too? Dad's always talking about you,' he added. 'I think every letter had something about the incredible Miss O'Halloran.'

'He was probably swearing at me.'

'Only sometimes. Did you really tell him to pay the native stockmen wages?'

'Of course.'

'Did he yell at you?'

'No. He said that if he did, their money would go to the Native Protectorate's Trust Fund. They'd never get a penny.'

'You've been company for him. I'm grateful. He must have been lonely with Bertram and me away.'

About as lonely as a king in his empire, she thought, but didn't say. She stood and brushed the crumbs off her skirt. 'I'd love to come to lunch.'

'Good. What's your favourite pudding?'

'What? Oh, apple pie.'

'I'll ask Mrs Murphy to make one.'

He cupped his hands to help her up onto Timber. She didn't need it, but liked it nonetheless. At once he stared, then pointed through the trees. 'Crikey … look at that.'

She followed his gaze, then drew in her breath. For a second she thought it was an earthquake, the land quivering, then she saw that the movement was birds, giant birds, emus, their brown and black flickering through the trees.

There must be hundreds of them, she thought. She had never seen so many emus here before. Now they flooded across the landscape. What had brought them here?

'Drought.' He said the word as she thought it. 'It's gone on so long the whole world seems to be drying up. They're heading for the river.'

The river was Drinkwater land. 'What will you do?' The enormous birds didn't even glance at them and the horses, intent, desperate, pounding their great feet toward the scent of water.

'Get rid of them. We can spare them the water. Can't spare the feed.'

She shivered. He meant he'd shoot them — or enough to scare the others away. He was right. If she owned Drinkwater she'd be ordering Mr Sampson to do the same; she would be out helping him and the boys.

Impossible to let sheep starve so that emus could feed. Shiftless to let your children starve when you could be trapping koalas for their fur.

But she was thoughtful as they rode back to Moura.

Chapter 41

Dear Matilda,

Thank you for your LOVELY long letter. I do so enjoy hearing all about your endeavours. I read your last letter out to the committee. They were SO interested, and send you their best wishes. We all pray that this dreadful drought will cease, and that our Lord will smile especially upon Moura, and send you green pastures.

Your foreman sounds a good, abstemious man, even though he is a native, though why I should say 'even though' I do not know, for Mrs Brothers and Mrs Richards are of native blood too, and are two of our most ASSIDUOUS members. Mrs Richards offered the committee her hospitality last meeting, and I assure you that her house though humble was SPOTLESSLY clean, and her scones were as light as my sister's.

I hope that your friend's shop is flourishing. Indeed, I believe you are blessed, my dear. It is rare to find a man who will give you what you NEED, and not what he THINKS you need. I hope I do not speak out of place.

We had a most successful display at the referendum, twenty-four of our members, all in white with blue sashes, holding a banner most BEAUTIFULLY painted by Misses Edkins and Frobisher, with Votes for Women in blue against a white background. I am glad to say that even many of the MEN at the polling station came up to offer us their sincere good wishes.

Your most sincere friend,
Alice Thrush

⁓⁂◎

The Town Hall floor vibrated with the dancers' feet. Up above the dangling lanterns jiggled too, making the shadows leap and sway.

Just three fiddles, the bows swooping back and forth like the players were using a cross-cut saw, and an old piano, slightly out of tune, but it was the beat that mattered. The rhythm was caught by a hundred dancers: old men with snow-white whiskers; young women with shining frocks; older women in high-buttoned black, their skin leathery from years of sun and work. And there were children of all ages, the girls in much-mended skirts but carefully curled hair, dancing with girls in what might have been their grandma's best, cut down to almost fit them, and the boys with bare feet or in their father's boots looking embarrassed from the sidelines.

Men outnumbered women but that didn't matter either. Old farmers danced with each other, stomping out the beat, their boots held together by string. The room smelled of sweat and scones and of the strong tea brewing in the big pots on the tables along the back.

She had imagined chandeliers, waltzes, an orchestra ... nothing like this. But how could the Town Hall have suddenly grown chandeliers?

People glanced at them, whispered about them. She could feel the gossip spread across the room like butter over toast.

It didn't matter. This was ... *fun*, an experience she hardly recognised. How long had it been since she had simply had fun?

Not since she was a little girl hunting shells on the beach below Aunt Ann's, perhaps.

She'd already danced twice with James, self-conscious and trying to mind her steps at first, till the sheer enthusiasm of the feet and elbows about her washed that away.

It was a progressive barn dance now. She whirled from gnarled hands to young hands, from black hair shiny with hair oil to long white whiskers. The old bloke by the door, one of the pub-verandah regulars, still wore his hat — in fact, she'd never seen him without it.

She was around to James again. He caught her waist and whirled her. 'You're smiling! What are you thinking?'

She nodded over at the door. 'That man hasn't taken his hat off for forty years.'

'Sixty at least.'

She laughed. 'He smells like cheese.'

'I beg your pardon?'

'I said *cheese*,' she yelled. 'Maggoty cheese!'

James stepped back, pulling her out of the ring of dancers. 'Let's go and get you a cup of tea. We can't talk on the dance floor.'

They had talked all the way in, hay versus wheat for drought-feeding the sheep; about the merinos he'd seen at the Cape in Africa; how he'd arranged for more rams to be sent out ...

No one had ever talked to her about farming like that before. Mr Sampson wasn't one for conversation — not in English, at any rate; Mr Drinkwater just smiled at her opinions; and neither Mrs Ellsmore nor Miss Thrush were interested in sheep. Even Tommy …

She put the thought of Tommy away.

James drew her over to the tea table, skilfully manoeuvring through the crowd, then smiled at one of the women wielding the giant pots of tea. 'Two cups, please. Now, Miss O'Halloran, can I tempt you to a scone, a scone or a scone?'

'A scone, please. Not plum jam. The apricot jam ones.'

He led her to a seat, then stood while she sat, holding her tea cup, the scone on the saucer. He looked around. 'It's funny, I had expected things to have changed when I came back. But they haven't.'

'Not at all?'

'Oh, the library is bigger now, and there's a few more houses.' He grinned. 'More dust. Hard to tell the sheep from the dirt sometimes.'

'I thought the sheep looked like rocks at first.'

'Ah, yes. Dear old Gibber's Creek. Where the sheep look like rocks, and the rocks look like sheep, and so do the people.'

'What? Shh! Someone will hear you.' She tried not to laugh.

'I'm not serious. Or not totally. But most people are like sheep, aren't they?' He was serious now. 'Few people actually do things. The rest follow.'

She looked up at him. 'You're a doer?'

'Yes. And so's Father. Bertram …' He shrugged. 'Bertram has his Florence and his bank. But he couldn't have started the bank, though he'll run it well enough.' He met her eyes. 'You do things. The only girl I've ever met who does.'

She took a sip of tea to cover her embarrassment. 'Not many girls get the chance. And I haven't had much choice.'

'Of course you had.'

He was right. She might still be at the jam factory, worn and white-faced. If she'd done what James's father had first offered she might be a housemaid now, polishing the silver in someone else's home, not sitting with the crumbs of a scone and an empty tea cup. He took it from her, put it back on the table, then held out his hand.

'I think they're starting a waltz now. Do you waltz?'

'Not since I was ten years old. And that was just at Miss Thrush's School for Young Ladies.' She froze as the fiddlers suddenly worked out what tune they were meant to be playing, and the melody emerged.

'"Waltzing Matilda"! Not a waltz then, but perfect for dancing with you. Will you dance with me, Matilda?' He saw her expression. 'What's wrong?'

What could she say? *That song is about how your father trapped and killed mine?* Impossible. It would make their families seem like enemies.

Perhaps they had been once. And while Mr Drinkwater might have tried to trap and imprison her father, he had not meant to kill him. She realised suddenly that despite all that Mr Drinkwater had done, the old man was a friend; it was as strong a friendship as she had with Mr Sampson or Auntie Love, or even Tommy.

'The song … brings back memories,' she said instead.

'Ones that hurt?' He looked at her with concern. 'Come on outside. The fresh air will do you good.'

She nodded, glad to get away from the song. She was aware of eyes on them — young Miss O'Halloran walking outside with

Mr James Drinkwater — as he held the door open for her, then followed her, leaned against the wall and drew in a deep breath.

'Ah, the smell of home. Horse, er, droppings. Hot sheep in hot paddocks. You never get a smell like this in cities.'

She laughed, glad he wasn't asking why she couldn't stand the song. 'Your cousin Florence would say that's a good thing.'

'She and Bertram are well matched. I think Bertram must have been frightened by a sheep at an early age.'

'Poor Bertram.'

'Yes. Not for him the joys of dagging a hundred ewes before breakfast or tidying up a flyblown jumbuck.' He looked at her seriously. 'Has anyone ever told you you're a strange girl? No, sorry, I didn't mean it the way it sounded. Strange in a good way. The best way. An incredible girl. I don't know one in ten million who could have done what you have — taken over a farm, made a go of it with just a few natives to give you a hand.'

'More than a hand,' she said frankly. 'And those natives know more than I ever will.'

He shrugged. 'Natives can be good workers. But they need someone to keep them under control or they go walkabout on you.'

She wondered how to explain that she had never given Mr Sampson an order in her life; that he had more knowledge of sheep in his little finger than she'd ever know; that Auntie Love could understand the land like the minister reading from the Bible. But now wasn't the time to try. She decided to change the subject.

'Are Europe and South Africa so different from here?'

'Europe? Oh yes, it's different. Cities of smoke and fog and neat farms like patchwork quilts. I reckon most English farmers would die of shock if they saw the distances out here. South

Africa —' He looked into the distance. 'It's like here, a bit. Just more. More colour. More animals. Thousands of impala flowing like a river over the plain. Elephants drinking from the horse trough.'

'An elephant? You've seen elephants?'

He laughed. 'Almost as many as the emus. I watched a pair of lion cubs once track and bring down a mongoose, then their mothers woke up. Twenty minutes later they'd brought down a giraffe and were feasting on the insides.'

'You sound like you miss it.'

'I miss the colour,' he said honestly. 'Part of me wanted to stay there. The Boers need to be reminded that South Africa is part of the British Empire. This Boer War is necessary.'

Once more he seemed far away. 'I made some friends there who've joined up already.' He shrugged, then smiled at her again. 'Dad wanted me back. He's in his seventies now, although you'd hardly know it. And this is home. I know this place. It's funny: the first morning I woke up back at home I thought the southerly will come through this afternoon. I could never understand the land in South Africa that way. I knew this place was part of me, and I am part of it. Does that sound crazy?'

'No. I understand.'

'I think you do.'

He stared at her, till she grew embarrassed again. The piano still thumped inside, the bows scraped on the fiddles.

She shifted uncomfortably. 'We should go in.'

He smiled. 'Not yet.' He leaned against the verandah rail and watched her for a moment. 'You remember when we first met?' he said at last.

'At the train line?'

'Yes.' He looked her in the eye. 'We weren't really shooting natives. It was just a boast, to impress Cousin Florence. You know how boys are.'

She didn't, but she nodded anyway. 'Really?'

'Really.' He laughed softly. 'The last wild natives were taken to the reserve, oh, twenty years ago now. Only those who work on the stations are left.'

Except for Auntie Love, she thought. Was James really telling her the truth or what he understood she needed to hear? 'Truly?'

He laughed again. 'Really and truly, cross my heart and hope to die. Come on,' he took her hand. 'I suppose we must go in.'

'Must?'

He stroked her cheek with his fingers. 'If you don't want to stay outside.'

She flushed, suddenly aware of what he meant. 'No. No, I don't —'

'Don't worry.' To her surprise he held her hand to his lips. She pulled it away, but the place where he touched her burned.

His eyes were serious now. 'I won't do anything to hurt you. Ever. I promise you.' He touched her cheek again and added, 'You're far too precious.'

—⊸⟊⊙

It was impossible to sleep in the strange bed at Mrs Lacey's. The mattress was too soft, the noise of the town too loud. She was used to waking if she heard the sound of another human, even the soft feet of Auntie Love. Impossible to escape the noise of people here.

She sat up, and plumped the pillows behind her. The pillows were too soft also …

A clock struck a few houses away perhaps. She counted the beats. One, two, three, four ... she'd have to get up soon ... except here in town they slept in, she supposed, to six or even seven o'clock. Like she had done once, in the cottage by the sea, so long ago.

She realised suddenly why she couldn't sleep. What her mind couldn't let go.

James. His words: *You're far too precious*.

Impossible not to let her thoughts race ahead to what they might mean, the words you might say to someone you loved, perhaps even someone you might ask to marry you.

Once it would have seemed impossible; the gulf between them too wide. Now — well, Moura was scarcely Drinkwater, but it was more than just a cocky farm too. She had manners, she read books, knew how to dress. She was — respectable. Yes, exactly that.

People showed her respect. And she loved the land, in a way someone like Florence could never do. She'd be happy here, when most other women could not. His father liked her, enjoyed her visits to Drinkwater, would be happy to have her live there too.

Her fantasies took hold. To live at Drinkwater. It was the sort of house she had dreamed of as a child, listening to her mother's stories. No, not like that — she had never known a house like Drinkwater existed till she saw it. But in that instant she'd known she wanted it; she longed for the acres too, more than just the scrubby 600 her father owned at Moura.

James was the eldest son. It would be his. And hers. Her father's grandchildren would own it too.

There was a triumph of a sort in that. The grubby girl would be gone, the memory of the jam factory and Grinder's Alley, replaced by Mrs Drinkwater.

Mrs Drinkwater would never have to wait for her husband to come back from shearing or grubbing on the Mallee, like Mrs Heenan. Her children would never have to live on a market gardener's charity. Drought, fire, flood — Drinkwater would protect her from them all.

She pushed off the eiderdown and got out of bed, then dressed quickly, reaching behind to do up the laces of her stays, leaving them as loose as she could and still fit into her dress.

James would propose. She knew it. If she was respectable enough to marry, she was too respectable to toy with: not a neighbour, not someone his father knew. The dance last night had been a public admission he was courting her. James, touching her cheek, her hand …

James — who had lied.

She'd known it when he'd said *cross my heart and hope to die* so easily. She would have known it even if she hadn't remembered Mr Sampson's words, the day they had first met. *She found him dead …*

There were things Mr Sampson never told her — things Auntie Love kept secret too. But they never lied to her.

The lie had come so easily to James, with no notion that she might not believe him. James had lied before, and got away with it as well.

She opened the door, then trod softly down the hall. She needed to think about this, to talk about it.

She needed Tommy.

The shop was dark; the shed at the back too. City boy, sleeping in, she thought, looking at the grey line of almost dawn along the horizon. Back home she'd be stoking up the fire now. Or soon, anyhow, at the first kookaburra call.

She walked around to his kitchen door and knocked, quietly at first, then more loudly.

No response. She went around to his bedroom window, and rapped it sharply. 'Tommy! It's me! Wake up!'

She listened. No sound within. Suddenly anxious, she ran down to the shed. His bicycle was gone. She ran back, tried to peer in the window, but it was too dark to see. She hurried around to the front, then saw the notice on the door. *Closed till further notice. Leave all messages at Mr Doo's to be passed on.*

She read it again, unbelieving. He couldn't be gone. Not Tommy. Not without saying goodbye.

There's nothing for me here, he'd said. But he had his workshop, he had friends. He had ...

A repair shop, she thought. That bloke in the city had a factory making Tommy's float valves, but Tommy was still repairing ploughs.

Back in the city he could have a proper workshop, even electricity. He could meet with others like himself, and talk about inventions instead of sheep. Meet Hargreaves with his flying machine, all the others who were creating the wonders of today.

Tommy stayed here for me.

He had given up so much already to look after the girl who had rescued him at the factory. She couldn't expect him to stay here now, and give up even more for her.

Was she going to have to choose? Choose between living in a city with Tommy, and living with James, out here? She gazed at the horizon again, the flush of red burning across the sky. No, she couldn't live in the city now. Nor had Tommy even asked her to go with him.

And James …

Suddenly she heard Aunt Ann, as clear as if she was standing around the corner. She'd been talking to one of her friends, a few months before she died. 'It's a woman's secret, isn't it?' Aunt Ann had said. 'We can live quite comfortably without men. But no man can survive without a woman to wash his clothes.'

It wasn't true. She knew men who lived without a wife, who never washed their clothes, for that matter. But the heart of it — yes, Aunt Ann was right.

So she had a third choice too. To live alone, to farm alone. No, not alone. But without a husband at her side. No children to show how termites flew before the rain, how grass orchids spray up after fire, where the daisy tubers slept below the ground, waiting for rain, or for hands to dig them and roast them and wonder at their nuttiness, a gift of food from a dry land.

She walked slowly back toward Mrs Lacey's.

She was getting way ahead of herself, she knew. She'd only really talked to James three times, and who knew where Tommy had gone?

Perhaps he had just left for a few weeks, to talk to that patent lawyer about his inventions, to see if there were more he could sell.

He'll come back, she thought. Tommy has to come back. There was certainly no need to make a decision now.

But it was good to understand that she had choices that few other women might have. She had the land. And just now she knew it was the most important thing that she had ever had.

Chapter 42

Deer Miss Mateelda,

We is sheerin down the Barcoo, we will see yous wen we gets back, you need sumpin you ask fer Oconnor at the hotel, hes a good union man like yur pa. Heel do yous right.

There was a cove here, he shor 400 sheep in a day but it were a long day so I rekkon he cheeted, youd niver do 400 in winter.

I aint niver writted a letter before but Jonno, he writ reel good, he writ this for me, and Ginger Mack, he say he drop it in ter yous. Ill be seen you cum sheerin time.

With respeks,
Brian Gotobed

Bluy sezs to sez hullo.

Mrs Lacey handed the letter to her at breakfast — it was a scrap of brown paper, roughly folded like an envelope, and addressed *Give to Miss Mateelda Moura*. Strange to be served breakfast: lamb's fry and fried tomatoes, and what Aunt Ann would have called a 'knee-high stack of toast'.

'One of the men gave it to me to give to you at the dance last night. He's just got back from the Barcoo himself.'

So she's read it, thought Matilda.

Mrs Lacey looked at her with sharp blue eyes. 'You enjoyed yourself last night with Mr James?'

'Yes. Very much. He's picking me up in half an hour,' she added, aware that this too would be added to the town gossip. 'We're going out to lunch at Drinkwater. It's his father's birthday.'

'That will be nice,' said Mrs Lacey, wielding the teapot in triumph. Matilda could almost hear her telling Mrs Harrison at the grocer's: 'Lunch with his father then. She'll have a ring on her finger by Christmas, mark my words.'

No decisions, she thought. There is plenty of time to make decisions.

─ ❦ ─

It was strangely familiar, sitting in a motorcar, smelling the hot fuel scent, the chugging of the engine. But now James sat beside her, not Tommy. This car had a wheel instead of a steering lever, and a silver vase set in the dashboard, filled with a posy of rosebuds, only slightly wilted overnight.

The land scurried past them; a mob of roos startled at the noise, and dusty sheep ran into yet more dust. Poor things, she thought. They have enough to cope with without us scaring them.

She had made a pen wiper for Mr Drinkwater's birthday, in the shape of a sheep. She hoped he didn't think it childish, understood the joke. She patted her hair, suddenly nervous — stupid, she had been to Drinkwater dozens of times now, had eaten meals there, formal meals when Mrs Ellsmore was visiting, or casual lunches or morning tea with Mr Drinkwater and Mrs Murphy in the kitchen, when she'd happened to be there at mealtime.

Not like this. She plucked at her gloves, made sure she hadn't smudged them.

James noticed. 'You look beautiful. You know, when I saw you in the hotel dining room — you looked golden somehow. Not just the sunlight on your hair. You almost seemed to glow. Made every other woman fade away.'

A golden man. She heard her mother's words. Her mother had been seduced by a glimpse, a dream. But James knows who I am, she thought. She was beginning to think she knew him too.

That was the trouble.

Past the turn-off to Moura, the hills behind them now, down the slope then up the slight rise, and into the Drinkwater driveway. Distances are so small in a motorcar, she thought. Somehow the land seemed less real. All you smelled was leather and petrol. You couldn't feel the air on your skin.

The air shimmered above the homestead. The house looked almost unreal too, in its island of green rhododendrons, the tall Norfolk pines standing firm in the dust. The oak tree was bare, but the roof had been freshly painted for James's return, a deep strong red, and the verandah washed back to white. Even the driveway was smooth, the ruts filled in before they got too large.

James swung the car into the curve by the house, then turned off the engine. It muttered for a few seconds and died. She waited while he got out to open the door for her — she had to remind herself to wait, remembering Aunt Ann's lessons all those years before, though those were for a lady getting out of a carriage, of course, not a car — then trod up the stairs in front of him.

She smiled at herself, her fingernails scrubbed till they were clean, lace gloves, a new dress, made herself from the very latest pattern in the *Ladies' Own* magazine, white organza flaring out in a single big ruffle below the knee.

It felt right to be coming here like this; she was not a grubby child, ordered to stand and wait these days, but a young lady, an honoured guest in a house she knew.

'Scratch cocky! Scratch cocky!' The bird flapped its wings inside its cage.

Matilda peered down at it. 'Poor thing. It should be free.'

'The other birds would peck it to death. It wouldn't know how to be free now.' James put his finger through the bars of the cage and scratched the bird's head, then offered Matilda his arm. She took it, and the warmth of his body swept away her doubts. She only knew that she was here, with him.

What would it be like to kiss him?

They walked into the hall together. That felt right as well. He placed his hat on the stand as the smell of roast lamb floated down toward them. Potatoes, she thought, pumpkin ... I hope Mrs Murphy has made her apple pie.

'James?' The drawing room door opened. Mr Drinkwater appeared, a pipe in his hand. He stared. 'Matilda!'

Why did he look so puzzled? No, astonished. What was wrong? She turned to James. He was smiling. 'A surprise for you, Father. Happy birthday!'

Mr Drinkwater lowered his pipe. 'Yes. A surprise.' He looked from Matilda to James. 'What is this about?'

She felt as though she was three years old, and someone had burst her blue balloon. 'I ... I've come for lunch. I thought you expected me. Happy birthday,' she added lamely.

'Thank you. Of course, you are always welcome.'

Why is his voice so wary then? she thought.

He turned to James. 'I thought you went to the dance in town.'

'I did.' James seemed puzzled too. 'I took Miss O'Halloran there.'

The old man flushed with anger. 'And how did Gibber's Creek like that, eh?'

'They were fascinated,' said James evenly.

'I imagine they gossip about everything a Drinkwater does — or Miss O'Halloran. Did anyone say anything?'

James frowned. 'Not to our faces. Father, it's only small-town gossip. You might as well ask the sun not to rise. What on earth is the matter?'

'Why didn't you tell me?' The voice was clipped.

'Because I am not a child, to tell my father everything I do. Because I assumed any guest of mine would be welcome in my home. Because I wanted to surprise you on your birthday.'

'You've done that all right.' His voice was grim now.

'Father ... I don't understand. You are upsetting Miss O'Halloran.'

'Miss O'Halloran has to realise that —' He stopped, as though searching for the words. 'Much as I value her as a neighbour, I will not have her attending dances with my son.'

'What!' James stared. 'How dare you?'

'This is my house! I will say what I like!'

Matilda looked from one to the other in distress, the faces so alike in their anger.

What was happening here?

'I ... I had better go. James, would you mind driving me home?' She couldn't walk to Moura in this dress. Well, she could, but it would take hours and ruin the dress. It was two days' work, and more than she should have spent of her savings ...

'I will drive you back when we've had lunch.'

'Really. There's no need. Please. I'd prefer to go now.'

'Not until we get this clear. Father, this is the girl I intend to marry. Is she welcome in my home or isn't she?'

Matilda gazed at him, startled. 'James.'

He put his arm around her waist, which was protective but embarrassing too.

'James, I haven't … we haven't —'

Mr Drinkwater's voice cut through hers. 'You will marry no one without my permission.'

'I will be damned! I will marry who I like —'

'Please.' Matilda moved away from James's arm, toward the door. 'James, I … I don't want to hear this.'

'You shouldn't have to.' He put his arm around her shoulders this time. 'Come on, I'll take you home.' He looked back at his father. 'And when I get back we will have this out.'

~ ⊛ ~

They were silent till they reached the end of the driveway. James's face was white about the lips; his knuckles too were white on the wheel. He is furious, she thought, too furious even to speak.

She felt … she didn't know what she felt. Humiliated. Betrayed. Disappointed — the lunch she had so looked forward to snatched from her. Angry too. James had no right to spring talk of marriage on her — and even less right to assume she would agree.

Or did he? He had been courting her, obviously and publicly. Why should he think that any girl would accept his attentions, then turn him down? He was rich and he was handsome. She had made it clear she felt a bond between them.

She shook her head, realising it was Mr Drinkwater's reaction that hurt the most. Did he think she wasn't good enough for his son?

'James?'

'Yes?'

'You said … you said you intended to marry me.'

His face softened a little. 'I do. And I will.'

'You might have asked me before telling your father.'

She waited for his anger to explode again. It didn't.

He looked at her ruefully. 'I'll go down on bended knee to you, I promise. I'm sorry. It was just Father wanting to be in control.'

She nodded, trying to smile. He still seemed to expect that her answer would be yes. But for some reason she couldn't melt like a heroine in a novel from the library; couldn't say, 'I love you, James. I want to marry you.' She needed to get home, get out of her stays and this dress, to walk up the hills, perhaps, look at the land and try to think. She couldn't think now, in the car so close to James.

'I thought your father liked me,' she said instead.

'He does. He talks of you often. Used to write to me, telling me about you standing up with all the others at the sheep sale. He admires you.'

'Then what was wrong?'

'He was probably angry because I didn't tell him beforehand, ask his permission. Maybe he feels I'm trying to take over too much, too soon. He's been boss of his own place for so long.' He took a deep breath, then reached over from the steering wheel to pat her hand. 'Don't worry. I'll work it out. It's all bluster and blather with Father, then his temper's over and the sun comes out.'

Like his son, she thought. She had a sudden image of Mr Drinkwater, with grandchildren at his knee. Why shouldn't those children be hers?

'Matilda. Darling Matilda.'

She didn't feel like anyone's darling, just then. He smiled at her. She forced herself to smile back.

This has to be right, she thought. The two of us, wanting the same things. She was strong enough to cope with James Drinkwater and his father.

The motorcar swept between the cliffs. He stopped by the house, then held her hand after he helped her out. She watched him as he leaned forward, kissed her cheek and then her lips. He tasted of peppermint. His lips were warm.

It was the first such kiss she had ever had. Once she worked out where to put her nose she wanted it to last forever.

He stood back and touched her cheek. 'I love you,' he said. 'I think I have always loved you. A woman who can stand by my side, face fire or drought.'

The words could have come from one of her novels. As if he could *always* have loved her. He'd been dreadful at first. But how like James, she thought, to know exactly the sweetest thing to say. 'I ... I love you too.' It's true, she thought. She loved his strength, the way he'd stretched out under the tree, the way he laughed with her, the way he made her feel, kissing her and saying she was beautiful.

But it wasn't the whole truth. She loved him, but not quite all of him. Why could she be so honest with others, and not with him? Was loving most of him enough for marriage?

'I'll see you tomorrow. It will all be sorted out then.' He bent, and kissed her again.

It worked better this time.

She watched the car as it vanished in the dust between the cliffs, till the sound of the engine was lost behind the ridge.

Only then did she pick up the carpetbag holding her dancing dress, her dancing slippers and the pen wiper in its small ignored parcel, and walk inside.

Chapter 43

Dear Mrs Thompson,

I hope you are well, and your family too.

I hope you don't mind my writing to you, but I don't know Tommy's address or if he is staying with you. Would you mind very much giving him this note? I would like to tell him how sorry I am about our quarrel, and how grateful I am for everything he has done for me.

I hope I do not put you to any trouble. With many thanks,

Yours sincerely,

Matilda O'Halloran

An engine growled up the driveway. James!

She had expected him all morning. She'd been awake half the night, trying to work things out.

She would tell him she needed time, she had decided. He had offered to go down on bended knee ... well then, he could go down on bended knee at Christmas. By Christmas they would know each other better — or she would at least know her own mind. By Christmas Mr Drinkwater would be used to the idea.

She glanced at her hair in the mirror, then lifted her skirts — no working trousers and boots today — and slipped outside as the motorcar pulled to a stop.

It was Mr Drinkwater. He looked older than yesterday, his eyes lost in his wrinkles. 'Where is my son?'

Where's that jolly jumbuck you've got in your tucker bag? She thrust the song away. 'James?'

'Don't play silly with me, missy.'

'I wasn't. James isn't here.'

'Of course he's here.'

'He isn't!' She waved her hand. 'Look around if you don't trust me. There's only one horse in the yards. Do you think I've hidden his horse too?' Suddenly she realised why he was here. 'You mean James isn't at home?'

He scowled at her. 'His bed hasn't been slept in. No sign of his horse. And he's packed his things.'

She said slowly, 'You thought he had come here to me?' The insult stung — that he thought she would let a man stay overnight. 'You … you old …'

'Old biscuit? Where else would he go?'

'I don't know. But I will. He'll let me know.'

'I imagine that he will.' He considered her. 'Look, Matilda.' She could see he was trying to keep his temper in check. 'The boy and I quarrelled, I admit it. I admit I want something else for my son. Is that so wrong?'

'Am I so bad?'

'You're wrong for him,' he said harshly. 'Neither of you can see it, but you are.'

344

She thrust her own doubts away. 'It's our choice. Not yours. Your son is not a boy. He's a man. You made your life — a different one from what your father expected. Why can't you let him make his?'

She saw something in his expression. Oh, I know you too, you old biscuit, she thought. You are so like your son. 'What did you say to him yesterday? What did you say to make James leave?'

For a moment she thought he wasn't going to answer. Then he said, 'I told him he could choose. You or Drinkwater. If he marries you the place will go to Bertram.'

Fury filled her like the flood down the river — anger for the property as much as for the man. 'You … you stupid old man!'

He stared at her. Good! How long had it been since anyone — apart from maybe James — had spoken to him like this?

'Bertram is a … a slug. He doesn't even like the bush! It's James's heart. It's not fair to the place either. You can't give land to someone who doesn't love it — understand it.'

'Then James will know which to choose.'

The stupidity of it made her want to stamp her foot. 'Mr Drinkwater … if someone gave you an ultimatum like that, what would you do? Would you give in?'

He took his hat off, almost, she thought, like he was pleading. 'Then you do it. Let him go.'

'Whatever happens between me and your son is our business. Can you understand that? Not yours.'

'If it's money you want —'

She gasped as though he had thrown a bucket of water over her. 'You are lower than a snake's belly. Get out. And don't come back.'

'Matilda … Matilda, I apologise.'

'Apologise to your son. I don't want to hear it.' She turned and went inside.

Chapter 44

My very dear Matilda,

It seems I am always apologising to you, first for my father's unforgivable behaviour and now for mine. I left Drinkwater in a rage last Saturday night, too late to see you and, if I am honest, too furious also. Nor did I want to risk gossip if anyone saw me going to your home at night.

To put it briefly, Father told me to choose between you and Drinkwater. I told him to, well, never mind that now. The important thing is that I love you, and have no intention of bowing to Father's temper in this or any other matter.

I'm heading up-country to my chum Feather's place. We were at school together. It's remote, and I'm not sure how often I can get a letter out. But I need to be away so Father can calm down. He needs me at Drinkwater, and he knows it. If you need to write to me, it's care of Beecroft Station, via Umbergumbie.

I hope to see you soon. Till then, will you wear this for me? It belonged to my grandmother, my mother's mother.

Yours, always,

James

She put the letter down, almost in a dream, then opened the tiny box. The ring was gold, with a blue stone. A sapphire, she supposed. Was it an engagement ring? Once more he hadn't asked, had just assumed.

She tried it on her left ring finger automatically. It was a bit loose, but it fitted. If she wore it she'd need to get it resized or wrap a bit of cloth around her finger.

She took the ring off, and stared at it. If she wore it she would be admitting to everyone who saw it that they were engaged. James obviously thought that they already were.

She placed the ring back in its box, then moved into the bedroom, reaching behind to undo the hooks on her dress. No need to wear a dress now that James wouldn't see her. She would change into her trousers, put out hay for the sheep.

Her hands were shaking. She took a breath and tried to open the hooks again.

A sound rumbled through the valley now. A motorcar. Of course Mr Drinkwater would know a letter had come for her. All mail passed through Drinkwater. And yet he hadn't opened it.

She hesitated, then opened the box again, and slid the ring onto her third finger, clenching her fingers so it didn't fall off.

This time she put the kettle on while she was waiting for Mr Drinkwater to come in.

'Matilda.' He stood at the doorway; he was looking even older. His eyes were shadowed. She had forgotten that she had told him not to come back.

'Mr Drinkwater. Sit down. I'll make some tea.'

She gestured with her left hand, so he saw the ring. His eyes widened, but he didn't comment. He looked around the house. 'Is the old woman here?'

'No.' Auntie Love was none of his business either.

He sat at the table, waiting while she handed him his cup of tea. 'You have a letter,' he said abruptly.

'Yes.'

'From James?'

'I'm sure you examined the handwriting before you let it come here.'

'What does it say?'

Anger made her voice sharp. 'You gave your son a choice. He's made it.'

He shut his eyes, looking so tired she almost relented, told him that she hadn't made up her mind, that James could come home. But she had put the ring on, and if James came back the arguments would just begin again.

'You can write to him care of Beecroft Station, via Umbergumbie,' she said instead.

'Feather's place?' He nodded. 'Thank you. I'm not going to change my mind, though.'

Why was he being so stubborn? It couldn't just be because he hadn't been asked, nor because she wasn't a wealthy bride. Once again she had the feeling that she had been told the truth, but not the whole truth.

Suddenly she had had all she could stand of the Drinkwaters.

'I need to check the water troughs,' she said abruptly. 'Please, stay and finish your tea.'

'What? Oh, of course. I must be going.' He stood up. 'Thank you, Matilda.'

It was all too much. 'For once in your life, can't you do the right thing?'

'I am,' he said heavily. 'Don't you see? I am.'

Chapter 45

Dear Mrs Thompson,

I hope you are well.

I do not know if you got my last letter. I would very much like to get in touch with Tommy. Could you please ask him to write to me? There are things I really would like to talk to him about.

She stared at the words. She couldn't plead with Tommy to come back like that. It wasn't fair.

She crumbled up the piece of paper. Paper was precious, but if she used this again even for a grocery list someone in town might read it.

She tried on a fresh sheet of paper.

Dear Mrs Thompson,

I hope you are well.

I do not know if you got my last letter. I would very much like to reach Tommy. Could you please ask him to write to me? Please tell him everything is well here, we even had a shower of rain last week.

Was that better?

She dipped the pen in the inkwell again, then put it down. She'd try to write tomorrow.

Maybe tomorrow there would be another letter from James. He'd written every week, though sometimes two letters arrived together. He'd told her he rode fifty miles each Saturday to get to the mail.

She looked at the ring on her finger. It tied her to him, yet she had been the one who put it on, who even wrapped a rag around her finger to make it fit. I can take it off any time I want to, she thought.

She didn't think she had ever felt so alone.

This wasn't getting the hens fed, the eggs collected, the cow milked. She stood up from the table, then stared.

Auntie Love smiled at her from the sofa, Hey You at her feet. 'Auntie!'

It was so good to feel the thin brown arms about her, to smell the gum leaves and smoke in her hair. Mum's dress looked no more worn than when she'd seen it last. 'Where have you been?'

Auntie laughed. She stood up, then calmly opened the chest to get flour to make damper.

Suddenly the valley felt right again.

It was a cold winter, the sky too high and clear to keep the warmth in the soil. The scanty grass seemed hardly to feed the sheep at all. They grew so thin that Matilda bought hay for the lambing ewes, and left bales by the water troughs every three days.

The morning sunlight flickered through the trees as she walked back toward the valley. The land was quieter in winter, most birds saving their songs for spring, the cicadas' summer duty done. A currawong's long liquid note drifted out from the valley, a branch cracked somewhere and fell, and behind her a steady *snick, snick, snick* ...

She turned. It was a bicycle, coming up the track. Happiness, pure as the sunlight, poured through her at the sight of his dear familiar face. He looked different — grey serge trousers, white shirt, a waistcoat, even a bowler hat — but somehow totally the same.

'Tommy!' She ran to him, beaming. 'Tommy, I've missed you so much!'

She meant to hug him, but the expression on his face stopped her. She took a step back and he stopped his bicycle. 'How are you? Where have you been?'

'Setting up a place of my own.'

A place of his own means a workshop, she thought, not a home.

'Got a loan from the bank.'

Why didn't he smile? Why didn't he say he'd missed her too?

'Good,' she said hesitantly. 'Come on up to the house. Auntie Love is here, so you don't have to eat my cooking.'

He shook his head. 'Need to get back to catch the train. Just came to settle things up, see that you're all right.'

'Of course I'm all right —' She broke off as he stared at the ring on her finger.

'Mrs Lacey said you were engaged. I wanted to know if it was true.'

'I'm not engaged. Well, not officially. I don't even know ... Tommy, it's been so difficult —'

'Is that his ring?'

'Yes. But ...' How could she explain to him what she didn't even understand herself? But if she could just talk to him maybe she could sort it out. 'Tommy, please, come and have a cup of tea.'

'No time.' He looked down at the watch attached by a chain to his waistcoat pocket. 'I've got to go. If you ever need anything you can write to me at Mum's. She'll always know where I am.'

'Tommy, please, can't you catch another train? Just stay a few days?'

Somehow she had to find the words. Tommy of all people could help her through her confusion. They had talked about so much together, for so many years. Why couldn't they talk about this too?

But he was already turning the bicycle.

Suddenly she remembered her father's words. He had wanted to plead, to kneel in the dust, as he watched his wife and daughter leave. But he hadn't, because it was best for them.

She could run after him. If she kept calling surely he would turn back. She just had to say she needed help and Tommy would be there ...

Instead she stood in the middle of the road, watching him get smaller and smaller as he pedalled back to town.

Chapter 46

Dearest Matilda,

It was wonderful to get your last letter. I've been getting the hump badly, these last few weeks. Feather is a good chap, but I'm not cut out to work on someone else's place.

Still no word from Father. I'm writing to him today too. He is stubborn as a donkey sometimes. I plan to head south and stay with Bertram and Florence for a while, so you can write to me there.

My love always,
James

PS I saw brolgas dance yesterday afternoon, a whole great mob of them, and thought of you.

Matilda put the letter in the chest with the others. It was good to hear from James. Of course it was good to hear from him, she told herself.

But it didn't help the hurt place inside that there was no letter from Tommy. Was he working in his city workshop? Did he miss Gibber's Creek at all or ever think of her?

She sat on the rug and watched Auntie Love lying on the sofa, placidly spinning strings of bark into rope. If only marriage and love and friendship were as easy to sort out as spinning. She said impulsively, 'Auntie, who were you married to?'

For a moment she was sure she had said the wrong thing. She had assumed from the small grave that Auntie had been married to a Drinkwater stockman. But women could have babies without being married ... Yet the ring that Auntie had worn that incredible time in front of Mr Drinkwater had looked like a wedding ring.

Had she offended her by asking? Maybe Auntie couldn't talk about him, not if he was dead. But Auntie just shrugged, not even looking up.

'Did you love him?'

Auntie did look up at that. 'Oh, yes.'

'Does being in love always hurt? Is it always so confusing?'

Auntie seemed to be hunting for words. 'It hurt,' she said at last. 'It's good, but it hurt bad sometime.'

'Did your husband die, like your baby?' asked Matilda gently.

'No. Baby die, I had to leave. Can't stay where people die. Got to leave their spirit free.'

'You mean you left Drinkwater because your daughter died?'

Auntie nodded, staring at her weaving again.

And his ghost may be heard as you pass by that billabong, thought Matilda, suddenly glad that no one had died here at her house. The whispers from the dead were loud enough, sometimes, without their ghosts haunting the place too. 'What about your husband? Did he leave Drinkwater with you?'

Again there was no answer.

Never the whole truth, thought Matilda. Had the Drinkwaters or their men killed her husband? Was that why Auntie refused to say more? I'm not a child now. I can bear these things. Why won't people tell me?

'Auntie, where do you go when you're not here? Do you go bush? Or do you have another home?'

'My home is here.'

'But when you go away —'

Auntie Love put down her weaving, and looked at her for a while. All at once she stood up, and shuffled toward the door. Matilda followed her, mystified.

Auntie signalled to Hey You to stay on the verandah. She used the railing to steady herself down the stairs, but once on the ground she was firmer. She walked a little way, then looked at Matilda, smiling.

'What is it? What do you want me to see?'

Auntie gestured at the ground.

'I don't see anything. Oh.' There were Matilda's footprints in the dust. But there was no sign Auntie had been there at all.

Excitement thrilled through her. 'How do you do that?'

Auntie gestured for Matilda to take her shoes off. She lifted a callused foot, with its wide-spaced toes, then placed it down again, onto its outward side, then did the same with the other foot. She took two paces, then smiled at Matilda. 'You try.'

The dust was cold and dry underfoot. She took a few steps, then looked back. She could just see two smudged imprints, but her other steps seemed to have vanished on the ground.

'Auntie Love! I did it!'

She looked around. Auntie Love was gone.

There had been no time for her to walk away. Surely the old woman could no longer run. But there were no hiding places either, just a few thin trees on either side of the track.

'Auntie Love! Auntie Love!'

'Here.'

Matilda jumped. One second there had been no one, then suddenly there she was, standing by a tree, only a couple of yards away. Surely the old woman couldn't make herself invisible?

Auntie looked at her seriously. Slowly she began to vanish again.

But not quite, not while Matilda stared right at her. The old woman stood side on to the trees, her shadow and her shape blending with theirs. One arm was raised, the other lowered, so she was no longer human in form, her head down, her eyes shut. Matilda had never seen anyone so still.

Auntie opened her eyes. All at once she was back.

'Can I do that too?' whispered Matilda.

Auntie nodded. She gestured for Matilda to come closer, then took her arms, bent her fingers into position ...

I am here, but not here, thought Matilda. I am a rock, a tree. There was no one but Auntie to see her, but somehow she knew that if anyone came up the track, they would see no one, not her, not the old woman.

She shivered, and the spell was broken. She stared around at the limp leaves of the trees, the shadowed cliffs, the strong shapes of the tree trunks.

Had Auntie Love ever been away at all?

Chapter 47

OCTOBER 1899

My very dear Matilda,

I am writing this in haste, so please excuse the scrawl. I have only just discovered that Bertram has stopped my letters reaching you. He gave instructions, would you believe, for the butler to hand them to him, when I left your letters with the rest of the mail to be posted. Bertram said it was his duty to Father.

Bertram now has a black eye, and I am posting this myself, and cursing myself for a fool for letting Bertram hoodwink me.

I haven't been able to settle since I left Drinkwater and you. I can't hack a job on a property where I can't be the boss, and I can't see myself working in an office, either. Which left one choice.

I sail tomorrow, as one of 'the soldiers of the Queen', off to fight the Boers. It is a good fight, one that we need to win. If I hadn't felt a duty to the old man I'd have stayed in South Africa with my friends there.

Don't worry about me, dear girl. I can look after myself. I am still sure that Father will come round. Bertram could never manage

Drinkwater — he'd sell up like a shot, and Father knows it. Father will never let the place leave the family.

Maybe this is what I should have been doing, all along. We'll have the Boers where we want them soon enough. This time next year we will be together again. Till then I am your adoring,

James

She stared at the words, not quite believing they could say what she had read.

Which left one choice. But James himself had said that everyone had choices. Enlisting to fight the Boers was the choice he'd wanted to make. He had left without telling her, without asking what she thought, just as he had assumed that she would marry him.

She looked at the ring. What should she do now? You couldn't write to a man about to go to war and say *I don't know if I want to marry you*. It was impossible to hurt him like that.

Suddenly the true horror of it hit her. James, about to face the enemy, a Boer with a rifle hunting him down, like James perhaps had once hunted others here. James hurt, bleeding, calling out in agony, even killed …

She was angry it hurt so much, furious with him and with herself. 'I love you!' she shouted, not caring if Auntie heard her, down where she was milking the cow. She heard the echo from the cliffs. *Love you … love you …*

How dare he desert her like this? How dare he vanish, leaving so much pain?

Suddenly she heard the sound of the motorcar. Mr Drinkwater would know she had got a letter, perhaps had received one himself or heard from Bertram.

She looked over at the cow byre. There was no sign of Auntie

Love. Matilda smiled, knowing it was deliberate, knowing this time how it was done.

The car drew up at the steps. Mr Drinkwater got out, looking frail as a sheet of paperbark. He stepped slowly up to the verandah. 'You've heard from James?'

'Yes.'

'Bertram wrote to me. Tell me it isn't true.'

He looked so vulnerable her anger vanished. 'Come inside,' she said gently. 'I'll show you the letter.'

Her ring flashed in the light from the doorway as she handed him the piece of paper, trying not to see the eagerness with which he took it, then busied herself with tea leaves and the pot.

He had read it and re-read it by the time she poured tea for both of them, and sat opposite him. His eyes were closed in pain. The tin roof creaked above her, as the sun came out from behind a cloud. He was an old man who had lost his son, lost him forever, perhaps. They had both lost him, for a while at least.

Funny — she had thought that if she married James she would never be like Mrs Heenan, waiting, waiting. Now she was waiting for something far more worrying than a shearer on a bender.

I can cope with waiting, she thought. But I can't stand the thought of James being hurt.

'Thank you,' Mr Drinkwater said at last.

'What for?'

'For letting me read your letter. For not accusing me —' He broke off.

'There's not much point now.'

'No.' He stared at the ring on her finger. 'Will you ...?'

It must be hard to have to ask. She said gently, 'I'll show you any other letters. Of course.'

'Matilda ... this makes no difference to how I feel.'

359

'I know.'

He drained his tea and stood up, then hesitated and put out his hand. She took it. It was almost as though they were sealing a deal about some sheep.

'James will be all right,' she said. She didn't know if she was comforting him or herself.

Christmas came. No word from Tommy, not even a card. She had sent one to his mother's house, saying *Merry Christmas with love from Matilda*. But there had been no reply. Mr Gotobed and his mates were away. No visit even from the Sampsons — perhaps they thought she would spend Christmas at Drinkwater. The whole district seemed to know that James had enlisted and that he and Matilda were engaged. It was her fault, she knew, for wearing his ring. At least no one outside the family seemed to know about the quarrel with his father.

Matilda killed a young rooster, and Auntie Love stuffed it. It was tough, not quite young enough or maybe cooked too fast. They ate it with roast potatoes and pumpkin, the first of the beans and young corn. The only other sign of celebration was the pot of ginger from Mr Doo and Patricia.

A note arrived on Boxing Day, delivered by one of the stockmen, asking her to dinner at Drinkwater on New Year's Eve.

Was the old man lonely? There had been no more letters yet. She supposed James was still at sea.

She scribbled a note in return: *Yes, I would like to come, no need to send the car* — she would ride over, ride back by moonlight. She could cope with dinner, she thought, but not with staying the night, nor with being in the motorcar without James.

It was hard to leave Auntie behind. Auntie was used to being alone, but she was like a shadow these days, as though if the sun moved you might find she wasn't there.

It was even harder sitting in the Drinkwater drawing room, neither she nor her host talking about what was most on their minds.

They ate roast duck and Mrs Murphy's lemon shape. They spoke of the weather, the price of wool, the defeat of the Labor government in Queensland, after governing the state for less than a week. They were on opposite sides politically, but comfortably so, in this at least. Sheep — and James — meant more to them both than politicians.

It wasn't till she was leaving that she said what she'd been wondering how to say the whole evening. 'We need to dag the sheep next week. Would you prefer not to have my stock in your shed now?'

He looked startled. 'Why would you think —' He stopped, his mouth twisted. 'The sheep are still welcome here. You are welcome.'

'Then why would it be so very bad to have me as a daughter-in-law?'

She had expected anger again. It didn't come. He simply said, 'My dear, you do not understand.'

'You're right. I don't. Why ... why haven't you threatened me, like James? You could make my life much harder, and you know it.'

'Because it wouldn't work.' He hesitated, then leaned over and kissed her cheek. He smelled of cigars and the whisky he had been drinking. 'Happy new year, my dear. Happy new century. May it bring rain and a new nation and happiness for us all.'

And bring James home, she thought. She kissed him back, then went out to where one of the men was holding her horse.

Chapter 48

SEPTEMBER 1900

My darling Matilda,

Well, I am still alive and in good heart. You may have read that we held onto Elands River. I tell you it was a rum do: by the end of the first day half the horses and cattle were dead — saw thirty of the poor blighters killed with just one shell — and we thought we were for it too. You've never seen so many men dig in so fast.

After four days old de la Rey, the Boer commander, sent us word he'd let us Australians through with safe conduct if we'd surrender. Lieut. Colonel Horse sent back: 'If you want the supplies we are guarding, you had better come and get them.' He is a good egg, and no mistake, a white man through and through.

We kept expecting the Brits to come and relieve us. But they marched them up the hill and marched them down again, as the nursery song goes — neither hide nor hair of them did we see.

De la Rey offered us terms again. We sent back: 'If de la Rey wants our camp, why does he not come and take it? We will be

*pleased to meet him and his men, and promise them a great
reception at the end of a toasting fork. Australians will never
surrender. Australia forever!'*

*Finally I gather Kitchener himself heard that we were still
holding out, and at last brought 10,000 troops to our assistance.
I tell you, it is good to be in Pretoria again, to see real food and
have a bath and see women again, but none of the nurses can hold
a candle to you, Matilda my darling.*

*I have made good friends here. You would like them — well,
most of them, perhaps! I have to show you this country one day.
Till then, I am your ever loving,*

James

Matilda put the letter carefully back into its envelope. She'd
take it up to Drinkwater this afternoon, to show it to the old
man.

She guessed that he too checked the newspaper casualty lists,
looking for James's name. The letters from him were good, but
they took so long to get here, weeks and even months sometimes
after they had been written. The casualty lists were sent by
telegram, and were the only real news they had, apart from the
scanty war reports in the papers.

Slowly she had been accepting that they really would be
married, when the war was over. Perhaps, she thought, it was
easier to love James wholeheartedly when he wasn't here. It was
a future that just made sense. They would run the two properties
together. Whatever her doubts about James, she knew that she
wouldn't be able to bear seeing him married to another woman,
another woman ruling Drinkwater.

'Matilda.'

She looked up, startled. Auntie Love hardly ever used her name. Hey You sat at her feet, panting from the heat. He was grey about the muzzle now, an old dog with an old woman.

'Auntie, are you all right?'

Auntie Love had been silent the past few weeks, as though she had forgotten all her language. Matilda wondered if she'd had yet another apoplexy, for her hands were clumsy too.

'Go and lie down,' said Matilda gently. 'I'll make you some tea and toast. I won't burn it this time, I promise.'

Auntie Love shook her head. She held out her hand, and Matilda took it. The fingers felt like sparrow bones. Auntie Love began to walk, each step as slow as honey dripping into the bucket, her breath shallow.

She should be in bed, thought Matilda, or at least resting out on the verandah. But even now there was something that made it impossible to argue with Auntie Love.

Down the steps they went, then up the slope toward the cave. Hey You padded silently at her feet. They were walking so slowly it seemed a dream, the air shimmering heat around them. Nothing moved, except an eagle, high up above the cliffs, riding on the wind.

Step, step, step ... Auntie Love was even slower now, but she didn't stop to catch her breath. It was as though she knew just how slowly she must walk to keep going.

Up the path ... Matilda looked back. The house sat like a doll's house, its iron roof glaring in the sun. Her father's wooden slats had weathered to the same colour as the rocks.

At last they reached the cave. Here, finally, Auntie Love paused, looking down at the valley. Hey You lay down in the shade of a rock, as though he had been told to stay. Auntie Love let go of Matilda's hand, and bent down, into the darkness.

Matilda followed. Once again, inside, her eyes quickly got used to the dimness. She waited to see what Auntie would do. Was there something hidden here, something else her father had left that she hadn't found? Or did Auntie want to see the stream maybe?

But to her surprise Auntie Love moved over to the wall, the one where streams of light glowed through holes from outside. She bent toward the lowest one, and crawled inside.

Matilda watched her feet vanish. What if there was a snake in there or … She took a breath, and crawled after her.

The passageway was less than a yard — a wiggle on her stomach and she was through. She stood, light glowing around her, and caught her breath.

She was in a small chamber, a few yards wide, high and bright as though the walls themselves shone light.

It was impossible, like a small sun beneath the earth. And then she saw that the light came from more holes higher up in the cave wall. The real sun must be at just the right angle in the sky, this hour, this day, she thought, to shine down here, to turn the tiny cave to gold.

She didn't think it was coincidence.

She gazed around. The floor was mud, even now when the world outside was dry. Water must seep through the rock. Behind her, and on either side, the walls were hard as glass and pale, as though the rock had melted or water turned solid. But the wall in front …

There were handprints. Hundreds of hands, thousands perhaps, some almost hidden behind the white layers of rock, others fresher, as though they had been left yesterday, but when she stretched out a finger the image didn't smudge; it was smooth and rock-hard as well.

As she watched, Auntie Love bent down, and pressed her hand into the mud, and then against the wall. When she took her hand away another print was left, fresh and unfaded.

She nodded at Matilda.

'You want me to do it too?'

Another nod. Matilda felt the damp clay clutch her hand; she pulled it free of stickiness, then held it against the wall. The rock felt strangely warm — from the sunlight, she supposed.

She glanced at Auntie Love, wondering if there was anything else. But the old woman just turned and bent down, her breath coming in shallow pants, to push herself through the crevice.

It was strange being outside again. As though she had been hours in the cave, not minutes. The valley below looked brighter, clearer than she had ever seen it, the shine of tree trunks, the depth of shadows in the cliff.

My eyes are used to darkness, she thought, and knew that was the true answer, but not the whole truth. Hey You got to his feet, still panting, and pressed against Auntie Love's thin legs.

Auntie Love stared at the world again too. Suddenly she turned to Matilda. 'Rain coming,' said Auntie Love.

Matilda glanced up at the sky automatically. 'The ants aren't swarming,' she said. 'No flying termites either. And the kookaburras aren't calling the right way for rain.'

'Not rain now.' Auntie Love shook her head, as though trying to find the words she needed, then held up her hand, three fingers extended. 'After three cold time, rain will come. Good rain. Dry will go.'

Matilda tried to understand. Did Auntie Love mean the drought would end in three winters' time? But the drought was never going to end. All she had ever known was drought.

Impossible that the world could be green again, the dry rocky creeks covered with water.

Impossible for anyone to know that far ahead. She looked at Auntie Love, surveying the world, fragile but serene. No, not impossible for Auntie Love.

Auntie Love took her hand. Slowly, slowly they walked down the path, Matilda watchful with each step, in case the old lady slipped. Her breathing was shallow and even louder than Hey You's. Her hand felt almost like it wasn't there.

Matilda had expected to head for the house. But instead Auntie Love walked down the track between the cliffs. Were they going to the Sampsons' house?

Suddenly she turned the other way. She kept on walking, around the ridge and down the hills, toward the flat plain on the other side, away from the river, away from Drinkwater and Moura.

Is this where Auntie went sometimes? wondered Matilda.

'Auntie ... you have to come back to the house. Let me look after you.'

The old woman looked at her. She lifted her hand and stroked Matilda's cheek. She smiled, suddenly younger, her teeth strong and white. Then she put her hand down and she was old again, a hollowed gum tree with only a few green leaves, already turning brown.

'You stay,' said Auntie Love, to Matilda, not to the dog. 'Not come now. You stay.' She took another step, then looked back to make sure Matilda had obeyed.

She wanted to cry, 'Don't go. Don't leave me all alone.'

So many had left her: Mum, Aunt Ann, her father, Tommy, James so far away.

She couldn't speak. Auntie Love had so little strength. Just enough, perhaps, for what she was doing now.

The sun was high above them. The world was shadowless. The air shimmered between the trees. The land was dappled with leaves and bark, the thin shape of Auntie Love stepping slowly away, her dog at her heels. Matilda watched. And between one blink and the next, the old lady was gone.

She could run after her. But she wouldn't. Auntie Love had given her so much. She couldn't disobey her now.

So she waited, sitting down, her back against a tree, watching the ants trickle out from the roots then clamber back, taking tiny seeds into their nest. She waited till the shadows grew longer than the trees.

Something moved behind her. It was Hey You. The old dog climbed onto her lap and lay there, whining softly. Matilda hugged him, her tears wet against his fur. Finally she stood, and walked back toward the house. This time the dog followed her.

Chapter 49

Dear Matilda,

Well, we are a new nation indeed! My sister and I were in the crowd at the park to see Lord Hopetoun read the declaration from Her Majesty. We left here still in the dark, and I am glad we did, for I have NEVER seen crowds like this.

According to the paper there were troops of many nations, and a choir of 15,000 children — we were close enough to hear them sing, it was the sweetest sound that I have ever heard.

We were close enough to even hear some of the speeches, though the wind blew many of the words away. 'One people, one flag, one destiny.' Oh, my dear, I DID hear that, and as you can imagine the tears flowed. I was glad I had taken a second pocket handkerchief. I had my umbrella too — SO useful to keep a place in a crowd, especially if men have been IMBIBING. However I did not need it, for not only was the crowd well behaved but the sun shone the whole day through, as though it knew it was shining for our hopes and dreams.

*Later we watched the procession move through the streets, led by
a band of shearers. My dear, I thought of you of course, and of your
father. It was so RIGHT that the shearers led today, for indeed our
country has followed where they have led. After came brass bands
and our brave troops marching. We waved our handkerchiefs and
sang with the crowd 'Soldiers of the Queen' and I thought of your
gallant James too.*

*This evening the committee will have a small celebration supper
at our house. I have baked a Victoria sponge, and my sister her
Empire cake, with ingredients from every state of our fair land.
I DO wish you could have joined us, my dear. I wish that your
dear aunt could have seen this day.*

Your faithful friend,
Alice Thrush

-·#Ø©-

She hadn't gone to town for the Federation celebrations. She
couldn't, not alone.

Alone. She had never been so alone. She worked with Mr
Sampson, but had never been close to his family — they were
silent when she was near, unsure of her language perhaps, as she
was even more ignorant of theirs.

She had never really minded being alone at Moura before,
even though she'd been lonely. There had always been the
knowledge that at any moment Tommy might arrive, grinning on
his bicycle, that Auntie Love might appear, a gift of oil-rich grass
seeds, or tiny red-brown native cherries, or the long purple fruit
that grew up in the cliffs.

She hadn't realised how much she had always felt Auntie
Love's protection around her. Even more than Tommy, it had

been as though the old woman would always be there if she was needed.

She had told Mr Sampson what had happened. He had nodded, as though it was no surprise. He had probably guessed as soon as he saw Hey You at Matilda's heels. He added that he and Elsie would 'take care of things'. Matilda supposed that meant whatever their people did for a funeral. But he offered no more, and she hadn't liked to ask.

Mr Drinkwater had asked after the old woman a week later. Perhaps one of the stockmen had told him of Auntie Love's disappearance. She had told him briefly that Auntie Love had died, that she didn't know where she was buried. She hadn't added that she didn't even know if she had been buried at all.

She had never wanted to put flowers on Mum's or Dad's graves, or Aunt Ann's. The heart of them was with her, and what they had loved, not in the soil. Auntie Love was all around her too. But that didn't help the loneliness.

Sometimes the words of the song came to her. She wished she had never heard them, but everyone it seemed sang it now. *And his ghost may be heard as you pass by that billabong …*

I would even welcome a ghost's company now, she thought.

She sat on the verandah, fondled Hey You's ears and watched the sheep, nosing at the trough of cobs of corn. She should write to James, give him news of home, the Federation celebrations, the short storm three days ago. Tell him his father was well, the news James would expect her to send.

And yet … James wrote when he could, she knew, and in each letter he sent his love, talked about the time they would be together. But he was there, and she was here. Other men had come home, their days of war over, their duty done, though the Boers were a long way from beaten yet. But James had stayed.

At first she thought he was waiting till his father apologised, wrote and said he would agree to their marriage. Now she suspected that even if he did it would make no difference. James would stay till the war was won.

And I wait here, she thought. My whole life is waiting. Waiting for rain, waiting for James, for marriage and for children, waiting like women have always waited for their men to come back from war or shearing.

She stood up. She was sick of waiting ... and there were people she *could* see. Peter Sampson's new wife, only a few years older than her. She bit her lip. No, it would be too hard to be with newly married happiness.

Instead she changed into a wide-skirted serge skirt and white blouse, suitable for riding, with stockings and pantaloons and high-buttoned black boots, her straw hat securely attached to her hair with half a dozen hat pins. She saddled Timber, and made her way to town.

~❦~

The Doos' Prosperity Hardware Store now occupied two shopfronts, with big sheds out the back around a central gravelled courtyard: one shed for sacks of feed, another for hay, a giant bay of farm machinery, metal pipes and shelves of tools.

It was a long way from the vegetable cart.

Patricia sat at the end of the dark wood counter, adding sums in the ledger book, one eye on the baby sleeping in the pram, the other on the young man advising a local farmer about a new plough. She was dressed like any other prosperous shopkeeper's wife, in a dark serge narrow-belted skirt, a white high-necked blouse, and with her hair pinned fashionably about her face. She closed the book as Matilda came in.

'Nei hao, zai gun gei hao le ma?' Matilda pronounced the words carefully.

'Yai hao.' Patricia stood up and pushed the pram into the room behind the shop. 'Come. I will make tea.'

They sat at the oilcloth-covered table, sipping the strangely fragrant tea from the thin china cups. Patricia eyed her shrewdly. 'You have cried.'

'No. I mean … yes.'

'What wrong then?'

Matilda shrugged, staring into her tea cup. 'I think … I just need someone to talk to. Someone who isn't a sheep.'

Patricia nodded thoughtfully. 'I am not sheep. You come to sewing circle then. Every second Thursday afternoon.'

'Sewing circle?'

Patricia shrugged. 'We sew. Sometimes we pod peas. We talk.'

'And they …' Matilda wondered how to tactfully ask if the other women had invited her, a Chinese woman, to join them.

'They not ask me to come. Ladies talk about it by the counter. I say, I like to go. They do not know how to say, "We do not want you there". So I go.' She gave a slight smile. 'Sometimes they forget, oh, for maybe five minutes, that I am Chinese.'

'Then why do you go?'

Patricia put down her tea, and gazed into the pram. 'I go for my children. New parliament will pass law; no more Chinese come here now. So, who will my son marry? Lots of Chinese men, few Chinese girl. The women see that Mr Doo and Mrs Doo do not run opium den, do not white slave or worship idols. One day maybe they will see that my son is a man, not that he Chinese.'

'And by then you and Mr Doo will own half the town.'

'Oh yes. So, you will come to sewing afternoon?'

Matilda stood up. 'Yes, I'll come.'

'Good.' Patricia hesitated. 'People talk about a girl living alone too. Not talk so much if they meet her every second Thursday.'

'Patricia, will you teach me more Chinese?'

'No. Sewing afternoon is much better for you.'

They smiled at each other, understanding, as Mr Doo came in, and Patricia rose to make fresh tea.

—⁂—

She felt better, riding home, the sweet clop of hooves below her, the afternoon shadows turning the trees blue, the bare land gold, not brown. She had friends, her farm, the green valley with its silver water. Time would pass. One day she would have a husband too, and children.

She tried to imagine a time when she and James might live together, their children at their sides. She would never be alone then.

And if Mr Drinkwater never gave his consent? She and James would still have Moura, small though it was. And they could make it bigger ...

A realisation swept through her, so obvious she wondered why it hadn't occurred to her before.

She knew when it would rain.

It was Auntie Love's last gift to her. She believed in it like she believed the sun would rise every morning.

In three winters' time it would rain.

When it rained the price of land would rise. The price of sheep too. Wool fetched a good price now — armies needed uniforms

375

of wool, especially with fewer sheep after so many years of drought. But no one was buying sheep now, except to slaughter for meat.

She gazed around the paddocks on either side, worn to their bones by drought, the idea growing.

She needed to buy land now — all the land she could. There were plenty who wanted to sell, who had abandoned their farms years ago, given up hope they could ever make a block of thistles and cockatoos keep a family.

Then at the end of next summer she should buy sheep — hundreds of sheep, or thousands if she could manage it, with enough hay and grain to keep them for a month or two. Then when it rained and everyone had grass she would be rich. She could sell the surplus sheep to pay her debts.

Moura could be twice the size by then — or bigger yet. Moura could rival Drinkwater, even if it was smaller, its carrying capacity greater with pipes and water troughs, with irrigated forage crops.

She and James could build the farm up together, breeding the best sheep in the country. They might even buy Drinkwater one day, or most of it, if Mr Drinkwater never forgave them and left it to Bertram as he had threatened.

If Moura was bigger Mr Drinkwater would have no power over them at all.

How much money did she have? Enough to double Moura, at least, with land prices so low, as long as she didn't try to buy too much of the more expensive land along the river. Enough income to pay the interest on a two-year loan, if the price of wool stayed high. For the first time she hoped the war in South Africa would last long enough to keep her wool cheques plump.

But did banks lend money to women? Sometimes — but not

when they were nineteen. And not, she suspected, without a male guarantor, even with Moura as security.

Moura ... if she mortgaged Moura to buy land and sheep she might lose the lot.

But it *would* rain. Suddenly she knew it with an even greater certainty than she had felt when she'd heard Auntie Love's words. For the first time the land felt like it was waiting, the trees sitting dormant, not even blooming in the spring. Waiting, like her, for rain.

She pressed her heels into Timber's flanks, so that he broke into a canter. She felt like flying, but it wasn't fair to him to go any faster.

She would be twenty-one by the end of next year. Time enough to buy the land then, to buy the sheep, to convince James to act as guarantor for her, even if he had to send a telegram to the bank to do it next time he was in Pretoria.

It would be hard to convince him that an old native woman would be right about the drought breaking, impossible perhaps by mail. But she was sure he'd agree to guarantee a loan if she thought she could make it pay — especially if it meant they could outdo his father.

In three years she would be done with waiting. In three years she could be rich.

Chapter 50

JANUARY 1902

Dearest James,

I really hope that you are well. It has been more than six months without a letter from you. Your father checks the newspapers for casualties, and every time we are incredibly relieved not to see your name. I am sure your letters will arrive soon — the last lot arrived three together. I suppose the mail has to wait till someone can take it to a ship coming to Australia.

All is good here. Moura is officially 1,500 acres since the sale of McSweeney's place went through. It has been a hot dry summer — not even a storm for the past three months, but the spring still flows here in my valley.

You remember I told you about planting the spring wheat, one of Mr Farrer's new strains? It was hard keeping the water up to it, even with our pipes. Mr Sampson and the boys took it in turns to guard it day and night to keep the crop from the roos and cockatoos. Even I took a turn — you would be surprised how good a shot I can be, though the noise is really all that is needed to drive the roos away.

We do not have a heading machine, so could not harvest the grain to sell, but we made a good grain-rich first cut of hay, and stored it in the silo, then took a second and third cut of hay from it too, to store in the old shearing shed. The sheep are grazing the stubble now. It should keep them going for another week at least, before we have to start hand-feeding them again.

There is not much other news. Your father and I have an invitation to look at a new steam tractor next Sunday after church. It is strange, he almost treats me as your fiancée. Sometimes I think he is simply waiting till you come home to tell you he will accept our marriage. Other times I wonder if he just doesn't want to have his family's private affairs gossiped about.

The new Australian flag flies now over the Town Hall. I do not know if you will have seen it yet. It has the Union Jack in one corner and the Southern Cross. I liked the design with wool bales and gum trees best, but my father would have liked the Southern Cross. I remember him telling me it would be on our flag one day, and of how he told the time at night by watching 'the cross turn over'. Your father, though, thinks the official flag the best.

I had better take this down before old Jack passes with the mail or I won't be able to post it till next week. I will write again, as always. Stay safe, dear James.

With love,
Matilda

She held a candle in the embers of the stove for a moment, pressed a blob of wax onto the envelope to seal it, then wrote the address: *Lieutenant James Drinkwater, Her Majesty's Service, Bushveldt Carbineers via Pretoria, South Africa.*

She didn't bother saddling Timber — the big horse was quiet enough to ride just with his bridle, especially down to the mail box on the road. Hey You ran at the horse's heels, casting an expert eye over the sheep as they passed. His coat was strongly flecked with grey now, and he slept a lot of the time too, but still padded at her heels when she went out to check the stock, or worked in the corn or vegetables, unless she told him to stay. He was a shadow dog, accustomed to stay with his master, his loyalty to her now.

It was still impossible to realise she would never see the old woman again. Even now she would see a flicker of movement between the trees and expect the old woman to trudge out through the dust on those hard, splayed, ever-silent feet.

The road stretched white and dusty on either side of the mail box. Would she never see a speck in the distance that was Tommy, bicycling out from town? She had just shoved out the spider who lived in the letter box, and stuck up the stick that meant 'mail to be collected' when she noticed a rising cloud of dust on the road from Drinkwater.

A horse and rider galloped into view.

She pulled Timber around, and waited for the rider to pass. It was rare to see a galloping horse — cantering or trotting, but no one galloped for long distances, except in a race.

She recognised the man as he drew closer. One of Mr Drinkwater's stockmen, Henries, that was his name, a white man who she suspected was mostly drunk. He looked drunk now as he reined his horse up next to her. 'Miz O'Halloran!'

'What is it?'

'You got to come. Come now. Mr Drinkwater, he's taken sick.'

'You need the doctor!'

The man nodded, out of breath. 'Goin' ter get 'im now. But he wants you. Mr Drinkwater sez, tell you.'

'I'll go there now. And slow down. You want to kill that horse before you reach town?'

She dug her knees in to bring Timber to a canter, Hey You running at their heels. Half her mind was filled with worry for the old man; the other, unbiddable, was thinking, if Mr Drinkwater died now what would happen to his land?

She glanced down at Hey You. The dog was panting, but refusing to lag behind. She pulled her horse up, then lugged the dog up before her, holding him on the horse with one hand while she held the reins with the other. It was awkward, but there was no help for it — Hey You would run till his heart burst rather than be left.

Two stockmen sat on the verandah as she rode up the Drinkwater drive: unthinkable, at any other time — workers went round the back. But they were looking out for her. One took Hey You from her and put him down, the other took the reins.

She ran up the stairs, Hey You at her heels. She stopped when they reached the verandah. 'Sit. Good dog.'

'Good dog. Good dog.' The cockatoo danced on its perch. Hey You lay panting by the front door. I'll have to ask Mrs Murphy to bring him water, she thought, or will the stockmen do it?

She had forgotten to ask where Mr Drinkwater was. But the door to the parlour was open. He lay on the sofa, still in his work clothes, his boots on the floor beside him, his eyes closed. But they opened as she came in.

She kneeled beside him. 'What's wrong?'

His breathing was laboured, his face white under its tan and sweating with pain. He made a vague gesture toward his heart.

'I'm sorry. Don't talk. The doctor's coming.'

'Nothing he can do.' The whisper was almost too faint to hear.

'Shh. We'll see.' She pulled up a chair, sat and took his hands. They felt cold. Working hands, one nail black, the tip of his little finger gone, despite his wealth.

He took a deeper breath, and then another as though it hurt to breathe. 'On the table. Read it ...'

For a moment she didn't understand, then saw the mail on the table, a scatter of letters, a newspaper, one letter opened, good paper, written in a hand she didn't recognise, with a newspaper cutting next to it.

'My dear ... my dear, I'm sorry.'

Suddenly she knew. 'James?'

But there has been no battle lately, she thought, no casualty list. No telegram to say he had been killed or injured. No, she thought, I won't believe it. He's going to come home. I will marry him.

Tears slipped along the wrinkles under the old man's eyes. He shut them tighter, as though he could stop the flow.

'Shh. Lie quiet.' She forced herself to settle the cushions under his head before she took the letter and the newspaper cutting from the table. The headline stopped her before she could even glance at the letter.

Australian Shot by Firing Squad and then the smaller headline *Prime Minister Protests.*

Pretoria, South Africa
    At 6 a.m. Australian Lieutenant James Drinkwater of the Bushveldt Carbineers was shot by firing squad after a sentence of

death was proclaimed by a British High Command Court-Martial for having shot two Boer officers who had surrendered.

Her legs turned to water. She sat, staring at the paper, trying to make the words say something different.

Lieutenant Drinkwater had pleaded not guilty to all charges, claiming that he was following the orders of Lord Kitchener in shooting all Boer rebels who wore the British uniform. No such written orders, however, were produced at his court-martial.

Prime Minister Barton has sent a telegram to the British High Command expressing outrage at the trial and execution of an Australian without informing the Australian government, and demanding that a copy of the records of the court-martial, claimed to be missing, be at once sent to Melbourne. It is understood that even Lieutenant Drinkwater's family was not informed, despite a statement by the British High Command that a telegram had been sent to them.

Lieutenant Drinkwater is the son of Cecil Drinkwater, one of the largest landholders in the county of St Andrews. He was born in ...

She put the cutting down. Later she would read it again and again, trying to tease out whatever details she could imagine. Now the skeleton of fact was enough.

James was dead. Her heart seemed to thud the word. *Dead. Dead. Dead.*

She wanted to howl like a dingo, run to the river and scream and scream. She wanted to claw her face so that the physical pain would stop the pain inside.

She couldn't. She owed him more than that. But she couldn't stop the tears that ran down her face.

She glanced over at the sofa. Mr Drinkwater lay with his eyes shut, breathing shallowly, a pale blue ring about his mouth. She took the letter, then sat on the floor beside him, her hand on his cold one. I should have washed, she thought vaguely. I would have scrubbed my hands if I'd known that I was coming here.

But his hands were as ingrained with dirt as hers.

She lifted up the letter and began to read. It was written in good black ink, with the rounded neat letters of an expensive fountain pen.

Dear Father,

I am sorry to send you such sad tidings. It was with shock that I opened this morning's newspaper. I can only be glad that I was still at the breakfast table, and not at the bank.

I enclose the cutting for you, as I expect the newspapers will not reach you till the next week's post. I wish I could have brought this dreadful news in person, but as you will understand my social and business positions mean that I can no longer allow myself to be associated in any way with the name of Drinkwater.

James's actions have brought unspeakable shame on our family and will have extreme consequences both personally and professionally. I will not speak of the horror of James's crime, only that we must all act as fast as is possible to disassociate ourselves from him.

Florence and I have discussed this, and we think it best if I immediately take her family's name, and the name of the bank — Ellsmore.

It is unfortunate that the property, too, uses the Drinkwater name that has been so tarnished. Florence and I feel that it would be best if you came to us as soon as possible, so that we can bear this together. Drinkwater must be sold as quickly as it is practicable. I most strongly hope that you will take the Ellsmore name as well. After a suitable period you might buy a house near us and Aunt Ellen.

I am sorry to intrude on your grief with these details, but we have to be practical if any honour is to be salvaged from this debacle.

I have good friends in the leading business houses of this city, and I am sure that as long as we take steps at once to show we disassociate ourselves entirely from James, they will show sympathy and stand by us.

Florence and I will expect to see you on Thursday's train, but if you decide to motor instead please inform us by telegram. Otherwise I will meet you at the station. This is hard for us, Father, but we can weather it. Florence sends her love and utmost sympathy, as do I.

Your affectionate son,
Bertram

Her hand shook too much to hold the letter; she laid it on the floor. She wanted to stamp on it, to dirty it with her boots. But it was Mr Drinkwater's letter, not hers.

'Tear it up.' The voice was soft, but sure. It was as though he had read her thoughts.

'Are you sure?' She reached into her sleeve for her handkerchief, and wiped her eyes. The handkerchief came away dust-stained. The girl with the grubby face, she thought. Oh, James.

'Burn it. There are matches on the table.'

She found them by his pipe, struck one, then held the paper over the fireplace as it vanished in ash and smoke.

'There. Gone.'

His eyes opened. 'Tell me what you think.'

'I think that Bertram is a cockroach. I'd like to turn him into ashes too.'

A ghost of a chuckle. 'I am glad he isn't here then. We are in enough trouble —' He gasped: the pain was suddenly too much.

'Don't talk.'

'Must talk. Do you ... James ...'

'Do I think James was guilty? No! It says in the paper that he said he acted under orders. That's enough for me.'

She saw his face relax. She had said the right thing.

And yet ... the image came to her of James's eyes, so wide and blue, as he said, 'We didn't really shoot them, you know.' James, his confidence so great that he would think himself justified in any lie.

She sat for twenty minutes perhaps, as the old man breathed shallowly but steadily beside her. Mrs Murphy put her head in twice, but Matilda put her fingers to her lips.

At last he said, 'Will you stay?'

'Of course.'

'Not just tonight. I need ... the property needs —'

She wouldn't humiliate him by making him say he needed help. 'I'll be here.'

She waited till the doctor bustled in, his bag in his hand, then slipped outside to ask Mrs Murphy to get one of the men to drive her to Moura, to fetch her things — she didn't want a stockman rummaging in her underwear — and to ask Mr Sampson to come in the morning.

Some time later there would be time to cry properly, to walk this land that James would never see again, to shriek and scream her loss. Not now. Too many people needed her now. So did the farm that James had loved. The honesty of that love, at least, she had never doubted.

She poured herself a cup of dark brown tea from the pot Mrs Murphy kept always warm on the side of the kitchen fire, then went back to hear the doctor's verdict.

Chapter 51

MARCH 1902

Dear Mrs Ellsmore,

Thank you for your kind enquiry about Mr Drinkwater. He is improving daily, and able to sit up for long periods now, but I do not think he is strong enough yet to hear that Bertram will not speak to him unless he changes his name. It will only make him angry. Please, if you can, convince Bertram not to be so stubborn, and to see how much his father grieves. Nor will Mr Drinkwater ever sell his property to a stranger.

He and I remain proud of James, who fought bravely for the Empire that he believed in so much. We will acknowledge him with pride.

Thank you for your good wishes, and the kindness you have shown me in the past. I do understand how your first loyalty must be with your daughter now.

Yours sincerely,
Matilda O'Halloran

Mr Drinkwater peered at Matilda from his pillows. 'I'm going to live. For a while at any rate.'

Matilda sat on the chair beside his bed. 'That's what the doctor says. If you stay quiet there is no reason you shouldn't manage for years yet.'

He gave the ghost of a snort. 'Why not just say I'm mostly dead?'

'Your son is dead. You are alive. Be grateful for it.'

He stared out the window. 'James's death is my fault.'

She buried her face in her hands, not because she was crying, but because she couldn't cry. The unshed tears were almost impossible to bear. When at last she spoke her voice was muffled. 'You didn't kill him.'

'No need to spare a sick old man.'

She looked up, her face hard and white. 'I'm not sparing you because you're sick. You killed my father, as surely as if you shot him. I don't know how many others have died so you could get your way. But James — no, you didn't kill him.'

'If I hadn't forbidden your marriage —'

'Then James would have stayed, for a while. He was happy to be back and looking forward to working Drinkwater. But he loved *challenge*. Can you really see him staying here, working the land you've already tamed, while his friends were fighting over there?'

She took a deep breath. 'If you had been different — if you had really needed him, he might have stayed. If I had been different, a sweet girl like Florence perhaps, he'd have stayed to look after me.'

He gave one of his snorts, stronger this time. 'If you were a simpering miss he'd never have wanted you.'

'No. James died …' Her voice broke. She took a deep breath and tried again. 'James died for the same reason my father died. Because there wasn't justice to protect him. At least this time our government protested what the English did to James. Maybe one day there'll be new laws …'

She stopped again, gazed outside at the giant oak tree by the window, just starting to turn flame red. 'You know,' she went on, 'it's easy to think of the … the big side of this. Justice, equality. It's easier to talk of justice and new laws than to think of James.'

There was silence from the bed. At last he said, 'Perhaps that is why your father was so passionate about his union and federation. He could fight for one big cause, instead of face the hundred small ones.'

She looked at him surprised. 'You sound as though you liked him, even at the end.'

'What? Of course I liked him, girl. Knew him all his life.'

'But I thought you hated each other.'

'Hate? No, never that. We argued enough, though. Anger eating us both, at the end, till we both did things we shouldn't have.' He shut his eyes. 'I grieved for him, girl. More than you can ever know.'

His voice was growing weaker. She stood. 'I'm sorry. You need quiet.'

'No. I need to talk. I am glad that you forgive me, even if I can't forgive myself. Matilda, I can't run the place like this.'

She didn't bother to deny it. 'Your foreman?'

'Farrell? He does what he's told. If you don't tell him he won't do anything.' He added abruptly, 'I want you to stay.'

'What?'

'Look at me. I have given more than sixty years to this land,' he said fiercely. 'Now help me keep it until I die.'

She said slowly, 'You want me to act as your … your foreman?'

'No. I can hire foremen. As my partner.'

'A partner?' She sat down again. 'What sort of partner?'

'The same as you and Sampson. You carry out my orders. We share the profit.'

'That's not what happens with Mr Sampson,' she said dryly. 'He runs Moura as much as I do. We have different skills, that's all.' She looked at him for a few moments. 'I can run this place, but it would have to be my way.'

'Why did I suspect you would say that? We will argue it out, then, when your way isn't mine.'

'That is going to be a lot of arguments.'

He gave the ghost of a smile. 'I look forward to them.'

She looked at him consideringly, trying to see how it could work. Sharing the running of the place with a husband was one thing. Running it as a woman was another. 'The men won't like it.'

'Make them accept it. Move your things here, today. The place has been leaderless too long.'

'Stay here?'

'Yes. You can run Moura from here, but you can't run this place from Moura.'

He was right. The sheds were here; the men.

She knew she should ask for time to think it over. But suddenly it seemed right, as though she had known this would happen from the first moment she had seen the place. 'On one condition.'

'What?'

'I can't do this alone. I need Mr Sampson as foreman, equal to Mr Farrell.'

'Sampson? You can't put a native over white men.'

'Mr Sampson,' said Matilda.

He gave a silent laugh. 'It's up to you. But you won't get Farrell sharing his job with a native.'

She stood. 'We'll see.'

The men stood in the courtyard behind the kitchen. Mr Farrell's hat was pulled down low over his eyes, and his arms were folded; the six white stockmen and the eight dark-skinned ones were standing to one side. All were staring at her and at Mr Sampson, their faces watchful, their legs far apart in that instinctive male challenge. Two of them chewed tobacco, as though to say they didn't think enough of her to spit it out.

She tried to keep her voice steady. 'You have probably guessed why I am here. I'm sorry Mr Drinkwater isn't well enough to tell you himself. He has asked me to run the property as his partner.'

Mr Farrell raised the brim of his hat a little. 'Don't you worry yourself, miss. We'll do all right.'

Anger sparked at his tone, but she tried not to show it. 'I know we will do all right. But there will be changes. I may do things differently from the way they've been done in the past.'

'What sort of things?' Mr Farrell's tone had more resentment than interest.

'Lucerne down on the flat by the river, to begin with. We can use windmills to get the water up to irrigate it.'

'Spending the boss's money already, are ya?'

'Mr Farrell, are you prepared to work for me or not?'

'No. An' I'm not takin' orders from no native, neither.' He gestured at the cluster of men. 'An' they won't, neither.'

'They can speak for themselves. Well? Who is staying, and who is going?'

Mr Farrell looked at her with fury. 'No one is talkin' about goin'. But I ain't doin' nothin' without the boss's say-so.'

'I am the boss. So do you stay or go?' She could never let them know how nervous she was really feeling.

'Go,' said Mr Farrell. 'Me an' all the boys. You go tell the boss that, and see if he still wants you to give orders then.'

She knew she could use her anger as a weapon, as she had when the swaggies tried to steal her things, so many years ago now. 'You're sacked. Mr Sampson, you're foreman of Drinkwater as well as Moura now. Farrell, pack your things and be gone by lunchtime. You can take your horse,' she added.

She put her hands behind her back so they wouldn't see them tremble, and looked around at the stunned faces. 'Anyone else who doesn't like it is to be off Drinkwater land by sundown. And Moura. Anyone here tomorrow will be working for me.'

She turned her back on them, slowly, deliberately, her heart thudding like a horse's hooves, and strode away.

—⚬⚬⚬—

She was eating lunch in Mr Drinkwater's room when Mrs Murphy tapped on the door. 'Miss Matilda? Sampson wants to see you in the kitchen.'

'Mr Sampson.'

Mrs Murphy looked at her for a second, then nodded. 'Mr Sampson.'

'Tell him to come up here. Mrs Murphy … is your husband staying? I'd be sorry to lose him. And you.'

The big woman gave a small smile. 'Murphy will do what I tell him. We've got our house nice here now. I ain't leaving it. So he ain't either.'

'I … thank you, Mrs Murphy. Please tell him I'm glad. And ask Mr Sampson to come up.'

She looked back to see Mr Drinkwater smiling. It was the first real smile he had given since he had heard of James's death. 'You're enjoying this,' she accused.

'Life hasn't been this interesting since your father called me a pock-faced old, er … biscuit and tried to get every man on the place to strike.'

'My father was right.'

'And you're his daughter.' He nodded as the door opened. 'Sampson.'

'*Mr* Sampson,' said Matilda.

The old man looked at Mr Sampson assessingly, then nodded. 'Mr Sampson.'

'Mr Drinkwater.' Not 'Boss', Matilda noticed. 'Sorry you're crook.'

'Well?' asked Matilda. 'How many are staying?'

'Farrell, Grahams, Fat Harry and young Spud have left. The rest,' he shrugged, 'they're staying. For now.'

'Can we manage?'

'For now.' He hesitated, glanced at Mr Drinkwater, then back at her. He pulled a letter out of his pocket. 'This came for you. Peter brought it up from Moura.'

A once-white envelope, creased and stained. Her hand shook as she took it.

The handwriting was James's.

'Thank you,' she said quietly. 'I'll be down in a minute. Mrs Murphy will give you a cup of tea. We'll go through what needs to be done then.'

He nodded, and then shut the door behind him.

James. She held the letter against her cheek, forgetting where she was and who was with her. She opened it carefully, trying not to tear the paper, then remembered the old man in the bed. Another shock might kill him.

He was staring at her, his knuckles white as they gripped his sheet.

She longed to run with it, to read it herself first in private, over and over till every word was hers. Instead she forced herself to take the old man's hand and kiss his cheek before she began to read it out loud.

Chapter 52

Matilda my darling,

I am giving this to a mate who will see that it gets posted. The powers that be have forbidden my lawyer to pass on any personal messages from me to the outside world.

By the time this reaches you I imagine you and Father will already have heard of my death. They take me to the firing squad tomorrow. I am more sorry than I can say that you will probably have to hear of it before I can tell you what really happened. I know however that I can trust you and Father not to believe the worst.

The two Boers I shot were scoundrels, rotters of the worst order. They shot a friend of mine, the best mate there ever was, but worse than that: when we found his body it was obvious that he had been tortured, in the worst and most hideous ways. Both Boers I shot were dressed in British uniform, the better to trick our people into coming close.

I acted at that time, and at all times, on the direct orders of

General Kitchener to shoot any Boer found in British uniform. The British wish to have those orders forgotten now, to appease the Boer authorities and make peace. I and every right-thinking man of the Empire would refuse any peace with those curs.

Please tell Father that I doubt I will have a chance to write more than this one letter. Tell him I am sorry for the quarrel between us, and the way it has turned out, but tell him I could never feel any regret for my choice of wife. Tell him that I died with honour, an Australian to my heart and bone. Once I would have said 'an Englishman' but I hold the English officers in no honour now.

My darling, give my love to Father and to Drinkwater, and most of all to you. When they take me out tomorrow I will ask them not to blindfold me. Instead I will be seeing you, among the trees of Drinkwater.

All my love, my darling,
James

The letter sat in the pocket of her shirt — her new shirt, a man's shirt, not an old one of her father's. Ginger Murphy had driven her to town in the Drinkwater car.

She bought shirts and trousers from the men's section at the General Store, feeling eyes upon her, the first time she had dared to buy men's clothes for herself. The district was already gossiping about her. Let them gossip about this too.

Mr Doo himself took her order for three windmills, a dozen stock troughs and lengths of piping, all on the Drinkwater account. She reckoned she could double the carrying capacity in six months — if she could find the men to do the necessary work.

But even Mr Doo and Patricia said nothing about James or Drinkwater, though they made polite conversation about the lack of rain.

What could they say? *Congratulations on taking over the station from a sick, sad old man? We are so sorry your fiancé was shot as a murderer by the English?*

What words could anyone possibly have for what had happened to her or Mr Drinkwater in the past two months?

The stares bored into her all along the street. It was good to sit back on the leather seats of the motorcar, see the last of the houses vanish behind them on the road, see the familiar arch of branches out the window again. It was good to drive past land she had walked over herding sheep to be shorn or dagged, or to gather the ewes for joining with the rams, land she had watched with Auntie Love, seeing the seasons change. Not just the heat and cold but the more complex seasons that Auntie had shown her, each signalling itself in different ways.

This was her land, hers to understand with a depth that a man like Farrell could never comprehend; hers to plan for in a way that he would never have done. Her land …

She bit her lip. Would the old man still let her manage Drinkwater when he grew stronger? Or would he take back the partnership even sooner, if a lack of stockmen meant his sheep couldn't be dagged or even kept from straying over the Drinkwater boundaries?

We need more fences, she thought. I should have put in an order for that new barbed wire. More fences meant fewer men to herd the sheep, more control over joining, lambing.

Fences needed men to put them up.

The car slowed down. She peered ahead. There was a wagon in front of them — a familiar wagon. Mr Murphy began to swerve around it.

'No. Stop.'

He drew the car to the edge of the road, fifty yards past the wagon. Matilda got out, and waited for it to draw closer again. Two men sat on the front seat; three sat in the back on their swags.

'Mr Gotobed!'

'Hello, girly.' Mr Gotobed spat out a plug of tobacco. 'Bad do about your young man.'

'Man's got a right to shoot the enemy,' said Bluey.

Curry and Rice swung himself out of the wagon, and shook Matilda's hand, as though she was a man. 'I reckon that Kitchener ought to be strung up.'

Matilda said nothing. There *were* words to say about James, she realised. These words, said with understanding.

'Heard you were lookin' for stockmen,' said Mr Gotobed. 'Two quid a week and all found, right?'

'One pound ten shillings,' she said automatically, then, 'You want a job? But you're shearers.'

Mr Gotobed shrugged. 'Man gets tired of travelling from shed to shed. Time we settled down.'

'Man's got a right to settle down,' said Bluey.

'Told Tiger and Jessup here that your dad were a right good 'un. A union man to the end.' Mr Gotobed pulled out another plug of tobacco and began to chew it. 'I were union rep down on the Barcoo. They'll work where I work.'

'You understand that you'll take orders from me,' said Matilda slowly. 'And Mr Sampson is foreman now.'

'Old Sampson?' Mr Gotobed exchanged glances with the others. 'Well, he joined the union, didn't he? Stood up to old Drinkwater too. Reckon we can give him a go. Two quid a week, right?'

'One pound ten shillings. Ten pound bonus after shearing. If you've earned it. Fruitcake for smoko.'

'You're on,' said Mr Gotobed. He paused, 'That Mrs Murphy's fruitcake or yours?'

'Mrs Murphy's.'

Mr Gotobed nodded. 'No offence, missy ... er, Boss. But her cake's better 'n yours.' He tipped his hat to her, then climbed back into the wagon. He lifted the reins, then paused. 'I reckon your dad'd be proud of you.'

The horse began to walk, the wagon wheels rolling in the dust.

Matilda watched them go; the breeze was whispering the song again.

'*And his ghost may be heard as you pass by that billabong ...*'

The billabong was gone, but her father, it seemed, watched over her still.

Chapter 53

My dear Matilda,

We have DONE it! You should have been with us yesterday when we heard the news. Sister baked her sponge cake and I opened the last of the elderberry cordial and EVERYONE in the League brought a plate. My dear, we simply FEASTED, and sang songs and toasted the Uniform Franchise Act and Lord Hopetoun and DEAR Mr Deakin until quite ten o'clock at night, and then had to call taxi cabs to take everyone home, and it is quite a haul up the hill for the poor horses.

Just think, next year you and I and the women of Australia will actually VOTE for the next federal government! I have heard too that Miss Goldstein of the United Council for Women's Suffrage intends to stand for the Senate in Victoria. We of the Women's Temperance and Suffrage League must hurry and find our OWN candidates.

I will write more fully next week, my dear. Just now I am almost too excited to hold my pen to paper. It has been more than

twenty years of struggle, but we have DONE it! Now if we can
only win the crusade against spirituous liquor too.

Yours in all joy,
Alice Thrush

—§§©

The westerly battered the windows, and sent the tree branches rattling against the roof. The drawing-room candle flames flickered in the draughts. Matilda stood up. 'I'll get a lantern from the kitchen. You can't read in this.'

Mr Drinkwater nodded, his eyes on the ledgers in front of him. Every Friday they checked the accounts together, and she told him her plans for the next week.

He was able to come downstairs now, though any exertion made him pant. He drank more whisky than she liked — more even, she suspected, than he'd drunk before. He said it eased the pain in his heart. She suspected he drank to make other pain bearable as well.

He was quieter these days, and not just from his illness. He was also stooped so far over that for the first time he was shorter than Matilda. But she thought he was content.

She looked out the window at the sunset as she placed a lantern on a mat on the polished table.

Was she content as well? Happy, sometimes, certainly, watching the ducks rise off the river in the early morning light or the sheep trail back to the water troughs at dusk.

Fulfilled — yes, she felt that too. They'd be able to keep all the lambs this spring — less income to begin with but it would be more than repaid after next year's wool clip. Despite the worsening drought both the bigger Moura and Drinkwater were doing far better than any of the properties around.

Mr Drinkwater moved back to lie on the sofa. The wind's dust and heat were hard on him. 'So what's happening next week?'

She moved to an armchair next to him. 'I want to write to a new lot of agents in England.'

He looked at her under his bushy eyebrows. 'What's wrong with the agents we've got? They gave us the best price yet last year.'

'Nothing, probably. Wool of all classes has been getting higher prices these last two years, but those rams have made a real difference to our quality. It won't hurt to have two offers for our clips next year.'

'Very well.' He reached for his whisky. 'What would you have done if I'd said no?'

'Argued till you said yes. Anyway, you don't say no. You argue till I agree you're right.'

'A healthy discussion is not an argument.' He lay back against his cushions. 'First time I've really been able to talk about the place to anyone.'

She stared. 'Not James?'

'He was a boy. Then when he was a man ...' He looked down into his glass. 'We had three weeks, and one of them he spent chasing you.'

She had to change the subject. 'Your wife didn't talk about farming?'

He gave a bark of laughter. 'Margaret? No. She hated it out here. You asked once how many I've killed. Well, maybe she was one of them. Died when Bertram was born, but I think it was the loneliness and heat that killed her.'

She thought of her own mother. 'She could have gone back to the city.'

'I wanted my boys here, and she didn't want to leave them.'
His voice trailed off. 'Justice of a kind, I suppose. Now I have
neither of them.'

'Give me a mortgage on Moura.'

'What!'

She almost smiled. She could never have found a better way
to change his mood. 'I want to borrow 600 pounds. Moura is
worth that.'

'In the right hands,' he said slowly. 'I doubt a bank would give
you 600 pounds for it.'

'That's why I'm asking you.'

'No, it isn't. The bank won't lend to a woman. Not even you.'

'Mr Hawkins might, just to make me stop pestering him.'

'Possibly. But he still has to answer to head office. So, why do
you want 600 pounds?'

'To buy more stock next winter. More land.'

He stared at her. 'You're already running the biggest spread in
the district. How much land do you want, girl?'

She tried to find the words to answer. 'You built up this place.
I'm just running it — running it well, but it's still yours. Moura
— well, it was Dad's before it was mine. I want something of
my own.'

'Buying land with money borrowed from me isn't exactly
doing it on your own,' he said frankly.

'It would be if it was a real loan, with interest. I'll pay it back
within two years. If I can't, then Moura is yours.'

'You're insane. You can't make 600 pounds in two years.'

'I think I can. Well, will you lend me the money?'

'Only if you tell me how you think you can make 600 pounds.'

There was no point hiding it from him. 'The drought is going
to break next winter.'

'What?' He peered at her from under his white eyebrows. 'Why are you so sure it will rain, girl?' Then he added, 'Was it Love?'

At first she thought he meant 'love' — her love for James or the land. She had always thought of Auntie Love as Auntie, never Love.

She could lie or refuse to tell him. 'Yes.'

He lay back again, his eyes shut. 'Old Love, eh? Well, she'll be right.'

She hadn't expected that.

He shut his eyes, smiling at the memory. 'Love told me when it was going to rain way back in the forties. That was how I made my money, first time round. Every man and his dog was selling sheep for less than they'd bring as tallow. You could buy a farm for a spit and a handshake. Love said it would rain.' He opened his eyes. 'So I borrowed and I bought every sheep I could. And then it rained.'

She stared at him. 'Auntie Love made you rich?'

'No. That was the beginning though. The gold rushes sent the price of meat up, and then the war in Crimea meant the price of wool rose too. Money means you can make more money. But that first fortune — that came from Love.'

'She was your housekeeper?'

'No. She was my wife.'

She stared. 'But … but that's impossible.'

'Is it? Look in the desk drawer. No, not that one, the other one.' He took the sketch that she pulled out, gazed at it, then passed it back to her.

It was of a young woman, brown eyes, black hair in curls down to her shoulders, a white dress, with lace. She was beautiful, and there was a hint of the old woman she would become too.

'You were really married to Auntie Love?'

He lay back, his eyes distant with memory. 'Yes. Married properly too. Minister only came every three years back then. Didn't want to marry us. But in the end he did.'

Matilda tried to work out the dates. 'But she can't have been Bertram's mother, or James's.'

'No, of course not. I married Margaret, oh, thirty years ago now. Love left me after … after our daughter died. Just walked out one morning. Never said a word, then she was gone.'

She said slowly, 'Her people can't stay where someone has died.'

He stared at her. 'What?'

He looked out the window — looked further than that, she thought. 'I didn't know that. If only I'd known back then. I thought it was me, kept trying to think what I could do to get her back. I'd done things she hadn't liked …'

'Of course,' said Matilda wryly.

'I rode the entire district, day after day. Kept thinking for years she might come back to me. If she was alive she would come back, that's what I told myself. She'd just gone walkabout. Took ten years maybe before I gave up hope. I never saw her again till the day at your house.'

'The time she took off her clothes?'

'That was Love telling me who she was. We had a dozen years together, and every one of them I spent trying to turn her into a white woman. She wore dresses for me, but I never could get her into shoes, except on our wedding day.'

He smiled again at the memory. 'She wore them for me then. I found the dogs chewing them the next day. Love never argued. She just did things. If I went too much my own way she'd just go native on me. Take off her clothes, all except the ring I gave her, put on those necklaces of hers.' He shook his head. 'She was my wife. My one real wife. There has never been anyone like Love.'

He looked around the polished wood of his drawing room, the velvet curtains with their golden tassels. 'I wonder what life would have been like if I'd known. I'd have built another house for her. How could I not have known?'

Because you didn't listen, thought Matilda. Just like your son. You loved her, but you only heard what you wanted to hear.

'Mr Drinkwater, Auntie Love was still alive when you married again.'

'So I am a bigamist. Or was. Yes, my dear, I do realise that. Marrying Margaret was a risk. But not much of one, even with the faint chance that Love was alive. It wasn't usual for white men to marry natives, not legally at any rate. The minister who married us was long gone by then, safe back in England.'

'Then Bertram and James were bast—' She couldn't say the word.

His lips twitched. 'Biscuits? Illegitimate? Yes. It didn't matter. I can leave my wealth to anyone I want to.'

'So that's why you didn't want Auntie around,' she said slowly. 'In case she told anyone she was your wife. That James and Bertram were … illegitimate.'

'No. Never in a million years. Love would never have turned on me like that. I could have had her sent away just by clicking my fingers, and you know it. I just wanted her back. Can you understand? Never mind that the district had changed, never mind what my sons or sister thought.'

She remembered the strength, the love of the woman they had both known. 'Yes,' she said softly. 'I can understand.'

He was silent for a moment. 'I loved her,' he said abruptly. 'That's what I called her. Love. Half killed me when she left.'

He had named her after his own feelings, she thought. Had he even once truly understood hers?

'But you still went shooting natives?'

He snorted. 'That has nothing to do with it. Love wasn't some wild native. She learned English. Wore proper clothes.' He smiled. 'Most of the time.' He looked out at the hills again without speaking. At last he said, 'You looked after her.'

'She looked after me.'

'Maybe she needed that, more than the tending when she was ill. So,' his eyes were sharp and blue, 'you want to buy land from poor unsuspecting, er ... *biscuits* who don't know it's going to rain. And you want to buy us sheep.'

'Us?'

He nodded. 'I'll take the mortgage on Moura. But in return you'll buy sheep for me before it rains next winter too.' He smiled, almost the man she had first met, nearly eight years ago. 'I'm not too old to make another fortune, girl. Not yet.'

Chapter 54

Dear Mrs Hindmarsh,

I do hope you and your husband are well, and that it was a wonderful honeymoon. It still seems strange not to write to 'Miss Thrush'!

It was a lovely wedding. You looked so beautiful in your navy-blue dress.

It was strange being back in the city. It is bigger and dirtier and noisier even than I remember, but in a funny way smaller too. I have been used to hills and cliffs, and even the tallest building seems small after them.

On the last morning I took a cab and had the driver take me past Aunt Ann's house. It was good to see the garden so well loved. I think another happy family must live there now. We went past Mrs Dawkins's too, but she no longer lives there. Even the factory where I used to work is a mechanic's shop.

I also tried to find my friend Tommy's mother — she used to live only a few streets from the factory — but the neighbours said that she moved three years ago, and they didn't have her new address.

It was a little sad and strange to see the old places, but I still enjoyed the visit enormously, and bought a shockingly expensive hat. It is white with green and white feathers. I had myself measured for green shoes to match it, and a silk dress with a green skirt and white bolero, and an evening dress of grey silk shot through with blue. Hopefully the parcel will reach me any day now, so I can astonish Gibber's Creek with my city finery.

It is good to be back at Drinkwater. Mr Drinkwater managed with Mrs Murphy to care for him, and Mr Sampson of course is a tower of strength, but I think they were as glad to see me as I was to see them.

I have put the piece of your wedding cake under my pillow, as you instructed, but I am afraid I have had no dreams of the man I might marry.

I suspect I terrify most of the local men — there is a story that I once challenged a man to a bare-fisted fight and won, which I assure you is not true! But truthfully there are no men now you can compare to the men that I have known — except your Alfred, of course. Please apologise to him if I ever talked in his mathematics class, and tell him how useful I find the fruits of his lessons now.

I wish you both the very, very best,

Matilda O'Halloran

It was cold in the solicitor's office; the room's tiny windows didn't let in much sun. Matilda signed her name, then handed over the bank draft.

'Congratulations, Miss O'Halloran. Another farm to add to your ... collection.'

He doesn't sound very congratulatory, she thought. This was the fifth parcel of land she had bought in the last year, and each time he had looked gloomier, as though he could see one of his best clients going bankrupt.

She stood up. 'Will you remind them that they are welcome to stay in the house, as we agreed? I'll guarantee all jobs as long as they want it.'

Mr Reynolds shook his head. 'The family is glad to be free of the place, Miss O'Halloran. I can't blame them.' He opened the door for her. The wind gusted in, bringing dust and the scent of dried horse droppings and hard paddocks.

And you think I've lost my mind, thought Matilda, beginning to walk down the wooden footpath in front of the shops, her hat doing its best to escape down the road despite her hand and hat pins. She had been offered more places than she was able to buy, the last few months.

It had been the hottest, driest summer anyone could remember. Even the river stopped flowing, the pools between the sandbanks edged with algae. She had been buying hay for Drinkwater and Moura and her other properties since Christmas, then when there was no more hay to buy, corn, then even wheat.

And she was buying more land, when any sane person wanted to sell. Even Mr Sampson had shaken his head when she'd suggested he might buy land now, using his savings and part of Mr Drinkwater's loan. Not even the assurance that Auntie Love had said it would rain had changed his mind.

She'd felt guilty with the first purchase. But not now. The owners were too glad to get their money. And even she was beginning to doubt.

She bent down and turned the crank handle of the motorcar then, when the engine caught, ran quickly around to the driver's seat and let out the clutch. She'd taught herself to drive this summer, as a distraction from the drought. The problem with drought, she thought, turning the lever to edge the motorcar out into the road, was that there was so little to do. You fed and you watered and you waited.

The engine purred under the bonnet. Ginger Murphy had soon learned what a motor needed to keep it happy. Matilda still preferred a horse, but going to town meant wearing a dress, with stays and pantaloons and shoes with heels, and that meant a sidesaddle on a horse. The car was easier.

It was good to get out of town. Too many stares and curious looks. She hadn't gone to the ladies' sewing circle since James's death. What did she have in common with those women with their children and kitchens anyway? Let them gossip about her. Patricia needed to fit in. Matilda didn't. She'd wear her difference with pride.

A cloud of dust hung about the car. Half the trees on the Moura hill looked dead, the wattles already turning back to bark and dirt, the gums like ringbarked ghosts. But weather had killed these, not men. Even the trees still living were thin topped, as though they had cast off their leaves like unwanted petticoats.

The ground was bare; the tussocks had been nibbled to the ground. The sheep droppings, the leavings of roo and wombat and wallaby, had shrivelled into small pellets too, covering the ground instead of grass.

It's going to rain, she thought. It has to.

The days followed each other, the sun rising and setting in a haze of red dust, each so much the same it was as though the land had forgotten how to change.

There was no one to talk to, not about what mattered most. Mr Drinkwater too was watching the horizon, waiting for the strings of cotton in the sky that would say that rain was near.

She wrote another letter to Tommy. She had nowhere to send them to, but she wrote them anyway. She told him about the land, cracking as the last moisture was sucked into the sky. She told him about the sheep, sitting under the trees all day, waiting for the few hours of cool to eat. She told him she missed him. Then she burned the letter in the fire in the drawing room when no one was looking.

Stupid, writing to someone who could never read her letter. But somehow it filled a need she couldn't quite describe.

She had never heard from him since that last stupid quarrel on the road. When the shock of James's death had eased, she'd begun to hope that he might at least write her a letter of condolence. He must have read about the court-martial, like the rest of Australia. But even then there'd been no word.

When she read the newspaper sometimes she hoped she might see his name, and an article about the inventor of a moving picture camera, maybe, or a racing driver. But she had never seen him mentioned. He had vanished as surely as all the others that she had loved: more surely, perhaps, for she knew roughly where the others now rested.

Her only comfort was that it was unlikely that he had died. His mother would surely have written to her about that. None of her letters to Tommy care of his mother had been returned. Which meant that she — and Tommy — had received them, read them and chosen not to answer.

It hurt that he had never answered. It hurt even more to realise that she must have caused the pain that meant he wouldn't answer.

⁓✲◎

Hey You died. He had slept beside her bed at Drinkwater, despite Mr Drinkwater's insistence that sheep dogs stay outside. His body was cold and already stiff when she woke. He had died at her side, guarding her, she thought, just like Auntie Love.

She sat on the mat and held his furry body on her lap and cried. She hugged him as she never had when he was alive. He wasn't a dog for hugging.

Then she carried him downstairs.

⁓✲◎

July came, with frost that put white whiskers on the sheep droppings and dewdrop icicles on the new barbed-wire fences. The icicles melted at midday, the only moisture the land had seen for almost a year. Sheep, rabbits, wallabies and roos all clustered around the drinking troughs and river pools of Drinkwater and Moura. She even saw a black snake share a pool with a wombat and a dozen sheep, each carefully ignoring the other species. The wind blew hard and cold.

It didn't rain.

By August she knew she was going to have to sell some stock. She had borrowed another hundred pounds from Mr Drinkwater to pay for her share of feed. She couldn't borrow more. Even Mr Drinkwater, she thought, must be running low on funds. Had he had to borrow himself? She managed the property. His other investments were his own.

414

If she sold stock she'd need to let some of the men go too, and there were no jobs for them to go to. The land was running empty, dying for lack of rain.

I could offer to put them on board only, she thought. At least that way they wouldn't starve. A day's work a week in return for rations. They could pick up a few shillings maybe selling rabbit skins or koala fur …

She looked at the sky, the bare hard sky. I'll wait till September, she thought. On 1 September I'll have to tell the men.

There was no reason to deliver the meat to the house up in the gorge. Mr Sampson could easily drop it in. But she liked to go up there once a fortnight, to the gentler security between the cliffs.

Peter Sampson lived there now with his quiet wife, an ex-housemaid from the property where he'd worked before. She dressed and spoke like a white woman, and her skin was paler than her husband's too. Matilda assumed her father had been white, and her grandfather, perhaps. She and Peter Sampson had three children now, and had added a new room onto the house.

She hadn't minded — much. Thelma kept the house well. The vegetable garden provided for all of Drinkwater now — carrots and cabbages grew better here, sheltered from the winds.

Peter could have brought the vegetables down to Mrs Murphy too. But she wanted to be up here, remembering, as she pulled up beetroot, stripped the stalks of Brussels sprouts. Remembering Mr Doo, in the days when they shared almost no language, showing her how to dig the first small patch; Tommy, balancing the steel piping somehow on his bicycle, and his clever hands fitting it together; Auntie Love, showing her goanna tracks and so much else.

Auntie Love, saying it would rain.

Should I have believed you, Auntie? she thought. You seemed to know so much. But I was just a child when I met you. When you are a child you think the ones you love are always right.

And Auntie had been dying when she had made her prophecy. Perhaps this time even Auntie had been wrong.

The sack was full, enough vegetables for the next days' stews and roasts. She left it lying on the cold soil, and climbed up to the spring. There was no need to keep it swept clear of animal dung now. Peter kept the fence around it well repaired. But it seemed the right thing to check it every fortnight, a promise kept to Auntie.

The stock trough below the spring was full, the float valves automatically letting water flow when it was needed. Tommy's system still works, she thought. She wished she could let him know, could thank him for this gift, still giving so many years after he had left. The spring ...

She stared. For the first time in all the years she'd been here, the spring was overflowing, seeping down a few yards into the bed of tumbled rocks below.

Why? How? The spring was fed by the river underground. But there had been no rain to make that river rise for thousands of miles. The spring hadn't ever risen before, not even when the river flooded after the fire.

She gazed at the spring, as though it might suddenly go back to the barely visible seep it should be. But the trickle continued, clear and steady till it vanished in the rocks.

She looked up at the cliffs, suddenly eager. Were there other changes she hadn't seen? There was a new white streak down the rock face — a wedgetail eagle's nest? They hadn't nested last year — or she hadn't seen any young, only the two giant parent birds circling above the gorge. Had they decided that this summer would be rich enough in rabbits and baby wallabies to feed their young?

She began to scramble up the rocks, then stopped, and looked at the ground instead. Yes, there were wallaby tracks, heading away from water. She followed them, soon finding the faint path, the hairs under the rock that showed which way the wallabies had come. She stopped as soon as she saw them. They saw her too: heads up, bounding away swiftly up the cliffs, as though their feet could grip onto rock.

But she'd had enough time to see their bulging pouches. The wallabies too knew that it would rain.

She took a breath, and then another. She could almost smell it now: moisture, flying this way from the sea.

Or maybe it was her imagination. It didn't matter. For now she knew the rain would come.

⁓🐚

The termites flew in a black cloud above the homestead, swept up in the wind then fluttering down, losing their wings and crawling into every crevice, into her hair, her eyes, down the neck of her dress, till she finally retreated to bed and the mosquito net.

The wind blew even stronger the next day, the sky a hard tight blue. It was still blue when thunder rumbled, so deep, so far away it was as though the earth had spoken, not the sky. Lightning ripped the sky even before the clouds arrived — green clouds, edged with purple. And then the hail.

Hail so loud it shook the roof, thunder that made it impossible to speak. The earth was white in minutes. Mrs Murphy held a saucepan out of the door and drew it back after a moment. Inside were balls of hail bigger than walnuts, rippled a bluish white.

The hail piled up against the house, against the trunks of trees. And then it stopped.

The rain began with the dusk, so light at first it was almost mist, a thin moisture on her face. By the time they had eaten dinner it was washing at the windows. The wind blew again, suddenly now, splashing drops against the house, the gusts strong enough to blow the candles out. They went to bed by lantern light, having left saucepans around the house to catch the drips.

It rained.

The storm was over the next morning. This was simply rain; there was no wind, nor even a breeze. The leaves hung limply in the downpour as though too sodden to move. The grey streaks merged into one so the whole air was grey, the earth turning silver below it.

The ridges vanished behind a haze of white. Even the cliffs were hidden. The world was simply water. Frogs yelled in an ecstasy of fluid.

The dry stones down from the Moura spring became a creek rushing toward the river, and then a river and finally a flood, clear and purposeful, as if the water needed to find its way from the earth down to the river proper.

The river roared below the homestead, not the shout of a flash flood but a steady vibration you felt through your feet and skin, a noise that filled the air at first, then you grew used to it. This was how the world was now, with the song of the water.

It rained, and then it rained some more.

It was as if the world had held its breath until it was soaked with water. White tree bark turned grey, then green and orange, peeling off in giant sheets, and new leaves shone red. The sheep looked stunned, as though they had never dreamed of wet like this; it took them a week to learn to stand under the trees, their backs to the wind. Even then they looked offended, and not sure quite how to walk or lie with wet and heavy wool.

Grass grew overnight, and then the flowers. Mosquitoes bred in small black clouds. Suddenly the land was white again instead of green, but this time it was the heads of daisies, so pale yellow the colour vanished when you saw them massed. Tiny pink flowers on thin stems, lichen springing from the rocks. Orange fungi sprang from dead tree trunks. Other tree trunks turned from skeletons to bushes of growth by morning.

Matilda helped Mr Drinkwater out onto the verandah. They sat together on the chairs her father had made, which she had brought up from Moura when she moved here, looking out at the green acres and the sheep with lush feed they hardly knew how to eat.

There was no need to speak. The river said it all, and the seed heads on the grass. This was a gift from the land, the sky and Auntie Love.

Chapter 55

Mr Drinkwater still read the newspapers before the rest of the household, when they arrived with each week's mail. He liked the crispness of an unread paper. It was almost dusk when Matilda bathed and changed for dinner, then went down for the evening drink on the verandah with Mr Drinkwater: his usual whisky for him, Mrs Murphy's lemonade for her.

Mr Drinkwater wasn't down yet, but the papers lay on the table, with the whisky decanter, the jug of lemonade under a doily to keep out the flies, the glasses.

'Scratch cocky,' ordered the cockatoo. She obeyed, scratching his crest, making sure he didn't bite her fingers, checking he had plenty of the sunflower seeds he loved. She longed to let him out, but he was Mr Drinkwater's bird, not hers.

She sat and leafed through the newspapers — the damage from the October floods was being repaired (it was still strange to be in a world where floods happened at least each year); a record wool clip had been exported this year, and a new record for wheat export too; the story of the infamous Kelly gang was to be told in moving pictures. How strange it would be to see pictures that moved ...

She was about to pass over the social pages when a photo caught her eye.

Tommy. Tommy in a dark suit, with a waistcoat and gold chain. Tommy in a tall top hat. She pulled her eyes to the caption.

Inventor and businessman Mr T. Thompson and Mrs Thompson, attending the demonstration of the new lifesaving reel, invented by Mr Lyster Ormsby, Captain of Bondi Lifesavers.

Mrs Thompson. Not Tommy's mother, but a young woman, in a straw hat with daisies around the brim, and ribbons. She held Tommy's arm, as though she didn't want them to be separated in the crowd, that so formally dressed crowd standing on the sand in their silks and their stiff collars and their boaters and top hats.

Matilda put down the paper and stared out at the Drinkwater paddocks. So Tommy was married. Her Tommy.

Not hers. It hurt, as though someone had attacked her with a pair of shears, severing the two of them like fleece from a sheep. But it was stupid to feel that way. He had been gone for so long now. And part of her felt a strange gladness that he was happy. The man in the paper looked fulfilled.

And his wife ... She looked at the paper again. She was looking at Tommy, not the lifesavers, with a smile that said that Tommy was more important than anything else could be. A good wife, a suitable wife, a wife for a businessman and inventor, not a woman who wore trousers and yelled at her stockmen.

Maybe in a week or a month, she thought, the pain will go. James's death no longer hurt, except when she thought of the loss, his laughing brightness gone from the world. Tommy was happy. That was what mattered now.

Mr Drinkwater's stick tapped on the floor behind her. He lowered himself carefully onto a chair.

'So you saw it,' he said.

She nodded.

'Pity. I liked him. You'd have been good together, one day.'

'One day?'

'You were both very young, my dear,' he said gently. 'Yes, you were both enormously capable too. But both of you still needed to find the confidence to cope with each other's strength.'

'Well, I know who I am now.' She touched the photo gently, as though she was almost touching Tommy himself. 'I think he's found what he needs too.'

She folded the paper away, hoping he wouldn't ask for it again. She would cut the picture out, put it in Aunt Ann's Bible. It was the only picture she had of Tommy. It would hurt to look at for a while, but in ten years, twenty, when she was an old woman maybe, she could take it out and say, 'That was my friend.'

They sat watching the paddocks together.

'I still think I will wake up and see it brown,' he said at last.

She was glad to talk about something else. 'It was drought most of my life, though I didn't know it till I came here.' She forced herself to smile. 'I suppose if the drought had come any earlier I wouldn't have been born. Dad would never have got married.'

'If there had been no drought you'd never have come here. You're a gift to me from the drought. Like many things. The drought gave us much more than it took.'

She looked at him enquiringly.

'If there had been no drought there'd have been no shearers' strike, no union. If times had been better no one would have worried about tariffs between the states or kanakas coming in to take white men's jobs. Without all of that we'd still be a collection of states, bumbling along side by side. The drought gave us Australia.'

He reached for her hand, and squeezed it briefly. His hand felt papery, but warm and comforting. 'Maybe as you get older you see your gifts for what they are. You and Love and Drinkwater. The land gave me them all.'

It had been unfamiliar, at first, living without drought. This was a new land — one where rain came regularly, where grass grew and new trees sprouted. But the bones of the land she knew were still there under the lushness.

The older sheep grazed steadily, their noses down, as though each blade of grass was precious. Their lambs nosed out the best, most luscious tussocks, and played king of the castle on any rocks, no longer bound to spend all their energy finding food.

The roos bred faster than the sheep; the rabbits bred even faster — a sea of white tails raced away when Matilda took a lantern out at night. She read every farming magazine she could to discover a way of stopping them, and longed for Tommy's ingenuity so she could trap them.

She hadn't looked at the photo again. But she refused to envy his wife. If James had chosen South Africa, she had chosen to stay here, not run after Tommy's bicycle and call, 'Take me with you. I want to be with you.'

This was who she was.

The best way to trap rabbits, according to the *Agricultural Weekly*, was to make a V-shaped fence each side of the most distant waterhole or trough, where the rabbits would gather to drink at night. Pull a gate across the top of the V and you had them.

The new fencer was waiting for her in the kitchen, eating a slice of Mrs Murphy's date loaf and drinking tea from a mug — no matter what Matilda said Mrs Murphy believed that china cups were strictly for those who had 'drawing room' tea. He stood up as Matilda came in.

'Ma'am.'

She smiled. It was a nice change from 'Mornin' Boss'. He was a good-looking young man too, if you ignored the shaggy beard. She felt his eyes assessing her, and flushed slightly. The Drinkwater workers were used to her trousers now, but newcomers still found men's clothes on a woman a shock.

'Mr Gotobed says you've been working down the Mallee.'

'Yes, ma'am,' he said again.

'Mr Gotobed will show you where we've pegged out the fence line. Should be easy work till you come to the ridge — it's shale there: crowbar work, I'm afraid.'

The young man gave a pleasant grin. 'I don't mind crowbar work, ma'am.'

'Good. Everything all right in your quarters?'

'Yes, ma'am. Never seen men's quarters with a bathroom before.'

It had taken three days of arguing with Mr Drinkwater before he'd agreed to put that in, though Matilda suspected he'd held

424

out for an extra day just for the pleasure of showing he was still boss too.

'I'll let you get on with it.' She turned to go.

'Ma'am?'

She looked back. 'Yes?'

'The men say there's a dance in town this Friday night,' he said slowly.

'There usually is.'

'Are you going?'

She shook her head, smiling. 'No.'

'You should go, miss.' Matilda looked at Mrs Murphy in surprise. The older woman smiled at her from the stove where she was stirring the Irish stew for lunch. 'Do you good to have a night out, miss.'

Matilda was silent. Mrs Murphy usually never offered an opinion — she kept them for her husband and sons when she went home at night. But Matilda knew what she was really saying. It was time to leave the ghosts behind.

I like my ghosts, she thought. James, Dad, Auntie Love, Mum, Aunt Ann … They'd approve of who I am now.

But it had been months since she had gone beyond the Drinkwater–Moura boundaries except for business. The men she had loved were gone, in their different ways both lost to her. She wasn't sure she wanted to spend time with another man — not yet. But it *was* time to join the world again. Every one of her ghosts, she realised, would probably tell her: 'Go and dance.' What harm was there in going into town to dance?

'All right. I will.'

The young man grinned again. 'Grand. I'll be waiting for you at five o'clock.' He headed out the door.

Matilda glanced at Mrs Murphy. Had he misunderstood, thought that she had agreed to let him 'take her to the dance' instead of simply driving in together? No, impossible. She was the boss. He was just being kind.

Mrs Murphy smiled at her Irish stew.

--※◎

She dressed carefully in a gown she hadn't worn since Christmas: not an evening dress with a low neck, the sort she changed into these days for dinner with Mr Drinkwater, partly to give the old man pleasure and partly because despite her comfortable work clothes she also loved the feel and drape of silk, of satin and brocade. I'm my mother's daughter too, she thought.

But ordinary townsfolk didn't wear silk dinner dresses. Tonight's frock was pale blue muslin, its bodice embroidered with darker blue flowers, with lace at the neck and in three tiers low on the skirt. A pretty dress, she thought as she secured her hair with the extra pins needed for dancing, but not one that called out, 'Look at me! I'm the rich Miss O'Halloran of Drinkwater.'

She glanced down at her jewelled timepiece on its silver chain. Mr Drinkwater had given it to her for her last birthday. Five o'clock. She hurried down the stairs, then into the drawing room to kiss the old man's bald spot. 'I won't be late.'

'Be as late as you want,' he said mildly. 'I'm glad you're going out, my dear.'

So he, too, thought she let her ghosts rule. She smiled, and walked out onto the verandah.

The buggy was waiting in front of the steps. The young man stood next to it. Matilda stared at him in dismay.

The shaggy beard was gone. His skin looked pale and slightly raw where he had shaved it too close. His hair was trimmed, and slicked down with hair oil. Even his suit looked new.

No, she thought. I can't do this. Can't give a man hope that I would be interested in someone like him. Not because he wasn't rich, but because even in the short time she had known him she'd seen he simply didn't have the strength, the dreams, the … the backbone of the men that she'd loved and had admired.

He smiled at her, and held out his hand to help her up into the buggy. If the two of them appeared at the dance like this the gossip would be all over the district by smoko tomorrow.

'Hoy, Boss, wait for us!'

She sighed with relief — or would have if her stays had let her — as Mr Gotobed limped around the corner of the house, Curry and Rice clicking the wagon reins behind him.

'Hey you, young Rogers. Buggy ain't no use for a dance. How's we all goin' ter fit in?' Mr Gotobed bowed low to Matilda. 'Yer look as pretty as a peacock with two tails, Boss. Ma'am, yer carriage awaits yer.'

'You're a darling,' said Matilda. She caught his eye. He had known exactly what was going on, and exactly how to save her too.

She smiled at the young man, safe now. 'Come on. We don't want to be late. You're looking grand tonight,' she added. 'I'm sure every girl in the hall will want to dance with you.'

'I bags the first dance with you, Boss,' said Mr Gotobed.

'Of course,' said Matilda.

Chapter 56

FEBRUARY 1910

To Mr Smith
Elder and Sons
Sydney

Dear Mr Smith,
   *Having read of the new electric shearing device invented by
Mr Faulkner, I would be glad if you could let me know the
specifications and cost of such a machine. If the price is reasonable
I would like to order sufficient for 30 stands for Drinkwater.*

Yours sincerely,
Miss M. O'Halloran

What would my father have thought of an electric shearing
machine? she wondered, licking the envelope. What would he
have thought of the coal strike, crippling transport across New
South Wales and Victoria, stopping even steamships carrying
wool? The miners wanted more money and safety underground.
She wanted her wool to get to England ...

So much had changed, she thought, running her eyes over the newspaper. Women lifesavers, women telegraph operators, wireless transmissions, old Queen Victoria dead and King Edward on the throne, cable trams and telephones, aeroplanes.

So much was still the same too — Mr Canning the Central Australian surveyor defending his chaining of the natives he used to establish his route across the country; the New South Wales government's new law threatening twelve months' prison for anyone who threatened 'essential services' with a strike; children still slaved in factories, some for no wages at all.

It was Wednesday, mail day, and, as well as the latest papers, old Jack had brought the post from town, which included a letter from Mrs Hindmarsh, a box of vegetable seeds and a dozen new apple trees that Matilda had ordered from Green's catalogue for the Drinkwater garden, a copy of *The Bulletin*, along with the sacks and tins and boxes of groceries for the rations that were part of the men's wages.

Matilda had hauled old Bluey out of his bunk — he'd lie there all day drinking rum for his arthritis if no one pushed him out into the sunlight — and given him the trees to plant and promised to read him the new union monthly after work. Then she had checked the stores were safely locked in the farm shop, and the seeds in their rat-proof box for spring planting, and given Mr Drinkwater the newspapers.

Now she sat at the table in the drawing room, while he lay on the sofa. He was no weaker these days, but no stronger either. He had begun to greet her at breakfast every morning with, 'Another morning and I'm still alive.'

He had withdrawn even further from the world, not even questioning her decisions for the farm and most times not even showing curiosity. She missed their discussions, his insights.

But he still enjoyed the papers every week, the brief window on the world.

Now he peered at her over his broadsheet. 'Says here that there's another entry for the 5,000-pound competition to build an all-Australian flying machine.'

Matilda looked up from the account book. 'What's his name?'

'John Duigan.'

'Oh.' She had thought it might be Tommy. There had been no other mention of him in the newspapers. 'Inventor and businessman' could have meant anything. It's an exciting time for men like Tommy, she thought, the world of horses and steam giving way to machines and electricity, humans taking to the sky as well as the sea and land. 'Any other news?'

'A concert in town. Excerpts from a thrilling performance in *Madam Butterfly*.' He looked at her over his glasses. 'Are you going?'

She smiled. 'No. The only butterflies I'm interested in are the ones laying caterpillar eggs on my feed turnips.'

'There are other reasons to go to a concert,' he said mildly.

'I know. But none that concern me.'

'My dear, there is more to life than turnips. Or looking after an old biscuit like me.'

She put down the account book and smiled. 'I've grown fond of the old biscuit.'

'But still … I wouldn't expect you to move out if you married,' he said suddenly. 'In fact, the opposite.'

'You want me to marry a good farm manager for you? Sorry, Mr Sampson is already married.'

'I would quite like a child about the place,' he said softly.

She walked across and kissed him. 'I'm sorry. But no one has asked me lately.'

'You terrify them,' said Mr Drinkwater dryly. 'There is a rumour that when that nice land surveyor took you to the Mayor's Gala you fixed the engine when his motor broke down.'

'Someone had to. He didn't know a carburettor from a radiator. Who told you that?'

'Mrs Murphy, who got it from her sister Sarah.'

'Has Mrs Murphy told you anything else?'

'Just that one of the new hands has been complaining about you appearing in the shearing shed while they're dagging the sheep.'

'It's my shed — sorry, your shed. I'll appear when I want to.'

'No women allowed.'

'I'm not a woman. I'm the boss.'

'That,' he said softly, 'is what I'm afraid of.'

'I'm sorry.' She smiled at him ruefully. 'I can put on a skirt again. But I just can't see myself ever giving control of the place to a man.'

'That is evident.'

She said nothing, looking out the window. She could see the shearing shed from here, and beyond the garden the pale green winter grass and the darker patch of the experimental turnip crop. She wouldn't plant them next year; the sheep weren't really fond of turnips.

If James had lived, would she have sat here sewing while he gave orders to the men?

'That new man down in the shed says sharp-tongued women need a man's belt to keep them in line.'

She grinned. 'Did he now? Mrs Murphy tell you that too?'

He nodded. 'Got it from her husband, who got it from Mr Gotobed. Where are you going?'

Her grin grew wider. 'To see Mrs Murphy.'

Mrs Murphy was rolling pastry at the big wood table. Matilda had bought a new stove for her last year, a double-sided one like the model Tommy had invented, though this was more than twice the size of the one in her old house.

'Mrs Murphy?'

'Yes, Miss Matilda?'

'I don't suppose you have any sheep tongues?'

Mrs Murphy looked surprised. 'I do indeed, miss. I was going to cook them in a nice white sauce for lunch. Got them all chopped, soaking in vinegar.'

'Cold lamb and salad will be fine.' Matilda swept the tongues out of the meat safe and into a bowl, then marched down the back steps and out toward the shearing shed. The dogs got to their feet, and followed her.

The shed quietened at the sound of her boots on the steps. 'Ducks on the pond,' yelled someone, the classic call if a woman invaded the shed.

'Quack,' shouted Matilda loudly. She strode inside. The men straightened, gazing at her, shears in their hands, sheep poised between their knees, the classer staring at her from the bins, the tar boy almost dropping his bucket in surprise.

'You. Come here.'

The man let go of his sheep, his mouth dropping open. He walked toward her.

'Heard you don't think much of a woman with a sharp tongue.'

'I ... er ...' stuttered the man.

'I've got a present for you,' said Matilda sweetly. She upended the bowl on the man's head. The squishier bits of tongue cascaded off his head and onto his shirt. He gave a yell as the vinegar stung his eyes and the grazes on his arms. 'Extra vinegar, just to make it sharp for you.'

She gazed around. 'Anyone else want a serving?'

No one answered. The men were silent as she strode out. She was halfway down the ramp when she heard Mr Gotobed's voice raised in song. '*Waltzing Matilda, Waltzing Matilda* …'

From anyone else it would have been an insult. From him it was a compliment — and a way of decreasing the embarrassment for a man bested by a woman. The other voices joined in.

'*You'll come a-waltzing Matilda with me* …'

Suddenly she began to laugh. She was still laughing when she heard the motorcar.

The car was almost at the house when Matilda emerged from the garden — a shiny, big green one. Her first thought was that it was Tommy — he always loved green. Why shouldn't he bring his wife back to the place he'd lived for years? Take her to meet an old friend too … She broke into a run as the dogs began to bark.

The chauffeur was just closing the back door. A woman already stood beside the car, wearing a tight, pale cream skirt with an even tighter long blue jacket and a wisp of a hat with feathers. Two children stood either side of her, perhaps eight and ten years old, the girl dressed identically to her mother (Poor child. How could you jump — or even walk — in a skirt like that? thought Matilda.) and the boy in a blue and white sailor suit, with a straw hat.

A man got out of the other passenger's seat. Even from behind she could see that he wasn't Tommy, but he was familiar too. He was tall, in a dark suit and a top hat; his back was to her as she rounded the house.

Matilda stopped, her breath frozen. James!

Thoughts tumbled through her head. His body was never shipped home; no one trustworthy had even seen it. Had it been a mistake all along? He had left the army, married in South Africa, been too embarrassed to let her know?

Even as she thought it she dismissed it. James would never have lacked the courage to tell her, or his father, that he had married someone else. Then the man turned and she saw that it was Bertram.

He looked older, and his mouth was firmer than it had been when she'd seen him last. This was a man used to being in control. He lifted his hat politely. 'Good morning, Miss O'Halloran.'

'Good morning, Mr … Ellsmore, isn't it?'

His mouth tightened. Of course she knew the name that he had taken. But he nodded politely. 'Miss O'Halloran. You know my wife, I think?'

'We have never met properly. Good morning, Mrs Ellsmore.'

The woman inclined her head. 'Our children, Cecil and Ellen. Say good morning to Miss O'Halloran, children. Mr Drinkwater's grandchildren,' she added carefully. She met Matilda's eye, then looked warily at the dogs, sitting at Matilda's feet and staring at the newcomers.

'Good morning, Miss O'Halloran.' The two children looked curious, and excited too.

She forced a smile. 'Welcome. Don't worry,' she added to the children, as Dusty and Splodge — Hey You's sons, she hoped, thinking fleetingly of the old dog buried under the oak tree —

sniffed at the children's neat, buttoned boots. 'The dogs don't bite. Well, only rabbits.'

Bertram stiffened. 'I do not think my father's grandchildren need you to welcome them to my home.' He gestured to the chauffeur to take the car around the back and unload the luggage.

'You're staying? But please, use the front door,' she said to the chauffeur. 'We only use the back to bring in the meat now.'

The man looked from her to Bertram. 'The back,' said Bertram. The chauffeur nodded, and slipped into the driver's seat to drive the car around the back.

'Scratch cocky!' yelled the cockatoo.

Bertram and Florence led their children up the verandah steps.

She could have followed them. This was her home now, after all. But the reunion between Mr Drinkwater and his son should be private. The first time he met his grandchildren too.

Her heart ached. By now she might have had children of her own, even the same age as these. Children to show the mysteries of the river in the cave, how black swans flew south after the rain. Children to read a bedtime story to, instead of reading about union meetings to a mob of shearers ...

She turned, and went in the kitchen door. 'There'll be four more for lunch, Mrs Murphy. Mr Bertram and his wife and children and the chauffeur as well — I don't know his name. I suppose he'll eat in here.'

Mrs Murphy nodded. 'I always keep the spare rooms made up, miss. I'll ask a couple of the wives to give me a hand for a few days. I'd better take some water up to their rooms ...' She hesitated. 'Do you know how long they will be staying, Miss Matilda?'

Matilda shook her head. 'I'm sorry about the tongues for lunch. Can you manage?'

'Plenty of cold lamb, and there's lettuce hearts for a salad and orange slices and pickled cucumbers and beetroot. I'm doing a cauliflower cheese, and there's rice shape with bottled plums for afters.'

'Wonderful. You're a gem, Mrs Murphy. I hope this won't be too much work for you.'

'Bless you, love, I don't mind. Plenty to give me a hand if I need it.' She looked at Matilda shrewdly. 'Hope Mr Bertram isn't going to make trouble, miss.'

No need to say what the trouble might be. Matilda nodded, and climbed the stairs to her room, to change into a dress … she sighed … and stays.

Lunch was stilted. Mr Drinkwater looked pale, his breath short as he sat at the head of the table, but his eyes were soft when he looked at his grandchildren, who were politely chewing their cold lamb. Florence had sat in Matilda's usual place at the other end, as though as the wife of the only son it was her right. Matilda supposed it was.

'How was the wool clip this year?'

Matilda opened her mouth to reply, then closed it. Bertram was carefully addressing all questions about the farm to his father. There was no point forcing a quarrel now.

'Excellent.'

Matilda noticed he gave no details. Mr Drinkwater's mind was still sharp, but he had lost his memory for figures.

Bertram nodded. 'The pastures are very green.' He looked

carefully down at his plate. 'We will have to visit more often. The children need to learn about the place that will be theirs one day.'

Matilda drew her breath in sharply. So it was out — the real motive for coming here today. To make sure that an aging father still left his property to his son — or if not, to his grandchildren — instead of to the interloper, the girl with the grubby face.

Mr Drinkwater smiled at the girl and boy. 'Do you want to be farmers?'

The girl — Ellen — looked up. 'I want to be an engine driver.'

'Nonsense,' said her mother. 'Girls don't drive engines.'

'Cecil?' asked Mr Drinkwater.

The boy hesitated, glancing at his father. 'Yes, please, sir.'

'You don't sound convinced,' said Mr Drinkwater dryly.

The boy looked from his grandfather to his father, then back again. 'I want to fly an aeroplane.'

Mr Drinkwater laughed, clearly delighted. 'I doubt you get your sense of adventure from your father.' He put his crumpled napkin back on the table. 'There will be enough money for you to buy your own train engine if you like, my dear, and for you to have your aeroplanes. Now if you don't mind, I will lie down a while. We will meet again before dinner.'

Bertram looked annoyed. 'You may leave the table,' he said to the children. 'Mrs Murphy will give you your pudding in the kitchen.'

Mr Drinkwater watched the children leave the room, then stood up. Bertram stood too.

'Then you intend to leave the farm to the children?'

Of course he will leave his land to his grandchildren, thought Matilda, trying to ignore the stab to her heart. But don't press him now, you slug. Let him think you've come because you love him — love the land — not just for money.

Mr Drinkwater looked at his son kindly. 'I hope their inheritance will be enough to establish them however they would like. But I'm afraid there is no farm to leave them.'

'No farm? Father, really —'

'I sold Drinkwater to Miss O'Halloran last year. Now if you'll excuse me.' He took his cane and walked from the room.

Matilda sat in shock for a second. She glanced at Bertram. His mouth hung open like a fish. Florence too looked stunned.

Matilda stood too. 'I need to check down at the sheds.'

She didn't, but it was an excuse to go, to let Bertram and Florence absorb the news in private. She also had to speak to Mr Drinkwater if he wanted her to keep up this pretence. She heard Bertram's voice rise in protest as she shut the door.

~ ❦ ~

She wasn't going anywhere, though, until she had changed. How did women manage to even breathe? she thought crossly, trying to open the hooks. A knock sounded on her bedroom door. She grabbed her dressing gown and pulled the belt tight, and opened it.

It was Mr Drinkwater. She held the door open further and he limped in then lowered himself into the armless chair by the dressing table. 'You looked very nice at luncheon.'

She grinned. 'I wasn't going to appear before your family in trousers. Not at the table, anyway.'

'You are my family,' he said.

Tears stung suddenly. 'I'm glad.' She bit her lip. 'Thank you for what you said to Bertram. It'll stop him countermanding my orders while he's here. But I do understand that Drinkwater will go to your family. I've always known.'

'As I said, you *are* my family.'

She stared at him. 'I don't understand.'

He smiled. 'I think by now Drinkwater is as much yours as mine. I got the land by squatting here, clearing the trees, making it my own. You've made it yours too.' He shrugged. 'It's time we made it legal. I could leave it to you in my will, but Bertram would contest it, and might well win. It is best to sell it to you now. Don't worry — the price won't be anything you can't afford. You've more than earned part of this place already. I'll send Murphy into town to tell the lawyer to draw up the papers. We'll have it settled by the end of the week.' He looked at her sardonically. 'I expect I shall survive till then.'

It was almost impossible to speak. Impossible even to comprehend it yet. 'You … you old biscuit. You'll live to be 150.'

He stood, then stepped over to kiss her cheek. 'I think parts of me will have worn out before then. But thank you for putting up with Bertram and Florence, my dear. He is a fool. He always was. But he is still my son. And the children.' His face softened. 'They are darlings, aren't they? And they shall certainly have enough to buy their engines and their aeroplanes, or whatever else they want that their father thinks they shouldn't have.'

'There is no way I can ever thank you,' said Matilda softly. 'And our partnership stays. Half of all profit for each of us.'

'Of course. Where would you be without my guidance? I should miss our arguments, as well.'

He met her eyes. 'You know, even today, if James was alive, I would be against your marriage. But long before he died you were closer to me than I could have imagined any daughter being.'

He let himself out of the room, shutting the door behind him. Matilda sat, her stays still half untied. It was a while before she realised she was crying.

Chapter 57

Dear Matilda,

I do hope you will join us for luncheon on Saturday, to celebrate the engagement of our son George to Miss Helen Underhill, of Melbourne. There will be tennis afterward, if you would care to play.

Your sincere friend,

Patricia Doo

So George was engaged. Matilda put the thick cream invitation down on the verandah table. She hoped his fiancée was a nice girl. A strong girl too, who could cope with the problems her mixed marriage would bring. But money eased problems. She smiled at the formal wording of the note — one of Patricia's children must have written it — and at the pleasure it would be to see her and her husband, to play tennis on their new court, to wear her tennis dress, with its daring ruffled skirt inches above her ankles.

There was a tennis court next to the church now too, so the churchgoers could play after services each Sunday, the men and women taking it in turns to use the parish hall to change out of their Sunday-best clothes.

Strange to remember the days when there had been a service only once every two months, when town and church had been impossibly far away for most of the district. Now there were a fair few cars, and many bicycles, and more horses than ever before now there was grass to feed them. Almost everyone had some form of transport. The desperate isolation that so many women and their children had faced was gradually ending, for most at least.

She had been dreaming of the past last night; she felt bleary today. She and Tommy had climbed the path to the cave together. She was twelve again, and he fifteen. He had been flying a kite, a giant white one that soared above the valley, which then turned into a giant white eagle that had flown off toward the river.

Nonsense, like all dreams. Tommy was long ago now. Yet her father, Auntie Love, Aunt Ann and her mother were still with her and the world they had given her all around. They were dead, and Tommy was alive. Why was it so strange that she still sometimes felt his presence too?

'Hello, cocky!' The cockatoo waddled toward her, back and forth on his perch. She reached in to scratch his head, then stopped, and reached for the door latch instead.

She opened the cage door, and waited.

The cockatoo stared at her, then at the open door, then back at her.

He is waiting for me to shut it again, to put in more seed or water, she thought. 'Come on, boy. Or girl, whichever you are.' She put her hand into the cage, next to the perch, to encourage it.

The cockatoo bit her wrist. A speck of blood appeared, but she kept her hand still. At last he stepped onto her hand, clutching her index finger with his claws. Slowly, very slowly, she drew him out, then rested her elbow on the arm of the chair. The bird didn't hesitate now. It stepped over onto the chair, then jumped down onto the floor, flapping its wings as it walked over to the edge of the verandah.

'He'll never fly.'

She'd thought he was inside, asleep on the sofa. She stood up — slowly, so she didn't startle the bird — and helped him sit down in his chair. 'He might.'

'He's been in that cage for forty years.' Mr Drinkwater waved a hand irritably. 'No, I don't need a rug over my legs. I'm not an invalid.'

Of course he was. And of course she couldn't tell him so. They watched the bird flap its wings again, using them to glide down to the ground.

'See?' said Mr Drinkwater.

'I'll leave the cage door open. He can come back if he likes.' She reached in and found a handful of seed, then threw it out onto the grass.

'The dogs'll get him —' he began, just as Dusty galloped around the side of the house. The dog gave a startled woof, then bounded toward the bird.

'Scratch cocky!'

Suddenly the bird was airborne, with a vast fluttering of wings. It made it to the lower branches of the Chinese tallow-wood tree, the new green leaves just showing. It glared down at the dog. 'Scratch cocky!' it yelled malevolently.

Matilda laughed. 'I bet in a month or two it'll fly off with the next mob of cockatoos that passes.'

'You mean the ones that come to steal our apples? More likely it'll teach the lot of them to hang around for a handout.' Mr Drinkwater peered at her over the reading glasses he had begun to wear. 'You're planning to put out seed for it, aren't you?'

'And water,' said Matilda cheerfully. 'It's worked for you for forty years, entertaining your visitors. We owe it a pension.'

Suddenly he laughed too. 'Go on!' he yelled to the bird. 'Fly! Who knows what you'll find over the hills? A fortune, a wife and baby birds —' He stopped.

'I expect an apple orchard's a fortune to a mob of cockatoos,' said Matilda. 'Or a paddock of ripe corn. Hopefully not ours.'

'I was wondering if we should put lucerne in down on the river paddocks.' Mr Drinkwater still looked at the bird. 'It's doing well higher up. They say lucerne roots are deep enough to survive when river flats get flooded.'

'It's an idea.' It had been hard watching their corn wash away last flood, and so much of their best soil too. Floods were part of their lives now. 'Let's give it a go. I have a feeling we're in for another deluge, and soon.'

She watched as the bird flapped its way up to a higher branch. We never really know the future, she thought. One day the door is closed, and then it's open. But at least thanks to Auntie Love she had some feeling for what the land might bring next.

She smiled at the man beside her. He was smiling too, watching the bird, remembering ... what? she wondered. How he had flown from the safe world of his father's house in Sydney? All that he had found and done? His wives, his children ...

She clicked her fingers to tell the dog to come up onto the verandah, then stood up. 'Will I tell Mrs Murphy we'll have lunch out here? That way we can see where it flies next.'

Chapter 58

SEPTEMBER 1914

Dear Grandpapa,

I hope you are well.

Thank you for the money for the aeroplane ride! It was the most wonderful birthday present ever. Mama didn't want me to go up in the plane at first, but I said it was your present, so she had to let me. The plane bumped forever over the grass, so I thought it would never get up into the air, then suddenly it wasn't bumping and we were flying! I wish you could have seen us. All the cows looked like tiny toys and so did the house. The pilot said I have an 'excellent stomach'. I wasn't scared at all, even when we looped the loop, which he says he hardly ever does with passengers in case they get sick.

Cecil has decided he does not want to fly aeroplanes now. He did not know they went so high up. He says he is going to explore the Amazon instead, if you will send him a ticket for the boat, and . fight a boa constrictor. If he wins, he will send you its head.

It was a good birthday. Mama gave me a new dress with yellow ribbons, and Papa gave me a new book for sketches. It has a kangaroo-leather cover and is very fine. Cecil gave me a box of chocolates, which I do not think is fair, as he will eat half of them and Mama will object if I do not share, but I will try to keep them hidden from him.

They were all good presents but I like yours best. Do you think I could have flying lessons for my next birthday? It will have to be another pilot though, because he is going to fight the Huns in Flanders with aeroplanes.

Please give my kind regards to Miss O'Halloran, and thank her for organising the plane ride for me. Mama would never have done it.

Your loving granddaughter,
Ellen

Mr Drinkwater's bedroom smelled of bay rum for his hair and the bitter brown medicine in the bottle by the bed. Matilda thought the old man was asleep at first, but he opened his eyes as she walked toward the bed.

She bent down as he whispered to her, 'The old biscuit is crumbling.'

'Shh.' She smoothed his pillow. 'No need to talk.'

She sat on the chair next to his bed — polished wood, a cushioned back and seat, so different from the chairs her father had made. But they were made with love, she thought. And then: maybe, somewhere, this chair was too. His skin felt like cool parchment when she took his hand.

'Left the place to you in my will,' he whispered.

'Thank you.' She leaned over and kissed his cheek. No point reminding him that she already owned the place, that he had transferred it to her four years before. In his mind the land was his, and always would be.

'You'll look after it. You won't leave? Love left me. Did I tell you Love left me?'

'I won't leave you. I'll be here, by your bed.'

His breathing grew shallower. She thought he was asleep or unconscious, when one bright blue eye opened. 'Sing to me. So I know you're here. Not that song,' he added.

'What song?'

'The one about the swagman.'

'I wasn't going to,' she said gently.

So he too had made the connection between the song and those tragic, confused moments at the billabong all those years before.

How long had he known about it? she wondered. Had he felt the same pain as she had when first hearing it?

She sang another ballad instead, softly, almost under her breath, held his hand in hers, watched his face relax until he slept.

No, this wasn't sleep. His breathing was too hoarse. He began to pant, like a dog, his failing lungs straining to get air. She was glad he was unconscious, didn't know of his body's last desperate attempts to live.

His hand was limp, but still she held it. She watched as his breathing changed again, and then the sudden slackness as it faded, and life finally drained away.

She had been closer to this man than any person in her life, perhaps. So many kinds of love, she thought.

She bent down to kiss his cheek. 'Sleep well, old biscuit,' she said softly. 'I'll tend your land. I promise.'

Mrs Murphy was polishing the side table in the hall as she came out. Waiting, thought Matilda. 'He's gone.'

The housekeeper reached over and hugged her. 'We'll miss him,' was all she said.

'Yes,' said Matilda. Her tears had been shed while she watched him die. Now, strangely, she just felt the peace she had seen on the old man's face at the end.

Mrs Murphy straightened. 'I'll get Murphy to tell the funeral parlour then.'

'Tell them to bring the coffin here. They can hold the service in the church, but he's to stay here till he's buried.'

She would need to send a telegram to Bertram, but she knew the funeral instructions in the old man's will. Mr Drinkwater would lie next to his wife — his second wife — and the tiny daughter he'd never known. But James rested elsewhere, as did Auntie Love.

It was funny, she thought, but she never felt James's ghost about the place, as she did sometimes with her father. James's heart was with his friends, in a far-off land under another hot sun. Not here, despite his letters. Not with her.

Mr Drinkwater's ghost might roam here, though. She smiled at the thought. She hoped it would be content. She thought it would. If I ever smell whisky on the verandah, old biscuit, she thought, I'll think of you.

And Auntie Love ... Matilda's smile grew deeper. There was no ghost of Auntie Love. Just the land.

She walked out onto the wide verandah and sat on one of the cane chairs. She missed the cockatoo, but was glad that it was free.

The afternoon sun was setting red behind the hills. Suddenly a longing came to see the cave again, to place her handprint again on the wall among the others. She'd ride up to the valley tomorrow, see her father's house, walk up the path again …

'He gone?'

It was Mr Sampson. She nodded. He took off his hat and sat in the chair next to hers. 'What now?'

She looked at him, surprised. 'The same as always. Why should it change?'

'Things always change.' He gazed out across the paddocks too. 'The boys are enlistin' in the army. Says they are goin' to fight the Hun.'

'What?' She'd never have expected this. Two of the younger stockmen had joined up when war was declared, but she had never thought that the Sampson boys might go. 'But will they …?'

'Will they take natives in the army? I reckon. Maybe if we fight with the whiteys long enough they'll forget the colour of our skin.' He shrugged. 'I reckon the boys want to see something of the world too.'

'Mr Sampson …' So much to say. No way to say it either. 'This place is their home. No matter how long they're away, this place is here for them.'

'Good-oh.' He was silent a while and then said, 'There's things you need to know, now the old man's gone. Things I reckon he never told you. Things no one can tell you now, but me.'

She stared. It wasn't like Mr Sampson to say things. He did things. He didn't talk. Or if he did, it wasn't to her.

'What things?'

'Auntie Love, for starters.'

'Mr Drinkwater told me they'd been married.'

He shook his head. 'Not that. You never guess why she stayed with you?'

448

She looked at him, surprised. 'She wanted to look after me, to show me what to do. Women's business. I was the only girl around.'

'That weren't it. Your dad ...' He took a breath. 'Your dad were her grandson. And that makes you her great-granddaughter.'

'What? No! Dad was a white man.'

But even as she said it she thought of the brown eyes, the shape of his face. Her eyes. Her face. The colour of his skin, which she had thought came from the sun.

And suddenly it all made sense, like shards of light coming together to make a single beam.

'He were three-quarter white. His grandpa was the man in there.'

The long-ago words came flooding back to her. *I'll never let you marry him.*

Was it the native blood the old man didn't want in his family? No, she thought. Not that at all. James was my ... my half-great-uncle? Could you marry your half-great-uncle?

It didn't matter. Hadn't now for many years. Whatever reasons he'd had for forbidding her marriage, he had loved her at the end. Closer than a daughter, than a great-granddaughter too. A partner in what they both held dearest in life.

And yes, you old biscuit, you were right, she thought. She and James had been too alike ever to have married happily, quite aside from the family connection. There was too much of Mr Drinkwater in them both. She had got on with the old man because he *was* old, and had learned his wisdom by the time their friendship grew. But she and James ... within a year they'd have been yelling about some decision on the farm. Two years later she'd have been left with the housekeeping and the children while he rode about his acres — and beyond.

She shook her head. The past had suddenly become another country, not the one she'd thought she knew.

'Who were Dad's parents?'

'The old man's first daughter, Rachel. She died when your pa was born. His father,' Mr Sampson shrugged. 'His name were O'Halloran. A white man. Worked on a place downriver from here. She moved there when they married. Then when she died the old man brought your dad back here.'

She looked at the skin on her wrist, trying to work it out. She was one-sixteenth native. Enough to give her brown eyes and a slightly darker skin easy to mistake for a touch of sun, especially with her blonde hair making her look white.

How many knew she was part native? There must have been some men who had known her father when he was young. Had they never mentioned it out of respect for him? Or her?

So this is who I am, she thought. Why did I never guess?

'What happened to Dad's father?' she asked at last.

'Don't know. He stuck around Drinkwater for a few years, then lit out somewhere. Ain't heard from him since. My ma and pa brought up your dad, mostly.'

'Not Mr Drinkwater?'

'He paid for his schoolin', stuff like that.'

But not boarding school, she thought. Not like his white sons. Was that the real reason her father had founded the union here? To show his grandfather that he couldn't always be the boss?

The old biscuit would have made me a maid, she thought, because I was part native. But he looked out for me. He loved my father, even when they quarrelled, just as he loved James.

Exactly what had been happening between those two at that

billabong, that final day? What undercurrents had she been too young, too ignorant to decipher?

They had told her the truth, her father and her great-grandfather. But never the whole truth. No whole truth till now.

A breeze gusted past the house. The sun had vanished now, but the red haze still lingered in the sky. 'So I'm … I'm really a Drinkwater.'

Did it even matter?

She looked at the man next to her, so carefully gazing away.

It mattered.

'You're my … cousin?'

'I reckon. More or less.'

She'd had family all along then, just without knowing it. Family who knew she belonged to them. She belonged on this land too. She wanted to hug him, but he had never been a man for hugs.

I had them from Auntie Love though, she thought. But she wasn't my auntie. She was my great-grandma.

Mr Sampson stood up. 'I'd best be goin'. Elsie will wonder where I am.'

'Does Elsie know?'

'She knows.' He held out his hand.

Matilda shook it. 'Thank you,' she said simply. 'I don't know what to say, except I'm glad. Glad you're my cousin. Glad the boys are family too.'

'Always were,' said Mr Sampson, and she realised he didn't mean by blood. He and Mr Gotobed, Bluey, Curry and Rice: they had been her family for years, had stood by her to let her become who she was now.

Suddenly she came to a decision. 'Mr Sampson … could you ask the boys to wait a bit before they join up? Please?'

He looked at her questioningly.

'I want to sell the sheep. Just keep the rams, a few of the best ewes.' She tried to find words to explain the feeling that had been growing the last few months.

Now when the whole of Drinkwater was finally hers she understood that the land was never hers; it wasn't Mr Sampson's either. The land belonged to itself; theirs to live with, to work, to cherish. But when we are gone, she thought, the land will still be here, changed perhaps, but here as it was before we came.

How long had it been since she had seen the yam daisies flowering after rain? The sheep had eaten both blooms and roots, like they ate the young trees too. How long since a mob of roos had bounded in a tide toward the hills?

'It's not just the boys going. Not the old man's death, either, though that's part of it. The land needs rest. A rest from sheep, from grazing. It's tired.'

And I'm tired too, she thought. We both need time.

The old biscuit would never have done this. Nor, she thought, would her father. But Auntie Love would have understood, maybe Aunt Ann too. Perhaps the folk were right who said a woman couldn't run a station. Men wanted profit from the land. A woman wanted to tend it.

No, she thought. That's not right either. I wanted success all right. Maybe I will again. But not just now.

'There's plenty in the bank to keep the place going. When the boys come back,' she added, 'well, we'll work out what to do then. Split the properties up, maybe, if you or the boys want farms of your own.'

Her heart beat like the soldier's recruiting drum at the thought. Could she let control of part of Moura and Drinkwater go? She didn't know. She'd have to try.

He gazed at her, his brown eyes so like her father's. Like hers. 'I didn't tell you for that.'

'I know.'

He was silent a while, and then he nodded.

She stayed in the chair long after he had gone. What battles had happened on these acres? Whatever they were, she was descended from both sides.

The land was silent now, apart from the far-off baa of a sheep, a bleating lamb strayed from its mother, the chortle of a kookaburra down by the river.

She was alone, but at last, she thought, not lonely. Was this what Auntie Love had felt, walking with her land? She would never be lonely now, not with the hills, the whispers of the trees.

She sat until the light had faded from the sky, and the stars were shining like pinholes in the velvet. She sat till the cross turned over. And then she went inside.

Chapter 59

Dear Peter,

It was good to get your postcard, and to know that despite all the losses at Gallipoli you and the Drinkwater boys are still safe and well. We all pray that you remain so. I hope the cake reaches you safely. Mrs Murphy made it, not me, so it will be good. She sends her best wishes and regards too.

Things are fine here. Too many rabbits — I've had Mr Gotobed and Bluey setting traps. Curry and Rice wants to get ferrets, but I do not know. We might end up with too many ferrets as well as rabbits. We had rain last week, nearly half an inch, so everything is green, despite the bunnies.

May the war soon be over, and you all home safe. My love and all my best wishes to you and the other men from Gibber's Creek and Drinkwater,

Matilda O'Halloran

The sunlight on her face woke her, streaming between the curtains. She'd been out by moonlight the night before, checking on the lambing ewes. One of them was straining. It had been nearly dawn when she'd finally got the first of the lambs out — a big male, followed quickly by a smaller female.

She dressed quickly — she was back to trousers now, the dresses hung up in her wardrobe for her rare days in town — splashed water on her face from the china bowl, then hurried out to the kitchen. Elsie was lifting the kettle from the stove. Matilda could tell the news from her face. Elsie's eyes were red from crying, but she was smiling too.

'He's all right?'

Elsie nodded. 'Mrs Murphy saw the latest casualty lists at the post office, and sent a note out with old Jack. None of the boys on it.' She pointed to a postcard on the table. 'A new card from Michael. Just says he's well, that's all. But …'

But at least we know he was alive when he wrote it, thought Matilda, as Elsie poured water into the pot, then slipped the cosy on. She and Mr Sampson had moved into the homestead when their sons pretended to be part Indian so they could join up, and Ginger and Mrs Murphy shifted into town the year before.

It was a curiously empty land now: most of the sheep were gone, most of the men as well. But the roos were building up again, now the sheep no longer ate all the grass. She wondered as she ate her scrambled eggs whether the koalas would reclaim the trees as well. Elsie sat at the table opposite, sipping her tea, nibbling toast to keep her company, her eyes straying to her new postcard.

How could a war so far away be so close to them as well? Damn the Turks and Germans, Matilda thought, and damn the British too. They had killed James and now they were killing

455

others. But she had never spoken the words aloud. Tell the truth, she thought, but not the whole truth. Sometimes it's wisest not to let the whole truth show.

The sound of a car woke her from her thoughts. The dogs began to bark in the courtyard. She glanced at Elsie. 'Mr Sampson take the car to town?'

Elsie shook her head. 'Mr Murphy's got to come out and look at it, remember? Wouldn't start last week.'

Shows how long since I have been anywhere, thought Matilda.

She took her plate to the sink, scraped the leftover eggs into the hens' bucket, then strode out down the hallway to the verandah just as the car came to the end of the driveway.

It was a bigger car than any in Gibber's Creek, long and blue, a carriage for passengers and a big leather-covered area for luggage behind. A well-dressed man held the steering wheel, with a girl in white and blue next to him. A uniformed chauffeur sat in the back seat, looking embarrassed.

She walked down the steps and waited for the car to stop. Who would drive themselves, and put their chauffeur in the back seat?

The car braked silently almost at her feet. The driver looked out.

It was Tommy.

Her breath seemed to leave her.

He looked the same. He might just have bicycled up from town, instead of driving in the shiny car.

He should look older, she thought. Where is his grey hair? We are both so much older now.

And then she realised: he was only thirty-six. It was she who felt old at thirty-three, so much of her life spent as an adult instead of a child, bearing the responsibilities of others.

She forced herself to walk toward the car. No, he wasn't quite the same. His face looked stronger, quieter, somehow more himself. The scar had faded, though it still pulled slightly at his mouth. But the smile was the same, the smile for her, another smile for the young girl who sat by his side.

Half her life had passed since she had last seen this man, but somehow she could feel the friendship was still there, the trust between them.

Where was his wife?

I don't care, she thought. I will be friends with his wife too. But I won't lose a friend again now.

The girl put her head out the window. She was about ten years old, red curls spilling out under her hat. 'Is that Matilda? Really truly? The girl in the song?'

Tommy nodded at the girl. 'That's Matilda. Really truly. Say hello politely now.'

The girl scrambled out of the car, blue boots under a practical blue skirt. She curtseyed neatly, then beamed up at Matilda. This is a girl who is used to being loved, thought Matilda wistfully.

'Good afternoon, Miss O'Halloran,' she said, then added quickly, 'We learned the song about your father at school. But I was the only one who knew about you!'

'How did you know it was about me?'

'Dad told me, of course. We stayed at the hotel in town last night. They know all about you too. I asked.'

Tommy was out of the car now. He looked at Matilda warily. 'Matilda, this is Anna. My daughter.'

'I'm glad to meet you, Anna.'

'I'm glad to meet you too! I can play "Waltzing Matilda" on the piano, you know. With both hands!'

'Can you really?'

'Ahem.' The chauffeur cleared his throat politely. 'Shall I unload the luggage, sir?'

The girl looked at Matilda hopefully. 'Can we stay? Dad wasn't sure. Please? He said you have horses and dogs and lots of sheep, and I'll see kangaroos.'

Her heart seemed to have stopped. She nodded in a daze to the chauffeur. 'Please, take the suitcases inside. No, don't go round the back.' She smiled slightly. 'Everyone uses the front door here.'

The chauffeur looked shocked. This was worse, it seemed, than riding in the back seat. He pulled open the hatch and carried up the first two cases, his back stiff with disapproval.

She looked at Tommy over Anna's head. 'There is a piano inside if you'd like to play it. It's the first room on the right. Your father and I can hear it out here.'

'Oh, thank you!' She was gone in a flash of blue skirt and white petticoat, her boots stamping up the steps.

Matilda heard the clang as the piano was opened and the first bars of music. If she listened closely she could almost make out the tune.

'She's only been learning for a year,' said Tommy apologetically.

Matilda smiled. 'At least she's enthusiastic.'

The girl began to sing. *'Once a jolly swagman ...'*

'I didn't know you knew,' she added quietly.

'That the song was about your father? I guessed. It isn't hard. The swaggie, three troopers, the squatter and a billabong. But they never mentioned you.'

'No. The songs rarely mention the women.'

She started slowly toward the verandah, with him beside her. 'Where's her mother?'

458

'She died,' he said gently. 'Anna's brother too. Diphtheria. They both died a year ago.'

'I'm sorry.' She found that she meant it: sorrow for his loss; sorrow for what Anna must have felt; and sorrow for the pain that she herself had known as well.

'I am too. We had been married over a year when I heard about James.' He added, 'Mary was ... gentle.'

She smiled. 'Not like me.'

'No. Not like you.'

She led the way up onto the verandah. 'I saw your photo in the paper, years ago. You both looked happy. I wanted to write to you, tell you I was glad for you, but I didn't have your address.'

'Matilda, I'm sorry. Sorry to vanish. Sorry I couldn't fight for you or accept you as you were. I was hurt and I was angry. I thought you had married James, and by the time I knew you hadn't ...' He hesitated. 'I can't say I am sorry I married Mary. I'm not. I wouldn't have married her if you were still in my life. But it was a good marriage, and a loving one.'

'I'm glad.' She was glad that she meant that too. She sat in one of the verandah chairs.

He sat in the one next to her. 'I remember these chairs.'

'The ones my father made. I brought them from Moura when I came here.'

'I went to Moura first. They said at the hotel that you own Drinkwater now, but I didn't know you had moved here.'

'You were looking for me?'

'I was looking for you.'

She nodded at the car. 'Did you make that?'

He laughed, leaning back. 'No. I made my money in radios. The ones the poor blighters are using in the trenches now, in fact.'

'So you're rich?'

'I'm rich. I gather so are you.'

'Yes.'

He looked at her, seriously again. The piano pounded from inside, though the girl had stopped singing. Matilda wondered if the tune she was playing was still 'Waltzing Matilda'.

'Why have you come now?'

'I thought you might need help. I keep in touch with some of my old mates from here. I know it's hard on most farms now. So many men gone to the army.'

'Just as you always came to help me before?'

He flushed. 'Not that you always needed it. And I couldn't for a while. It wouldn't have been fair to Mary.'

'But now you can?'

'Now I can.'

He had waited a year out of respect for the woman who had been his wife. She found that she was glad of that too. This was the Tommy she had known: the bone-deep integrity. Tommy who was true to his friends, and true to his wife, as well.

She sat back, staring at her acres, almost empty of sheep. Saplings were growing again, olive heads taller than the grass.

'No, I don't need help. Not that sort of help, anyway.' She met his eyes. He was still Tommy. The one person in all the world, she thought, who will always tell me the whole truth, even if it hurt. Why had she never realised that friendship was the deepest kind of love? 'But I would still like you to stay.'

'For how long?' His voice was cautious.

She smiled, knowing this time that she had to say it for him. 'Forever, if you want to.' Tommy would never tell her she was beautiful. Never say sweet words that might come from a novel.

'You never danced with me,' she said suddenly. 'Never. Not even once.'

'I don't dance.' He met her eyes. 'You didn't understand, back then. I never asked you because I didn't dare.'

He lifted his scarred hand. The scar had faded like the one on his face, though the fingers were still slightly twisted.

'So you left?'

'Tommy Thompson couldn't compete with a James Drinkwater.'

'Matilda O'Halloran couldn't compete with electric generators in a city.'

He stared at her. 'Electric generators are portable, you know. There is nothing I can do in the city I can't do here, with a bit of money to lubricate things.'

It was like the first shaft of sunlight gleaming along the river. Suddenly she saw what marriage might be like: not two people sharing one life, managing a farm together, but two lives, linked by love and trust.

He was still looking at her. 'Matilda, would you really have chosen me instead if I'd stayed?'

She looked at her hands, then back at him. She would tell the truth too. The whole truth, just as she always had. 'I don't know. You never gave me a chance to find out.'

He hesitated. She could see he was choosing his words with care. 'Maybe if you'd chosen me, we mightn't have been happy. Not then. I had to be your protector in those days. I was Mary's protector too.'

'And I've never been someone to be shut up in a cage, even a loving one?' She smiled. 'But things are different for Mr T. Thompson, inventor and businessman? I kept your photo,' she added. 'It was the only thing I had of you. Except the car, of course … do you know it still runs? Well, almost. And the stock troughs and — and everything really.'

She stood up, then held out her hand to him. 'Will you dance with me now?'

He looked startled. '"Waltzing Matilda"?'

'Exactly that,' she said.

He smiled. 'I may not dance, but I know that tune isn't a waltz.'

She laughed. 'I don't think you can tell the difference when Anna plays it.'

'True.' He took her hand in his, then put his other hand on her waist, looking into her eyes. 'Darling Matilda. I've been driving the last twenty miles trying to talk to Anna and all the while thinking: what if she sends me packing? Should I have brought you flowers, a basket of fruit?'

'Just you will do. And Anna.'

'That's what I hoped. Will you waltz with me, Matilda?'

She felt like soaring with the cockatoos over her acres, yelling happiness to the world. But a waltz would do to start with.

Inside the girl began to sing the song again. Suddenly it was as though other voices joined her, the whisper of the river, the laughter of the wind. Matilda wondered what Anna would think about a cave and a wall of hands upon a rock.

Matilda put her other hand onto Tommy's shoulder. He felt as warm as the hills, and as solid. 'Let's waltz.'

Notes on the Text

A Waltz for Matilda is fiction, put together from historical facts. There was a swagman and a billabong. I have known women like Matilda, her Aunt Ann and Auntie Love: the women who helped create our history but are so often forgotten by it. The drought, the strikes, the campaigns for federation and new laws were much as I have described them here. Most of all the land and its lore are based on the land that is my home. Like Matilda, I have watched it and loved it, seen its changes and been part of its endless generosity.

In one respect, though, I have departed from historical record. The episode that inspired the song 'Waltzing Matilda' happened in Queensland. While I have carefully not mentioned where this book is set, it isn't Queensland. This book is a love song to a nation, but also to a land. The land in this book is the one I know.

This is why I have deliberately not specified which 'city' Matilda travels from. It could be one of many. Nor have I given the exact date of the referendum that led to Federation, as they took place at different times in different states. This is a book about a nation, not one state.

'Waltzing Matilda'

'Waltzing Matilda' is Australia's national song — though not its national anthem — but few Australians know that it commemorates a real event: the death of a shearer who was suspected of burning down a shearing shed in the shearers' strike of the 1890s.

'Waltzing Matilda' was written by Banjo Paterson, a poet who helped make the bush and the outback seem romantic to people in the city.

Andrew Barton 'Banjo' Paterson, CBE (1864–1941) grew up on his family's property beyond Yass, New South Wales (his nickname 'Banjo' came from one of his father's favourite horses). Although he was born on a farm and loved the bush and wrote about it, he mostly lived in the city, working as a solicitor. His first book of ballads, *The Man from Snowy River and Other Verses*, was published in 1895 and became a smash-hit.

In 1895 Paterson also went to stay with the Macpherson family on their property, Dagworth Station, just over sixty miles north-west of the town of Winton in Queensland. He and Bob Macpherson rode around the station and Paterson heard the story of how the Macphersons' shearing shed had just been burned — and how a swagman–shearer who was believed to have been part of the disturbance, 'Frenchy' Hoffmeister, had been found dead at a nearby camp.

Inspired, Paterson wrote the words of 'Waltzing Matilda'. Christina Macpherson provided the music, based on a tune she'd heard at the Warrnambool country races (probably the old

Scottish tune 'Thou Bonnie Wood of Craigie-Lea'). Soon everyone in the Winton district was singing the song and, not long after, most of Australia was too. But as with the women in this book, Christina Macpherson's contribution to what became our national song has mostly been forgotten.

Soon there were several versions of the song being sung, long before the song was first published in 1903. That first printed version is slightly different from the song I learnt as a child, and both versions have been included in this book to acknowledge the many versions that were around, even by 1910.

'Waltzing Matilda' came to symbolise the ways the new nation of Australia thought of itself: courageous, contemptuous of authority and with our hearts in the bush. The fact that most Australians lived in cities and towns, even back in those days, and preferred safe jobs to wandering the bush, didn't matter then and doesn't seem to now.

I have always loved the song, but for many years have wondered at parts of it. How could the swaggie grab a jumbuck and force it into his tucker bag? I was once a sheep farmer, and remember vividly being dragged on my stomach along a road by a stroppy ram as I gripped onto its leg. Trust me: it is very hard to catch a ram, unless you have it pinned in a yard. Sheep have four legs to pull away from you, and can easily overbalance a human with only two.

But a poddy — a sheep that has been orphaned and brought up by humans — is easily caught, in fact can be hard to get away from.

And what of the squatter and the troopers? The history of the time suggests they must have *planned* to arrest the swaggie — distances were large, and it's an enormous coincidence that so many troopers just happened by that billabong.

Where did the poddy come from? Perhaps they had planted the sheep, to tempt the man into grabbing it. Who was the squatter? And how did the world know what happened, there at that billabong, over a hundred years ago? Did one of the troopers tell the story in guilt and shame? I suspect that Banjo Paterson wrote about a frame-up — and that he and his listeners back then knew it. Nowadays the real significance of the song has been partly lost.

The 1880s to the 1930s was a time of many poems and songs about the right of workers to join together to get better conditions. 'Waltzing Matilda' was just one of them; another was 'The Ballad of Joe Hill', the United States song that also spoke of an unjustly accused union man whose ghost reappears to inspire others.

We mostly think of Australia's 1800s as a time of spreading rural stations, shearers and stockmen, and men panning for gold. But even then, most Australians lived in cities, and back then conditions in factories were as horrendous as they were in the United States and Europe: dangerous or even deadly machinery; impossibly long hours; small wages that weren't enough for a family or even one person to eat well, much less pay rent; no holidays except Christmas Day and Sundays; no sick leave or pensions when you got old; and no compensation if you suffered an accident at work. Servants had easier conditions, but they usually only got an afternoon off a month, although considerate employers might let them go to church on Sunday mornings — as long as they sat at the back, and had got up before dawn to put on Sunday dinner and get their chores done.

But Australia was settled as much by people who had rebelled against authority, whether as criminals or as political protestors, as it had been by 'respectable' immigrants. The new colonies had some of the earliest trade unions in the world. Even by the 1830s, shipwrights and then other craftsmen banded together to fight for better working conditions.

In the 1880s conditions for most people in Australia grew harder. The land was starting to show scars from decades of hard treatment. The native grasses were being eaten out as, especially in dry times, sheep nibbled the grass so close to the ground that the local perennial grasses died. A long and desperate drought lasted from the mid-1880s to the early 1900s in most parts of Australia. Prices for wheat and wool crashed too. The state governments had borrowed to fund projects when times were good. Now they weren't able to repay their loans, and work on government projects stopped.

People lost their jobs; employers dropped wages and expected longer working hours. Strikes spread across the country in the late 1880s — ships' officers, seamen, waterside workers, shearers, miners and many others announced they would stop working until their conditions improved. The colonial governments and their police forces supported the employers. And the bitterness between workers on the one side and employers on the other grew.

By the mid-1880s soup kitchens had to be set up in Sydney and Adelaide to feed the starving workers and their families. And by the early 1890s the Australian colonies were in a serious economic depression.

The swagmen took to the roads and tracks outback looking for work and a cheaper way to live. A swaggie had a spare pair of trousers, comb and towel wrapped up in his swag, or 'Matilda', or blanket, strapped to his back, with a billy — an old tin with a handle of fencing wire — in one hand and a hessian sack containing some flour and tea and sugar in the other.

This is a book about the land, as well as people. These days we often forget to take the effect of the environment into account. Even as I write this, economists around the world are expressing surprise at the 'negative growth figures' caused by the 2010 cold winter in the northern hemisphere — you can't build houses when snowbound, and much else stops too. But few appear to have figured such possibilities into their forecasts.

If there had been no major 1880s–1903 drought there might not have been the shearers' strike that was such a major part of the beginning of the labour movement. There might not have been the bank crashes, the hard economic times that led to demands to drop taxes between the states, the uniform immigration policies.

If it hadn't been for the drought — and the men, waltzing their Matildas — we might still be a loose association of states, and not a nation.

THE SHEARERS' UNION

In July 1886 the Shearers' Union was formed after squatters wanted to lower the rate of pay. The shearers were also angry because squatters would claim that a sheep hadn't been shorn properly and then refuse to pay anything for the rest of the sheep that had been shorn.

Of all the unions, the Shearers' Union was the most militant. Members refused to work at stations around Barcaldine, in Queensland, unless the Squatters' Association met their demands for better conditions. In January 1891 the union called out 200 shearers and rouseabouts as a protest against working with non-union shearers. The strike lasted till 7 August, when the last of the shearers went back to work, after the leaders of the strike had been arrested for conspiracy and sentenced to three years' gaol. But strikes broke out on other properties for many years, either for better wages and conditions or to protest against property owners employing non-union labour.

The Journey to Federation

Members of the various unions had realised that they all wanted much the same thing: an eight-hour working day, a minimum wage for all men and women, workers' causes represented in parliament, and a way of settling (arbitrating) disputes between unions and employers, instead of using strikes and lockouts, where unionists were locked out without pay and others were employed in their place. The first meeting of the Australian Labour Federation General Council was held in Brisbane on 31 August 1890.

Could the unionists' dreams be fulfilled with a new national government? Many other Australians hoped the same thing: that a united Australia would mean free trade between the states, helping bring prosperity back again, and that a new federal government would give the vote to women, ensure young children went to school, rather than work in factories, and other just laws.

But other reasons were more selfish: the desire to stop anyone who wasn't white and English-speaking from entering or settling in the country. This was partly to stop the (slave) 'kanaka' labourers who had been brought to Australia mostly to work the sugar fields — their low wages meant that there were no jobs for white workers — and to stop competition from Chinese migration.

Our nation's founders also wanted uniform tariffs (taxes) on goods coming into Australia to help Australian factories, so they could charge higher prices and pay higher wages. And they were seeking a government that could bring all states together on major projects from defence to building railways.

Australia was built on idealism — and on self-interest. Men over twenty-one could vote in the first federal election; women couldn't, although the first parliament voted to give them the vote. Only British citizens could vote, and Aboriginal Australians were not counted as British citizens. South Australia had allowed white women and Aboriginal men to vote, but even they weren't given the right to vote in a federal parliament. And Aboriginal Australians were not included in the census.

When Australians today talk of our 'constitutional rights' they often assume that we have the rights that are enshrined in the American constitution. We don't. Our only 'right' is freedom of religion — and that was really only meant to allow Catholics the same rights as Protestant Christians. It's likely that if those who drew up our constitution ever suspected that Australia might have a large number of people practising non-Christian religions, they would have excluded them from this constitutional right.

Our nation was created by idealists. But their ideals weren't all ones that most modern Australians would agree with.

'BREAKER' MORANT

James Drinkwater's fate of course is based on that of Harry 'Breaker' Morant, who was tried and shot for killing Boer commandos who might, or might not, have already surrendered, but who had killed and possibly horrendously mutilated his friend. (Morant was accused of other crimes too, but those charges were dropped.) Breaker Morant's story is fascinating, but too long to go into here; and, apart from his final fate, he and the James in this book had nothing else in common.

Breaker Morant's story however is important: the Australian government and public were infuriated over the British government's refusal to officially inform them about the Breaker Morant case; the official records were lost — or possibly deliberately mislaid — and even his next of kin weren't officially informed of his sentence.

The feeling that justice had not been done to an Australian by a British military court resulted in the ruling that, from then on, all Australian service people would be tried by Australian military tribunals. In World War I many British soldiers were shot for cowardice, when they were simply suffering from shellshock or unbearable horror at what they faced. No Australian in World War I was shot for cowardice and, from then until today, Australian forces remain under direct Australian command, even if general control of the operation is given to an ally.

This led to greater emphasis on 'Australian units within joint forces' — and the Anzac legend. It was also the start of a growing feeling that we were Australians, not British. While most Australians fervently supported the 'Empire' in World War I, there was still a feeling of distrust — often justified — about the competency of British officers and the feeling that Australian troops might be more 'dispensable' than British ones.

THE BOER WAR

The Boer War (1899–1902) was about which of two European countries, England or Holland, was going to control South Africa. Most of the fighting was between the farming descendants of the Dutch settlers — the Boers — and the British army.

The conflict had nothing to do with Australia, but we were part of the British Empire, so Australians flocked to fight. The Boer farmers fought the British army by hiding, ambushing them, then retreating to the country they knew so well.

About 20,000 Australian men served in the Boer War and about eighty Australian women as nurses. It is difficult to know exact numbers as some men enlisted more than once. Other regiments were 'irregulars' and their men weren't counted in official numbers. It was an enormous number, though, for such a small nation. Most families had someone fighting or knew someone who was.

About 600 Australians died and six were awarded the Victoria Cross for their Boer War service.

CONVEYOR BELTS

In this book Tommy invents the conveyor belt before Henry Ford in the United States. In fact many inventions and achievements — like the Wright brothers' first manned flight — were based on articles by other people or invented several times. At that time a young man like Tommy could have easily created a conveyor belt and later written about it, so that it was adopted elsewhere.

HONEY

As a beekeeper, many years ago, I mostly took honey from our hives in mid to late summer. These were European bees, long-bodied and golden, not the smaller and mostly stingless native bees, which are either almost black or a bright clear blue. (The blue bees don't form hives and prefer to collect nectar from blue flowers.)

It has been over twenty-five years since I collected 'sugar bag', or wild honey, and even then it may have been from wild European bees. There are still purebred native bees in Australia, but in the area where I live there are only native 'blue bees' — solitary ones that are not good for sugar bag. Sugar bag is collected just after the local gum-tree flowering. Here this is in August or September, although there isn't a massive flowering every year, and some years the flowers don't contain much nectar.

The bees' behaviour, though, tells you how much honey you can take without danger of taking too much and killing the hive. It would take a whole book to explain this properly, but one way is to see how many young bees there are — they have hairy legs that collect pollen to feed to more young bees. A sudden increase in fluffy-legged bees means that the hive is hatching a lot of young and expecting good honey flow soon. Honey colour varies a lot, depending on what the bees have been feeding on.

NATIVE FRUITS

There are hundreds of good native fruits and vegetables — possibly thousands that I have never heard of. I haven't given the names of them here because it is very easy to mistake a tasty berry for one that might kill you, though each is based on a native plant that I harvest at the time Matilda gathers them in this book. Some fruits should only be eaten when they are at a particular stage of ripeness or they can be toxic, and others should be tasted first. Bitter or almond-smelling ones should be thrown away as they may be poisonous enough to kill you, while others on a bush nearby that look almost exactly the same may be sweet and can be eaten. Identifying the 'good' fruits needs at the very least photos and a map for each fruit, plus a few paragraphs of information. Even better, you need to be shown by someone who knows the land and how its fruits can change from year to year, or decade to decade.

EATING SNAKE, SWAN AND GOANNA

Do not try this.

It's illegal — all native animals are protected. It may also kill you — both snakes and goannas have poison glands. While it is possible to eat the meat, you have to know exactly what you are doing or you may end up dead. There is also increasingly less land for wildlife, and we need to cherish what we have — even if, like snakes, they can just possibly kill us too.

It is also illegal to eat swan, though early settlers did. I never have, but am told by a friend, who did once eat swan for Christmas dinner more than half a century ago when her bush parents were very poor indeed, that swan meat is very tough, though a large swan can have quite a lot of meat on it.

TURNING INVISIBLE

The techniques that Auntie Love used to leave no tracks and become invisible were shown to me decades ago. They are of course more complex than I've written here — it's much easier to demonstrate in person than write down. I have only tried the invisibility once, to frighten a group of trespassers. It worked so well I scared myself too!

I have never tried it again, partly because it did scare me a little, but also because if it didn't work I'd look stupid, standing stock-still trying to become a tree. Like everything from making a good cake to the five-times table, I expect turning invisible needs practice.

How to tell when it will rain

The ways of looking at the land to tell if there will be rain, or good grass, or bushfire, are just a few of the many strategies those who live with the land and watch it can use to tell what will happen — anywhere from tomorrow to two or even more years' time. I only know the signs that the land where I live tells me. These will be different in other areas. As I have said before, while this is a book about all of Australia, the land in the book is the land where I live. We are a small nation, but a very big country, made up of many regions, each with its own weather, climate and lore.

Sheep

The methods of treating fly strike and other sheep instructions in this book are those of the 1890s. *Do not use them* — they can be dangerous for both sheep and humans.

Seeds in raisins

Old recipes for fruitcakes and puddings tell you to take the seeds out of the raisins. These days most raisins have the seeds removed or they are from newer varieties of fruit that have small seeds. But old raisins had big seeds, almost like apple pips, and if the seeds weren't taken out you had to spit them out, which was bad manners.

THE WOMEN'S TEMPERANCE AND SUFFRAGE LEAGUE

There was no such league, though there were temperance leagues and women's suffrage leagues, and very often they would have the same members. For convenience I have joined them in this book.

These days many people drink alcohol without drinking too much or too often. But back in the 1800s drunkenness was not just common but the norm for many men after work. Many, perhaps most, shearers drank their entire pay cheque then moved onto another shed where they would have board and lodging till they could have another 'bender'. In the days when few women had the chance of a paying job, families suffered extreme hardship and frequent violence from men's alcoholism.

The Temperance Movement didn't want people to stop enjoying themselves. They helped women feed and educate their families, fought for the vote for women and for equal rights for Aboriginal Australians. My paternal grandmother, Jean MacPherson French, was a member of one such league, and fought diligently for the right of Aboriginal Australians to vote and to be counted in the census. It was her phrase that I have borrowed, spoken after a visit to an Aboriginal comrade's home: 'It was spotlessly clean! Spotless!' There was no greater compliment my grandmother could pay ... except perhaps when she spoke of Aboriginal poet Oodgeroo of the Noonuccal people to say: 'Australia has finally found its Robbie Burns.' I wish that she — and the other women who gave me so much — could have read this book.

DYING

Many characters in this book die. This is what happened a hundred years ago — people died more often, and younger, than they do now in Australia. Women and children were especially vulnerable, with no antibiotics, no vaccination for polio, measles, whooping cough, diphtheria and other great killers, and poor medical hygiene in childbirth.

HEY YOU

Hey You would have been part dingo, part cattle dog. The Australian cattle dog (also called the Queensland heeler, or the red or blue heeler) was recognised as a separate breed by 1890. Its ancestors include the dingo, an English herding breed called the Smithfield and the smooth-coated Blue Merle collie.

THE SONG AT MR O'HALLORAN'S FUNERAL

This song, 'The Song of the Union Man', comes from *Shearers' Record Newspaper*, January 1890, as recorded in *Sydney Folklore* — Section 2: Labour History.

HENRY LAWSON

Henry Lawson spent little time 'out bush', but his poems and stories described the bush as it really was, unlike other romantic stories made up about it. There are many phrases in this book that are used in homage to his work, from Mrs Heenan being 'past caring' to 'Grinder's Alley'.

THE CHINESE WORDS IN THE TEXT

Matilda would have assumed that there was only one Chinese language. Chinese migrants to Australia in the 1800s came from many areas and used several languages. Two of these are used in this book, assuming that Mr Ah Ching and Mr Doo's family came from different regions of China.

My grateful thanks to a dear friend, for providing the words in the text that a Chinese man might have used in Australia in the 1890s, and the information about the bow that Matilda makes in chapter one. If I have used them in the wrong context the mistakes are mine, not hers.

Note: These are not as the words would be used or spelled these days, but are from 1890 or even earlier.

Qing An: a suitable greeting from a young girl to an older man

Duo xie: words of thanks

Gai ri zai lai, qing zou hao: 'Come back some day and take care on your way home, please'

RACISM

Once more, I apologise for the racist terms used and assumptions made by some of the characters in this book. There is no way to show the rural Australia of the 1890s — or the effects of that racism — without them. If anything, I have enormously softened both the racist language and the racist assumptions likely to have been made — much of which I remember from my own childhood, decades later.

Several readers have questioned the phrase 'just one buck' used by the Drinkwater boys to describe killing an Aboriginal man. I have heard the word — and 'doe' for a woman — used several times, including once by ex-Prime Minister Mr Malcolm Fraser, when he was interviewed about the often deadly racism that horrified him in his youth and helped convince him to work to combat it.

Aboriginal men, women and children were still being hunted out of farming areas in the 1890s, often in retaliation for eating the sheep or cattle that were taking the place of the native animals that had once grazed those same lands. The false accusation that 'natives' were cannibals was a common one in the 1890s.

Aboriginal men, such as Peter and Michael Sampson in this book, even had to lie about their heritage to join the army. It wasn't until 1917, when the army was desperate for men, that Aboriginal Australians were allowed to openly join up.

To say 'I am proud to be Australian' in no way describes the depth of love and identification I have for this land. But it is worth remembering that our country united to become one nation partly to keep out those who weren't white English speakers, and that the religious freedom mentioned in our constitution was meant to ensure that Irish Catholics were free to worship, rather than the many religions of today's Australia.

Our constitution has changed since Federation — notably in order to give women the vote. Our nation has changed too. But we can still perhaps understand it better if we know where we have come from. The past is not always comfortable, but it is part of who we are.

Acknowledgements

A Waltz for Matilda could not have been written without the wisdom of seven generations of women, some only slightly disguised in this book. My great-grandmother Emily Shèldon, great-great-aunt Nin Edwards, grandmothers Thelma Edwards and Jean MacPherson, and mother, Val French, are the women of the Temperance and Suffrage League, who fought — and in my mother's case still fights — for their ideals. The women of our family tend to be long lived, and pass on their stories — and their passions — to many generations.

Auntie Love is many women, some of whose names I don't know or don't have permission to give, but who include Oodgeroo of the Noonuccal people (I knew her as Kath Walker), Maureen Watson and the others who tried to pass on to rootless city kids a sense of land and of belonging, as well as Neeta Davis and Jean Hobbins. Miss Thrush and Gillian Pauli have nothing in common except the dedication and generosity they gave to their students. I suspect that Peg Job and Virginia Hooker — both of whom listen tolerantly to the latest historical obsession for at least an hour more than politeness and friendship require — are somewhere in this book too. The young Matilda owes much to tens of thousands of letters from young people. Young people — like Matilda — often see the world with a clarity that adults are too preoccupied to remember.

A Waltz for Matilda has also been blessed with the 'two Kates' — Kate O'Donnell, who began the work on this manuscript, and left for the birth of her bonny boy, Clem, and Kate Burnitt, who took over in a seamless transition, checking and rechecking every phrase, making sure that the vision in my mind's eye was intelligible for the reader. Liz Kemp brought the brilliance of her insight to the first draft of this book. I am a far better writer for knowing that Liz, with her critic's eye, will read the manuscript.

This book is also partly the vision of two other exceptional women: HarperCollins associate publisher Lisa Berryman, and friend (and volunteer editorial advisor) Noël Pratt. Lisa is the rock of my professional life; Noël is the rock of friendship, wisdom and generosity. This book owes more to Lisa and Noël than I can express.

Titles by Jackie French

Historical
Somewhere Around the Corner • Dancing with Ben Hall
Daughter of the Regiment • Soldier on the Hill • Hitler's Daughter
Lady Dance • How the Finnegans Saved the Ship
The White Ship • Valley of Gold • Tom Appleby, Convict Boy
They Came on Viking Ships • Macbeth and Son • Pharaoh
A Rose for the Anzac Boys • The Night They Stormed Eureka
Oracle • Nanberry: Black Brother White • Pennies forHitler
I am Juliet • To Love a Sunburnt Country

Fiction
Rain Stones • Walking the Boundaries • The Secret Beach
Summerland • A Wombat Named Bosco • Beyond the Boundaries
The Warrior: The Story of a Wombat
The Book of Unicorns • Tajore Arkle
Missing You, Love Sara • Dark Wind Blowing
Ride the Wild Wind: The Golden Pony and Other Stories
Refuge • The Book of Horses and Unicorns

Non-fiction
Seasons of Content • How the Aliens from Alpha Centauri
Invaded My Maths Class and Turned Me into a Writer
How to Guzzle Your Garden • The Book of Challenges
Stamp, Stomp, Whomp • The Fascinating History of Your Lunch
Big Burps, Bare Bums and Other Bad-Mannered Blunders
To the Moon and Back • Rocket Your Child into Reading
The Secret World of Wombats
How High Can a Kangaroo Hop? • A Year in the Valley
Let the Land Speak: How the Land Created Our Nation
I Spy a Great Reader

The Animal Stars Series
The Goat Who Sailed the World • The Dog Who Loved a Queen
The Camel Who Crossed Australia
The Donkey Who Carried the Wounded
The Horse Who Bit a Bushranger
Dingo: The Dog Who Conquered a Continent

The Matilda Saga
1. A Waltz for Matilda • 2. The Girl from Snowy River
3. The Road to Gundagai

The Secret Histories Series
Birrung: The Secret Friend

Outlands Trilogy
In the Blood • Blood Moon • Flesh and Blood

School for Heroes Series
Lessons for a Werewolf Warrior • Dance of the Deadly Dinosaurs

Wacky Families Series
1. My Dog the Dinosaur • 2. My Mum the Pirate
3. My Dad the Dragon • 4. My Uncle Gus the Garden Gnome
5. My Uncle Wal the Werewolf • 6. My Gran the Gorilla
7. My Auntie Chook the Vampire Chicken • 8. My Pa the Polar Bear

Phredde Series
1. A Phaery Named Phredde
2. Phredde and a Frog Named Bruce
3. Phredde and the Zombie Librarian
4. Phredde and the Temple of Gloom
5. Phredde and the Leopard-Skin Librarian
6. Phredde and the Purple Pyramid
7. Phredde and the Vampire Footy Team
8. Phredde and the Ghostly Underpants

Picture Books
Diary of a Wombat (with Bruce Whatley)
Pete the Sheep (with Bruce Whatley)
Josephine Wants to Dance (with Bruce Whatley)
The Shaggy Gully Times (with Bruce Whatley)
Emily and the Big Bad Bunyip (with Bruce Whatley)
Baby Wombat's Week (with Bruce Whatley)
Queen Victoria's Underpants (with Bruce Whatley)
The Tomorrow Book (with Sue deGennaro)
Christmas Wombat (with Bruce Whatley)
A Day to Remember (with Mark Wilson)
Queen Victoria's Christmas (with Bruce Whatley)
Dinosaurs Love Cheese (with Nina Rycroft)
The Hairy-Nosed Wombats Find a New Home (with Sue deGennaro)
Good Dog Hank (with Nina Rycroft)
The Beach They Called Gallipoli (with Bruce Whatley)

Jackie French is an award-winning writer, wombat negotiator and the Australian Children's Laureate for 2014–2015. She is regarded as one of Australia's most popular children's authors and writes across all genres — from picture books, history, fantasy, ecology and sci-fi to her much loved historical fiction. 'Share a Story' is the primary philosophy behind Jackie's two-year term as Laureate.

You can visit Jackie's website at:
www.jackiefrench.com